Cynthia Harrod-Eagles is the author of the hugely popular Morland Dynasty novels, which have captivated and enthralled readers for decades. She is also the author of the contemporary Bill Slider mystery series, as well as her recent series, Ashmore Castle, and War at Home, which is an epic family drama set against the backdrop of World War I. Cynthia's passions are music, wine, horses, architecture and the English countryside.

Also by Cynthia Harrod-Eagles

Ashmore Castle series

The Secrets of Ashmore Castle
The Affairs of Ashmore Castle
The Mistress of Ashmore Castle
The Fortunes of Ashmore Castle

The Morland Dynasty series

The Founding	The Hidden Shore
The Dark Rose	The Winter Journey
The Princeling	The Outcast
The Oak Apple	The Mirage
The Black Pearl	The Cause
The Long Shadow	The Homecoming
The Chevalier	The Question
The Maiden	The Dream Kingdom
The Flood-Tide	The Restless Sea
The Tangled Thread	The White Road
The Emperor	The Burning Roses
The Victory	The Measure of Days
The Regency	The Foreign Field
The Campaigners	The Fallen Kings
The Reckoning	The Dancing Years
The Devil's Horse	The Winding Road
The Poison Tree	The Phoenix
The Abyss	The Gathering Storm

War at Home series

Goodbye Piccadilly: War at Home, 1914
Keep the Home Fires Burning: War at Home, 1915
The Land of My Dreams: War at Home, 1916
The Long, Long Trail: War at Home, 1917
Till the Boys Come Home: War at Home, 1918
Pack Up Your Troubles: War at Home, 1919

The Fortunes of Ashmore Castle

Cynthia Harrod-Eagles

SPHERE

SPHERE

First published in Great Britain in 2025 by Sphere

1 3 5 7 9 10 8 6 4 2

Copyright © Cynthia Harrod-Eagles 2025

The moral right of the author has been asserted.

All characters and events in this publication, other than those
clearly in the public domain, are fictitious and any resemblance
to real persons, living or dead, is purely coincidental.

All rights reserved. No part of this publication may be reproduced, stored
in a retrieval system, or transmitted, in any form or by any means, without
the prior permission in writing of the publisher, nor be otherwise
circulated in any form of binding or cover other than that in which
it is published and without a similar condition including this
condition being imposed on the subsequent purchaser.

A CIP catalogue record for this book is available from the British Library.

ISBN 978-1-4087-3427-8

Typeset in Plantin by Palimpsest Book Production Limited, Falkirk, Stirlingshire
Printed and bound in Great Britain by Clays Ltd, Elcograf S.p.A.

Papers used by Sphere are from well-managed forests
and other responsible sources.

Sphere
An imprint of
Little, Brown Book Group
Carmelite House
50 Victoria Embankment
London
EC4Y 0DZ

The authorised representative
in the EEA is
Hachette Ireland
8 Castlecourt Centre
Dublin 15, D15 XTP3, Ireland
(email: info@hbgi.ie)

An Hachette UK Company
www.hachette.co.uk

www.littlebrown.co.uk

For Tony, always

DRAMATIS PERSONAE

AT ASHMORE CASTLE

The family
Giles Tallant, 6th Earl of Stainton
  — his wife Kitty, the countess
    — their baby sons Louis, Lord Ayton, and Alexander
  — his eldest sister Linda, widow of Viscount Cordwell
    — her children Arabella and Arthur
  — his brother Richard
  — his sister Rachel
  — his sister Alice
  — his widowed grandmother, Victoire (Grandmère)
  — his grandfather's half-brother Sebastian (Uncle Sebastian)
  — his widowed mother Maud, the dowager countess
    — her brother Fergus, 9th Earl of Leake
    — her sister Caroline, widow of Sir James Manningtree (Aunt Caroline)
    — her sister Victoria (Aunt Vicky), Princess of Wittenstein-Glücksberg
    — her cousins Cecily and Gordon Tullamore
      — their children Angus, Beata, Fritz, Gussie, Ben, Mannox, Mary

The male servants
Afton, butler and valet to the earl
Crooks, valet to Mr Sebastian and Mr Richard
Footmen William, Cyril, Sam
House boys Wilfrid, Eddie
Peason, head gardener
Allsuch, under gardener
Cox, Wilf, gardeners' boys

The female servants
Mrs Webster, the housekeeper
Miss Hatto, maid to the countess
Miss Taylor, maid to the dowager
Housemaids Rose, Daisy, Doris, Ellen, Mabel, Tilda, Milly, Addy, Ada, Mildred
Dory, sewing maid
Mrs Terry (Ida), the cook
Brigid, Aggie, Debbie, Kathleen, Ivy, kitchen maids; Biddy, scullery maid
Miss Kettel, the governess
Nanny Pawley
Nursery maid Jessie

In the stables
Giddins, head man
Archer, groom to the earl
Josh Brandom, groom to the young ladies
Stable boys Timmy, Oscar, George, Bobby
Coachmen John Manley, Joe Green

On the estate
Markham, land agent
Adeane, bailiff
Moresby, solicitor

Saddler, gamekeeper
Gale, estate carpenter
Axe Brandom (brother to Josh) woodsman

In the village
Dr Bannister, rector of St Peter's Church

Physician, Dr Arbogast, Dr Welkes

Miss Violet Eddowes, philanthropist
— her butler Moss
— her cook Mrs Grape, her maid Betty

IN MARKET HARBOROUGH

Nina, Kitty's best friend
— her husband Joseph Cowling, an industrialist
— Decius Blake, his right-hand man
— her housekeeper Mrs Deering
— her maid Tina
— her groom Daughters
— her friend and neighbour Lady 'Bobby' Wharfedale
— Bobby's husband Aubrey
— Bobby's brother Adam Denbigh
— her friend Lady Clemmie Leacock

IN LONDON

Molly Sands, piano teacher, once lover of the 5th Earl
— Chloë, her daughter
Sir Thomas Burton, impresario, Grandmère's cicisbeo
Henry 'Mawes' Morris, cartoonist, Mr Cowling's friend
— his wife Isabel and daughter Lepida

CHAPTER ONE

December 1904

Hospitality was one of the duties of an earl, but Giles, Earl of Stainton, felt that the arrival of two unexpected guests on Christmas Eve was asking rather much of his forbearance.

Uncle Fergus, his mother's younger brother, had frequently stayed at the Castle, though never before without warning. He liked his comfort, so he preferred his hosts to have plenty of notice before he descended on them. But what young Angus Tullamore, merely a second or third cousin, was doing there was a mystery. Before Giles could even begin to interrogate Tullamore, his uncle, who had never surprised anyone in his life, stunned the company by announcing that he was going to be married.

Warming his tail at the fire he said, 'Miss Lombardi – Giulia – has consented to be my wife. I'm for ever indebted to you, Giles: if you hadn't invited her to Rachel's ball, I should never have met her! It took me an age, I can tell you, to pluck up the courage to ask. I never in the world thought she would say yes. But as soon as I saw her, I knew there could never be any other woman for me.'

Giles was still grasping after the right words to respond. His sister Linda got in first. 'But there never *has* been any other woman for you!' she cried in outrage. 'You've never

.est interest in females. It's ridiculous to start
, at your age? It's – it's *unseemly*!'
,iles blenched at her rudeness.
,as unabashed. 'Oh, don't pretend you're not
the same!' she snapped. 'He's been caught, that's what . is! An adventuress after his money. Really, Uncle, some painted trollop has only to flatter you and—'

'Now, now! Come, come!' Fergus interrupted her, more surprised than offended. 'No need for that sort of language. I'm not so hideous, am I, that no decent female would have me? I've had my share of admirers over the years, I can tell you. Fact of the matter is, I could have married a dozen times by now if I'd wanted.'

'But you never *have* wanted!' Linda raged. 'That's the whole point! You've been perfectly happy being single, and at your age you ought to be settled in your ways, not making a fool of yourself over some—'

'Linda, that's enough,' Giles admonished sharply.

She rounded on him. 'You're not going to side with him? It's bad enough with Mother's burlesque marriage, without another member of the family bringing ridicule on us.'

Their widowed mother was even then on her honeymoon with the German prince who had unexpectedly taken a fancy to her.

Fergus was looking wounded now, and Giles had to put an end to it. He took Linda's arm in a grip that was intended to hurt, and said quietly, but forcefully, 'Stop this, or leave the room.'

She opened her mouth, then closed it again, seeing he meant business. Uncle Sebastian had oozed up beside her, and caught Giles's eye with a nod that said, *I'll deal with her if she starts again.*

Now Kitty, the countess, from her position by the Christmas tree where she was preventing her younger son, Alexander, from pulling off the baubles, said in just the right sort of warm, interested voice, 'We're so pleased for you, Uncle. Do tell us all about it.'

The slight cloud cleared from Fergus's face. He was a man of very little conceit: he liked most people, so he assumed most people liked him, and rarely took umbrage at anything. 'Oh, from the moment I saw her, it was like being struck by lightning,' he said, beaming again. 'She's so beautiful – and clever, too. I never thought she'd favour me, but when I went and called on her and her parents in Florence, they received me so kindly I started to hope.'

'Is that why you went to look at your house in Venice?' Kitty asked.

'Yes, exactly. And I've spent months having it put to rights, because, you know, I had to have *something* to offer if I was to ask for her hand.'

'You have three houses in this country,' Richard reminded him drily. 'But I expect the Ca' Scozzesi tipped the balance.'

'Well, I didn't like the idea of tearing her entirely from her native land,' said Fergus.

'And who doesn't like Venice?' Richard said.

'I am a very ordinary fellow,' Fergus said, 'but I'm glad I do at least have the wherewithal to make her comfortable, if that counts for anything.'

Linda could be silent no longer. 'For God's sake, it counts for everything! Your estate, your fortune and your title? That's the whole point! Don't you see—' The sentence broke off with a sort of squeak, and Giles guessed that Sebastian had pinched her, hard.

'It's wonderful news, Uncle, and calls for champagne,' Giles said. He could do no less, though the announcement had disconcerted him as much as Linda, though for different reasons.

Afton was just coming in, with footmen William and Sam behind him. He had anticipated, as a good butler should, that champagne would be wanted, and had brought it, and glasses, and plates of the little savoury biscuits, *moulinets*, that Mrs Terry made down in the kitchen, having begged the recipe from the earl's grandmother's French cook. They went very well with champagne.

There was a pleasant little bustle of pouring and serving. While that was going on, Richard said, 'So, Uncle Fergus, when is the wedding to be? And *where* is it to be? Are we invited?'

'The thing of it is, you see,' said Fergus, 'that a young woman marries from her own home. That's the rule, ain't it? And also, there's the question of . . .' He cleared his throat, looking slightly awkward. 'Naturally enough, they are Roman Catholics. Italy, you know – pretty much home of it, what? So the wedding has to be in one of their churches. We're going to tie the knot in Florence.'

'Don't *you* have to be a Roman Catholic as well?' Giles's youngest sister Alice asked.

'Ah! Nail on the head, my dear. That's partly what I've been doing over there all these months. Getting m'self accepted into their Church.'

There was a brief, surprised silence.

'Don't you *mind*?' Alice asked, but with an innocent frankness that did not offend.

'Never been a great one for church,' Fergus said. 'One religion's as good as another to me, so if it makes Giulia happy . . . More important, makes her parents happy. Same God, as I understand it, different words, that's all.'

'But that's not— It's more than— Oh, my God!' Linda's intervention ended in a choking sound and she fled from the room.

The champagne had been distributed, and Giles now proposed a toast – 'To Fergus and Giulia!' – which was drunk.

Alice asked, 'So we won't get to see you married, Uncle?'

'Weddings are overrated,' Richard said, to comfort her. 'Too much crying.'

'People enjoy the crying,' Alice said. 'And it's not *obligatory*.'

'Just coming to that.' Fergus made himself heard. 'Wedding itself will be small and quiet, in Florence, but then we'll come to London and have a slap-up celebration, and you'll all come to that.'

'When will that be?' Kitty asked.

'March,' Fergus said. 'Wedding in February. A few weeks in Paris so she can buy clothes. Then London. Some legal things to tie up. Then I'll show her round my estates, lie of the land and so forth, then back to London for the Season. She's looking forward to that. Culture, you know,' he added vaguely.

'Well, that's something to put into the diary,' Sebastian said. 'A grand party in March.' He raised his glass again. 'Wishing you every happiness.'

'Hear, hear,' said Richard. 'You're an inspiration to us all, Uncle.'

At that Alice gave him a questioning look, but didn't follow it up.

When Kitty was dressed she sent Hatto away, crossed the dressing-room to Giles's bedroom, and found him in his shirt-sleeves. She thought how handsome he was, even when screwing up his face in the mirror as he wrestled with his tie.

'Shall I do it?' she said.

He turned, dropped his hands, raised his chin, and she stepped close, feeling the warmth of his body radiate through the dress shirt, his breath stir her hair. Since the birth of her second son, he had rarely visited her at night. It was possible he never would again, and it was a melancholy thought, because she was still in love with him. *Suppose*, she thought, *I were just to slip my finger in between two of the buttons . . . how hot and smooth the skin of his chest would feel . . .*

She gave the bow a final tweak and stepped back, and he inspected the result in the mirror. 'Have you come to quarrel with me?' he asked. She didn't answer and he turned to her. 'I saw you look at me, when her name was mentioned. I knew you would.'

'I saw that you didn't like it,' Kitty replied.

'No, I didn't like it, but not for the reason you seem to suspect.' On their honeymoon in Italy, Kitty had been jealous of his closeness to Giulia, and had let him know it. 'I have always felt like a big brother to her. And since she wouldn't have met him if I hadn't invited her to the ball, I feel responsible.'

'She's a grown woman. She can choose for herself.'

'He's too old for her.'

'He can't be more than forty.'

'Forty-one,' Giles said. 'She can't possibly love him.'

She gave a small, wry smile. 'Of course, you are such an advocate for marrying for love,' she said.

'Oh, Kitty!'

She waved away the protest. 'It's a prudent match, and he's a kind man. What's your real objection?'

He could have refused to answer. But he suspected she still thought he had romantic feelings about Giulia, and he owed it to her to dispel any misapprehension.

'I want her to be happy, just as I would Rachel or Alice. I hate to think she would tie herself in a loveless match purely for money.'

'Because that would make you think less of her? But women have to make these decisions. I don't despise Nina for marrying Mr Cowling. What else was she to do?'

He turned away to hide the wryness of his mouth at the mention of her dearest friend, who had married a wealthy industrialist twice her age. Giles's hopeless feelings for Nina had to be kept deeply buried because, yes, he had married Kitty for her fortune, but he was fond of her and had no wish ever to hurt her. He hid his face by keeping his back turned while he put on his jacket. 'I am not in love with

Giulia, Kitty,' he said. 'I never have been. You do believe that, don't you?' She didn't answer. He turned to face her. She was frowning a little, deep in thought, but she did not seem distressed. 'I'm going down,' he said. 'Are you coming?'

She shook herself back from her thoughts. 'You go. I'll come when the bell rings.' And she went back through the dressing-room door.

Alice dressed herself, except on very formal occasions, and it hadn't taken her long to put on her dark green tartan dress and wind her daytime plait into a chignon. Ready, she went upstairs to the old schoolroom, which she and Rachel used as a sitting-room. The dogs, which had been lying outside Giles's room, came rushing to her, longing for company, and followed her upstairs. Since Kitty had taken over the running of the house, there was always a good fire kept in the old schoolroom. When her mother had ruled, fires had been rationed.

She sat on the rug with a dog either side of her and stared into the flames. Her thoughts went, like a bird flying home, to the last time she had seen Axe, and they had kissed. It was the first time she had ever kissed a man. To remember it, to relive it, was her one comfort, because she knew she must not see him again. He was the estate woodsman; she was Lady Alice, sister of the earl. If anyone found out about their deep and tender friendship, they would destroy him. She longed for him, ached for him, but she knew they had been lucky so far. In a country district like this, secrets could not be kept. She must never go back there, to the one place where she felt belonging.

She had always been a cheerful, practical sort of girl, not given to thinking about herself, but she was coming to realise that her upbringing had left her lonely. Her father had always been a distant, rather frightening figure. Her mother noticed her rarely, and then only to criticise. Giles and Richard were hardly ever at home. She'd had Rachel for a companion, but Rachel had always been a different kind of girl. Rachel was prettier than Alice; her hair was always tidy, her hands always clean; she was quiet and ladylike; she loved parties and balls. She'd always wanted to get married and have lots of children. Grown-ups had approved of Rachel.

All Alice had wanted was to be left alone to ride and run about with the dogs, to read books and to draw. Her feelings for Axe had crept up on her. At first she was just glad there was someone who liked her. Then she began to appreciate someone who did not either treat her distantly, because she was gentry, or patronise her because she was young and female. He treated her as an equal: that in itself was a wonder. The realisation that they were of different sexes – or, rather, the realisation that it mattered – had come to her only lately. As a child of fifteen she had known, vaguely, that people would disapprove of her friendship with him. Now she was eighteen, the matter was much more serious. What she wanted she would not be allowed to have; and the consequences to him would be disastrous.

She had grown up; and it made her shake her head in wonder to think how much Rachel had longed for adulthood, because to her it was no pleasure at all.

The dogs jumped up, hearing Rachel's light footsteps an instant before she did. 'I thought I'd find you here! Oh, Alice, you shouldn't sit on the floor! You'll get dog hairs all over your skirt.'

'You do look pretty,' Alice said, to distract her. Rachel's dress was emerald green silk with a wide, deep lace collar almost like a bertha. Her hair was in a soft mound on top of her head and she was wearing earrings.

'Do I? Angus likes green – it's his favourite colour. Oh, Alice, he's *here*! Isn't it wonderful? Isn't he just the handsomest man in the world?' Rachel sat in the nearest chair, clasping her hands to her breast; her eyes shone in the firelight.

'He's very nice,' Alice said, 'but what *is* he doing here? He wasn't invited.'

'He's come for me,' Rachel said impressively.

'Oh, goodness! "So stately his form and so lovely her face . . ." Well, that part's right. He is quite stately. Good shoulders – and I remember from seeing him in a kilt that he has good legs, too.'

'What are you *talking* about?' Rachel said impatiently.

'Don't you remember the poem about Young Lochinvar? How he snatched up his love behind him on the saddle and galloped away with her? Are you going to gallop away with Angus?'

'I'll tell you if you'll just listen for a moment,' Rachel said. 'It isn't in the least funny.'

'I never thought it was,' said Alice. 'Go on.'

'Well, his father wants him to marry Diana Huntley. And her parents want it as well.'

'And what does Diana Huntley want?'

'I'm sure she wants to marry Angus – who wouldn't? He's argued and argued with his father and pleaded to be allowed to marry me, and his father simply won't listen. And just two days ago he told Angus that the Huntleys were coming to spend Christmas at Craigend, and that Angus was to propose to her during the visit. He said everyone was expecting it. Angus thought it would be shocking to be having the row when the Huntleys were there, in front of Diana and everything, so he packed a bag and slipped out, and he's been travelling for two days. Oh, and just as he was getting down from the train at Canons Ashmore, there was Uncle Fergus getting out of the first class. Angus had travelled third, to save money. We'd sent a carriage for Uncle, of course, so that's how they arrived together. Luckily, Uncle didn't ask him any questions.'

'Uncle Fergus never asks questions. But I expect he'd quite approve of Angus being Young Lochinvar, seeing as he's in love himself. But Mama wouldn't approve of Angus being here.'

Some of Rachel's euphoria evaporated. 'No, she's against us too. Oh dear, what are we to do?'

'What's Angus's plan?'

'I'm not sure he has one. I haven't had much chance to talk to him yet, just a few words in the hall while everyone was fussing over Uncle's news. But he swears he won't marry anyone but me. At least we can have Christmas together. And there's the hunt on Boxing Day – Giles will have to lend him a horse. Then the ball at the Grange on the day after. Oh, to dance with him again! He dances like an angel.'

'I know. "Never a hall such a galliard did grace".'

'What?' Rachel asked, but did not wait for an answer. 'It's so different dancing with the person you love. You can't imagine.'

Alice felt sad for them both. 'Don't get too hopeful, will you? If they're all against it, it probably won't happen. In stories true love triumphs and they live happily ever after, but real life isn't like that. In real life, marriage is like our mother and our father, or Linda and poor Lord Cordwell.'

Rachel was stubborn. 'But Angus has shown them he absolutely *will not* marry Diana Huntley. So Sir Gordon will *have* to agree.'

'But there's still Mama. And you know she never changes her mind about anything.'

Giles trotted down the stairs to the drawing-room, feeling hard done by. He absolutely was *not* in love with Giulia Lombardi, said his internal monologue, and it was unfair of Kitty to suspect him. Yes, he admired Giulia's intellect and enjoyed her conversation. *Had* enjoyed it. Since that awkward moment on the ship coming back from Alexandria when the tipping of the vessel had thrown her into his arms and he had kissed her, she had been notably cold towards him.

Richard, in whom later he had confided, had said it was not the kiss that had upset Giulia, but his apologising for it afterwards. He did not understand that, but it was a fact that Giulia had snubbed him at the ball, had actually refused to dance with him. Now he was worried that her accepting Uncle Fergus was somehow connected. He was anxious for her well-being, that was all. It was too bad of Kitty to be giving him Looks across the room at the mention of Giulia's name!

The bell hadn't gone yet and he was expecting to be the only one down, but Angus was lurking near the Christmas tree, evidently hoping to waylay him. Ah, yes, Giles thought, he could legitimately be angry about Angus.

The young man got his word in first, smiling anxiously. 'I was hoping to see you, sir. I wanted to have a private word with you.'

'And I want to have a private word with *you*,' Giles said grimly. 'What the devil are you doing here?'

'Well, sir—'

'For God's sake stop calling me "sir".'

Angus blushed. 'I thought, with you being the earl, head of the family—'

'Not of your family. Your mother is my mother's aunt so I suppose it makes us cousins of some sort – is it second, third, or once removed? I've never understood all that business. I am, however, responsible for Rachel while she's under my roof. And to save you time: I know, because my mother told me, that you and Rachel have taken a fancy to each other and want to marry.'

'It's more than a fancy. I love her, and she loves me,' Angus protested.

'My mother also told me that both she and your father are dead set against the match. Rachel is under age and her mother is her legal guardian, so I must revert to my original question. *What the devil are you doing here?*' Another thought occurred to him. 'Do your family know where you are?'

'Not precisely,' Angus admitted. 'I mean, I expect Father will have guessed, but I didn't exactly *tell* anyone—'

'You had a row and stormed out,' Giles gathered. 'You hot-headed young idiot! What sort of good do you think that will do?'

'You don't understand – my father was trying to force me to propose to Diana Huntley. She and her parents were coming to stay for Christmas and he said I must do it while they were there.'

'Go on,' Giles said. He began to feel sorry for him. He knew what it was to be forced into marrying.

'I just couldn't,' Angus said wretchedly. 'I told Father I didn't love Diana, but he said marriage was nothing to do with love. He said young people couldn't be expected to know better than their elders what was good for them. So I—'

'Ran away.'

Angus reddened. 'It sounds paltry when you say it like that. But I couldn't think what else to do. I thought—'

'Did you? It seems to me there wasn't a great deal of thinking going on at all. Well, the first thing we have to do is let your parents know where you are. Oh, don't look at me like that – unless he has a flying carpet he can't suddenly turn up here – at least, not until after Christmas.'

The clattering of nails on the marble floor of the hall heralded the arrival of the dogs, Tiger and Isaac, who dashed in to romp fawningly round Giles and then Angus in a serpentine of adoration. Giles guessed they had been with Alice and Rachel in the schoolroom, which meant that the girls could not be far behind.

'Now, look here, Angus,' he said. 'My mother is determined on a grand marriage for Rachel. She was only allowed to come here for Christmas on condition that I wouldn't permit any correspondence or clandestine meetings between you two. So you've put me in the dickens of a position.'

'I'm sorry, sir – but I really do love her.'

'Yes, yes, take that as read. Well, this isn't correspondence, and as a meeting it's hardly clandestine. And I can't bring myself to turn you out into the snow. But while you're here, you're not to be creeping away together for secret talks – and certainly not for kisses – or you'll make a liar of me. You'll see her and talk to her only in the public rooms with the rest of us present.'

'I understand,' Angus said. 'Thank you, sir – Cousin Giles.'

'But you had better do some serious thinking. You have a few days' respite. Make good use of them. And now, here the girls are, so no more of this. I'll have another talk with you later.'

After a fast run, the hounds checked at a spinney, and Nina pulled Jewel up. They had gone so fast there were only a couple of other riders, both of them men, between her and the hunt servants. Her face was stinging from the passage of the wind. The short December day was declining and the air had taken on a chill; the sky was pink behind the bare branches of the trees.

A moment later, Adam Denbigh arrived and halted Talleyrand beside her in a cloud of steaming breath. 'Good God,' he said, 'what was that about? The expression "neck or nothing" comes to mind. My heart was in my mouth.'

She leaned forward and patted Jewel's neck. 'He went like a bird, didn't he?'

'That's not the point,' Adam began.

Fortunately – since he seemed to be about to deliver a lecture that she would not have taken well from him – his sister, Nina's friend Bobby, Lady Wharfedale, rode up. She had lost her hat and her hair was coming loose. Zephyr was blowing like a train, but her eyes were sparkling. 'What a run!' she cried. 'It must have been ten miles if it was a yard! The way you took that blackthorn with the ditch in front! I funked it and went by the gate.'

'I was just going to mention that,' said Adam. 'It was a wild thing to do, when you didn't know what was on the other side. Reckless, in fact.'

'Oh, Adam!' Bobby said, exasperated. 'She was wonderful! You sound like Mr Cowling.'

Even Nina rarely used her husband's first name. He was, somehow, quintessentially Mr Cowling. At this mention of him, she turned her head away.

Adam didn't notice. 'It's you who's always saying how dangerous riding side-saddle is,' he said to Bobby. 'Suppose Jewel had stumbled on landing and fallen? Nina could have been trapped underneath him.'

'But that's the whole point!' Bobby cried. 'We shouldn't be *forced* to ride side-saddle. Why should men tell us what we can do and can't do? You can't turn the argument on its head and say it's a reason never to go out of a walk! If women had—'

The hunt secretary interrupted them, riding up and touching his hat. 'Hounds have lost him,' he told them, 'and the master's decided to call it a day.'

'Just as well, really,' Adam said, as the secretary rode off to spread the word. 'It's getting damned cold.'

There was a glittery feeling to the air as the sun sank and the frost began to fall. The sound of conversation rose as the field said their goodnights, thoughts turning to hot tea and hot baths. The grooms rode up: Hoday handed Bobby her hat, while Daughters said to Nina, 'Better keep him moving, missus. We don't want chills.'

Nina thought he gave her a rather disapproving look, and wondered whether it was for her previous fast riding or the current coffee-housing. 'Yes, you're right,' she said. 'We're going now.' She looked around. 'Anyone know where we are?'

Bobby knew every inch of the country. She pointed her whip. 'See that line of elms over there? That's a lane that comes out on the Langton road, just above Skinner's Farm. Then it's about three miles home.'

The drawback with hunting was having to hack home afterwards when you and the horse were tired and night was coming on. It was necessary to trot most of the way so that the horses didn't get cold, and trotting side-saddle was terribly uncomfortable. Bobby found them a track that led to a gate into the lane, and then they kept to the verges as much as possible, trotting through the gathering gloom and the uncanny stillness of a winter evening. Every sensible creature was indoors, and only the owls skimmed the dusk fields like velvet shadows.

When they turned onto the Langton road, the verge was wide enough to ride two abreast. Bobby fell in beside Nina as they walked for a bit to rest the horses' backs, and said, 'Kipper's right about one thing, though.' Kipper was her childhood name for Adam. 'You were riding rather more recklessly than usual. Has something happened?'

'No. Why? What should happen?' Nina said.

'That's a very evasive answer. Has Mr Cowling said something to you?' Nina's quick glance told her she had hit the bull. 'Did he try to stop you coming out?'

'No, of course not. He likes me to hunt, as long as it's side-saddle. He thinks I look elegant.'

'There is something wrong, though, isn't there? Tell me what's upset you.'

Nina was silent, and then she sighed. 'I can't. I wish I could, but I can't.'

'You can tell me anything,' Bobby insisted.

Not this, Nina thought. 'We should probably trot again. It's getting really cold, isn't it?'

They trotted. Nina had knives in her back; her hands were numb, despite her gloves. The cottages they passed showed yellow squares of lamplight, making her think of butter melting on hot toast. Invisible in its kennel, a dog barked sharply as they passed, the rattle of its chain ringing clear in the unnatural stillness of the frost.

★ ★ ★

They passed Welland Hall first. Nina resisted all appeals to come in and take tea, and rode on to Wriothesby House with Daughters a polite distance behind, her mind a pleasant blank of tiredness. She had half hoped to slip in unnoticed, but her terrier, Trump, had been without her all day, and came scurrying from the kitchen, barking excitedly.

That brought Mr Cowling from the small parlour that he used as a business-room, newspaper in his hand, as eager as Trump for her return, but less sure of his welcome.

'There you are!' he said, with studied heartiness. 'Was it a good day?'

'A lot of blank draws,' she said, crouching down to caress the dog, 'but then we had a very good run. Bobby thought it was a ten-miler, but I think a bit less. Eight, perhaps. Very fast, at any rate.'

'Good, good,' Cowling said. 'And the horse went well?'

'Perfectly.' She knew he wanted to talk about the thing she didn't want to talk about. 'I'll go up and have my bath,' she said.

'Have a cup of tea first,' he urged. 'And a muffin. You must be starved.'

'No, I think I'll bathe first. I'm a bit stiff.' She began to turn away, tried to forestall him with a neutral comment. 'I'm glad we have a proper bathroom now, and hot water from a tap. No need to have a servant toiling upstairs with cans.'

'Nina,' Cowling said urgently. 'I want to talk to you. I *must* talk to you.'

She didn't meet his eyes. 'Not now,' she said.

But he stepped close and laid a hand on her arm. 'I know you're upset about what I said.' He kept his voice low since they were still standing in the entrance hall. 'I didn't mean to offend you. I thought it would make things all right between us. I'm such a clumsy fool. I wish to God now I'd never said it, seeing how upset you are. Won't you forgive me? I can't bear to see you like this.'

'There's nothing to forgive,' she said, trying to be natural, but knowing it sounded brittle. 'I'm not offended or upset.'

'But you won't look at me,' he said miserably.

If you focused on the bridge of a person's nose, you seemed to them to be meeting their eyes, without actually doing so. She forced a smile. 'You see? Nothing's wrong, Joseph.' She made herself use his Christian name, hoping it would please him.

But his expression remained troubled. 'Go and have your bath, then,' he said at last. 'I'll ring for fresh tea when you come down.'

She went upstairs, dread weighing her as much as the weariness of her legs. He would talk about it over tea, she thought, and she would have to endure it.

It was all still so raw. As she sat in the hot water and soaped herself, with Trump perched on a chair beside the bath, ready to dive in in case of accidents, she thought about that dreadful moment on Christmas morning when he had apologised for not being able to perform properly in bed. He had apologised for failing her.

'You must have expected, when we got married, that there would soon be a baby on the way,' he had ploughed on against the mute protest of her silence. 'It's natural for a woman to want babies. God knows, I want them too. A son, to hand on my business to. And a daughter would be nice too, for the fun of it. It must be hard for you, especially when your friend Kitty has two. You want to hold a precious little bundle of your own in your arms.'

'Lots of people don't have children,' she'd said, trying to stop him.

He hadn't even acknowledged that she'd spoken. 'I wouldn't be surprised if that's not what's behind this restlessness of yours – talking about votes for women and wanting to ride across, and so on. A childless woman lacks proper occupation. I know you get these ideas from Lady

Wharfedale, but I expect she finds you fertile ground, given that you've an empty nursery. It grieves me to the bone that I can't give you the child you crave. But this is what I think we can do about it. I think it will make things come out all right for us.'

And despite her urgent desire that he should not, he had gone on to tell her his idea. If she were to get what he could not give her from someone else, he would cherish that child like his own, and never a word about the true situation would ever cross his lips to her, the child or anyone else. 'You'd be giving me what I want too – a son to carry on my name, so there'd be no wrong in it for you. And I know you have the good taste to choose a right 'un, and the sense and good manners to be discreet about it.'

'Please don't! Please don't talk like this,' Nina said desperately.

He gave her a wry, sad, loving smile that came close to breaking her heart. 'I wouldn't want to know anything about it. I would never ask. I would hope that, whoever he was, you wouldn't go falling in love with him – aye, that's the risk from my point of view! But I'd never speak of it. Only, one day you'd come and tell me there was a little one on the way, and I'd be as pleased and proud as could be.'

'*Please* don't say any more,' she begged.

'And when that little one came, I'd be the best papa that there's ever been in the world. I'd love it like I love you, Nina. Wife.'

'Stop, please stop. I can't bear any more. It's – it's impossible!'

'Not impossible at all. It's a way to put things right. I won't say any more now, but think about it. You needn't tell me what you decide. I don't want to know details. Better that way. Just one day present me with a child, and I'll be as happy as a king.'

He had changed the subject then, but it had been a strained

Christmas Day, and since then she had been in a turmoil of shock and shame, anguish that he should love her so much that he would suggest such a thing. And guilt, searing guilt that her thoughts had flown briefly and, oh, so wrongly to a certain person – a man she had no right ever to think about – and what bliss it would be to have a child of his.

She had been awkward in Mr Cowling's presence ever since, and could not meet his eyes. She had been forced, most unwillingly, to think about the scheme. How had he envisaged it happening? How in the name of God would she initiate such a transaction and with whom? To solicit it merely as a practical measure was unthinkable and shameful. He must have meant her actually to have an *affaire du coeur*; but that way lay terrible danger, heartbreak and, surely, the ruin of all Mr Cowling's hopes. How could they live together after that? But they would have to. The water cooled around her and she imagined the ghastly tangle that would result.

They were married. A man could petition for divorce for a wife's adultery, but Mr Cowling would never do that. It was not that it was extremely expensive – he was a rich man – but that it was also shameful, and would result in social death for both of them. He wouldn't do that to her. And a woman could not divorce a man or even leave him, having no money of her own. And, besides, she did not want to break his heart. She was not in love with him, but she cared for him.

Her aunt, who had brought her up after her parents died, had counselled her to think carefully before accepting Mr Cowling. Nina had believed she had done so, but how could she have anticipated his problem? If she'd had a child by him, things would have been different.. With a child, children of her own, and a kind husband who was also a fond papa, she thought she could have been happy. But as it was, she was lonely. His love for her was a responsibility, not a joy. It did not fulfil her.

Eventually she had to go down and face him. He was in the drawing-room. The lamps were lit, the curtains drawn, the fire bright: a scene of domestic comfort. He stood up as she entered, and came to her, smiling, to take her hand and lead her to the fire.

'Now then, my darling, come to the warmth. And don't look so anxious. We're not going to speak of that subject ever again. I want us to be comfortable, like we were before. We can be, can't we? I should never have suggested such a thing and I hope that you'll forgive me and put it entirely out of your mind.' And he added, with emphasis, 'I've put it out of mine.'

She smiled and said what was necessary. But she didn't think he had. He might have shut the idea away in a separate room in his head, but it was still there, and she believed he still half hoped she would act on it.

CHAPTER TWO

A telegram had been sent off to Craigend on Boxing Day. On the morning of the twenty-eighth, Giles received a reply, and called Angus and Rachel into the library after breakfast. Through the Christmas festivities, the meet on Boxing Day and the ball at the Grange, he had kept an eye on them, but they had shown no tendency to try to slip out of the room. Angus had been particularly good with Linda's children, played chess with Uncle Sebastian, and made up fours at bridge to keep Uncle Fergus happy. At the Grange he had danced with Rachel only a seemly amount. Giles was impressed with his steadiness.

'I've had a telegram from Sir Gordon,' Giles said. 'He is very seriously displeased, and demands that you go home immediately.'

Angus had expected that. 'I'm not going to give in to him. I'm a grown man, I can make my own decisions.'

'He's still your father,' Giles said.

'But my life is my own to live as I see fit.' He grew a little angry. 'If he thinks behaving like a – like a *tyrant* will make me any more likely to come to heel, he mistakes me!'

'Please don't rant at me. I'm only the messenger. Obviously he has anticipated your answer because he says if you don't go home the consequences will be severe.'

Angus was silent. Rachel looked up at him and said, 'What consequences?'

Giles answered for him. 'Financial ones, I assume.' What other power did a man have over a grown son?

'Money doesn't matter, does it?' she said.

'Of course it does,' Giles said impatiently. 'Don't talk like an idiot.'

Rachel blushed. 'You sound like Mama. All she cares about is how rich a person is. She wants to marry me to a Russian prince and talks about jewels and carriages and so on. But I love Angus, and he loves me. That's what's important.'

'Next you'll tell me you'd be happy to be poor and live in a hovel,' Giles said. 'You, who've never mended your own clothes or cooked your own food.'

'I can sew,' Rachel retorted. 'And I could learn to cook,' she added less certainly. 'You're just being disagreeable and trying to make me give him up. Well, I won't!'

'You wouldn't have to live in a hovel,' Angus said. 'I'd look after you.'

'That rather begs the question, doesn't it?' Giles said. 'How exactly *would* you support a wife?'

'I'd find something,' Angus declared. 'I'm not afraid of hard work. I've helped in my father's business for years, I must have skills I can use.'

'Hmm. I don't think you have the least idea how expensive my sister would be. You'd need a pretty damn good position.'

Angus eyed Giles cautiously. 'I suppose *you* wouldn't—'

'You suppose right,' Giles interrupted grimly.

Rachel looked at him eagerly. 'Oh, Giles, you could give Angus a job on the estate! Then we wouldn't have to go far away from you all. A job and a little cottage. Angus is terribly clever. He'd be a tremendous help to you.'

'No, Rachel.' Giles stopped her, feeling like a wicked stepfather. 'How can I help you, after I gave our mother my word that I'd keep you two apart? Even if I wanted to – and I don't.'

'You don't?' Rachel's lip trembled.

'Not as things stand.' He noticed that they had instinctively moved a step closer to each other and gave an inward sigh. 'I can't order you to go home,' he said to Angus, 'but I strongly advise it. Talk to your father, see if you can't find a way through.'

'I *have* talked to him,' Angus said. 'He doesn't listen. All he wants is his own way.'

'I see a family resemblance,' Giles said.

'I won't give him up,' Rachel said. 'And I won't marry anyone else. Mama can't make me.'

'But she can separate you for another two years, and do you really think you'll last that long?'

Rachel began to cry, but quietly. She and Angus were standing so close together now she was able to slip her hand into his.

'You'd both do better to give up this nonsense,' he concluded.

'I'm afraid we can't do that, sir,' Angus said, a trifle glumly.

'I see.' Giles was standing by his desk, and picked up a pencil, put it down again, drummed his fingers briefly on the leather surface, picked up the pencil again, thinking. 'Well, I can't let you stay here,' he said to Angus. 'I gave my word, and I've stretched it already. You can remain for today, but you must leave tomorrow. I can't do any more for you. Now I'm going downstairs and you can follow when you're ready. Mind, if you haven't appeared in ten minutes, I'll come back up and chase you down.'

He walked out of the room, closing the door behind him. When he reached the stairs he realised he still had the pencil in his hands, and was surprised to find that it was snapped in two.

'Cup of tea, Mr Afton?'

Afton, passing the open door to the housekeeper's room, paused. 'Thank you, Mrs Webster. That would be most agreeable.'

As he walked in, his sharp eyes noted that the table in front of her was already laid with two cups, so the invitation hadn't been spur-of-the-moment. Brigid appeared almost instantly with the filled pot, and put it down in front of Mrs Webster without a word.

'This is very nice,' he said, taking the offered seat. 'You've made this room very cosy.'

'As the Duke of Wellington said, any fool can be *un*comfortable,' she said, preparing to pour. 'Milk in first or afterwards?'

'I understood it was always first?'

'For the finest bone china, yes, to prevent cracking. I'm afraid these cups aren't quite so dainty. Bread and butter, or cake?'

'Bread and butter, please,' Afton said. 'I believe "Cake is rarely seen at the best houses nowadays."'

'I beg your pardon?' Mrs Webster looked startled.

'I was quoting. From a play.' Evidently it rang no bells with her, and remembering that mention of Oscar Wilde was largely frowned on since his imprisonment for gross indecency, he did not enlighten her. Instead, he looked round. 'What a lot of photographs you have.' They were framed and displayed all along the mantelpiece and the windowsill, and clustered on a small table in the corner.

'I come from a large family. My father was one of seven and my mother was one of nine, so I have cousins galore, and four brothers of my own, and most of them are married and have children.'

'Might I enquire whether there was a Mr Webster?'

'I've never been married,' she said. 'But that's not for other ears. I don't discuss personal matters with the lower servants.'

'I beg your pardon if I was impertinent.'

'Not at all. I don't mind *your* asking. What about you, Mr Afton? Do you have much family?'

'I never married either. The opportunity never arose. It's

difficult for people in our position, isn't it? And I have no family.'

'None at all?' The way she said it made him think of Lady Bracknell. He imagined her saying, 'To have few relatives may be regarded as a misfortune. To have none looks like carelessness.' He had seen *The Importance of Being Earnest* at the St James's Theatre during its opening run, before the author had fallen into disgrace, and it had made him laugh so much – because he recognised so many of the characters from real life – he had gone twice. Wilde, of course, was dead now. He wondered if his work would ever be performed again. It seemed a shame to lose works of genius because of the frailty of their creator. How many great artists had a private life that would bear close scrutiny?

But Mrs Webster was waiting for an answer. 'None I know about. I was a foundling. Left in a box on the steps of the poorhouse.'

Mrs Webster threw a glance at the open door, then lowered her voice. 'If I might offer a little advice, I shouldn't mention that to anyone else. Your secret is safe with me, but the other servants . . . Uneducated people have strong prejudices, and servants in particular like things to be a certain way.'

'A butler who was a foundling wouldn't do?'

'He would not. And you're already coming to the position from the wrong direction,' she said. 'You were a valet. A butler ought to have started as a boot-boy and worked his way up through footman and under-butler: that's the proper way. His parents should have been in service too, for preference. They want you to be like their idea of a butler. It's how they make sense of the world.'

Afton smiled. 'It's a form of play-acting, isn't it? Are you fond of the theatre?'

She shook her head indulgently. 'When do you think I'd have the time to go? And living out here in the country, there's none to go to. I did once see a pantomime at Drury

Lane,' she added, 'when I was about ten years old. It was a Christmas treat. There were harlequins and a giant goose, as I remember. And a demon king. And a dog that did tricks. Dear me. It was . . . very entertaining.'

'I never went to one, but I remember seeing the bill-posters for the pantomime when I was a child. The walls would be papered with them in the weeks leading up to Christmas.' He paused. 'Quite a different Christmas we've had here this year.'

'Rather too many surprises for the smooth running of the house,' she said.

'It was very pleasing news,' he suggested, 'about Lord Leake's getting married.' She gave a cautious assent. He leaned forward. 'Tell me, why was Lady Linda so angry about it?'

He thought she might not answer, but she lowered her voice again and said, 'You see, Lord Leake has been a bachelor for so long everyone assumed he'd stay that way.'

'Yes, I gathered that.'

'And he's very wealthy, and none of his estate is entailed. Lady Linda's late husband inherited nothing but debts, so she's been banking on Lord Leake leaving everything to her children, seeing he hadn't anyone else to leave it to.'

Afton considered. 'Wouldn't there be other claims on him, from other members of the family?'

'I gather from Rose, who maids her when she's here, that she's always considered everyone else was taken care of. When the idea formed in her mind, Lord Giles was the heir to this estate, and Mr Richard was in the army so he didn't need anything.'

'And their young ladyships?'

'She supposed the Ashmore estate would take care of them. It's a pity the dowager wasn't here – she'd have jumped on Lady Linda right away. His lordship is too soft.'

'He is quite upset about Lady Rachel's situation.'

'Yes, it would be a very unwise match. Reckless, in fact.'

'I don't think that's why he's upset,' Afton said. 'He doesn't like having to be harsh with her, and he rather likes Mr Tullamore.'

'I'm afraid there's an unfortunate streak of the romantic in his lordship. It must be all that digging up of history. They were always falling in love with the wrong people in history times, weren't they?'

Afton gave her an impish grin. 'I can assure you there's nothing romantic about digging about in tombs – all heat and dust and flies, and bad food, and sand getting into everything. How fastidious gentlemen can bring themselves to do it . . . !'

'It's reverting to childhood, that's what it is,' Mrs Webster said, amused. 'There never was a little boy who didn't want to mess about with mud pies and get himself filthy.'

'I think you may have put your finger on it,' said Afton.

'Of course I have. Another cup?'

'Thank you.' He watched her pour. 'I really am enjoying this. Ours is a lonely calling – having to hold ourselves aloof. It's nice to have a conversation with an equal for a change.'

'I was just thinking the same,' she said. 'Your predecessor, Mr Moss – he was a very fine butler, but not a great one for conversation. He liked to *tell* you things. It's not the same.'

'Indeed it's not.'

'Will you have a piece of cake?' She eased a slice onto a plate for him. 'Lady Rachel's all smiles now,' she reverted, 'but she'll soon have them wiped off when her dowager ladyship finds out Mr Tullamore's been here.'

'How will she find out? Surely his lordship won't tell her?'

She gave him a canny look. 'Oh, she'll know all right. If no-one else tells her, Lord Leake will. She's his big sister and he writes to her regularly. She's going to come down like a thunderbolt, I can tell you. Lady Rachel had better watch out.'

Fergus and Angus left the same morning, sharing the carriage to the station. Fergus was on the way to visit friends for the

New Year, to spread the good news of his betrothal before returning to Italy. Angus was going to London.

He'd had a private talk with Richard in the afternoon of his last day.

'I know I have to go home and face the music,' he said, 'but I don't want to go until after the Huntleys have left.'

'I don't blame you,' Richard said. It was just after luncheon. It had turned unexpectedly mild, and the air was damp and milky, echoing with rooks supposing prematurely that spring was on the way. He was going down to the stables to check on the horses and, seeing the furrowing of Angus's brow throughout the meal, had invited him to go along, so as to give him the opportunity to unburden. Their feet crunched on the damp gravel, and the air smelt of wet grass and leaf-mould.

'You see, I know my father is going to make a tremendous fuss,' Angus said, 'and it would be awful if he did it while they were still there.'

'Yes,' said Richard. 'Humiliating for Miss Huntley, for one thing.'

Angus reddened. 'I feel an absolute cad, but I can't help it. It would be worse if I married her feeling as I do, and made her miserable, wouldn't it?'

It wasn't a rhetorical question. Richard slowed his pace so they shouldn't get to the stable yard too soon. 'No-one likes to be rejected,' he said. 'But it depends on her feelings for you. Does she love you?'

'I don't think so,' Angus said, frowning in thought. 'It's hard to say – she's one of those terribly composed girls who doesn't show much, but I honestly don't see how she can. We've spent so little time together. I think she's just very obedient. And . . .' He hesitated.

'And?'

'Well, girls think differently about marriage, don't they? I mean, they know they *have* to get married to someone or other.'

'So when will it be safe to go home?'

'I'm pretty sure he said the Huntleys were leaving after Twelfth Night because there was a house party at the Culrosses' he and Mother were going to. And I know he has to be in Edinburgh on the Monday for business, and Mother will probably stay on at Craigend because she doesn't like Edinburgh in the winter. So if I could tackle him in Edinburgh I wouldn't have to upset her.'

They paused in the gateway to the stables. A horse somewhere was banging a door with an impatient forefoot. 'Giles is saying you have to leave tomorrow,' Richard said, 'so you'll need a burrow to lurk in for a week or ten days.'

'It's awkward,' Angus said. 'I have a little rhino, but I don't know how long it will have to last, and hotels are expensive.'

'Well, if you want to wait out your time in London, I know of a cheap place that's clean and decent – I've stayed there myself. It's near Victoria station. I'll write down the direction for you.'

'I say, thanks awfully! You're a tremendous brick.'

'Best not to tell Giles, though – he thinks you should go straight back, and he'll curse me for interfering.'

'I won't say anything.'

'And since I have to go up to London in the new year, I'll even take you out for supper one evening, and you can talk over your plans with me. If you have any.'

Angus's answer was a sigh.

Though tearful at Angus's departure, Rachel did not seem desolate. In fact, her tears soon dried and she went about with a glow of secret happiness, which suggested to Giles there had been some powerful reassurances given during their farewells. He deliberately hadn't asked for any promises from the lovers not to communicate. He hoped that what he didn't know would not compromise his honour.

He came in one afternoon from the library, where he had

been looking at accounts, and paused for a moment in the doorway of the drawing-room. Alice and Rachel had their heads together, exchanging secrets. When he sat down and took up a newspaper, Kitty came and joined him.

'I saw you looking at them,' she said. 'I hope Rachel's not plotting to run away.'

Giles looked up. 'I don't think she has the pluck for that. More likely they're plotting how she and Tullamore can write to each other.'

'You're not going to try and stop them?'

'Not as long as I don't know about it. I'm damned if I can see why I should be my mother's policeman.'

'So you think they should be allowed to marry?' Kitty smiled. 'I was afraid you were against it.'

'I *am*, as things stand. If he had his father's approval and money, it would be a fair match. But it's not up to me. I just wish I weren't stuck in the middle of it.'

'At least now Uncle Fergus has gone, Linda's complaints have subsided,' she said. 'She hasn't cornered you in the library for days.'

'I told her in no uncertain terms it was nothing to do with me, and I wouldn't hear another word about it. But she won't have given up. I'm pretty sure she's written to Mother, urging her to stop the match.'

'Poor Giles,' Kitty said.

He raised an eyebrow. 'Don't you mean poor Linda?'

'She makes her own troubles. You have yours thrust upon you.'

He looked at her cautiously, but she was smiling – a little, teasing smile. He warmed towards her. 'You are far too understanding of other people's problems.'

'Only yours,' she said. 'And yours are mine.'

Rachel's glow lasted until the arrival of the telegram, all the way from St Petersburg, on New Year's Day. It was addressed to Giles, and since the dowager's new husband, Prince Paul of Usingen, was very wealthy, she had not bothered to restrict her words to the minimum.

ANY FURTHER COMMUNICATION BETWEEN RACHEL AND TULLAMORE ABSOLUTELY FORBIDDEN + AM SURPRISED AT YOU FOR ALLOWING IT + AS SHE CANNOT BE TRUSTED SHE IS TO COME BACK TO ME PENDING MARRIAGE TO BE ARRANGED + AM SENDING TAYLOR TO ACCOMPANY HER ARRIVING JAN 5TH + HAVE RACHEL PACKED AND READY FOR IMMEDIATE DEPARTURE + DO NOT FAIL ME IN THIS GILES ++ PSS USINGEN

Rachel paled as she read it. Giles thought irritably that there was nothing more likely to provoke her into running away than the threat of an immediate marriage to a stranger in St Petersburg. But Mother had never had the slightest acquaintance with tact.

'I won't go!' she cried, her eyes filling with tears. 'Giles, you won't let her make me?'

He realised that he should have taken the telegram out of the room to read, and sent for Rachel, rather than reading it at the breakfast table, because now everyone wanted to know what was in it. Rachel had already passed it to Kitty, and both Alice and Linda had risen from their seats to look over her shoulder.

Alice didn't speak, only bit her lip in distress, but Linda said loudly, 'A marriage? This must be the Russian prince. Oh, you lucky girl! You'll have so many clothes. They do things in style in Russia. They change four and five times a day, I believe.'

'It's inhuman!' Kitty exclaimed, pushing away Linda's hand as she tried to take the telegram from her. 'Giles, you must do something.'

'Angus said I can't be forced to marry,' Rachel said with a sob in her voice. 'He said it's the *law*.'

It went on round the table. 'Not even signed "Mother",' Richard mused. 'Is there some sort of creature that eats its own young?'

'Giles?' Kitty urged.

'She's her guardian. *That*'s the law,' Giles said. 'I don't see what I can do.'

Sebastian looked up from reading the flimsy message of doom. 'Delay,' he said. All heads turned. Rachel wiped her eyes on her napkin and looked at him with faint hope.

'Delay?' Giles queried.

'Miss Taylor will have been travelling for days. It would be cruel to make her turn around and go straight back.'

'She'll probably have passages booked,' Giles said doubtfully.

'Passages can be changed. Meanwhile, think. Plan. Negotiate. Come, Giles, show a little gumption. The game's not over until stumps are drawn.'

Rachel rose and ran round the table to give him a damp kiss. 'Do you really think something can be done?'

'We'll see, Puss, we'll see.' He met Giles's eyes and gave the faintest of shrugs. Even if, in the long run, the result was the same, it shouldn't be done in this way.

Giles understood the message. 'Right,' he said. 'Delay.'

And you never knew what might happen. The dowager might change her mind. The unknown Russian might change his. Rachel might fall out of love, or Tullamore come into an unexpected fortune. A flaming meteor might destroy the earth and all their problems with it.

And it was certainly true that his mother a thousand miles away in Russia was less worrying than his mother actually in the house.

London was locked in fog. It came up from the Thames and met the chimney smoke coiling down to form a still grey blanket that muffled sounds and reduced vision to inches. It made haloes round the streetlamps, beaded the railings and bare tree branches with dirty drops, condensed on the roads and pavements and made them slippery. The sharp smell of horse-dung mixed with the sulphur of coal fires and the throat-clutching tang from exhaust pipes. Motor-buses loomed suddenly like mastodons, their headlights like glowing eyes. Timid pedestrians felt their way along railings; muttered curses told where bolder ones had collided with lampposts, pillarboxes or each other.

When Richard came up from the Underground at Piccadilly, there was a policeman with a flare directing traffic around the circus, which helped him get across. But he had to feel his way along the wall through Air Street and Lower John Street, and only knew he had reached Golden Square by the sudden sense of open space. Crossing to the centre he bumped into a horse and apologised to it, let the cart pass, then felt his way round the railings of the garden, glad that he knew the geography from his many visits.

'I'm lucky to have got here alive,' he told Molly Sands when he gained her drawing-room. 'You see before you an explorer winning through against fearsome odds. Like those fellows on the *Discovery* expedition in the Antarctic. I feel quite unexpectedly dauntless.'

'You're such a fool!' she laughed.

'And unlike them, I didn't have dogs . . . To think when I got up this morning I was merely intending to toddle through the metropolis like an ordinary cit to visit the most beautiful woman in the world.' He caught her face in both hands so that his kiss landed on her lips and not her cheek.

She allowed one kiss and then pulled away. 'Is it very bad out there?'

'Fog, even more than snow, makes the familiar unfamiliar. And – ugh! – how it smells!'

'I'll make you a cup of tea. The kettle's hot – it won't take a minute to boil.'

'Hot water we need, but I have something better to put it in.' From one pocket he drew a flat quarter-bottle of rum, from another a lemon. '*Et voilà!* I assumed you would have sugar. A rum toddy will go some way to convincing my feet they still belong to the rest of me. You've no pupil?'

'Not this morning. I have one this afternoon, but he might not arrive if the fog's as bad as you say.'

'Then you can have one with me.'

'I can't have rum on my breath if he does arrive.'

'It will have dissipated by then,' he assured her. He made himself comfortable in a chair by the fire and she pushed the kettle on its trivet back over the coals. It was cosily domestic. How he wished . . .

'You came up yesterday, I suppose,' she said, with her back to him.

'Last night. You are my first priority. You might show a little gladness to see me! My vanity is quite bruised.'

She turned her head to look at him. 'Oh, I am very glad. I feel as though if I looked out of the window the sun would be shining.'

He grinned. 'Better! Well, shall I tell you all the news? We've had exciting doings all over Christmas.'

He told her about Uncle Fergus and Angus, and his mother's telegram.

'Who is Taylor?' she asked.

'The mater's ferocious lady's maid. Been with her centuries, and from what I observe they detest each other, and exist in a bracing atmosphere of barely concealed animosity. It's just like my mother to despatch the poor woman on a double journey of a thousand miles in the depths of winter. And just like Taylor to obey.'

'A desire for martyrdom?'

'Something like that. Hating Mother keeps her going, and undeserved suffering increases her self-regard.'

Molly laughed. 'You're embroidering to entertain me.'

'Perhaps a little. Well, Uncle Sebastian's idea was to take pity on Taylor and make her stay a few days to get over the journey, thus delaying Rachel's departure in the hope that something would happen. And, blow me down, it did! Taylor stepped down from the railway carriage at Canons Ashmore onto a patch of ice, slipped and fell, and broke her leg.'

'Oh, the poor woman!'

'Yes, frightening, and very painful, I believe. I wouldn't have wished it on her. But she's now at the Castle with a great plaster cast like an elephant's foot on her lower leg, and obviously unable to escort Rachel back to St Petersburg.'

'So what's going to happen?' Molly asked, pouring water onto the rum. The aromatic smell lifted into the air.

'There was an exchange of telegrams. Mother demanded Giles send Rachel with one of his own servants and he said he had none to spare. Then Mother said she would come herself but it could not be yet as she had too many engagements. And there it was left.'

'So you don't know when she might arrive?'

'No, she's hanging over us like the threat of an avalanche, with everyone hoping if they don't make any sudden noises she'll stay put. I suppose she's bound to be in London in March for Uncle Fergus's celebration. That gives Tullamore a few weeks to try to sort matters out with his father. One has to feel sorry for him.'

'Yes, it must be very hard for a young man to be told he has to marry a beautiful girl with lots of money, follow a well-paid career and inherit a fortune.' She handed him a toddy and sat down opposite him.

He looked at her sternly. 'You've missed out the part about being in love with someone else. I know what it's like not to be able to marry the woman you love.'

'The cases are not the same.'

'No, mine is the settled affection of a mature mind, and Tullamore's – well, I'm fond of Rachel, but she is rather a silly girl. Quite what Tullamore sees in her I don't know. But, still, he *does* see it, and they make a pretty couple, so it seems unnecessarily cruel to keep them apart.'

'And you're seeing him tonight? Do you hope to ease the path of True Love?'

Richard was thoughtful. 'I'm not sure there's anything I can do, except encourage him to devise a plan in case his pa won't budge. He's going down next week to face the dragon, and one hopes that paternal affection will surge up at the sight of him. He is a pretty boy.'

'And if it doesn't?'

'Ah. Then, I suppose, if he still wants to marry Rachel, he'll have to find himself another career.'

'And there's your mother to think about.'

He gave a rueful grin. 'I was trying not to! But, yes, she won't be reconciled to the idea. Rachel would have to hold out against extreme pressure for two years until she's twenty-one – which would give Tullamore time to set up a career and save up some jingle. But whether she has the pluck to resist . . .' He shrugged.

'So is that what brought you to London?'

'No, I came up to see you. It's been a long three weeks.'

'Tell the truth.'

'It's true. Also I have some milk business to attend to. I promised Tullamore I'd see him before he went north – and I've a letter from Rachel for him. And, last but not least, I brought Alice up to stay with Aunt Caroline and see about enrolling at the Slade School. She's really good, you know!' he said, his face animating. 'And Giles, bless him, has said he'll pay for it, because I'm positive Mother won't.'

'Will she agree to Alice going? From what you've told me about her, I'd have thought she'd be against it.'

'We haven't asked her yet. One crisis at a time! But she's never really cared for Alice, doesn't see her making a glittering marriage. So she probably won't mind what she does, as long as she doesn't make a scandal. All her hopes were pinned on Rachel – and she certainly was the debutante of the Season. It's enough to make one feel almost sorry for her.'

'For Rachel?'

'No, for Mother. Wouldn't it be dreadful to have it in her grasp to see Rachel a princess, then have it snatched away at the last moment? And Rachel's the sort of girl to be swayed by the last person she spoke to. If she met this prince she might be perfectly happy to marry him. Tullamore had better run away with her before she's forced to go to St Petersburg or he might lose her entirely.'

'Richard Tallant! You can't possible recommend elopement!'

'Oh, is that what I did? Speaking of which, how is Chloë?'

She looked serious. 'That isn't funny.'

'I'm sorry. You know I am prone to sacrifice all for a *bon mot*. Forgive me. Is there any more talk of a European tour?'

'No, because Sir Thomas is still down in the country with his wife, but I'm sure he hasn't given up the idea. He'll be back in Town any day, and then I suppose we shall see.'

'Sufficient unto the day,' Richard said. He looked at her keenly. 'It must be lonely here without Chloë. With nothing to occupy you all day but teaching scales to little children.'

'There's a little more to it than that.'

But he had seen it in her eyes, before she turned her face away. Such a confined and confining life, for a woman of taste and intelligence, he thought. He hated it for her, and he hated that he was unable to do anything about it. He wanted to take her away from the poky rooms and the barrenness of daily drudgery. But he had nothing to offer, no way to support her. His bad arm ached, as it often did in cold weather, but just now he chose to take it as a reproach, an injunction to start racking his useless brains and work out a plan. His situation, he realised, was not so dissimilar from Angus Tullamore's.

For the moment, however, all he could do was support her spirits. 'What time is your afternoon pupil coming or not coming?' he asked.

'Three o'clock.'

'Why didn't you say?' He drained his glass and jumped up. 'There's time for me to take you out to luncheon before then.'

'Don't you have business to attend to?'

'It can wait until tomorrow.'

'Tomorrow's Sunday.'

'Next week will do.'

'You are entirely reprehensible!'

He grinned. 'I'm so glad you noticed! As the old proverb says, never put off till tomorrow the pleasure you can have today.'

'That's not the version my mother taught me.'

CHAPTER THREE

'Are you sure, dear?' Aunt Caroline had kept asking. 'It sounds a very *odd* idea to me.'

That was before Alice showed her the pictures. She was silent for a long time, examining each with some care before passing them on to Grandmère, who happened to be visiting. Then she said, 'I had no idea you drew so well. These are remarkably lifelike.'

Having seen them all, she patted the sofa beside her, and when Alice sat she said earnestly, 'All the same, dear, I'm quite surprised that Giles has agreed to this. I'm afraid it will damage your chances.'

'My chances?' Alice asked blankly. She heard her grandmother give a little Gallic snort of amusement.

'Your marriage chances,' said Aunt Caroline. 'You see, it's one thing to sketch prettily, or play the piano, or embroider. Talents suitable for the drawing-room. But to be *trained* at a special school . . . That smacks of the professional. Men don't like their wives to be artistic to that degree. Except for artistic men, I suppose,' she corrected herself doubtfully. 'But, then, I couldn't recommend you attach yourself to an artistic man. They never have any money, you know. And they lead such erratic lives,' she mentioned vaguely. 'And they have a distressing tendency towards soft collars. Who was that artist fellow, Victoire, that Willy knew, and invited sometimes to dinner?

He wore a most peculiar kind of velvet jacket one evening, like Henry Irving playing *Hamlet*.'

'That *was* Henry Irving,' Grandmère said. 'Not a painter.'

Aunt Caroline missed the correction. 'Alice, dear, I'm afraid you would be giving up all hope of a good marriage if it were known that you had gone to acting school.'

'Art school, Aunty,' Alice corrected.

'Of course, I meant art school. But it's just the same thing. You might be classed along with actresses and ballet girls and – oh dear, I'm quite sure Maud won't like it. I'm surprised she hasn't forbidden you.'

Grandmère's sharp eyes divined from Alice's expression that permission hadn't yet been sought. 'But, *ma chère*,' she said, 'what do you mean to do with it when you have won your diploma, or whatever it shall be? Do you mean to sell paintings for money?'

Alice hastened to say, 'There are very respectable people who earn a living by painting. It isn't at all like acting. Princess Louise paints, and she's Queen Victoria's daughter!'

'I don't think she does it for a living, dear,' Aunt Caroline objected.

'Well, perhaps she doesn't have to. But she *could*. And she went to the National Art Training School. Then there's the Kemp-Welches – Margaret, Edith and Lucy. They're *terribly* respectable. And Lady Elizabeth Butler: Queen Victoria bought one of her paintings. For money.'

'In France, there was Rosa Bonheur,' Grandmère said, 'who was awarded the Légion d'honneur. The first female artist to receive it.' Her eyes twinkled naughtily, because Rosa Bonheur had led a famously irregular life, but she was sure Aunt Caroline would never have heard of her.

Aunt Caroline was looking besieged. 'Well, it might be as you say. I really don't know. But Maud won't like it, I'm sure of that. And, darling,' she turned back to Alice, '*who* will you marry?'

'I shan't worry about that just yet, Aunty. But Princess Louise married a duke.'

Grandmère chuckled. 'You have a talent, and it is rare. Anyone can marry. Remember, child, art lasts. Kisses do not.'

At those words, Alice's mind was seared by the memory of Axe's kiss. And a vision of him alone at his cottage, wondering why she didn't come any more. She had not dared to go and say goodbye to him. Grandmère noted the look of desolation that passed quickly over her face, but said nothing. It confirmed a suspicion she had formed. But great art so often came from suffering, and perhaps it was within Alice to make great art. One would see. For now, she must be encouraged – and kept from harm until it was seen how good she really was.

'She will live here with you while she studies,' she said to Aunt Caroline. 'Nothing could be more *convenable*. Who could object to it?'

'Maud could,' Aunt Caroline said gloomily. But then she cheered up. 'It will be nice to have a young person about the place again. And I'm sure studying won't take up all of your time. I shall take you about, Alice dear, and introduce you to people. Your mother, I'm afraid, sadly neglected that part of your upbringing.'

Alice caught her grandmother's eye in what appeared to be almost a wink, and wisely did not argue. 'That will be nice, Aunty,' she said.

The Tullamores' town house in Edinburgh was in Drummond Place, but Angus walked up to the office in Queen Street to find out where his father was that day. It turned out that Sir Gordon was there, so he had no time to brace himself and assemble his arguments, but was shown straight up to his father's room on the first floor.

It was a dreich day of heavy dark skies and freezing sleet, a day to be indoors, and there was a grand fire blazing under the enormous marble fireplace, and the many candles of the electric chandelier were reflecting gaily in the mirror over the mantelpiece. But his father was standing in front of the hearth with a face like a thunderstorm.

Angus said meekly, 'Hello, Father,' and braced himself.

At first it was very bad. Scalding words poured over him.

'Have you the least idea what an impossible position you put me in?'

'Thoughtless, irresponsible . . .'

'The appalling insult to our guests . . .'

'Your mother's feelings . . . great distress . . .'

'Shocking insult to Miss Huntley . . .'

'Brought shame on the family . . . Loss of Huntley's business . . . Never hold up our heads again . . .'

Angus endured, eyes lowered. Finally his father stopped for breath, and said, 'Have you *nothing* to say for yourself?'

'I'm sorry, Father,' Angus said.

'Sorry?' Sir Gordon bristled at the inadequacy. 'You're *sorry*? What in the Devil's name did you think you were doing?'

'I didn't know what else to do,' Angus explained desperately. 'I told you over and again that I couldn't marry Diana. I *begged* you to understand. I tried to reason with you—'

'*Reason* with me?' A bark of fury.

'But you wouldn't listen. If I'd stayed we just would have had the same awful row but in front of the Huntleys, which would have been much worse. So I *had* to go.'

Then Sir Gordon was off again. 'Selfish indifference to the name and honour of your family . . . Utterly careless of your mother's feelings . . . No thought to any convenience but your own . . .'

Bad as it was, Angus began after a while to sense a faint but growing bafflement in his father. After all, words hurt, but they did not actually change anything. Raw and sore inside, Angus felt it was coming to an end. His father ran out of steam at last and stood glaring at him in exhausted rage. 'I don't know what can be done to recover the situation,' he concluded, after a pause. '*Your* reputation is beyond salvage. You must bear the consequences of your actions. My concern now is to save what can be saved of the Tullamore dignity and the family's fortunes. The Huntley connection is lost. They will never forgive the insult, and there's already talk of a match between Diana and Peter Banchory.'

Angus's spirit lifted a very little. 'Then if there is no more question of my marrying Diana . . .' For a moment he thought of her with pity. Would she object to this sudden transfer of nuptials, or would she meekly comply? Had she viewed *him* with any more than the same compliance? He hoped, he really hoped, he had not broken her heart. He resumed, though his father's face was darkening again: '. . . then, I can marry Rachel, can't I?' No immediate answer. 'She's an earl's daughter. It's not a shameful match.'

'You may do as you please,' Sir Gordon said coldly. 'I wash my hands of you.' The way he said it did not sound like good news. 'At the Hogmanay festivities, George Culross proposed a connection. He has lumber and rail interests that would fit well with our coal. And he has a daughter, Fiona, nineteen and ready for marriage.'

'But—' Angus began.

'Fritz will be twenty-one in May. He will marry Fiona Culross and I shall make him my heir. He will take the general-manager position I was intending for you. In a year or two he'll be made partner, as you would have been, and he'll inherit everything when I die.'

'You're disinheriting me?' Angus said, aghast.

'I have already consulted Frampton. I cannot keep the title from you, though I would if I could. You do not deserve to use it, or the family name. I hope you will have the good manners not to presume upon the Tullamore credit, though I have little hope that you think aright on that subject, given your failings on every other front. For the rest, Frampton is drawing up a new will. Fritz will marry Miss Culross and take your place.'

It was what Angus had dreaded, but now it had come, he discovered he had never really believed it would happen. A pit opened under him. 'But what will I do?'

'I neither know nor care.'

'Father! That's ridiculous! I've been training to take over since I was ten years old. Fritz doesn't know the business.'

'You may go now.'

Angus opened his arms in a helpless gesture. 'Am I to have nothing?'

'There is a trunk at Drummond Place that was packed for you – your clothes and effects. McBane will give it to you. And whatever you have in your bank account you may keep. That's all. Go now. I don't wish to look at you any longer.'

Sir Gordon turned away and took up the poker to ruin the fire.

'This is ridiculous,' Angus said again, helplessly, but his father did not turn round. 'Can I at least take my leave of Mother and the little ones?' Aside from Fritz, and his sister Beata who had been married the year before, there were two younger sisters and two younger brothers at home, Augusta, Benedict, Mannox and Mary.

'They remain at Craigend,' said Sir Gordon, 'where you will *not* go. Your mother does not wish to see you. Please leave. You are no longer my son.'

There was nothing to do but obey. Dazed, bruised, he left the office and went out into the hateful weather. Edinburgh seemed black and hostile, the massive buildings turning their sooty shoulders on him in rejection. At Drummond Place he rang the doorbell, and the butler, McBane, opened the door. He seemed embarrassed and slid his eyes away as he said, 'The master said you might call for your trunk, sir. It's here.'

It was ready in the lobby between the outer door and the

inner glass doors. So he was not even to be allowed inside the house. The trunk was large and heavy.

'You'll be taking it to the railway station, I expect, sir?' said McBane.

Angus pulled himself together. 'I suppose so. I shall need a cab.'

'I'll send a boy down to the corner, sir,' said McBane. He summoned a scared-looking page, who scuttled off through the sleet, leaving them trying not to look at each other, frozen in a farcical tableau. Beyond the glass doors a maid passing on the way to the staircase with a pile of fresh linen threw Angus a look of apprehensive sympathy.

A motor-cab came, with the boy running behind, his jacket black with moisture and his hair gleaming with ice crystals. Between them Angus, McBane and the cabby got the trunk onto the luggage step, and Angus climbed into the back. The door of what had been his home closed on him; blinds were drawn in the upstairs rooms and it seemed to be shutting its eyes so as not to see him. He was borne away in the miserable wintry half-light, through a sleet that had thickened since he'd arrived and was driving sideways on a bitter wind.

Ellen, her cheeks pink with outrage, was holding forth to her fellow housemaids.

'Nothing's ever right for her! She complains about everything! I shall tell Mrs Webster. I wasn't put on this earth to fetch and carry for someone who doesn't even say thank you.'

Milly's eyes and mouth were round at the very thought of such daring. Addy looked impressed. Mildred sniffed – her nose was always running – and said, 'Sooner you than me.'

Encouraged, Ellen tossed her head. 'Well, she's only a servant, like us. She thinks she's so superior, but she's not going to treat me like a heathen slave! I shall tell Mrs Webster—'

Mrs Webster was suddenly there and Ellen stopped

abruptly. The housekeeper had an uncanny way of appearing when she was least wanted.

She surveyed Ellen with a cool and slightly menacing smile. 'Yes, Ellen? You'll tell Mrs Webster what?'

The other three bunched up closer to her, not so much in support but in an egging-her-on sort of way. It was always fun to watch one of your own catch it.

Ellen felt defiance was her only option. 'It's Miss Taylor. I don't see why I should wait on her when she's only a servant, same as me.' She was trembling slightly now with her own daring. 'She called me a name! She threw a hairbrush at me! Well, I'm not going to do it any more.'

Mrs Webster didn't shout. It was one of the things that made her more frightening. 'You will do exactly as you are told, Ellen. I will decide your tasks and you will carry them out without comment. Now get about your business, all of you. Milly, close your mouth. Addy, take that silly smile off yours. And, Mildred, wipe your nose. *Not on your sleeve, you appalling girl!* Where's your handkerchief?'

'Lost it, Mrs Webster,' Mildred sniffed dolefully.

Mrs Webster drew a plain square out of her pocket. 'Take this. It's clean. I will deduct sixpence from your wages for it. If you lose another one it will be a shilling. Now go!'

She watched them scuttle away with a thoughtful frown. Miss Taylor was a problem, a hitch in the smooth running of the house.

Rose, the head housemaid, joined her, having overheard everything from the nap closet, where she had been inspecting tablecloths. 'They should never have brought her here in the first place,' she said. 'The cottage hospital's the place for her.'

Mrs Webster agreed inwardly, but it wasn't for her to criticise what Upstairs decided. 'Well, she's here now, and we have to deal with the situation.'

Miss Taylor had been carried in, frightened and in pain, and the mistress had sent for the doctor and ordered her to be cared for. Once the leg was in plaster, it was obvious that Miss Taylor could not go back to her old room at the top of the house. Even when she was able to get out of bed and move about on crutches, so many stairs would be impossible. Mrs Terry, the cook, had volunteered to move out of her room, just along from the kitchen.

'I don't mind sleeping upstairs with the maids,' she said. 'As long as Biddy wakes me up a bit earlier.'

Biddy was the under scullery maid, the lowest creature in the house, and the first up in the morning, her job being to make up the big kitchen range, boil a kettle and wake Mrs Terry with a cup of tea before starting on the scrubbing. Biddy wasn't quite right in the head, but the life of the under scullery maid was such that no normal girl would stick at it. Mrs Terry treated her kindly, and Biddy had conceived a dog-like devotion to her, so it had worked out all right. She tended, as Mrs Terry called it, to 'go cluck' if she got flustered, but as long as she was given clear instructions and left alone to get on with the job, she was a good worker.

'Are you sure?' Mrs Webster had asked, because having your own bedroom was one of the perks of the cook's job, but Mrs Terry had said yes, it was quite all right.

So Miss Taylor had been installed in the cook's room, which Rose had said was enough to give anyone the willies, since the cook before Mrs Terry had suffered from melancholy and had hanged herself in that room. And even if you weren't superstitious, it was a gloomy sort of cell, lit only by one barred window high up in the wall. Between suffering and morphine, Miss Taylor had hardly noticed her surroundings at first, but now it seemed to be getting on her nerves. She was becoming increasingly irascible.

'You ought to ask the mistress to have her moved,' Rose said now. 'If you ask me, it's driving her barmy. You know how keen she always was on precedence. It must gall her to be in a cook's room when she's a lady's maid.'

'*Was*,' Mrs Webster corrected. Rose looked questioning, and she shrugged. 'Who knows what will happen? Her mistress might not take her back, and she must know it.'

'All the more reason to get her out of here.'

'I did hint it right at the beginning, but the mistress said we must take care of her, after all those years of service. I can't bring it up again.'

'Hmph,' said Rose. 'Well, then, I'd better have a word with Taylor and tell her to mind her manners.'

Mrs Webster sighed. 'You're probably the only person who could.'

'Oh, I don't mince my bones,' Rose said, with a toss of her head.

'But whether it will do any good . . .' Mrs Webster finished doubtfully.

Rose and Miss Taylor had served together for a long time, since the reign of the old master, and were, along with the dowager, the only ones who had known his darkest secret. It had given them a certain sort of invulnerability: the dowager was cold of heart and savage of temper and would dismiss at the drop of a hat anyone who displeased her. But Rose and Taylor could not be dismissed. They had kept the secret; they had to be kept.

Rose tapped on the door of the cook's room and went in, remembering for one brief flash how poor Deena had hung there, with purple face and black protruding tongue. Rose was unsentimental and did not believe in ghosts, but she thought she would not have wanted to have that room. Taylor, however, like Mrs Terry, had not actually seen the body, so perhaps it was different for them.

'It's only me,' Rose said, as she entered.

Miss Taylor, propped up in bed, scowled at her. 'Did I say come in? Is one to have *no* privacy?'

Rose gave her a sharp look. 'Not when "one" is having her

meals brought and her potty emptied and not a lick of work to do for it. When are you going to get out of bed?'

'I don't have to listen to your impertinence. Get out!'

Rose stood beside the bed and looked down at her, not without pity. She spoke with a degree less sharpness than was her wont. 'I know you're scared. Lord knows I would be, in your shoes. But you're not helping yourself. If it was me, I'd be doing everything I could to get back on my feet.'

'You know nothing about it,' Miss Taylor snapped.

'I know Dr Welkes says you're ready to walk with crutches. You got to start some time.'

'Oh, leave me alone!' Miss Taylor cried.

'Look, Taylor—'

'Don't call me that!'

'Well, Mary, then. Ha! You didn't know I knew your name was Mary, did you? Her ladyship's being nice to you at the moment, but you're not *her* maid, and sooner or later his lordship's going to ask your mistress what's to be done with you. And if you can say for certain what she'll decide, it's more than I'd answer for. So you'd better get back on your feet, and quick about it. And stop cussing the maids and throwing things at 'em.'

'I shouldn't have to endure their impudence,' Miss Taylor growled. 'They never would have dared when—'

'No, they wouldn't,' Rose agreed, but without sympathy.

'I won't be pitied!' Miss Taylor cried sharply.

'Well, *I'm* not pitying you,' Rose said. 'Seems to me you've got enough self-pity to be going on with. But you'd better snap out of it before Upstairs loses patience with you. That's all I've got to say.'

She turned to leave, seeing out of the corner of her eye Miss Taylor reaching for something to throw. But the only thing to hand was the Book of Common Prayer on the nightstand, and that was too small to do much damage. All the same, Rose turned at the door in time to catch it, and lobbed it neatly back onto Taylor's bed.

'You'll go to Hell, abusing the Good Book like that,' she remarked.

And as she closed the door behind her, she heard Miss Taylor say, 'I *am* in Hell.'

Left alone Mary Taylor stared at the ceiling and contemplated her wretchedness. Her leg still hurt a great deal, but Dr Welkes had stopped allowing her morphine, and the aspirin only helped a little, and gave her an acid stomach, which did nothing to improve her temper. Most of all, she hated her helplessness. She had always been proud and haughty with other servants and kept them in their place with cold looks and a sharp tongue. Now they dared to look at her with pity and say sugary things, as though she were old or an imbecile! So she abused them and threw things. Better they disliked her than felt sorry for her.

And there had been no word from her mistress. She knew Lady Maud did not like her. Well, *she* didn't like *her*, either. But she had grown old in her service, and she had been loyal, through thick and thin – mostly thin. That deserved loyalty in return.

A broken leg! What if she was never able to walk again? What if she walked, but with a limp? No lady would keep on a crippled maid, least of all Lady Maud.

A servant who had given long personal service to a noble family and could no longer work could expect to be kept on in the house and found something to do: fine sewing was the usual thing for a retired lady's maid, or fine laundry, or washing delicate ornaments. But her history with Lady Maud was complicated, and she was afraid the dowager would seize an excuse to be rid of the embarrassment of what Taylor knew. Rose had put her finger on it. The present Lady Stainton was being kind, but Taylor was not *her* servant.

The cold terror came over her, the fear that every servant faced at some point in their life. To fall so low: unable to work, no money and no way to support yourself, old and alone and helpless – then it was the Union Workhouse, and you would eke out your last days in shame and abject poverty, to die at last on a stained, straw-filled mattress with some toothless crone watching at your bedside for the chance to search you as soon as you were dead for anything of the slightest value. Some said they would even smother you to help you along, merely for the sake of a handkerchief or a petticoat.

She thought, now, with a small shiver of guilt, of how little pity she had spared old Moss, the butler, when he had collapsed with a heart-attack and his position at the Castle had been closed to him. He had been lucky enough to get a position down in the village with Miss Eddowes – a great step down in status, but at least he was still a butler, albeit with only a cook and a maid under him. He had been seen cleaning the front-door brass. Moss, cleaning brass! She had sneered at how low he had fallen. But there were lower places than that.

Silently she raged at her misfortune: at her mistress for sending her half across Europe in the middle of winter, at that patch of ice for being invisible, at the station staff for not removing it. Behind her eyes she felt the heat of tears gathering, but she would *not* cry. If another impertinent maid walked in, they should not find her weeping. She would save her tears for the middle of the night, the only time she could hope for privacy.

Alice's hopes plummeted when, on the 16th of January, they discovered that the Slade School had no vacancies: her dream seemed to have ended before it began. But Richard squeezed her hand, and proceeded to get into conversation with the porter. In his opinion, porters of these venerable establishments always knew everything. He took out his cigarette case, offered one to the fellow, lit his own and leaned his elbow comfortably on the desk, a man with all the time in the world to chat – and probably a half-crown in his pocket that might want a new home.

It transpired that London was full of art schools, and many of them now followed the lead of University College London and accepted women on equal terms with men.

'There's the Blackwood, sir,' the porter suggested. 'That might be just the job for you.'

The Edith Mary Blackwood School of Art, founded by the famous nineteenth-century landscapist, was in Old Burlington Street, just round the corner from the Royal Academy.

'It's a small establishment, sir, nicer for the young lady – more individual attention, you see. And all girls. I know that some parents prefer that.'

'Probably very popular then – perhaps over-subscribed?'

'I'm sure they'd make room for one more young lady, if circumstances were right.'

'I suppose he was hinting that it costs a lot more,' Richard said to Alice, as they walked away. 'But it still won't be a fraction of what Giles had to fork out for Rachel's come-out. And Old Burlington Street is even more convenient than the Slade. No distance at all from Berkeley Square – you can walk there.'

'I just wish we knew whether it's a really *good* school,' Alice said.

'Well, let's go and have a look at the place. See if they'll take you first. Then we can ask questions.'

He treated her to luncheon first at the Princes Restaurant on Piccadilly, because he said it was originally built for the Royal Institute of Painters in Water Colours, 'So it has appropriate connections.' The vast dining-room was elegant in white, red and gold, and fabulous with mirrors, gilding, moulding and chandeliers, all in the French Empire style, celestial painted panels on the ceiling and potted palms in niches. Richard observed Alice's expression and said, 'Enjoy it while you can. Once you're a jobbing painter you won't be able to afford places like this,' which made her laugh, when she had been on the verge of being overawed.

Old Burlington Street was only a step away. The Blackwood occupied a handsome double-fronted Georgian house, four storeys and a semi-basement, with nothing but a discreet brass plate outside to tell what it was. On enquiry within, they were directed to the room of the school's principal, whose name Alice recognised: Mary Ellen Brightwell was famous for her paintings of dogs and horses. She told Richard in an urgent whisper as they went up the stairs that he would recognise them if he saw them.

'Wait a minute – that painting of the little girl and the dog playing the piano together, that the cousins have in their drawing-room?'

'Yes, that's one of hers.'

Richard entered the sanctum with more confidence now he knew what he was dealing with. It seemed somehow insulting not to know *any* of a person's works when that person had dedicated their life to them. But the lady herself was not at all how he expected an artist to look. Where was the pale, spiritual face, the soulful eyes and flowing Rossetti locks, the billowy pre-Raphaelite gown? This was a short, round, homely-looking woman in a tweed skirt and sensible blouse, with the sort of ordinary, bumpy face anyone might have. She looked like a cook. But the bright, dark eyes were sharp, her handshake was firm and her voice was commanding. She invited them to sit and listened to Richard's exposition, and then looked with careful attention through Alice's portfolio.

She looked up at last. 'These are all your work?' she asked Alice.

'Yes, ma'am.'

'Who taught you?'

'Nobody. I taught myself.'

'You didn't have a drawing-master? You didn't do art at school?'

'I didn't go to school. I had a governess for a while, but nobody taught me. I just did it because I love it. But I want to be better.'

Mrs Brightwell smiled, and her face was transformed. No-one would have taken her for a cook just then. 'That's the right answer!' she said. 'You have talent, but you have much to learn. I'm glad you know it. I've no room for girls who think they know everything already. Are you prepared to work hard?'

'Oh, yes, ma'am. It's all I want.'

'Then I think we can take you. Term has begun already, but the young ladies have been settling in, so you won't have missed anything important. I suggest you come in on Friday to get your bearings, and start lessons on Monday. You're living nearby, you said?'

Richard answered. 'With our aunt, in Berkeley Square.'

'That is satisfactory. We have a few girls who board but I have no vacancies for a boarder at present. So now we need only discuss our fees.'

Alice had little idea of money, never having had to use it, so she didn't know whether the fee was high or not. Richard did not blink, but merely nodded and said, 'I assume a cheque will be acceptable.' And that was that.

But outside he said, 'I just hope Mother doesn't forbid this when she finally hears about it, because that fee's a stiff one and I'm pretty sure it won't be refundable. I'm not sure I'd even have the gall to ask – your Mrs Brightwell might look like one's granny, but I have the feeling she's tempered steel inside.'

'*My* Mrs Brightwell,' Alice said, and laughed with pleasure. 'I'm going to study art,' she said, hugging herself. 'I really am.'

★ ★ ★

Rachel was daydreaming over breakfast when Afton came in with the letters on a tray, and startled her back to the present by laying one beside her plate. If a bow could be said to convey emotion, his was sympathetic. She only said, 'Oh!' as she looked at it, but Kitty knew it was not an 'Oh!' of pleasure.

They were alone at the table. Richard was still in London with Alice; Giles had breakfasted earlier and gone out about his business; and Uncle Sebastian was at his own house in Henley for a few days. And Linda had gone to visit her long-suffering friends the Willoughbys on their estate in Somerset, in the hope of an invitation to go with them to Paris – Mrs Willoughby always went in February – while her children were upstairs at their lessons with Miss Kettel.

So it was up to Kitty to show an interest in her sister-in-law's affairs. 'Not bad news, I hope?' she said.

Rachel looked up tearfully. 'It's from Mama. She's—'

'Upset?' Kitty suggested, when Rachel didn't finish.

Rachel nodded, read to the end, then said, 'You can read it if you like. You can probably guess what it says anyway.'

It was not the sort of letter Kitty would have liked to receive – at the same age she had been even more shy and sensitive than Rachel. The words were so angry that at times the dowager's pen had stabbed right through the paper. At the end of the tirade, she forbade Rachel to see or correspond with Angus. Maud would come in person to fetch her as soon as was convenient. Until then she was to remain at the Castle and concentrate on her languages, both French and German, and practise on the piano every day, to ready herself for the prestigious marriage that was being arranged for her. She was also, the letter concluded, to look to her conscience and pray to be forgiven for her unfilial behaviour, which had caused her mother such distress, and a breakdown in health.

'Oh dear,' Kitty said, as she got to the end. Rachel was weeping now. Kitty was amazed at how she managed to do it without the contorted features, swollen eyes and red nose that afflicted ordinary mortals. She looked, if anything, even more beautiful when weeping. 'I'm sorry. It's not a nice letter to receive.'

'It's so unfair!' Rachel cried. 'I love him! She doesn't understand!'

Kitty thought her mother-in-law understood perfectly well, but simply did not regard Rachel's feelings as relevant. Maud's marriage had been arranged for her, and so had Linda's. Kitty's too – though in her case she had wanted to marry Giles more than anything. Girls of Rachel's rank married as they were directed, always had, always would.

'I'm sorry,' Kitty said again. 'But you know there's nothing to be done about it. Much better to put Angus out of your mind. You'll only make yourself miserable.'

'I don't want to marry a R-Russian,' Rachel grieved.

'He might be very nice,' Kitty said. 'And once you start having babies it will all be different.'

Rachel turned drowned blue eyes on her. 'Why do babies make it different?'

'Because you love them so much, you can't want any life where you didn't have them.'

Rachel dried her eyes daintily. 'I'll go upstairs now, if you don't mind,' she said, getting up, and added, 'To practise my French.'

She had always been a good girl, always obedient, because she had always hated to be scolded. But loving Angus had changed that. She was going to defy her mother. She was going to write to Angus. She would see him whenever the opportunity arose. And if necessary, she would run away with him. In the mean time, she realised she would have to allay suspicion. She wouldn't put it past her mother to have someone in the household who reported on her. So Rachel would improve her languages and piano and behave like a good, obedient girl – and hope fervently that Angus could come up with a plan before Mama came to England and kidnapped her.

CHAPTER FOUR

Back in London, Angus had been able to get a room in the same lodgings, which was lucky as he wouldn't have had any idea where else to go. And there he had retired from the world for a while to lick his wounds, dazed with the shock of such a violent rupture. He was like the survivor of an earthquake who crawls out from the rubble to find every trace of his village obliterated. All his landmarks were gone. He was young and strong and intelligent and he *would* come about, but it would take time to understand the terrible thing that had happened. For a while he could only sit and grieve.

He knew there was no way back. His father had the adamantine pride that would never back down. He was not destitute, however. His father had paid him an ample allowance in recent years, and he had not needed to spend much of it, so his bank account contained enough to live on modestly for a while. He could afford to take time to look around for something to do that would earn him enough to support a wife. He wouldn't be able to keep Rachel in the style of Ashmore Castle, of course, but he hoped eventually for a decent middle-class life in a neat house with at least a cook and a housemaid.

London was the place: lots of opportunities for a hard-working fellow to get ahead. Plenty of houses to choose from. In London they wouldn't need to keep a carriage. Rachel had family there. And there were all the resources and entertainments of London to enrich their lives.

He wrote to her, a letter full of hope and firm intentions. Her reply was by turns hopeful and despairing, fearful and determined, and urged him to hurry up and rescue her before her mother came back.

He was beginning to realise that marriage was a different matter when you didn't have a prosperous parent behind you, providing home, income and all the other wherewithals. But before he could become too discouraged, he received by the next post a friendly note from Richard inviting him round to tea at his aunt's house in Berkeley Square.

> Aunt Caroline doesn't know all the circumstances of your present predicament, but she won't ask awkward questions, so if you don't say anything either, all will be serene. Do come! I'm eager to hear how you are doing.

Aunt Caroline was an easy-going person, who had found that assuming everything was as it should be made for a comfortable life. She also loved to be visited and was fond of young people, so the appearance of Angus Tullamore in her drawing-room elicited no more questions than 'You're in Town on business, I suppose?'

To which Angus replied, 'Yes, ma'am.'

'How is your dear mother?'

He had anticipated that one, and said, 'Still at Craigend, ma'am.'

'Do call me Aunt Caroline,' she said. Angus's mother was in fact *her* aunt, but such entanglements weren't worth going into. She hadn't had much to do with the Tullamores over recent years – since her marriage the contact had always been more between them and Maud's family – but she was the right age to be an Aunt Caroline, and was quite prepared to accept her pleasant and good-looking young relative as a nephew.

He was glad to find he was not the only guest. Apart from Richard, there were some other young people – the Pelham girls, Isobel and Frances, and Peter Hayes-Wallace, all children of Caroline's old friends. And there was Mr Cowling, for whom she had conceived an inexplicable fancy the year before. He had taken a house on the opposite side of the square. A few days previously, he had called and left a card announcing his arrival in Town, and she had responded with a card of her own inviting him to come to tea.

She presented Angus to him. 'I don't think you have met? Mr Tullamore is a sort of cousin of mine – eldest son of Sir Gordon Tullamore—'

'Coal and shipping?' Cowling said, his sharp eyes assessing Angus and noting a slight stain of confusion.

'And property – yes, sir,' Angus said. 'Do you know him?'

'I've not met him, but I've heard of him, of course I have. Eldest son?'

Angus could only swallow, and nod.

'Mr Cowling is in business himself,' Aunt Caroline said helpfully. 'Boots and shoes and – and all sorts of other things.'

'A very useful fellow to know,' Richard added, giving Angus a pointed look.

Aunt Caroline thought this sounded rude. 'I assure you,' she said hastily, 'we value him for *himself*!'

Cowling gave her a twinkling look. 'Aye, sought after for my sparkling wit in drawing-rooms up and down the land, isn't that right, Lady Manningtree?'

Tea was brought in – a lavish one, Angus was glad to note, because he had been on poor grazing lately – and he had to do his duty to one of the Miss Pelhams, handing her things and sitting beside her and conversing. Richard was looking after the other sister, and Peter Hayes-Wallace was talking to Aunt Caroline, who had Mr Cowling on the other side of her. It was Hayes-Wallace who brought up the subject of Russia.

'What do you think, Mr Cowling, about this news of another assassination? My father told me about it this morning – Grand Duke Serge, the tsar's uncle. Blown to bits by a revolutionary's bomb.'

Miss Pelham gave a little gasp, and her teacup rattled in its saucer. 'Oh, how dreadful!'

He went on: 'Only last month there was an uprising in St Petersburg. Thousands marched on the Winter Palace and were shot down by the guards. Do you find such upheavals affect business, Mr Cowling?'

'I don't think this is a topic for the drawing-room, young man,' Cowling said. 'There are ladies present.'

But Aunt Caroline was answering: 'It's Serge's poor wife I feel sorry for – she was Princess Elisabeth of Hesse, you know, and sister to Princess Alix who is the present tsar's wife.' Genealogy was her passion. '*Their* brother, of course, is Grand Duke Ernie Hesse, who my sister Vicky knows very well. And your mother met him too, Richard, when she took Rachel over there. Says he's a most charming fellow: he thought Rachel a great beauty. He will be very upset by this – they are all very close, the Hesses. *And*,' she went on, 'the previous tsar's wife was Princess Dagmar of Denmark and sister to our own dear queen. They were apparently inseparable as children. Oh dear, so many connections between that unhappy country and ours! Poor Serge's sister, Grand Duchess Marie, married our Duke of Edinburgh – Prince Alfred. He was Queen Victoria's favourite son, I believe, and she was quite against the marriage at first, not liking the Russians much, but she took to the idea at last. And *her* mother – the Duchess of Edinburgh's, I mean – was also a Hesse, now I come to think of it. Princess Wilhelmine of Hesse. So you see!' she concluded triumphantly.

It was not terribly clear what she thought everyone would see, and there was a little silence. Then Hayes-Wallace repeated his question to Mr Cowling. 'Does Russian instability affect business much, sir?'

'Not directly,' Mr Cowling said. 'But I'd advise those with

shares in Russian railways or coal mines to think carefully. Your father,' he looked at Angus, 'does he trade much with Russia?'

'We don't sell coal to them,' Angus replied, 'but our ships – my father's shipping line, I mean – carry goods both to and from Russia, mostly lumber and furs *from*. Machinery, machine parts and luxury goods *to*. St Petersburg seems to have an insatiable appetite for English soap.'

He had tried to make it into a little joke, but Mr Cowling nodded without smiling. Angus felt uncomfortably that his eyes saw everything. He was sure he had noticed that little stumble over '*our* ships'.

But the conversation moved on, people changed seats, and some time later Angus found himself standing by the fireplace with Richard, who said, 'How are things going with you? Have you found yourself a position yet?'

'I've been looking,' Angus said. 'There are jobs I could have taken – general clerk, shop assistant, that sort of thing – but they wouldn't have paid enough for me to marry on. I'm not trained in anything specific, you see, like the law or engineering. I can keep accounts and I know my father's business inside out, but how to apply it elsewhere is the problem.'

'How to convince others you can apply it elsewhere, rather,' Richard said. 'I wonder if—'

He broke off as he realised that Mr Cowling had come up and was standing just beside him. Cowling nodded to him in a friendly manner. 'Now, I know something is going on,' he said. 'Heads together, lowered voices. Is this young man in trouble?'

Richard said, 'Not in trouble exactly, sir, but he needs a job. He needs someone to recognise his considerable abilities and take a chance on him.'

Angus was mortified. 'Oh, I say, Richard—'

Cowling made a negating gesture with his hand. 'Good employees are just as much a raw material to a business as coal and steel – and harder to find. Know much about import and export, lad? Bills of lading? Bonded warehouses?' Angus nodded to each. 'Come and see me tomorrow. Maybe I can help you.' He looked around. 'Attend to the ladies, now, young gentlemen. Lady Manningtree won't thank us for spoiling her tea-party.'

A sudden sleety squall sent two young women scurrying down Old Burlington Street, like blown leaves, huddling, arms linked, under one umbrella, hastening to gain the shelter of the house. The sleet gathered in balls in the gutter and bounced up from the pavement. Their hems and stockings were splashed and dirty.

When Alice had gone to be shown around in advance of starting at the Blackwood School, she had been met in the entrance hall by a tall young woman with a large-featured, handsome face, and a mass of curly dark hair as harsh as a pony's mane. Her eyes were dark brown like a pony's, too, and since Alice loved horses, she was instantly prepared to like her.

'Miss Tallant? I'm Miss Strachan. Mrs Brightwell asked me to show you everything.' She grinned infectiously. 'I've only just learned my own way around so I suppose she thinks it'll be fresh in my mind.'

'Are you a new girl?' Alice asked.

'Yes, I came last week. New to London, too – but I'm told you live here?'

'I'm staying with my aunt in Berkeley Square, but I really live down in the country, in Buckinghamshire.'

'Shropshire, me. I'm staying with friends of my parents. London quite took my breath away for the first few days. I'm so glad you're a country girl. All the others seem to be Town bred, and look down their noses if you're not, but they wouldn't last long where I come from.'

'My aunt had a maid once who didn't know that milk came from cows,' Alice said. 'She was so horrified when I told her, she wouldn't serve drawing-room tea if it meant she had to touch a milk jug.'

'What happened to her?'

'She left to work in a haberdasher's. My aunt was quite cross with me because otherwise she was a good maid.'

The tall young woman surveyed Alice with satisfaction. 'D'you know, Miss Tallant, I think we're going to be friends.'

'Oh, please, won't you call me Alice?' She had decided with Richard that she would not mention being *Lady* Alice in case it set her apart from the other girls.

'And you must call me Bron,' said Miss Strachan.

'Bron?'

'It's short for Bronte. My mother insisted on naming me Emily Bronte Strachan. I didn't like the name Emily, so I've always used the Bronte part. *Wuthering Heights* is Ma's favourite book. If I'd been a boy she was going to call me Heathcliff, so I suppose I came off lightly. Do you have any brothers and sisters?'

'Two of each, all older than me. What about you?'

'Two step-brothers, much younger. My pa died when I was little and my mother remarried.'

'My papa died too, three years ago. My mother married again and lives abroad now.'

'How amazing! We have so much in common.'

There was only one important question left for Alice to ask. 'Do you like horses? Do you ride?'

'Never out of the saddle at home. I do miss my darling Bayard.'

'I miss Pharaoh.'

'And my dog Bundle. He's a Jack Russell.'

'Oh,' Alice began, about to mention Axe's dog Dolly, but checked herself in time. And felt sad because that was one thing she couldn't share with her new friend. Bron was waiting for her to finish the sentence, so she said, 'Oh, I'd love to have a dog. Is he a ratter?'

'A champion.' Bron grinned again. 'Better not let the other girls hear us talking like this! They'd think we were very strange.'

Alice had always hated the idea of the typical debutante's life: to be paraded about, to make pointless conversation in drawing-rooms and ballrooms! The constant fitting of clothes, and changing of clothes, and thinking about clothes! The endless shopping for gloves and hats and pins and Poland water and stockings! And all for the getting of a husband, the ultimate prize.

School, by contrast, was everything she had dreamed of. It was wonderful to have a structure to her life, work to do, an opportunity to learn. It was so fulfilling that she didn't mind devoting other times to her kind aunt, who had her on her conscience. Aunt Caroline had been perplexed by Alice's wardrobe of sensible skirts and shirts, but was wise enough not to fuss too much. She contented herself with buying her one or two ready-made outfits and having the seams and hems gone over by hand. Alice showed her gratitude by fitting in cheerfully with Aunt Caroline's plans.

The Season had not yet started, and there were no balls, but there were enough families who lived in London all year for there to be card evenings, teas and informal dinners. Alice had not had a proper debut and it was moot whether she was really 'out' or not. It was enough, Aunt Caroline felt, to help her niece to acquire a little drawing-room polish, in case Maud should change her mind and bring her out after all. She had to admit that Alice was not awkward or shy. She seemed at ease in the company of older people – indeed, she was quite a hit with a certain sort of old gentleman who liked her pretty ways and were flattered by the attentive way in which she listened to their stories.

Meanwhile at the Blackwood, Alice was learning. The first term was given over to architectural drawing – no-one seemed to be able to tell her why this was the case, but it was traditional. She liked the fact that it required precision and care: she was better at it than Bron, who was inclined to be slapdash. 'I'm not going to be an engineer and build bridges! I can't see the point!' Bron would cry, when a wobbly line or a missed 'twiddle' condemned her work. But Alice thought it might be rather wonderful to design something in which intricacy and grace combined with huge strength. She daydreamed about submitting a plan for the likes of a Crystal Palace or Tower Bridge, and drew fanciful public buildings on the backs of her papers.

They did a great deal of copying, and had the drawings of Brunel, Gilbert Scott, Charles Barry, Bazalgette and Horace Jones put before them. One day they were escorted outside to draw the façade of Burlington House, the home of the Royal Academy.

'It's different drawing a building from life instead of copying a design,' she remarked to Bron.

'You can't call it "life" when it's nothing but a heap of stone and brick,' Bron objected.

'Oh, but buildings *are* alive in a sort of way,' Alice said 'They absorb life from the people using them.'

Mr Ffolliot, the old gentleman who taught this part of the course, happened to pass behind her at that moment, and said, 'You are quite right, Miss Tallant. I think you have a feeling for this sort of work.'

Alice blushed with pleasure, and Bron whispered, 'Next term we'll start botanical drawing with Miss Palgrave, and I'll come into my own. You'll see!'

Being busy kept her mind from home, and from missing Axe, and she tried honourably to keep it that way. But in bed at night, just before falling asleep, it tended to drift back to him. To indulge herself just with those few minutes, she decided, was perhaps allowed. There was no-one to harm by it but herself.

★ ★ ★

The two girls hurried up the steps and into the hall out of the sleet, and stood on the doormat, shaking themselves like dogs and laughing. Mrs Platt, the secretary, came out of the school office and gave them a severe look.

The school was very strict about decorum. They were required to behave in a seemly manner even when they were not in school. 'Wherever you are, you are ambassadors for the Blackwood!' they were told. They must never be seen without a hat and gloves, with untidy hair or unpolished shoes. Dress must be plain and modest. During the school day they wore what was called 'the overall', a cross between a pinafore and a smock in black glazed cotton, which protected their clothes and conferred a sort of uniform tidiness on them. They had to buy them from an outfitter in the Burlington Arcade.

'One would think we were novices in a convent,' Bron had complained to Alice once.

Now Mrs Platt surveyed them disapprovingly and said, 'Conduct, young ladies! Conduct! And you are dripping on the tiles. The servants have enough to do without making extra work for them. Go and get changed quickly.'

They suppressed their laughter until they were inside the cloakroom. 'Conduct, Miss Tallant, conduct!' Bron mocked.

They hung up their coats and hats and tied each other's overalls at the back. 'The school bow must be exactly six inches wide, Miss Strachan,' Alice intoned. 'Neither more nor less.'

'Both your eyes should be worn on the same side of the nose, Miss Tallant, not straddling the proboscis in that untidy way.'

'Oh, hush!' Alice gurgled. 'I've got a stitch!'

They stepped out of the cloakroom into the hall, and had to jump backwards as they were almost run into by someone clattering very fast down the stairs. He stopped dead and looked down at them. He seemed to be in his late thirties, dressed in a light-grey suit with an ochre waistcoat, soft collar and a flowing sort of tie in a loose bow. His hair was very dark, wavy, and also flowing, just over his collar at the back; his features were finely cut, and his eyes were an astonishing pale, bright blue.

'Young ladies?' he said, on a slightly questioning note. Bron flushed slightly, shifting her eyes away, but Alice forgot to look down and, staring at his face, was thinking how much she would like to draw him. 'Well, you'll know me again, won't you?' he said, addressing her. 'Miss . . .'

'Tallant,' she replied automatically, then managed to drag her eyes away. 'I'm sorry.'

'Sorry? You have an excellent name, don't apologise for it. We all desire talent.'

She glanced at him and saw he was staring at her in something of the way she had stared at him – as if to remember her features.

'I don't know you. First-year students?'

'Yes, sir,' Bron managed to answer.

'Then we shall meet again when you begin my classes. *À bientot, mesdemoiselles.*' He gave a theatrical bow, and continued on his way, walking with rapid steps towards the back of the house where an enormous glazed structure – originally the orangery – was now known as the Studio. So far, they hadn't used it – their lessons had been in the two classrooms upstairs.

'Who was that?' Alice asked, in an urgent undertone, as they trod up the stairs.

'Ivor Wentworth. He teaches figure studies. We're not allowed to do those yet.'

'Ivor Wentworth?' Alice said. 'But he's famous! I've seen pictures in the magazines. He does those wonderful paintings of Egyptian and Roman scenes. I can't believe he's so young!'

'Why not?' said Bron.

'I don't know. You always think famous people must be really old, don't you? Like Mr Ffolliot.'

'*He*'s not famous. Not properly. Isn't Mr Wentworth *handsome*?'

'He is. Very,' said Alice. She remembered his words, *We all desire talent*. He was just making a joke about her name, wasn't he? But when he said it he had looked at her in a certain way . . . 'Like a Greek god.'

'I don't think there was ever a Greek god called Ivor, was there?' Bron said. 'But he's like an angel. Glorious English angel.'

Angus presented himself at Mr Cowling's house on the other side of the square, telling himself not to hope for too much. The servant seemed to be expecting him, and conducted him straight to the business-room, where Mr Cowling, behind his desk, rose to his feet and invited Angus to sit. He looked him over for a nerve-racking age and, placing both his hands flat on the desk in front of him, he said, 'Now then, young man, let's have your story. What's this trouble you've got yourself into? And don't bother denying it, because I wasn't born yesterday.'

Angus was not sure how much detail he ought to give, but Mr Cowling had a very *absorbent* way of listening, alert, attentive and silent, which seemed to draw him out. When he finally stopped, Mr Cowling sat in silence for a few moments, as though reviewing the story in his head, and Angus made himself sit still and not fidget.

Finally Mr Cowling said, 'Well, I'm sorry to hear of such a falling-out between father and son. It's a puzzle. It's not as if you wanted to make a low marriage. An earl's daughter ought to be good enough for anyone, I'd have thought. What d'you think minded your father to take such a position?'

'He's my father, sir, and I don't wish to speak disrespectfully,' Angus began.

'Quite right. Honour thy father and thy mother, the Good Book says. But you may be open without being disrespectful, as long as what you say is the truth.'

'Well, then,' Angus said, a little awkwardly, 'the truth is that when my father gives an order he won't brook dissent.'

Mr Cowling frowned, the fingers of one hand drumming on the desk-top to aid thought. 'I don't know your father, but I know he's a successful man in his field. I admire that. I don't have a son.' For an instant he stopped, and a shadow briefly crossed his face. He resumed: 'But if I had, I should expect him to obey me.'

Angus's heart sank. Of course he would be on Father's side! 'Yes, sir,' he said.

'However.'

Angus's heart stopped sinking and hovered uncertainly.

'Would I force my son to marry when he'd a strong inclination another way? If that other way was not disgraceful in itself?'

The fingers drummed.

'I've no experience of buying influence that road – through ties of blood. I know high-up folk do it – aye, I know that well enough! And maybe it answers. I suppose it must, or they wouldn't do it, and it's been going on long enough.'

The heart began sinking again.

'Nine times out of ten it must pay. But then comes the tenth time.' Mr Cowling was looking at him now, searching his face for information. 'Are you sure your father won't budge?'

'Quite sure, sir. As far as he's concerned, I no longer exist. Even if I went now and said I'd seen the error of my ways and would marry as he chose, he wouldn't take me back, because that would be to show weakness.'

'Well, it passes me!' Mr Cowling muttered. 'If I only had a son, I'd make good sure to keep him by me, whatever it took.'

Angus's heart now didn't know which way to go, but on the whole it was looking upwards, sensing a peep of daylight.

'Now, I want to be sure if I help you I won't be treading

on anyone's toes. I don't like to make enemies in the world of business. And to come between father and son . . .' He shook his head. 'Tell me honestly, will your pa think I'm interfering in his family's private matters?'

'I'm sure he won't, sir. He won't care what happens to me. If he ever even hears about it, which I doubt, he'll only shrug and think you a fool for helping me.'

'Will he, by God!'

'Begging your pardon, sir.'

'We're all fools under God, Mr Tullamore, but each in his own way, and your pa's way is not mine. You seem to me a likely sort of young man and I've a mind to make use of you.'

'I'd be very grateful, sir.'

'Aye, you would, I've no doubt. Now, here's the thing: I've a lot of different businesses, and it's getting to the point where keeping an eye on all of them at once is difficult. So I'm minded to set up an office in London to pull all the threads together. There's my boots and shoes, which is where I started, and my art-silk stockings, and my share in the jam company. And there's a glove manufacturer in Nottingham I'm thinking about buying – they make leather gloves as well as fabric, and it wants shaking up, because the end result may be a glove either way, but the processes are different.'

'I imagine working in leather presents different problems,' Angus said, interested.

'It does, and working in leather is a thing I know a bit about! And I've a good supplier for the fine-grade hides, and I wouldn't mind putting a bit more business their way.'

'Luxury leather gloves ought to export well.'

'You've touched on it, lad. I want to get into export. I've seen it with the jam business – that's where the big money lies. You piqued my interest when you said the Russkies can't get enough of English soap.'

'English leather goods are very highly thought of, too. And paper goods – books and stationery and so on.'

'Paper, eh?' Cowling looked thoughtful, then shook himself. 'One thing at a time! Fine leather gloves and shoes are in my sights – and while I'm at it, what about leather pocket books and briefcases and portmanteaux? Factory space is easy enough to come by, hides I can get hold of. It's just a matter of tooling up.'

'And setting up the export lines,' Angus said. 'That takes a bit of time.'

'Time I've got, and money I've got. You have to invest to get it back, that's my motto, and I've a mind to invest in a shipping line of my own – why pay someone else to carry your goods if you can put 'em on your own ship? Now, there's a small shipping line I know of, working out of London Pool, a neat enough business but ready to expand if they can get the capital—'

'You wouldn't mean Mayer and Frank, would you, sir?'

'You know it?'

'I've heard the gossip,' he said. 'They've a good reputation, but these days if you don't expand you decline.'

'I knew I was right about you. I've a good eye, and I don't like to see something being wasted that can be put to good use – glove manufacturers or shipping lines or young men with a lot of their father's stubbornness about them. Aye, I've got your measure!' He smiled. 'Now, would you like to join me?'

'If you were to give me a chance, sir,' Angus said fervently, 'I promise you'd never regret it. What would you want me to do?'

'Set up my London office and, if you do it right, run it for me. It's a proper career I'm offering you.'

Angus's heart could get no higher now without exiting his body. He was almost beyond speech. 'Sir! Oh, sir!'

'Aye, that's me all right,' Cowling said humorously. 'I like to encourage ability – and reward it. Show me what you're made of, and I'll stick by you. You'll have to find me office premises. Furnish 'em. I'll need telephone and telegraph laid in. Set up communications with my other places. Find good staff. That's to start with. Then when it's all running smoothly, you'll look at the export and shipping side.'

Angus swallowed. 'My father's office was already running when I joined it. I've never had to set one up from scratch. I've never done anything like this before, sir – not on my own.'

'You won't be on your own, you noddy!' Cowling said pleasantly. 'I'm going to give you my secretary, Decius Blake, to begin with, till you find your way around. And I'll bring old Parkinson from my Northampton factory to help you as well for a few months. He's under-manager there, started at the bottom, and there's nothing much he doesn't know about – well, everything! I'll take you on on a three-month trial, and if you don't shape up, it's out you go with no hard feelings, eh? But if I'm any judge of character, you'll turn out to be just what I'm looking for.'

'I won't let you down, sir.'

'Right, then. I'll start you on five pounds a week—'

'Sir!' Angus gasped. It was very generous.

Cowling waved a hand. 'I'll need you to look smart if you're representing me, and you can't do that on a pittance. Where are you living?' Angus told him. 'Find yourself some decent lodgings somewhere around Eastcheap for a start. Once things are up and running you'll know better where to take a little place for yourself. Well, well, I think we've made a good start today.' He stood up and offered his hand. 'Next thing is to have a meeting with Decius and Parkinson and put a few things down on paper. I'll get them here next week. You see,' he added, 'if I had a London office we'd have somewhere proper to do the business!'

CHAPTER FIVE

It amused Richard to contrive a meeting between Rachel and Angus, though it had to be kept secret from Aunt Caroline – she would never go behind her sister's back. He suggested, quite truthfully, that Alice might like a visit from her sister, and Aunt Caroline obligingly wrote inviting Rachel to stay for a few days.

Richard offered to amuse Rachel on the Friday while Alice was at school. Aunt Caroline was surprised that he proposed taking her to the Victoria and Albert Museum. 'I don't think she's interested in old things, dear,' she said.

'It's not that sort of museum,' Richard said. 'There are some pretty things to look at. And a tea-room she'll certainly enjoy.'

That was no more than the truth, because he arranged for Angus to meet them there. He was interested in any case to hear about his interview with Mr Cowling.

'It sounds as if he means you to have a career with him. You could end up running a significant part of his business,' he said, when Angus had told all.

'That's what I'm hoping for,' said Angus. 'And if I can help him develop the export side—'

'It will make him even richer than he is already,' Richard finished for him. 'I don't think you'd find him ungenerous.'

'Then I'd be able to support a wife in decent style,' Angus said.

Rachel was gazing at him, torn between admiration and doubt. 'But—' she began.

'But,' Richard agreed. He owed it to his sister to keep a level head. 'There's still the question of our mother's permission. Which I can't imagine will be forthcoming.' He held out his hands like the two sides of a balance scale. 'A job in manufacturing and shipping. A Russian prince's estates.'

'Oh, *Richard*!' Rachel said reproachfully.

'You have to face it, old girl. The mater is no advocate for True Love.'

Rachel looked at Angus with swimming eyes. 'She'll never let me marry you.'

Angus reached for her hand across the table. 'You just have to hold on for another eighteen months. Once you're of age, you won't need her permission, and by then I'll be established in my career and have some money behind me. Only eighteen months more.'

Rachel gave him an adoring if watery look, but Richard knew – and probably the young couple did, too, deep in their hearts – that expecting Rachel to hold out against her mother was like expecting the ramparts of a sandcastle to hold back the tide. Once Maud's honeymoon was over she would take Rachel back to live with her in Germany, and Rachel would have no-one to stiffen her resolve.

'I'll hold on,' Rachel said. 'I really will.'

Angus could only squeeze her hand, with a bleak look.

'What was all that rumpus?' Rose asked, coming down the back stairs into Piccadilly – as they called the main connecting passage below stairs.

Afton paused to enlighten her. 'Little Lord Cordwell got into a fight with one of the stable boys, Timmy.'

Rose snorted. 'He wants beating, that boy.'

'Quite. Timmy called Lord Cordwell a blankety beggar-boy who was only here on sufferance.'

'No, I meant young Cordwell wants beating. I'd bet anything he started it. I heard him the other day making fun of Billy Watts's stammer. And what was he doing in the stables anyway, when he was supposed to be doing lessons?'

'I suppose he slipped away somehow.'

'That Miss Kettel can't control him, a big lummox like him. He's nearly nine years old. He ought to be sent away to school.'

'I agree. School would be the best thing for him.'

They both knew there was no money left in the Cordwell estate to pay for school. 'You should have a word with his lordship,' Rose said.

'It's not my place to suggest any such thing,' said Afton.

'There's bad blood in the Cordwells. His grandfather was a spendthrift and blew his brains out, and his father wasn't much better,' Rose said. 'Bad blood will out.'

'There's no such thing as bad blood,' Afton said stiffly.

Rose gave him a penetrating look. 'Says it right there in the Bible. The sins of the father will be visited on the children to the third and fourth generation. You can't argue with the Bible.'

'I'm sure his lordship is acquainted with the state of his own household and can make his own mind up,' said Afton.

The penetrating look did not waver. 'Well, if I catch him messing with my things again like he did last week I shall box his ears, and her ladyship can dismiss me if she wants.' She continued on her way, but turned a few steps past Afton to say quietly, 'You should have a word with his lordship, Mr Afton, place or no place, before that boy causes real trouble.'

Miss Taylor was able to get about on crutches now, which was a cause of irritation to Rose because she never knew where she was going to come across her. She found her poking about in the ironing room. She turned as Rose came in, and scowled. Her temper was as stretched as the head housemaid's. Dr Welkes had told her that her leg would heal in three or four months, but would she still have a position after that time?

'A whole basket of little Lord Ayton's things sitting here waiting to be ironed! Those nursery maids are shockingly idle! They should be done as soon as they are washed, not left for the creases to set in.'

'Not my business,' Rose said sharply. 'And not yours either.'

'The smooth running of the house is everyone's business. We never had slackness like this in Mrs Horsepool's day.' This was the housekeeper before Mrs Webster.

'You don't remember,' Rose told her. 'You were never down here except for meals. And it's time you started to get used to the stairs again. Your mistress is coming back next week, isn't she?'

Miss Taylor tossed her head, jammed the crutches into her armpits and heaved herself away instead of answering. To add to the worry of the Princess of Usingen coming back to the Castle was the unusual way she had announced it.

Everyone had expected Maud to go to London first, and probably to stay there until after Lord Leake's party. Also, when she came to the Castle, she normally only sent a telegram giving the train she would be on, so that the carriage could be sent to the station. But this time she had announced her return two weeks in advance, and by letter to Mrs Webster, with no mention of any stay in London, but an unusual degree of detail about the arrangements to be made.

The prince would sleep in the Queen's Bedroom – the state bedroom that Giles's father had occupied but which he had never cared for – and the portrait of the princess's first husband, the Earl of Stainton, which hung over the fireplace, was to be replaced with the daguerreotype of Queen Victoria from the morning-room. That much was understandable. But she went on to say the Van Dyck Room was to be prepared for her. It was named after the studio copy of the portrait of

Henrietta Maria of France in a magnificent dark blue silk gown, by Van Dyck, which had once hung over its mantelpiece, facing Charles I on horseback on the opposite wall. Both paintings had been sold by the late earl when he got into difficulties, but the name survived.

In addition the princess stipulated that she would have the state bed from the Tapestry Room; the yellow satin sofa and chairs from her old bedroom, along with the rosewood bonheur-du-jour from her former sitting-room; and the green porphyry fern stand from the library with an arrangement of flowers in the Roman vase from the Jade Room..

'What on earth is all this about?' Mrs Webster had said to Rose, perplexed. 'I've never known her to give orders like this. You've been here the longest, Rose – is this usual?'

'I've never known her to care a jot about what bedroom she used and what was in it,' Rose answered. 'If you ask me, she's just making trouble.'

'The state bed from the Tapestry Room?' said Mrs Webster. 'It's enormous! However can we move it?'

'The carpenter'll have to take it to bits and put it together again. It was done once before when the Empress Eugénie visited – Mr Sebastian will probably remember. That's three days' work for four men. If I was you, I'd check with his lordship. It's not as if she even lives here any more.'

Mrs Webster looked worried. 'But supposing it means she's moving back in? With the prince?'

'Then you'd definitely better check with his lordship. Maybe she's written to him as well,' said Rose.

The invitations to Fergus's post-wedding celebration had gone out, and the illustrateds had caught the romance of the story and had fallen into breathless superlatives. England's Most Eligible Bachelor Brings Home Italian Bride. Florentine Beauty Set To Dazzle London. Not since Helen of Troy captured the heart of Paris . . . Lord Leake, famously impervious to the most feted of English debutantes . . . Renaissance elegance and wit has cast a spell . . .

Lacking any likeness of Lord Leake's bride, one ingenious weekly had published the image of Da Vinci's *La Belle Ferronnière* to be going on with. *Lady's Realm* had managed to acquire a photograph of Lord and Lady Leake exiting the Meurice in Paris, but as she was wearing a hat with a veil and Lord Leake was holding an umbrella over both of them, there wasn't much to be seen.

The publishable facts were that Lord and Lady Leake were to stay at the Hambleton Hotel in Grosvenor Square where they would host a dinner for ninety followed by a ball to celebrate the nuptials that had taken place quietly in Florence. The less delicately minded publications were making estimates of how much it was all going to cost.

'Ninety at dinner! I had no idea Fergus knew so many people,' Aunt Caroline said to Giles, who had come up to Town to talk to his banker, Vogel.

'"His charming bachelor habit of moving from house to house during the Season proved him to be one of the best-known and most popular house-guests in the land,"' said Giles.

'Is that a quotation?' Aunt Caroline said, puzzled.

'From *Vanity Fair*. Lady Bexley showed it to me after church. I think she supposed I might be able to get her an invitation.'

'Oh dear, how embarrassing,' Aunt Caroline said.

'It was. She gushed.'

'I did invite them to stay here, of course,' Aunt Caroline went on, 'but I had no idea of the scale of his plans. I thought it was to be a neat dinner for immediate family. Excluding the children we'd have sat down twelve at table, a pleasant number I always think. I've had to see Madame Hortense about a new gown, and she doesn't like to be hurried. How dressy do you think it will be? Do you think I should get my tiara from the bank?'

'Aunty, I have no idea,' Giles said impatiently. 'Just be glad they're *not* staying here – imagine having the press gathered in front of your door day after day, photographing everyone going in or out.'

'Have you heard any more from Maud and the prince? I understand they're going straight down to Ashmore – probably wise after such a long journey. They'll need time to recover before the party. But will they want to stay here *after* the ball? You're all welcome, of course, but I need to know who will be staying. This is really a *very* small house. Eight bedrooms should be enough but not if married people want to sleep separately.' She looked anxious at the thought.

Giles smiled and patted her hand. 'You do have your troubles. Ask Grandmère to take Alice and Rachel for the night.'

'Oh, Alice!' Aunt Caroline cried, seeing a new problem. 'That child has *nothing* suitable for a dinner and ball like this. I shall have to wheedle Madame Hortense into making something for her. It will put her in a dreadful mood,' she sighed.

'Goodness, a dressmaker who gets upset by being asked to make dresses?'

'You don't understand. She's an artist, and artists are temperamental. Has Kitty something suitable? Tell her not to leave it to the last moment. Rachel will be all right – she had trunks full of things for her come-out last year.'

'I know. I paid for them,' Giles said drily.

London always made him feel tired, and talking to Vogel was not something he looked forward to, even though these days the financial news was good. Harvey's Jam – the business Kitty had inherited from her mother and brought him as a dowry – was making large profits since, with Mr Cowling's added investment, they had gone into five- and ten-pound tins for the export market. Everyone wanted jam, and the ingenious managing director, Charles Logan, was even now talking with the Colonial Office about supplying it to government installations and hospitals in India. Their prosperity seemed assured, and Vogel was a happy man, as far as he ever displayed emotion behind those gold-rimmed glasses; but numbers bothered Giles like flies, decisions made him sleepy, his stiff collar and tie grew tighter the longer he wore them, and London pavements made him feel as if he had two feet in each shoe. He was relieved to be going home.

The train soon left the suburbs behind and rattled into ever more bosky surroundings. Trees and hedges were starting to come into leaf, blurring the stark outlines of winter; and the pastures were always green in Buckinghamshire, the greenest of English counties. Just now he was inclined to welcome the rural peace. His mother coming home; rows over Rachel and Alice; this damned London dinner and ball; meeting Giulia again, as wife – wife! – of his uncle! Everything ahead of him seemed gauged to vex him. He had not wanted the earldom or the estate, but with a day in London irritating his mind, like grit inside a shoe, the thought of walking out into his own fields with a gun under his arm and the dogs at his heels, with no-one near by and no sound but the rooks in the spinney, made him realise there were compensations.

He hoped that when he got home he could change quickly and slip out into the dusk for a walk with Tiger and Isaac, but Linda had arrived back, had found her invitation, and was waiting for him.

'Giles! I have *nothing* to wear for this ball. It's going to be in every paper and magazine. The eyes of the whole nation will be on us. The family's reputation is at stake!'

'You mean you want a new gown.'

'I mean I *must have* a new gown. It's imperative!'

Ah, yes, Giles thought. In the list of things lining up to vex him, he had forgotten to include Linda.

The arrival of Maud and her new husband at Ashmore Castle was keenly anticipated in one quarter. Giddins, the head man, was in a bustle of pride and excitement. The dowager, now the Princess of Usingen – and if anyone deserved to be a princess it was her: she had always behaved as if she *was* one – demanded the highest standards, and it was his chance to show his mettle. The four matched dapple-greys (he wished they could be six, or even a royal eight) were washed and polished until they shone – and it was hard to get a grey to shine. He stood on a box to plait their manes himself; and when the team were perfect in every respect, he stationed two boys to keep watch behind them in case one of them should cock a tail: stable stains were the very worst thing with greys. If natural functions seemed imminent, a boy was to run in with a skip and intercept.

While not looking forward to the invasion, Mrs Webster was anxious not to have fault found. Her tension communicated itself to Afton, and between them they chivvied the servants and checked each other's work. Afton looked over the Queen's Bedroom almost as often as Mrs Webster did the Van Dyck, to make sure that anything that could possibly be wanted was in place.

Crooks, who had been valet to the old earl and now valeted Mr Sebastian, and Mr Richard when he was at home, was in a ferment of nerves in case he should be called upon to valet the prince.

'He'll have his own man,' Afton said.

'But nothing was mentioned about servants in the letter, was it? Suppose he *doesn't* bring a valet?'

'Then you'll manage. I have every faith in you.'

'It isn't that he's a prince, you understand, but that he's not English. He might have different requirements.'

'He's a man, Mr Crooks. We all put our trousers on one leg at a time.'

'That's just it, Mr Afton. I've been helping gentlemen into their trousers all my life, but it takes time to get to know their little ways. His late lordship, for instance—'

'I'm sure you'll come through if it should be needed,' Afton said quickly, and hurried away before he learned more about the late earl's nether garments than he wanted to.

Miss Taylor, grim-faced, had the opposite problem: suppose the princess arrived with a lady's maid, what would happen to her? She had been practising walking, but too much exertion made her leg ache abominably. Dr Welkes had taken off the cast, and had provided her with a brace to wear. She had let down her hems to brush the top of her foot, which hid the brace from sight, but he had told her to use a stick for a few weeks, and she was sure that even if the princess had not brought a maid, she would not allow a stick anywhere near her.

Kitty was dreading it, having always been afraid of her mother-in-law. All she could do was order the best meal possible (though March was not exactly an accommodating month) and instruct that the servants should all be lined up in front when the carriage came back from the station.

'At least it's not raining,' she remarked to Giles, as they waited inside the hall for the signal that the carriage was in sight. It was grey, mild and misty. The dogs came poking their noses up and swinging their iron-bar tails, hoping that all this activity portended a walk. 'Oh dear! She doesn't like dogs. Afton, can you take them away and shut them in somewhere?'

The boy they had stationed on the drive ran panting up. They walked out onto the front steps, and could see the carriage with the greys coming up the avenue, followed by the brake for the luggage and the closed cab from the station.

Giles said, 'It puts me in mind of the arrival of the Queen of Sheba, "with a very great retinue, with camels bearing spices, very much gold, and precious stones".'

'Oh, I wish she did have camels!' Alice said, from behind him. 'Shouldn't we be welcoming her with sackbuts and shawms?'

'I should think you'd not want to draw attention to yourself,' Linda told her severely. 'Neither of you,' she included Rachel in the opprobrium. 'If I was you I'd keep very quiet.'

'Is Grandma going to be cross?' her daughter Arabella asked.

'Not with you,' Linda said shortly. 'But don't speak unless spoken to.'

'I'm bored!' her son Arthur, Lord Cordwell, moaned. 'Why have we got to stand here all the time? I want to go in.'

'Ssh!' Kitty said sharply. She checked one last time. The maids in their morning grey, with caps; the footmen and boys in livery; old Frewing, the hall porter, proudly holding the door and at the back the nursery maids in blue with her sons, Louis and Alexander, decked in their best.

The greys, lifting their legs beautifully and arching their necks, drew the carriage up to the entrance and John Manley, the coachman, stopped it exactly at the centre. William the first footman moved into position to open the door and put down the step. Cyril, the second, ran round to the far side from which the tall, thin shape of the prince, wearing a voluminous greatcoat with a vast astrakhan collar and a Russian astrakhan hat, soon emerged and came round to help his princess out of the carriage.

And finally Giles's mother appeared, stepping down between the prince and William, in a mauve-grey wool coat, a grey hat with iridescent cock feathers, a mink cape and a huge mink muff. She straightened, shook away the prince's hand, and walked up to Giles, extending her neck, tortoise-like, for his dutiful kiss, and ignoring Kitty.

'Welcome to Ashmore, Mother,' Giles said. 'How was your journey? You're looking well.'

Actually, he thought, she was. She seemed to have put on a little flesh, and had some colour in her cheeks.

She gave him a cold look. 'I suppose that is your idea of a joke, Stainton.'

Well, he thought resignedly, I didn't expect her first words to me to be, 'It's wonderful to see you again, my son.'

Kitty actually preferred to be ignored, but if she was going to be told off, better to get it over with. 'We got your letter,' she said. 'We've prepared everything just as you asked.'

Maud gave her a look even colder. 'When I was mistress here, things were done as I ordered them to be. It was not necessary to mention it.'

Giles grew a little impatient. 'Have you come home simply to complain about everything, Mother dear?'

She drew herself up another inch. 'No. I have come home to die,' she said.

Down in Piccadilly, maids' heads were together. 'And then she said, "I came home to die,"' said Tilda, impressively.

Milly's eyes were round. 'Ooh! I never! Did she really?'

'You could have knocked me down with a feather!'

'She didn't say that,' said Doris. 'She said, "I came home *today*."'

Daisy was impatient. 'Don't be stupid. We know she came home today. We were there.'

'I thought she said, "I came home *tidy*,"' said Addy.

'Well, why would she say that?' Tilda said, annoyed at being cheated of her story.

'On account of his lordship had just asked her if she had a good journey,' said Addy, slowly, thinking it out. 'And she was lettin' him know she didn't get all blown about on the ship.'

'You're all idiots,' Daisy said. 'Tilda's right, she said she came home to die. I heard it clear.'

'But what can it mean?' Milly said.

Mrs Webster and Afton appeared at that moment and Afton said sternly, 'It's not for you to gossip about Upstairs. Get about your work.'

They scuttled away, and Afton said quietly to Mrs Webster,

'In fact, it's all they *do* have to gossip about, poor things. But discipline must be maintained.'

'Quite,' said Mrs Webster. 'You heard her say it, though, didn't you, Mr Afton?'

'You know her better than me. Is it the sort of thing she says – for effect, perhaps, or to gain sympathy?'

'Never. I couldn't have been more surprised.' She sighed. 'If it's true, it means she'll be here for a long stay, and great unpleasantness at the end of it.' She contemplated it glumly.

The house boy Wilfrid ran up and divided a message impartially between them. 'Luggage comin' in! Mountains of it. And two servants – foreign ones!'

Miss Taylor had positioned herself in the Van Dyck room, having left her stick outside. She could manage for short periods without it, and it was obviously impossible to fetch and carry and help someone undress while holding one.

A strange young woman entered bearing a valise, beamed nervously at Taylor and said, in a heavy accent, 'I am Elke, please.'

'I am Miss Taylor, her highness's personal attendant. Is that her bag for immediate use?'

'Please?'

'Put it down over there. I shall attend to it.'

'Please?'

Taylor conveyed her meaning by a violent jab of the finger, and the girl, still smiling, complied. It was at that moment that the princess entered the room. Elke curtsied.

Miss Taylor curtsied only to royalty. 'Welcome home, your highness,' she said.

Maud raised an eyebrow. 'What are you doing here?'

'I anticipated that your highness would require my services,' Taylor said, through rigid lips. 'I *am* your highness's personal attendant. And that young person does not appear to understand English.'

Maud looked at her for a long moment. 'Very well,' she said at last.

Miss Taylor's relief was so great her knees trembled, but she showed nothing in her face. She stepped forward, trying desperately not to limp, as Maud turned her back for her coat to be removed. The princess slipped off her mink and tossed it carelessly to Elke, who caught it deftly. 'Elke can assist you,' she said. She addressed a rapid sentence in German to the young woman, who replied, and left the room. 'Hot water?' she said.

'Coming at once,' said Miss Taylor.

'My dressing-gown is in that valise.'

Miss Taylor undressed the princess as far as her chemise, and helped her into her dressing-gown. Then Maud said, 'I shall rest on the bed. I'll ring for you when I want you.'

Miss Taylor bowed her head in acknowledgement. As she reached the door, the princess said, 'Oh – Taylor?'

She turned. 'Your highness?'

'I'm allowing you to keep your position only because I omitted to dismiss you when you so inconsiderately broke your leg and interrupted my plans. Don't let me down again.'

'What does she mean? She doesn't look ill,' Kitty said, having beckoned Giles into her bedroom, sending Hatto out so they could talk privately.

'I have no idea,' Giles said. 'Mother never talks about health, her own or anyone else's, so it's impossible to ask her.'

'But, Giles, we have to know if she needs any special arrangements.'

'She'll let you know soon enough if she wants something.'

Kitty shook her head. 'I'm just so shocked. I don't know what to think.' She looked at him sharply. 'Aren't you dreadfully upset? She *is* your mother.'

'I'm still trying to come to terms with the announcement,' Giles said. 'She's no age.'

'Do you think the prince knows?'

'It's hard to say. I don't think he heard what she said – he was a long way behind her. And his English isn't good.'

'Surely she would have told him first?'

'My mother is a rule to herself. Does he look like an adoring husband whose wife is dying? It's so hard to tell. He has that fixed, uncomprehending smile all the time, like a dog when you talk to it.'

'Oh, Giles!' Kitty said reproachfully.

'I'll try and talk to her this evening and find out more. But it won't be easy.'

Miss Taylor's face didn't show emotion. The lines in it were set, like the folds in a damask tablecloth that has been carefully put away in a chest for years. But anyone who knew her well would have seen that her eyes were gleaming with satisfaction when she came in to servants' dinner and said to Hatto, 'You must go lower. I believe my lady outranks yours.'

'*Your* lady?' Hatto queried.

'A princess outranks a countess.'

Mrs Webster said, 'What about that young person?' She nodded towards Elke, who was hovering uncertainly by the wall. 'I thought *she* was the princess's maid.'

Hatto had got up, and maids were shifting down the table in a ripple like a breeze passing over a wheatfield. Taylor took the vacated seat and said, with a hint of triumph, 'I've never seen her before. I expect she's a chambermaid taken on to attend her ladyship on the voyage. *I* am the princess's personal maid.'

Elke saw eyes on her, 'Please?' she said.

Rose shoved her firmly towards the last seat in the middle of the table. 'She doesn't understand a word of English,' she said, going to her own chair.

Webster lowered her voice. 'The prince's man doesn't either, but Mr Afton showed him to his place.' The valet, tall and thin like his master, but younger, dark-haired and balding at the front, sat impassively in the place next to Afton.

'How *is* her ladyship, Miss Taylor?' Rose asked.

'Her ladyship does not discuss her health.'

'I couldn't believe she said what she said, right out in front of everyone.'

'Well, I think it's terrible sad,' Milly said, with a sentimental sigh. 'And her only married a few months.'

'It's nice for her that she'll be able to spend her last days here,' Ellen said, 'instead of some nasty foreign place where she doesn't know anyone.'

'Days, Miss Taylor?' Mrs Webster asked, in a low voice. 'Or months? Was any indication given?'

Miss Taylor didn't bother to repeat her previous statement. She just gave Mrs Webster a withering look.

'Either way,' Rose said, 'it looks like you're not going to keep your job long. You celebrated too soon.'

'Do you see me celebrating?' Miss Taylor said, giving the withering look another outing.

'"My mistress outranks yours,"' Rose imitated her.

'That's enough, Rose,' Mrs Webster rebuked. 'Grace, Mr Afton?'

When amen was said, Mrs Webster started ladling soup, and Crooks picked up the bread basket and offered it to the German valet. 'Bread, Mr Usingen?'

He looked uncomprehending for a moment, and then said, 'Usingen. *Ja.*'

'I believe that means *yes*,' Crooks enlightened the table. 'In their language.'

'I think we got that, Mr Crooks,' Cyril said, 'on account of he nodded his head.'

The valet took a piece of bread, sniffed it uncertainly, and then said, '*Danke.*'

Crooks turned to translate this for everyone, and Mrs Webster said under her breath, 'Oh, this is going to be fun,' and then loudly, 'I wonder if the prince is going to stay here the whole time. Is your German good enough to ask that, Mr Crooks?'

'I fear not, Mrs Webster,' Crooks said. 'But no doubt we will be told of the arrangements when it is appropriate.'

Rose, passing soup plates down, said, 'Lady Linda speaks German. She'll get it out of one of them all right.'

'And you'll get it out of her,' Miss Hatto said, but so quietly no-one heard her.

At dinner, Kitty said to her mother-in-law, 'If there's anything we can do to make you more comfortable, you must tell us.'

Maud raised an eyebrow at her. 'Was my letter of instruction not clear?'

Kitty flinched at the rebuke, and looked down at her plate.

The prince said something in German.

The princess snapped, '*Auf Englisch!*'

Effortlessly, he said to Kitty, 'You have here a very pretty house, Lady Stainton. Do you make much stay in the country?'

Kitty gathered herself. 'We live here most of the time,' she said.

'I like very much to make stay in the country,' he persevered politely. 'It is of all things most agreeable. But ladies, I think, like to be in the town.' He smiled around the company. 'Ladies, I think, like the shopping and the theatre *und so weiter*. Is it not so, dear wife? In the Nevsky Prospekt in St Petersburg there were many fine shops. We look forward to return when the present *Schwierigkeiten* are ended.'

Giles met Kitty's eyes down the table. *He doesn't know*, he thought. *Surely he wouldn't talk like that if he knew?*

'Did you see much of the disorder in St Petersburg, sir?' Uncle Sebastian asked.

'No, we had left the day before the march on the Winter Palace.'

'That was lucky,' said Uncle Sebastian.

'The strikes were making life uncomfortable,' Maud said. 'When the electricity failed we accepted an invitation to stay with the Menshikovs in Crimea. The Crown Prince and Princess of Romania were there also, and they invited everyone to Bucharest.'

'The Cotroceni Palace is most comfortable,' the prince said. 'Much of improvement lately by King Karel has been made. Sinaia is more pretty, but a summer palace. The mountains are too cold in snow-time for my lady. But the crown prince has promised to invite us when summer comes,' he concluded blithely.

It was all very puzzling.

The princess, it was noted, ate very little at dinner, and when the cloth was drawn announced she was retiring. The prince rose as she did, and seemed almost to want to escort her, but after a rapid exchange in German he bowed her out of the room and sat again, leaving them to entertain him.

Rachel and Alice exchanged a look of relief: there would be no facing the music for them this evening, at least. But while they were still at dessert, a footman came in, approached Rachel's chair and murmured a message that made her turn immediately white.

'What is it?' Giles said, annoyed. Surely young Tullamore had not invaded the house again, uninvited, and at this hour.

Rachel was already rising. 'Mama has sent for me.'

She actually swayed on her feet. The other men had of course risen, and Richard steadied her and said quietly, 'Best get it over with. She can't kill you, you know.'

Rachel stared at him a moment with beseeching eyes, unable to articulate the many layers of foreboding in her mind. To withstand her mother's will was difficult at any time, but how could you defy a mother who was *dying*?

★ ★ ★

'Stop crying, Rachel,' Maud said irritably.

'I c-can't help it,' she sobbed. 'You're my m-mother. I don't want you to die!'

'It is a natural process. All life ends in death. *You* will die. There is nothing to make a fuss about.' Seeing that Rachel had used up the capacity of the dainty handkerchief, which was all a young lady expected to need at dinner, she rose from the settle and fetched another of her own, and gave it to her. 'Compose yourself. Control, Rachel! Control is everything. The Usingen motto is *vincit qui se vincit*. Do you know what that means? He succeeds who conquers himself. You would do well to adopt it. Dry your eyes, blow your nose and sit up straight.'

Rachel was a tender-hearted creature easily brought to tears. Even though she had always feared her mother, they had spent a great deal of time together the previous year, and being rarely scolded during that time had made her fonder of her stern parent – the only one she had left, after all. But obediently she mopped up, sat up, and tried to control the last hitching sobs.

'Now, as to your future,' Maud said. 'I do not know how long I have left – no, I forbid you to cry again! – so we must work quickly. Negotiations with Prince Suripov are well in hand, and fortunately he is very fond of England and is willing to come here for a binding betrothal ceremony. The wedding itself will have to take place in Russia and you will have to convert to the Russian Orthodox religion. If I should die before the wedding can take place, your stepfather will complete the arrangements, escort you to St Petersburg and attend you to the wedding. He will be your legal guardian until you marry.'

Rachel felt as though all the blood had drained out of her. Her lips felt numb. She could only stammer, 'But – but I don't want—'

Maud interrupted her, eyebrows shooting upwards. 'Do you understand what a brilliant match I have made for you?

Prince Suripov has connections all through the Russian Imperial court. His first wife was unable to give him a child, so—'

'His first wife?' Rachel gasped.

'He is a widower. What now? He is a little older than you, in his forties, but your youth is a great attraction. Give him a son, and he will be a kind and generous husband. You will like St Petersburg – a very civilised city.' She stopped, with a slight frown, remembering the recent troubles. But they would soon be dealt with. Russia went through these convulsions from time to time, the Suripovs had told her, but then everything settled down and the old order was restored.

Rachel gripped her hands together, summoned the dregs of her courage, and said, 'I won't do it.'

Frost settled on the air. 'I beg your pardon?'

'I won't go to Russia. I won't convert. I won't marry an old Russian prince I've never met.'

'Don't be foolish. You'll meet him at the betrothal.'

'I won't marry him,' Rachel cried desperately.

Maud regarded her thoughtfully for a moment. 'You'll deny your mother her dying wish?'

That ought to have clinched it, but, oddly, it strengthened Rachel's resolve. 'That's not fair! You know I—'

'Disobedience to your parent is a sin, are you aware of that?' Rachel's lips were trembling too much for her to answer. 'Is this about that foolish Tullamore boy?' Maud said, eyes narrowing.

'I love him!' Rachel cried. 'I'm going to marry him.'

'And how precisely is he to support a wife? I have it on good authority that his father has disinherited him.' Rachel was weeping again. 'You propose to choose a life of hardship and penury with that obscure boy rather than a life of ease and wealth with a man of rank and position? Are you insane, or merely an abject fool?'

'Mama, don't!'

'Kindly cease that disgusting exhibition. No, Rachel, I will not let you ruin your life. You are my daughter and you will marry as I see fit.'

'You can't make me! You can't make me!'

'Don't talk nonsense. Usingen will take you to Russia and you will forget all about your silly childish fancy – for that's all it is. I can't look at you in that state any longer. Go away now. You have wearied me beyond endurance. We'll speak again tomorrow.'

CHAPTER SIX

Up in the old schoolroom, Rachel wept on Alice's shoulder. When she was quiet at last, Alice said, 'Did she mention me?'

'No,' Rachel hiccuped. 'I suppose you'll get your turn.'

Alice gave her a handkerchief. 'Do you really not want to be a Russian princess and have jewels and carriages and furs and great houses?'

Rachel gave her a reproachful look. 'But I love Angus.'

'Why?'

'I don't know,' Rachel said. 'I just love him. I could never love anyone else.'

If her sister had come up with reasons, Alice might have doubted her, but she was aware of how love took you and didn't bother with whys and wherefores. It just *was*.

'Then you must resist.'

'But how can I refuse Mama's dying wish?'

'You must, that's all. If you feel you're starting to give in, we'll run away together.'

'Run away? Where to?'

'London, of course.'

Rachel looked doubtful. 'Aunt Caroline wouldn't side with me against Mama.'

'We won't go to her. We'll get jobs as chambermaids in a hotel – that way we'll have somewhere to live as well. Then, as soon as you're of age, you can marry Angus.'

'I don't think I'd like to be a chambermaid,' Rachel said.

'Well, perhaps you can get some other kind of work,' Alice said impatiently. 'The important thing is not to give in.'

Rachel still looked doubtful. The thought of working at a job and living in lodgings like ordinary people was frightening. She wouldn't know how to go on. People would tell her to do things and she wouldn't know how, and they'd get cross with her. Her clothes would get dirty and wear out. How could she buy food? She didn't know how much anything cost.

But the image of Angus's face came before her eyes in the nick of time. 'Angus will look after me,' she said. 'Angus knows how to do things.'

The next morning the princess was not down to breakfast: word came that she was over-tired and was remaining in bed. Rachel felt horribly guilty. Had she made her mother sicker?

The prince, in his halting English, attributed it to the strain of the long journey, and did not seem worried. 'Travelling is by all means tiring,' he told them.

'He doesn't know,' Richard said afterwards to Uncle Sebastian. 'I'm convinced of it. But how could Mother not tell him?'

'Because she hates talk about health matters,' Uncle Sebastian said.

Richard shook his head. 'One feels sorry for the poor man – he's obviously devoted to her. Do you think you ought to have a word with him?'

Uncle Sebastian looked alarmed. 'Come between a husband and wife? In any case, what could I tell him? *I* don't know what's wrong with her.'

As Mabel straightened up from putting her basket back in the cupboard in the housemaids' closet, the awareness of a looming presence behind her made her whip round defensively and squeak.

'*Genau wie eine Feldmaus!*' the valet said, smiling.

Mabel caught the 'mouse' in the answer and decided it wasn't threatening; besides, when a male creature smiled, she always smiled back. 'Oh, you startled me, Mr Usingen,' she said, giving him the title by which he was known below stairs.

'*Nein, nein.*' He jabbed himself vigorously in the chest with a forefinger and said, '*Adolf. Mein Name ist Adolf.*'

Even Mabel could not mistake that. 'Oh, Adolf? That's nice,' she said.

'*Und wie heißt du?*'

A pointing finger and questioning eyebrows meant she understood the question. 'I'm Mabel. Ma-bel,' she repeated, with slow clarity, as to the feeble-minded.

He said something else in German, still smiling, and putting out a hand to rub her upper arm appreciatively. Mabel filled her uniform plumply, and while not strictly pretty she had a round, healthy, pink face and shiny eyes, and men quite often smiled at her and found it hard to resist a stroke or a pinch. She knew where she was with this approach. Adolf was not bad-looking. Besides, he was a valet, and she had a very keen sense of hierarchy.

'It must be lonely for you, not speaking any English,' she said. A doubt struck her. 'You *don't* speak any English, do you?'

'*Du bist ein lustiges Mädchen,*' he said. '*Willst du auf meinem Schoß sitzen?*'

She smiled incomprehendingly, but he stepped closer and slid an arm round her waist, and she knew what that meant. 'Oh, you are a naughty man!'

'*Und du bist ein schmutziges Mädchen!*'

She giggled. 'You think I'm pretty?' she hazarded, from previous experience. That's what they usually said.

He smiled and nodded. '*Schmutzig.*'

She tried it. 'Shush . . . Shmush . . .'

'*Schmut-zig,*' he said with slow clarity and a smile that, had she been concentrating, she'd have noticed was a little menacing. His hand crept from her arm to her shoulder, with a drift of fingers towards her bosom.

'Shmoo-sig,' she copied carefully. And then the choreography fell into usual patterns.

'It's a growth,' Rose told Mrs Webster in the privacy of her room. 'Something of a dropsical nature. Lady Linda said she thought it might be liver.'

'But what are her symptoms? I thought liver made you yellow.'

'Well, it might not be liver. She has vomiting and light fevers, and swelling in the ab— What's it called?'

'Abdomen?'

'That's it. And tiredness and loss of appetite.'

'Sounds more like heart failure,' said Mrs Webster. 'I had an aunt went that way. Dropsy and extreme tiredness. Did Lady Linda mention what the doctor said about it?'

Rose gave her a look. 'She's not seen a doctor. You know what she's like.'

'So she doesn't know . . . ?'

'How long she's got left? No.'

'It seems unfair on the poor prince,' Mrs Webster said, after a moment. 'He ought to have the chance to say goodbye.'

It was for Giles, as host, to look after the prince while his mother kept to her chamber, and he took him out for a long walk with guns. Shooting was over, of course, but there were always pigeons, and the more of *them* they shot, the happier Saddler would be.

After luncheon he offered him a mount, and Richard, in response to an urgent rolling of the eyes at the luncheon table, joined the party and helped with the conversational burden. The prince rode well; he had proved himself an excellent shot, too. And when Richard, by trial and error, had discovered a subject that interested him, he waxed lyrical about his estate in Germany, the countryside, and German rural life. As his speech grew more animated he lapsed more often into German, but Richard's German was better than Giles's, and he was quicker at picking up meaning from context, so Giles was able to lapse into his own thoughts, which dwelt on what a horrid mess this was, how distressing it was going to be for everyone, and what would happen to his three sisters.

'What's happening?' Alice asked, as she entered the drawing-room before dinner. Everyone was looking tense. The atmosphere in the house was almost palpable, and everywhere there were servants being busy about nothing, a sure sign they were waiting for news of some sort. 'Is Mama not coming down to dinner?' she asked, when no-one answered her.

'*He*'s in there,' Linda said. 'In her room. They're having the most tremendous row.'

'I don't think we should be talking about it,' Kitty said.

'It's too late for discretion,' Richard said. 'The cat's well and truly out of the bag.'

'But what's *happened*?' Alice asked again.

'Uncle Sebastian had an attack of conscience,' Richard said. 'He took the prince for a game of billiards and put the whole thing to him. The prince looked horrified and rushed off to Van Dyck to have it out with her. Did you know Germans don't play snooker?'

'Don't be frivolous,' Giles rebuked. 'There's nothing amusing about any of this.'

'I didn't say I was amused.'

Sebastian walked in. 'I don't know how these things get about, but Crooks just asked me some very oblique questions.'

'They listen,' Richard said. 'My mother may believe servants are blind and deaf, but that doesn't make it true.' He looked at Linda. 'And of course my dear sister is thick as thieves with head housemaid Rose.'

Linda bristled. 'Are you accusing me of gossiping with servants?'

'Oh, please, don't let's quarrel.' Rachel was near tears. 'Mama's dreadfully ill and the poor prince does love her so. He must be so terribly upset.'

Afton appeared at the door and caught Kitty's eye.

'I think we should go in to dinner, and not wait for the prince,' she said.

'And as mistress of the house,' Giles said, going to her side, 'my wife hereby forbids any further discussion of this subject. Let's try to behave in a civilised manner at table.'

It was an unnerving thing to Giles to see his mother subdued. He had never known anyone make her do anything against her will. He supposed his father might have, but they had led such entirely separate lives, he had never seen it happen. Besides, he didn't suppose his father cared much what she did.

She came down to breakfast in the morning on the prince's arm and announced that she would be going to London after breakfast. She seemed disinclined to say more, but the prince gave her a nudging sort of look and she added without meeting any eyes, 'His highness wishes me to consult a physician.'

'That seems a good idea,' Kitty said tentatively. 'At least, then—'

Maud cut her off, shaking away sympathy as a dog shakes water from its coat. 'In accordance with his wishes I shall consult Sir Henry Felden. And that is all I wish to say on the matter. Kitty, will you give orders for the carriage? The prince and I will take the ten-thirty train.'

'Of course,' said Kitty. She wanted to say how glad she was that her mother-in-law was to consult a doctor; to say that perhaps the case was not hopeless as she believed, that perhaps there was something that could be done. But she didn't quite dare, and tried to put it all into a look. But Maud had turned away and didn't see it.

Sam was third footman and content with his lot. Though fair and good-looking, he was short, and most houses liked their footmen to be tall, so he was glad to get this job. He had also been illiterate when he arrived, and had struggled to hide the fact, but Mr Crooks had discovered his secret and had kindly given him lessons, so that he could now at least sound out the names on tins and packets and avoid mistakes like using blacklead on boots.

He was cleaning the silver when someone came into the plate room behind him. He looked round and saw it was the prince's valet. 'Can I help you with something, Mr Usingen?' he asked politely.

'Please call me Adolf,' the valet said.

Sam looked doubtful. 'We're not supposed to. Mr Moss was always very particular. Visiting valets are called by their master's name.'

'Who is Mr Moss?'

'He was the butler before. It's Mr Afton now.'

'Then *vielleicht* we need not trouble with Mr Moss's rules?' Adolf smiled. 'What is your name?'

'Sam,' said Sam, with a blush at so much attention. 'I didn't know you could speak English.'

'It is necessary in high German houses a little English to speak. Many times there are English guests and their servants.' He shrugged. 'So we learn. Do you speak a language?'

'Only English,' Sam said. 'I'm only third footman, so I don't have much to do with guests.'

Adolf gestured to the silver. 'You are busy, I think. I should not trouble you.'

'No, please, if there's something I can help you with,' Sam babbled. 'No trouble at all.'

'*Ach so.* To tell me the names of things, perhaps, if you will? This thing, for instance. *Wie heißt es?*'

'The epergne?' said Sam. 'It's an epergne.' He blushed at his own foolishness.

Adolf drew close and examined it. 'It is very – *verwickelt.*'

Sam glanced up under his eyelashes and guessed. 'Fancy? Yes, it's the dickens to clean. Getting into all the crevices . . .'

'A skilled job. Here, for instance.' He touched the convolutions of a bunch of grapes. Sam's gloved hand was holding the epergne just near there, and Adolf's hand brushed it. 'It must take you many hours of work.'

'We don't use it often. Only on grand occasions. But Mr Afton likes things to be kept ready, just in case.'

'I think he trusts you to this important work. You especially.'

Sam's blush, which had only just subsided, rose again. 'I'm only third footman. I'm not special.'

'But this – epergne – must be very valuable.' His hand moved again, and was definitely resting on Sam's.

Sam's Adam's apple rose and fell in his throat. 'I 'spect it is.'

Adolf's hand moved up to Sam's wrist, where a small area of bare skin showed between glove and cuff. 'What smooth skin you have,' he said.

Nothing but a muted squeak was able to escape the constriction of Sam's throat.

Kitty had dreaded her come-out, and had got through it only with the help of Nina at her side, encouraging her. Marriage and children had changed her, and she was able to meet strangers with some composure now. She even quite enjoyed the parties she and Giles gave themselves.

But arriving at the Hambleton Hotel for Fergus's dinner and ball brought back the old feelings. It was lit up like an ocean liner; carriages and motor-cars were queuing up to disgorge their fabulous freight; policemen were in attendance to control the crowd, which had gathered in expectation of a free spectacle.

'I won't know anyone,' she murmured anxiously to Giles.

He didn't hear her, or feel her hand tremble on his arm. He had his own concerns. He feared this first meeting with Giulia would be awkward, despite telling himself that she would surely have got over her annoyance with him by now

He and Kitty had come up that afternoon and gone to Aunt Caroline's to change. His mother and the prince had elected to stay at Claridge's, so there was room after all at the house for Uncle Sebastian, Richard, Linda and the girls to stay the night as well. Aunt Caroline was bringing Richard and the girls in her carriage; Linda and Uncle Sebastian were in another cab behind.

They shed their outer wrappings in the imposing foyer. March was a poor month for flowers, but there were tubs of gardenias and small orange trees in bloom, and the smell reminded him painfully of the house in Florence where he had been warmly welcomed for so many years: they had flowering lemon trees in the courtyard that served for a garden.

He felt Kitty's nervousness, and whispered perfunctorily, 'Don't worry, you look very nice.'

Kitty would have liked something more than 'nice'. Her ball gown of eau-de-nil satin was not new, but had been refreshed with appliquéd cream lace on the bodice, at the waist and around the hem, and elbow-length pleated chiffon sleeves with coloured ribbon edging. Hatto, when she had dressed her, had said fervently, 'You look *lovely*, my lady.' It was absurd to fear she was meeting a rival. But she could have wished Giles's attention was fully on her as they mounted the stairs, and she felt it was not.

There was Fergus, immaculate in tails, breeches and stockings, white satin waistcoat and white tie, a gardenia in his button-hole, looking younger, trimmer and very happy. And

Giulia, ravishing in a gown of silk taffeta in a rich yellow daringly trimmed with black silk fringe and black lace as fine as spider-web, diamonds round her throat and at her ears and a delicate diamond tiara in her piled-up black hair. Everyone else, Kitty thought, would fade into invisibility next to her. She greeted them both and passed on.

Giles, behind her, kissed Giulia's hand. Was he imagining that there was an edge of malice in her smile? He murmured a congratulation, and she said, 'Oh, but you must call me Aunt Giulia now. Do not forget that I am now your aunt, nephew Giles.'

No, she had not yet forgiven him.

Alice enjoyed the dinner, finding herself seated between two pleasant young men, sons of old friends of Uncle Fergus, who seemed to find her conversation sufficiently amusing, and were punctilious about turning between courses so that she never found herself with two backs-of-heads. The dinner itself was handsome – hors d'oeuvres, soup, fish, entrée, roast, game, sweet and dessert – and she managed to sample a little of everything, mindful that there was to be dancing afterwards. The most fashionable ladies were tightly corseted to achieve the required tiny waist. It was an odd thing, she reflected, to dine lavishly before a ball.

Looking around the table during a pause, she saw quite a Scottish contingent, including Aunt Cecily Tullamore with Sir Gordon and two of their children, Beata and Fritz; turning her head the other way she spotted Angus in comfortable conversation with Honor Eassie, daughter of a neighbouring house at Kincraig. Naturally, she thought, Angus would have been invited as well, but she hoped there would not be unpleasantness later. She searched for Rachel's face in the crowd and, by her expression, saw that she too had spotted Angus.

Her mother and the prince were very late arriving, and

were escorted after everyone was seated to the empty seats of honour, on either side of Fergus and Giulia. They were too far away for Alice to tell what her mother's mood might be, or whether she had seen either Rachel or Angus on her way to her chair. She hoped among so many guests they might pass unnoticed.

At one end of the vestibule in front of the ballroom, heavy velvet curtains hanging before a floor-to-ceiling window made a little secret alcove. In the hiatus between dinner and ball, Alice was following some of the other women upstairs when an urgent *hsst!* caught her attention and an arm whipped out to pull her inside.

'I'm so glad I spotted you,' Angus said. 'My father's here. I don't want a scene so I'm hiding.'

'I wondered where you'd got to,' Alice said. 'But you can't stay here all night.'

'No, I shall have to slip away before the dancing starts. But I can't go without talking to Rachel. Do you think you could bring her to me here, without anyone seeing?'

'Mama's bound to be keeping a pretty beady eye on her. But I'll try.'

'Oh, you are a brick! Thank you.'

'Make the most of it,' Alice said. 'She's still determined to marry her to the Russian prince.'

'Poor Rachel must be frantic. I wish I could suffer instead of her.'

'I thought you were,' Alice said, peeped round the curtain to see if it was safe, and left.

Giles did not have as much difficulty in securing a dance with Giulia as he had expected – then realised that it was probably because she wanted to torment him a little more.

'You are looking extremely beautiful tonight,' he said, as they glided away into the throng of dancers.

'It is agreeable to be able to buy nice clothes. My husband is generous and likes me to be well-dressed.'

She put a little emphasis on 'husband', and Giles flinched a little. 'Is that why you did it?'

'Why I did what?' she asked.

He missed the dangerous tone of her voice. 'Marry him.'

'*Maladetto! Io dovea da te fuggir!*' she said, in a low, grinding voice. 'You have not earned the right to insult me.'

'Oh, God, I didn't mean it like that! It's just that I'm trying to make sense of it.'

'It is not yours to make sense of,' she said, tossing her head so that the light lanced from the diamonds in her hair.

He was silent a moment. Then he said, very gently, 'Was my crime so terrible that you can never forgive me? I know I hurt your feelings, but—'

She interrupted him. 'Oh, what do you know of feelings, you? Man of ice and stone! Yes, they say the English are cold, heartless. *Quanto è vero!*'

'But what did I *do*?' he pleaded.

'Is it possible that you really don't know?'

'Let's say that I don't,' he suggested, hoping for enlightenment.

'You really don't know that since I was a girl I have been in love with you absolutely?'

He was silent a moment. 'I didn't know,' he said. 'But, Giulia, surely I never gave you to think that I—'

'Not until the Valley of the Kings.' Another silence. 'Don't you remember? *Il cielo di velluto, le stelle come diamanti,*' she said softly. 'Your voice caressing me in the darkness.'

'Giulia!'

Her voice was not angry now, but warm, inviting. 'Is it possible that you felt nothing? No, I can't believe that.'

'I'm a married man,' he said desperately.

The warmth disappeared. 'And now I am a married woman,' she said. 'So we are equal.' Her smile was malicious.

'You came so seldom to Italy, but now I am in England, we shall meet all the time.'

'Giulia—'

'You cannot refuse when your aunt summons you to visit her, can you?'

She laughed again, and fortunately for his sanity, the music stopped just then, saving him from finding something to say. He doubted he could have formed a coherent sentence.

In the seclusion of the alcove, Rachel and Angus exchanged hungry embraces and murmured endearments. 'It's so wretched that we can only meet like this,' he mourned. 'I want to claim you as my own before the world.'

Rachel clung to him. Her eyes were wet. 'She's dying. Mama's dying.'

'*What?*'

'It was the first thing she said when she got out of the carriage. "I've come home to die." She wants to have me married to the Russian before – before the end. But if she – goes first, the prince will finish things. He will be my legal guardian.'

'But that's outrageous!'

'She's my mother, and she's dying!' Rachel cried. 'I can't go against her now. How would you feel if it was your m-mother?'

He drew out his handkerchief and gently mopped her tears. 'My poor darling! It's dreadful. But it's your whole life at stake. You can't let her command you from beyond the grave.'

The word 'grave' made her cry even more. 'I don't want my mother to die!' she sobbed.

Angus held her in silence until the tears subsided.

'What are we to do?' she hiccuped dismally. 'It's hopeless.'

'No, it isn't,' he said. 'I have a position now, a good one. In a year or two I shall be able to keep you in comfort.'

'But it will be too late. I'll be married and living in Russia by then!'

He held her close, and said, 'If it comes to it, we'll have to go to Scotland. You're old enough to marry in Scotland without consent. And once we're married, they can't part us.'

She looked up at him, damply, but with hope. 'Is that true?'

'Yes. Scottish law and English law are different.'

'So – we could go now? Tonight!'

'The difficulty is that you have to live there for twenty-one days before you can marry. And if I disappeared for twenty-one days I'd lose my new position. And then I couldn't support you.'

She was silent, looking at him trustingly, waiting for him to solve the problem.

'Look,' he said at last, 'we'll do it if we really have to. I promise you. But let's wait a bit and see. She might change her mind. If she's really – you know – she might see things differently. It's bound to change your view of things, isn't it? But if it looks as though there's no other way, we'll go to Scotland and I'll just have to find another position – though I doubt I could find another as good. But we'll manage somehow.'

It was a chilly, damp and blowy evening, and Richard was not pleased to be dragged outside onto the terrace, where no-one else was foolish enough to be lingering. 'What on earth's got into you?' he grumbled.

'It's Giulia,' Giles said.

'Oh, Lord!' He fumbled for his cigarette case. 'Wait until I light a cigarillo . . . All right, carry on.'

Giles told him.

'Well, that explains a lot,' Richard said, at the end. 'A lifelong crush on you makes much more sense. She was madly in love with you, you kissed her and then rejected her. Of course she's furious. Hurt pride, broken heart, Italian passion heating the brew to boiling point.'

'But I swear I never encouraged her! I always treated her like a sister, nothing more!'

But he hesitated, remembering the warning given him by Mrs Antrobus in the Valley of the Kings. *Surely you must know she's in love with you*, she had said. He had dismissed it as female fantasy. *You treat her with a friendliness and a lack of formality that can only encourage her.* But they had always talked like that! He had told himself the woman simply didn't understand. *The way you sit and talk with her late into the night, your heads together and your voices lowered . . .* Now he remembered Giulia's recent words: *the sky like velvet, the stars like diamonds, your voice caressing me in the darkness . . .*

Giles put his hands to his head and groaned. 'Oh, God, what have I done?'

'I don't know, old dear. What *have* you done?' Richard asked calmly.

'Perhaps the setting was a little – romantic.' He gave a stilted description of those evenings.

Richard laughed mirthlessly 'And this was you not encouraging her?'

'It was just conversation. I never so much as touched her hand! And she knew I was married. How was I to know she was – harbouring thoughts? I thought she was more sensible than that!'

'I applaud your modesty, if not your common sense. You're not as handsome as me, but you're not bad-looking, and you've got a title. You really didn't think she fancied you?'

Giles was silent. His experience with women was very slight in any case. And since he had fallen hopelessly in love with Nina, he had shut thoughts of love and romance out of his head. Being immune to anyone else, he had arbitrarily assumed no-one else could fall in love with him. 'What am I to do?' he said.

Richard was still thinking. 'You don't suppose . . . ? Are

you thinking she married Uncle Fergus simply to get back at you?'

It was what he feared. 'I can't believe that of her,' he said uncomfortably.

'Poor old Uncle. You can see he's as in love as it gets.'

'Should I tell him?' Giles said miserably. 'Perhaps I ought to.'

'That his new-wedded bride wants to be off with a raggle-taggle gypsy? Are you mad?'

'But if she's deceived him—'

'I dare say most people getting married are deceived one way or another. The poor old beast is blissfully happy – why spoil it for him?'

'Then what *can* I do?'

'Nothing. Just behave yourself from now on. Exemplary uxoriousness is to be your motto – if you can pronounce it.'

'She said now she's my aunt, I'll have to come when she summons me.'

Richard laughed. 'Good Lord! Yes, I'd forgotten that! She's your aunt – how delicious! Mine too, if it comes to it. But look here,' he grew serious, 'even if there's nothing you can do, there's not much *she* can do. You can avoid her. They might not spend much time in England, and then there's his estates. And even when they're in London – well, you don't come up very often. *I'm* more likely to bump into them than you. And I think I can be trusted to resist her charms.'

Giles said nothing, thinking what a mess it was, how many people stood to be hurt, and how unfair it was that it should fall to his blame: he had never meant any harm.

Richard patted his arm, guessing his thoughts. 'I know, you're feeling unjustly put-upon. You really are rather dim when it comes to people, aren't you?'

Giles looked cross. 'For instance?'

'For instance, keeping me standing out here. The damp is taking the starch out of my collar-points.'

Giles was forced to smile. 'Let's go in, then. And thanks for listening to me.'

'Think nothing of it. You're as good as a one-act play any day.'

Alice and Rachel met at the side of the ballroom at the end of a dance. 'I've been dancing with everyone I can,' Rachel said, 'to allay Mama's suspicion. I don't want her to guess Angus was here.'

'Where is he now?'

'He said he was leaving, after we had our talk. But I haven't seen Mama and the prince anywhere.'

'They left when the ball started.'

Rachel looked disappointed. 'Then he could have stayed! We could have danced together.'

'I think you're forgetting *his* father and mother were here too.'

'Oh dear, yes. So he couldn't have. Why are people so difficult?'

Alice thought of her own secret love, in comparison with which the strictest parent would prefer their daughter to fancy Angus. 'I don't know,' she said. 'I wonder what news Mama had yesterday. When she saw Sir Henry Felden.'

'Oh, goodness, yes, that was yesterday.' Rachel frowned. 'Could it have been good news? If it was very bad, surely she wouldn't have come tonight at all.'

'But Uncle Fergus is her special pet, because of being a mother to him when he was a baby. I think she would come no matter what, for his sake, even if she didn't stay long.'

'But do you think she looked very low? Or not so badly?'

'I don't know,' Alice said. 'You know Mama – she never shows anything in her face.'

Giles found himself beside Uncle Fergus. 'This is a very grand occasion,' he said. 'You must be pleased with how it's going.'

'Except for your mother leaving early,' Uncle Fergus said. 'She said she had a headache. You don't suppose I've offended her, do you? I did wonder whether I ought to invite her and Usingen to the actual wedding, but I didn't think she'd want to make the journey just for that.'

'Perhaps she actually *had* a headache,' Giles said, concluding that the princess had not told him about her real situation.

'She never gets headaches,' Uncle Fergus said certainly. 'I suppose she doesn't approve of my choice of bride,' he went on, with a sigh. 'But she'll love her when she comes to know her. You must put in a good word, Giles – you know Lady Leake better than anyone. You've known her from a child.' He gave a little smirk. 'Funny to think she's now your aunt!'

'Believe me, that irony has not been lost on me,' Giles said.

'I can hardly believe she's chosen me when she could have had anyone. I don't know what she sees in me, but I shall dedicate my life to making her happy. Thank God I have fortune enough to give her anything she wants.'

It was unlucky that Linda passed at that moment, and overheard the last words. She glared at her uncle. 'I hope you know you have *ruined* my life!' she hissed, and stalked away.

'What was that about?' Uncle Fergus said in surprise.

'She was banking on your remaining a bachelor and leaving your fortune to her children.'

'Oh, is that it?' He thought a moment, and actually blushed a little. 'Of course, I *am* hoping Lady Leake and I will have children. Why not? She's young, and I'm in my prime. And Linda may be my niece, but I have no responsibility for Cordwell's dependants.'

'When you've anything in your pocket, there will always be people wanting to help themselves to it. Spend it on Giulia, that's my advice. It will be more enjoyable.'

★ ★ ★

He danced with Kitty. 'At last,' she said. 'Why is it so difficult to dance with one's own husband at these affairs?'

'Duty,' Giles said. He hoped she didn't want to talk – he was emotionally exhausted.

She was silent for a while, and then a gap opened in the crowd and she saw Giulia dancing with Lord George Alexander, the colour high in her cheeks as she gazed up at him, laughing at something he'd said. The gap closed again, and she said, 'I don't want to reopen old wounds, but I have to say something.'

He looked down at her wearily. 'Must you?'

'Oh, it's nothing bad! Just to say that I know now I've been foolish to be jealous of Giulia. I know it was just friendship, because she's so clever, and you don't have many clever people to talk to. It must be hard for you. I used to think, during our coming-out year, that you'd have been more suited to Nina than to me. You could talk to her so much more. If only she'd had any money—'

'Kitty, don't!'

'It's all right. I know you married me for my fortune. But we're happy enough now, aren't we? People say these things work out, and they do, don't they?'

'Oh, Kitty!' What was happy 'enough'? he wondered.

'I'm not going to be jealous of Giulia any more. It was silly of me and I'm over it. That's all I wanted to say.'

He looked down at her: smiling and at ease, a sweet-faced little matron, pretty as a kitten, mother of his two adored sons; and he thought how lucky he was. 'I don't know what I did to deserve you,' he said.

She looked up, and her smile was for him alone. 'I think it's always a matter of luck, isn't it, not deserving? I didn't deserve you, either, but here we are.'

There were many ways you could take that, he thought, as they danced on.

★ ★ ★

Caroline enjoyed the dinner and the ball, finding many old friends to talk to, and even dancing – once with someone who had been a beau of hers before she had married Manningtree. He had flirted with her, just a little, and she had enjoyed his subtle suggestion that if Sir James hadn't cut him out she might even now be Lady Flintshire. But she did not stay to the end. For one thing, the evening had been long and loud, and the solitary pleasures of her bed and a book had an irresistible attraction after ten o'clock. And for a second, she had not had a chance to talk to Maud since her consultation with Sir Henry Felden, and her leaving the ball right at the beginning was concerning.

She had known nothing of Maud's state of health until yesterday, when she had called in with the prince to say that they would be staying at Claridge's, and to drop her bombshell. She gave the news without emotion, and when Caroline had tried to express shock and sympathy had cut her off. Her attitude had always been 'Never complain, never explain.' There was no sense in even talking about things that could not be helped. But she had said that, to please Usingen, she would consult with Sir Henry that morning. 'And that's all I have to say.'

Caroline had known there was no point in asking her for any details as to what ailed her. She had eyed the prince and thought that if she could get him alone she could probably find out more – thanks to their sister Vicky's early marriage and many holidays at the Wachturm, her German was almost as good as Maud's – but they left immediately so there was no opportunity. But she had gathered from Maud's unspoken attitude that she did not think there was anything to be done, and the consultation was only to appease her husband.

As her maid prepared her for bed she thought about her sister, and how much harder their childhood would have been if Maud, the eldest, had not taken on the role of mother to them all, and how the strain of responsibility had hardened her already tough character into adamant. She could only hope that whatever it was Maud had, the end would not be too painful or difficult, and decided that it had been sensible to come home to die rather than in a foreign land. And she felt desperately sorry for the prince, to be losing his new bride so untimely.

She did not sleep well, and was up early the next morning. She went down to breakfast before last night's revellers were up. She was spreading toast with her favourite lime marmalade and thinking that she ought to visit Grandmère today, and break Maud's news to her gently, when Sebastian appeared, another early riser. With a subtle gesture she sent Forbes for fresh toast and coffee, and said, 'What an excellent occasion it was last night, don't you think?'

'Went off like a bomb,' Sebastian said. 'No-one else about?'

'I expect they'll all sleep late after so much dancing. I'm a little too tired myself for church this morning.'

Sebastian cleared his throat and said, 'Young Tullamore was there.'

'Oh dear. Why do things have to be so difficult?' Caroline said, unconsciously repeating Rachel.

'Can't think why Maud didn't settle her last year, when she was all the rage.'

'But I don't believe she had any suitable offers,' Caroline said. 'It was a question of dowry, you see.'

Sebastian's own youthful love had been scotched by the unsuitability of his choice. 'Awful lot of nonsense,' he rumbled.

Forbes returned with the coffee and they lapsed into silence, until they were roused from their thoughts by the undeniable sound of the street doorbell.

Caroline looked up. 'Who on earth can it be at this time of the morning?' It crossed her mind that it might be Angus, hoping for a word with Rachel. Who else would get up so early? Should she allow it, which would be disloyal to Maud? And really not in the children's best interests either, because there was no point in encouraging them when it was hopeless.

Moments later Forbes appeared at the door, looking put out – it wasn't right to show visitors into the morning-room – and admitting the Prince and Princess of Usingen.

Maud was fully and fashionably dressed and was looking less composed and calm than usual, with an unexpected amount of colour in her cheeks. And the prince was positively radiant, so Caroline rose to greet them with the happy conviction that it must be good news, that Sir Henry had been able to give some hope.

'No, I won't stay for breakfast,' Maud said, intercepting the enquiry and the order to Forbes. 'We are on our way back from church. I'm glad to find you alone.' Her look included Sebastian, so he didn't offer to leave. 'I have something to tell you and it will be easier without so many to hear it.'

'Come and sit down,' Caroline urged, gesturing towards the sofa and chairs in the bay window.

But Maud remained standing where she was, giving her an almost uncertain look. She waited until Forbes had left the room, and then nervously stripped off one glove, and fiddled with it between her fingers.

Caroline was disturbed all over again. It was unlike Maud to fidget. Perhaps it was bad news after all. 'It is something about – something Sir Henry said yesterday?' she urged.

'Yes,' said Maud. She glanced at Usingen, who smiled and nodded at her, encouragingly.

'Oh, do say that it is good news!' Caroline cried.

Maud recoiled slightly. 'Please, Caroline, restrain yourself. I cannot bear displays of emotion. My nerves are strained already.'

'Your nerves?' Sebastian said, in astonishment. 'I never knew you to have any.'

Maud ignored him. 'When I saw Sir Henry and explained

the symptoms he said he had little doubt as to the diagnosis but regarded an examination as essential.' She reddened even at the mention of it. One very good reason never to admit to illness was the horrible embarrassment of submitting to a strange man touching your body.

'And?' Caroline prompted. 'Please don't keep me in suspense!'

'It is not as I thought. The symptoms – perhaps at another time I might have guessed.' She gathered her courage. 'I am with child. I am going to have a baby.'

Usingen beamed as the words were finally spoken, nodded in delighted confirmation at the other two. He reached out and took her hand, and for a wonder she did not shake him off. The next words broke from her as if against her will, almost in a wail. 'I thought I was done with all that! It was the last thing I suspected.'

Usingen could contain himself no longer, and broke into a flood of delight in German. He had never been married before, had thought he had left it too late, his family and the whole estate had been afraid he would leave no heir, but his beloved Maud had agreed to marry him and he was so blessed, now everyone would be so happy, almost as happy as he was.

It was well that he filled the silence because Caroline was too astonished for words.

At last she said, 'I'm so glad you're not dying.'

Sebastian said, 'I'm glad the prince insisted on your seeing a physician. Congratulations, by the way, Usingen. I'd say let that be a lesson to you, Maudie, but I can't immediately think what the lesson would be.'

'Don't talk nonsense,' Maud rebuked him. And to her sister, who was moist about the eyes, 'I look to you to tell the rest of the family, and to tell them that I forbid any fuss. And now I'm going home.'

'But, Maud,' said Sebastian, urgently, as she turned away. 'You are pleased, aren't you?'

She turned and met his eyes with a look of utter perplexity. 'It was not what I expected,' she said at last. 'It will take time to understand.' She glanced at her husband. 'Usingen is pleased.'

He took her hand and drew it through his arm, beamed at her, and called her his *herzliebste Frauchen*.

'Yes, I should think he is,' Sebastian said.

Maud could not bear to talk to anyone. She could hardly bear to be in the same house as another soul. She was uncertain, wrong-footed, and riven with embarrassment – emotions she was not accustomed to in her rigidly controlled life.

Despite the fact that Usingen, having married her, wanted to affirm his passion for her far more often than she would have chosen, it had never occurred to her that she might conceive. She was over fifty, and her Monthly Visitor had been irregular for some time. Most of all, she had had no *intention* of having more children – and such was the force of her character that what she willed always came to pass..

The nausea, general feeling of unwellness, and then the swelling in the abdomen, were symptoms she recognised from a close friend of her mother whom she had witnessed die of a growth on the liver. Lady Wendell's death had been a grim backdrop to a period of her life that had culminated in her mother's death in childbed, and was engraved on her mind and her heart. In the grim watches of the night Maud had faced and come to terms with the prospect of her own dissolution. Fergus's wedding celebration gave her the excuse to return to London without telling Usingen – she could not face his anguish – and once there, she would stay to the end, which she assumed would not be long coming. Lady Wendell had lived only a few months: the disease took its victims rapidly.

She'd had no intention of telling anyone until the very end, when it would become obvious anyway. Above all things, she hated talk about health matters. But arriving at Ashmore, miserably uncomfortable and tired from the long journey, Stainton's annoying remark about her looking well had been the last straw and she had barked out that stupidly melodramatic statement.

And then came the long, exhausting scene with Usingen, at the end of which she had agreed to see a doctor. He had made it impossible for her to refuse. He had raged, and wept, pleaded his love for her, demanded in wounded tones how she could shut him out from something so vital, asked what she thought he must be feeling, claimed wildly that there was always hope. Hope, that insidious poison. Despair she knew could be coped with; but hope would kill you.

And now she was in this dreadful position, where she had told everyone she was dying when in fact she was harbouring new life. It was horribly, scaldingly embarrassing. She did not know how to have any conversation that was likely to arise. And at the end of it – a baby. Usingen was delighted, of course, and she was glad enough to please him. But to bear another child at her age? She'd had more than enough of that in her marriage to Willie Stainton. She was too old, she was too tired. She didn't *want* to do it. But there was no choice in the matter.

Most of all, she didn't want to talk about it. A convent at the top of a mountain where the nuns had taken a vow of silence – that was where she would have chosen to spend the rest of her pregnancy.

If only, if *only* she had not blurted out that she was dying! One moment's lapse had led to all this trouble. She had lived her life by suppressing all natural reaction, and lectured her children on the virtue of iron self-control at all times. Now, once people had got over the surprise of the news, they would be laughing at her behind her back. The pains of childbirth were as nothing beside the anguish of feeling foolish.

CHAPTER SEVEN

Sebastian, at the piano, saw a flicker of movement at the door, and lifted his head to say, 'Don't go! Come in and listen.'

Dory reappeared doubtfully. 'I mustn't.'

'Please,' he said. 'There's no harm in listening to a bit of music.' Still she hesitated, and he said beguilingly, 'I'll play you Chopin – the piece you like.'

'Just for a moment, then.' She came in and stood to the side of the door where she couldn't be seen from outside. He let his hands transition through some chords and arpeggios until they found the opening notes of the Berceuse. She folded her arms round the silk counterpane she was carrying – she was the sewing maid and repaired all the most delicate things in the house – and gazed at the empty air as she listened.

'What's that?' he asked, when he had finished and slid into another piece so as not to leave a gap she might depart in.

'It's the counterpane from Van Dyck. The one with tropical birds and such. The thread's badly worn in places. Her highness likes to rest on top of the bed, but she ought to have Miss Taylor take it off first.'

'Would you like me to tell her?'

Her eyes opened. 'What – and let her know I'd spoken to you about it?' And then she realised he was joking, and smiled. 'You shouldn't tease me.'

'You take your work so seriously.'

'It's the only way to do any work, isn't it?'

'You're right, of course. "Do the work as best you can, Though it's hard at whiles, Helping when you meet them, Lame dogs over stiles,"' he quoted.

She frowned. 'That's not how it goes.'

'I paraphrased to fit the occasion.'

'Anyway, why would you help a lame dog over a stile? Dogs go *under* stiles – I've seen 'em.'

'You must ask Charles Kingsley. I suspect he meant metaphorical lame dogs.'

'I've never met one of those. Our neighbours had a dog with three legs when I was a girl. It could run faster than all the other dogs.'

'There's a Kingsleyish message in that somewhere, if we could think of it. "Don't shoot the dog that's one leg short, it runs so fast, it can't be caught."'

She laughed. 'You're quick!'

'What's the talk below stairs?' he asked. He saw that she had relaxed, and was glad of it. He slithered into some Scarlatti, where you could fudge a little, since it all sounded much the same to the untrained ear.

'Oh, about her highness, of course. What a strange thing that she thought she was dying when she's really having a baby!'

'And very glad we all are about it.'

Dory nodded. It wasn't that the princess was beloved, but a birth was always better than a death. 'But what a queer mistake to make.'

'It's happened before, only the other way round. Queen Victoria had a lady's maid called Lady Flora Hastings, who suffered from nausea and headaches and a swollen abdomen. There was a scandal because she was unmarried and everyone thought she was pregnant, but it turned out that she had a growth on her liver.'

'Oh, the poor lady. What happened?'

'She died.'

'I don't like that story. Will her highness stay here to have the baby?'

'I imagine the prince will want her to go home. It's his heir, after all. He'll want it to be born in his house.'

'Will she take Lady Rachel with her?'

'Probably.'

She sighed. 'I wish she'd take Lady Linda and those children instead.'

'What's Arthur done now?'

'Caught a rat in the stables and let it loose in the kitchen. I thought Mrs Terry would have a nose bleed, she screamed so hard. She's all right with mice but she can't abide rats.'

'What happened?'

'The prince's man heard the racket and came in, grabbed a saucepan, whacked the poor thing and killed it, picked it up by the tail and threw it outside. Cool as a cucumber. The girls were all very impressed. They think he's a sort of hero. Even him not speaking English makes them wriggle.'

'Wriggle?'

'They think it's romantic.' He saw her mood change as she remembered where she was. 'I must go.'

'Not yet. It's been so long since we've had a chat like this,' he said. 'I miss you.'

'I miss you, too, but I mustn't,' she said, in a low voice. 'I ought to go away, get another position.'

'Please don't,' he said.

She shook her head, and was gone.

He played on without knowing what he was playing, thinking that the time had come. He had been putting it off, telling himself first that the Christmas season was in the way, then the weather, then Maud's strange drama. But the longer he waited, the more he risked losing her. She might just go one day, and not tell him where, so that he wouldn't be able to follow.

He must act.

★ ★ ★

Addy and Mabel passed each other on the first landing as they went between bedrooms with their housemaid's boxes.

'What you just done?' Mabel asked.

'Lady Mary's Room,' said Addy. 'You?'

'Jade Room. Lot of fussy stuff in there.'

'Mine's worse. Lady Linda's awful untidy,' Addy said. Linda always slept in Lady Mary when she was at the Castle. 'Here,' Addy remembered, 'there was a funny book on her nightstand, all in foreign.'

'That'll be German,' Mabel said. 'She knows German on account of visiting her aunty, her that married a German prince.'

'You mean her mother?'

'No, stupid! Princess Usingen's her mother, but she'd an aunty that married a German as well. When she was a child.'

'Oh,' said Addy, blankly. Then her face cleared. 'Here, that valet of the prince's is a nice gent.'

Mabel frowned. 'What sort of nice?'

Addy giggled. 'Oh – you know!'

'I don't know. What you been up to?'

'Nothing. Just a bit of a kiss and cuddle. No harm is there?'

'What? You as well?'

'What d'you mean?'

'I had a kiss and cuddle with him an' all.'

Addy looked disconcerted. 'But he said I was a pretty girl.'

'He said I was too, only he said it in German, on account of he doesn't speak no English.'

'Well, he talked English to me,' Addy said, bewildered.

Mabel took a step towards her, belligerently. 'You lay off him, Addy Coggins! I saw him first!'

'You never! Anyway, he said English to me, and that's better than German. So he must like me better.'

'Get off! He knows you're too stupid to understand German.'

'Well, so are you!'

Rose appeared in the corridor behind them and said furiously, 'What d'you think you're doing, bellowing away like fishwives? Shut your mouths and get about your work!'

Mabel had one last shaft to deliver before flouncing away. 'I know more German than you, anyway! *Shmoo-sig!* That's German for a pretty girl, so there!'

Rose maided Lady Linda at the Castle, as she didn't have a lady's maid of her own. When she was doing her hair that evening, she said, 'Can I ask you something, my lady?'

'Hmm?' said Linda, staring at her reflection, and thinking that when a lady reached thirty she ought to have diamond earrings. Diamonds close to the face gave it a sparkle.

'What's the German word for "pretty"?' Rose asked.

'*Hübsch*,' Linda said absently.

'Oh,' said Rose. 'So what's *shmoo-sig*, then?'

Linda frowned, dragged back from her diamond reverie. 'What? Do you mean *schmutzig*?'

'I expect so,' Rose said. 'What does that mean?'

'"Dirty",' said Linda. 'Why?'

'Oh, the German servants below stairs. Something that was said, that's all,' Rose said vaguely. 'It's a bit awkward them not speaking English.'

'Taylor speaks German well enough now,' Linda said dismissively. 'She can translate.'

'Yes, my lady. The tortoiseshell combs? Or the jet?'

Rose cornered Adolf in the visiting valet's room, where he was polishing the prince's boots.

'What have you been up to, Mr Usingen?' she demanded. 'Have you been bothering the housemaids?'

He turned and examined her slowly up and down with an undressing look. Rose, however, had dealt with that sort of thing too many times before and looked straight back. He said something in German that sounded like a denial.

She narrowed her eyes. 'You understood what I said, otherwise you couldn't have answered me. Speak English!'

'Oh, Miss Rose, you are very sharp,' he said. 'A rose has many thorns, is it not?'

'You're not the first man to say that, so don't think you're clever. And don't think you can smarm me, either.'

'I don't know what is *smarm*, but I have no interest in you, Miss Rose. You are . . .' He held his palms six inches apart and moved them up and down. 'I like girls who are . . .' Now he used the hands to describe a roundness that was almost a full circle. And he grinned.

Rose bristled. 'Oh, yes, I know your sort, Mr Usingen. Interfering with girls too silly to know better, getting your pleasure at their expense.'

He moved a step closer, looking insistently into her face. 'But I am not Mr Usingen. My name is Adolf. You must call me Adolf.'

'I'll call you with the back of my hand if you fiddle with my girls. I'll tell his lordship. I'll tell your master.'

He laughed. 'Oh, but you will not. There must not be a fuss. And housemaids do not speak to masters. It is not done.' He stepped closer again, and she held her ground, refusing to flinch from him, though they were almost nose to nose. 'You have much spirit, Rose of the thorns, I like that. Even though you are too *mager* for my taste, I like you.'

Like a snake striking, he seized her round the waist, pulled her close and fastened his lips to hers. She was wiry and strong from housework, but he was taller and more powerful, and she struggled in vain. When he released her she rubbed at her mouth furiously, bristling like a cat.

He only laughed. '*Ach so!*' he said. 'Now you have kissed me too, so you cannot complain about the others. You are as bad as them.'

She stared for a moment, then walked away. There was

nothing she could do or say that would enhance her dignity.

'Mr Usingen, can I have a word with you?'

Adolf turned and looked down at Afton as he stood in the doorway. '*Bitte?*' he said.

'Ah,' said Afton. 'Now we have a little problem to overcome. I don't speak German, but I know you speak English. However, if you refuse to, I can always ask Lady Linda to translate for us. Or her highness. Would you really like one of them to hear what I have to say?'

Adolf thought for a moment, then smiled. 'You are a clever man. And a handsome one! No doubt you are having pleasure with the maids yourself. If you tell me which ones you favour, I will leave them alone. There are plenty, enough for both.'

Afton gave him a look of distaste. 'We don't do things that way in this house.'

'That is hard to believe.'

'I don't really care what you believe, Mr Usingen. You will cease to interfere with the maids from this moment.'

Adolf looked almost merry. 'But, Mr Afton, what can you do?' He jumped into a mock pugilist pose. '*Handgreiflichkeiten?* But you, handsome man, clever man, you are also small man, smaller than me. It would not go well with you.'

Afton did not smile. 'I have no intention of fighting you, though if I did, you'd learn a thing or two. Where I grew up, we had to take care of ourselves. But if you do not leave the maids alone, I *will* go to my master, and he *will* speak to yours. You are abusing our hospitality, and that is an insult to my master, and thus to his mother, who is your master's wife. I think the prince will not care to have her insulted.'

Adolf sighed theatrically. 'I understand. You wish to keep all the maids for yourself. You are – how is it said? – dog in the manger. I will leave them alone, as you ask.' He twinkled at Afton. 'My friend, you should have the fat ones first. They are more *bequem*.'

Mrs Webster and Rose called all the maids together before servants' supper, crowding them into Mrs Webster's room and closing the doors. And under two sets of eagle eyes they listened in silence to the warning to steer clear of the German valet. Some of the maids had cast-down eyes, some were blushing – though that may simply have been because of the subject – and some simply looked bewildered.

'If he approaches you, just walk away. And if you have any trouble, come straight to me. But I warn you, anyone who goes along willingly with it will be dismissed straight away, without a character. We don't want girls of that sort here at the Castle.'

They filed out. Rose caught up with Mabel and said, 'I've something to say to you.'

'I've not done nothing,' Mabel said automatically.

'You think Mr Usingen was calling you a pretty girl? Men will say anything to get you to give them a fumble. And it wasn't even a compliment.'

'What are you talking about?'

'*Schmutzig* doesn't mean "pretty", you stupid girl. It means dirty.'

Shock was followed by fury in her round pink face. '*Well!*' she said, almost speechless.

Rose nodded. 'He was laughing at you. Now get about your work.'

Unseen in the shadow of the boot room, where he had turned off the light and opened the door just as the girls streamed out of Mrs Webster's room, Sam blinked back tears of chagrin.

The short way down to the village did not pass Hundon's farm, but Rose was not in a hurry, and found reasons to go the longer way. Well, it was a nice walk. She certainly didn't walk that way in the hope of seeing Michael Woodrow.

He had two cattle dogs now, Fly and Jess, and as she passed the gate one afternoon, allowing herself no more than a glance into the yard, Fly came running out with a single bark, and circled her as if trying to herd her in. She stooped to caress him – he was a black and white Border collie, his face white with a black patch round the eye, which gave him a comical look – and as she straightened, Woodrow emerged from the barn and saw her, smiled and approached her.

'Hello! I haven't seen you for ages. Come in! Are you in a hurry?'

'I can't stay long,' she said. Not for anything would she show eagerness.

'Please. There's something I want to show you.'

She turned into the yard, Fly frisking about her. 'Your sister at home?' she asked casually. His unmarried half-sister Martha kept house for him, and even he admitted she was an odd one. Rose had got the feeling she didn't like her, and avoided her when possible.

'No, she's gone down to the village. Come into the barn.'

In the sweet-smelling, dusty half-light he led her to a pen made of hurdles, and there in a bed of straw lay his other dog, Jess, with a litter of squirming puppies.

'Fly is the proud father.' Fly was pushing his nose through the bars in an interested way. Jess wrinkled her muzzle in a silent warning, and Michael pushed the dog back with his foot. 'He's terribly interested in them, but Jess isn't ready to let him near them yet.'

'They look big and healthy,' Rose commented. 'I expect they get lots of milk, with all the cows around.'

'Only mother's milk for now,' he said. 'But Jess has a saucer of fore-milk every day, to get her strength back.'

'Don't the cats get jealous? I thought that was their treat.'

'Oh, there's enough for all of them. We've twenty-six in

milk at the moment, plus four that are drying off.' They walked back outside to leave the bitch in peace, and stood outside the barn door in the cool, weak sunlight. A gusty March wind was banging a loose shutter somewhere, and blowing rooks about the sky, as if it had shaken them out of the stand of elms where they nested.

'You must be busy come milking time,' Rose said, to keep the conversation going. She liked the way the sun lines at his eye-corners were white in his brown face, and the way his mouse-fair hair grew a little tufty and unruly at the crown. His shoulders and neck were strong, and his hands, though work-roughened, were shapely.

'It's quite a problem,' he said. 'Good milkers are hard to come by, and they don't stick at it. Beattie Gale's a good girl – you know Beattie?'

'George Gale's daughter?' Gale was the estate carpenter. 'Yes of course.'

'Girls are lighter-handed than men, I prefer them. But girls keep going off and getting married. Half the time Martha and I have to make up the numbers. I wish we had machines to do the milking.'

Rose laughed. 'Machines? That's like something in a story.'

'Oh, no,' he said seriously. 'People have been patenting milking machines for years and years, but none of them really works perfectly. There are always problems.'

'How can a machine milk a cow?' Rose asked, thinking of a factory full of steam-driven looms and spinning jennies.

'Well, the early ones were just cups you fitted over the teats, connected to a hand pump, and they sucked the milk out. But continuous suction is uncomfortable for the cow. You see, when a calf nurses, it sucks and then pauses while it swallows, so there's a sort of pulsing action. And it pushes on the udder before it sucks to make the milk flow. What's needed is a machine that mimics what the calf does, but no-one's perfected it yet.'

'I should think not,' Rose said genially.

Seeing she was interested – or at least was pretending to be – he was pleased, and went on. 'And a machine that milks one cow at a time is still only half the battle. Ideally, you'd want a machine that milked several cows at once and passed the milk into a common container, sealed against contamination.'

'I see you've got some big ideas,' Rose said.

Woodrow smiled ruefully. 'I'm afraid I got up on my hobby-horse just then, and bored you.'

'It's not *boring*,' she said truthfully.

'But not a suitable subject for a lady.'

'I'm not made of paper. I can talk about cows' teats without fainting,' she said briskly. 'So that's your hobby-horse? Machines that milk?'

'Not only that. I want to bring method and science into dairy farming. Too often it's a muddy yard and manure-stained cows wandering into a dark, broken-down byre to be milked into a dirty bucket. I'd like everything to be clean and hygienic. Concrete floors and electric light. Find out by scientific observation which is the best sort of cow and what's the best way to look after it. Measure feed against milk output. Test for bacteria.'

'Doesn't sound much like farming,' Rose said.

'No, I know. To the average person, a farmer is a chap leaning over a gate with a straw in his mouth.'

'I'm not an average person,' she objected.

'I'm very well aware of that,' he said, and there was a moment when the air between them seemed to ripple, and Rose suddenly felt very warm, despite the cold wind. 'I say,' he began, 'I wonder if some time you'd like to—'

At that moment Fly barked and dashed past them, and they both turned to see Martha coming in through the gate with a basket on her arm. She scowled at the sight of them, and said, 'Got time to stand talking, have you? I just saw

Mrs Ogg and she says Bill's got a sore hand.' Bill Ogg was Woodrow's yard man. 'Tore it on a nail yesterday and now it's swelled up and gone bad. So he won't be milking tonight.' She looked at Rose. 'Can you milk?'

'I dare say I could,' she said with dignity, 'but I shall be busy. I must get on.' She started away, and Woodrow gave his sister a cross look and followed her.

'When's your next afternoon off? Come to tea.'

'Oh, I don't know,' Rose said. 'Your sister doesn't like me.'

'She doesn't like anyone. Pay no heed. Come and have tea, so we can talk properly.' He gave her an enticing smile. 'I can talk about other things than milking machines. Or farm improvements.'

'I don't mind what you talk about,' Rose said, and found herself smiling. And realised she had agreed to come to tea without actually saying it.

Fergus's plan to show his bride around his estates began with Cawburn Castle, his ancestral home in Northumberland, where he took her directly from London. He issued a wide invitation to the family to join them for a house party.

Maud accepted. 'I want you to see where I come from,' she told her husband. 'My childhood home.' The prince, still a little bemused and infinitely tender, agreed readily.

Caroline was frank. 'At this time of year? No, thank you. I still remember the chilblains I had when I was eleven.'

Giles refused politely for him and Kitty, saying that they already had engagements right up to Easter. 'He could have taken her round some friends' estates first, and gone north when the weather was better,' he said to Kitty. 'He's going to give her a poor idea of England.'

'I've never seen Cawburn,' Kitty said, but he didn't catch her slightly wistful tone.

'You haven't missed anything,' he said.

Only Linda was eager for the trip. She still wanted to

ingratiate herself with the prince. He was as rich as Giles, if not richer, and from what she had observed far less stingy.

Then Maud decreed that Rachel was to come with them. Rachel begged to be left behind, but Maud narrowed her eyes, suspecting some secret tryst was planned. 'Nonsense,' she said. 'Your place is with me. You were only allowed to stay at Ashmore to recover from your exertions, and I can see that you *are* recovered.'

Rachel went up to her room, and wrote a frantic letter to Angus, sprinkling the page with tears.

> I know if once she takes me out of England I am doomed. I don't know if she plans to come back to Ashmore before going to Germany. If she goes straight back to Germany, we must pass through London, and perhaps I can escape somehow from the station when we change trains. Oh, my love, I wish you were here to give me courage. I am so weak and foolish, but I will hold on to the best of my poor strength.

Kitty suggested hopefully to Linda that it would be good for Arabella and Arthur to see where their maternal family came from, but Linda replied shortly that since Fergus had seen fit to *marry* (she made it sound like a particularly egregious aberration) they had nothing to expect from Cawburn. The fact was that she had no intention of hampering herself with two children when she had successfully shrugged off that responsibility onto Giles, Kitty and Miss Kettel.

Cawburn Castle was set amid tall pine trees at the top of a steep cragside above a raging burn. It was built of grey stone and had a castellate, fortified air that appeared to set it in the time when the borderlands were wild and dangerous. In fact it dated only from the 1840s when Prince Albert, missing his homeland, had romanticised everything Scottish, and

Maud's grandfather had felt that Northumberland was close enough to Scotland to qualify. Inside, the fake-baronial had replaced the original baronial and was, in fact, more comfortable in many ways, wood panelling being cosier than bare stone walls, and edge-to-edge carpets an improvement over flagstones. But it was still a bleak place in winter, and the small resident staff were slow to respond to orders to light fires in *every* room and *keep* them burning brightly.

But Fergus could not bear the sight of his bride looking pinched and shivering. He ordered lavishly, chivvied both the old staff and the new who had been hired to augment them, and by the time the Usingen party arrived, things were looking more promising.

Giulia was determinedly gay. The journey north had been a severe trial to her, the trains slower and more uncomfortable with every change, and the final leg of the journey by carriage almost more than she could endure. The first sight of Cawburn could not fail to impress: massive, looming, romantic with its turrets, pinnacles and crenellations, like something out of a fairy story. She had married the lord of the castle, and this was only the first of his properties! But she was a child of the warm south, and what was within those towering walls made her wonder what on earth she had done, especially when the cruel wind came soughing round the walls, fingering its way under the doors and, worst of all, driving belches of smoke down the chimneys and into the rooms.

'It's only because the chimneys are cold, m'lady,' the housekeeper assured her. 'it'll be better by and by when they've warmed up.'

Giulia, huddled into the fur that had been one of her wedding presents, wondered if that would be in her lifetime, and pondered how people could live in places like this when they had the whole world to choose from. But she was too proud to regret the mad impulse that had made her accept Fergus's offer, and told herself that they would not be here for long. His other houses must be better than this; and if they weren't, well, there was London and there was Venice, and he was so besotted with her she was sure he would follow her desire. Which was never to be cold again.

In the mean time, she had a front to keep up. She had been angry and disappointed to learn that Giles would not be coming, but his mother was, and she must take back to him a report that Lady Leake could not have been happier and was basking in her fond husband's attentions and enjoying his resources.

Maud saw nothing wrong with the temperature. She had been brought up here and if, in her childhood, anyone had asked whether she was cold, she would not have understood the question. Comfort was never thought to be a requirement of a Forrest. She was unexpectedly glad to be back at Cawburn, and went from room to room remembering people and occasions, from window to window rediscovering views. Her husband revelled in her new-found communicativeness as she relived the nicer parts of her growing-up. He was delighted to see her happy.

Maud herself was surprised to realise that that was what she was. Contentment had not often come to her since at the age of nineteen she had married Willie Stainton. But Paul Usingen not only offered her security, he actually liked her. He was kind to her. He cared that she should be happy. And she found too that she was glad, despite the initial shock, to be carrying a child for him. She wanted – this was something quite new – to please him. This unexpected softening – she put it down to a curious effect of pregnancy – was alarming to her at first, until she realised that there was no longer any need for her to be hard all the time. There was nothing in particular that she had to strive for. She could, if she wanted, simply enjoy things. It was very odd.

★ ★ ★

More guests came every day, and the atmosphere grew jollier with each arrival, since both Fergus and Giulia were determined, if for different reasons, that everyone should have a good time. The house was very large, since the neighbours lived so far away, if they visited they had to stay the night. So there were plenty of bedrooms. And if southerners had been wary about visiting the wilds of Northumberland at that time of year, friends and relatives in Scotland had no such fears. Which was how Maud came down from resting on her bed one afternoon and discovered a bustle of welcome in the great hall for Sir Gordon Tullamore, accompanying his daughter Beata, now Lady Elrick, and her husband.

Sir Gordon was brushing snow from his shoulders and saying, 'I don't think it's settling. We saw a lot of deer on the way up, Leake – your people haven't been taking care of them. That's the trouble with being an absentee landlord.'

'Giulia thinks they're pretty,' Fergus said defensively, and sought to divert attention. 'Here's Maud. You haven't said hello to Maud.'

A stiffness came over Sir Gordon, but he bowed and said, 'Maud. Are you well?'

'Tolerably so, thank you.'

'I thought you had gone back to Germany.'

'Not yet. Fergus is my only brother. I must pay his bride suitable attention.'

'Quite so. Quite so. Beata, my dear, are you ready to go to your room?'

Beata had forgotten for the moment Maud's connection with the banishment of her brother, and was in any case newly enough married for her husband to push everything else out of her head. 'Oh, no, Papa, Roly and I must have a cup of tea first. It was a dreadful journey. The roads are terrible. Is there tea, Uncle Fergus?'

'As soon as you ring. Giulia, my dear, show our guests to the fire.'

'I'll go up, and join you shortly,' said Sir Gordon, and turned to the stairs, just as Rachel was coming down them. She stopped and blushed scarlet, then came on, and Sir Gordon, instead of waiting for her to step off at the bottom, started up, brushing past her without acknowledgement.

Maud's lips tightened; Beata looked embarrassed, remembering what she had forgotten. 'Oh dear, I hope there won't be unpleasantness,' she whispered to her husband.

Maud heard her. 'Unpleasantness?' she said coldly.

'We didn't know Rachel would be here,' Beata said awkwardly.

'Where should she be?' Maud demanded.

The prince, recognising the onset of conflict, stepped between them and offered each an arm. 'If I may be of service, dear ladies,' he said. 'To such a good fire to go on such a day is pleasant, not?'

Sir Roland Elrick took pity on Rachel, left standing, and offered her his arm, and she took it gratefully.

The atmosphere deteriorated slowly. Maud and Gordon Tullamore should have been on the same side: neither wanted the Angus-Rachel marriage. But because Rachel was an earl's daughter and Angus only a baronet's son, Maud had always believed it was for *her* to do the rejecting, not Tullamore. And it was not by *her* choice that Angus had been banished from the family and lost to his father (though she would have come down equally hard on disobedience) so it was rather too bad of Tullamore to treat her coolly.

For his part, Sir Gordon blamed Rachel for leading his son astray, and Maud for not bringing her up properly and controlling her.

In a large house with a large crowd of people things might have passed off without an explosion, but on one evening, to amuse his guests and show off Giulia, Fergus got together some musicians and arranged a ball after dinner. Sir Roland, seeing Rachel drooping in a corner, hiding herself from Tullamore's eye, was overcome by good manners and asked her to dance. She didn't really want to dance with Sir Gordon watching, but she appreciated the kindness, and she had always enjoyed Scottish dancing. It reminded her of Angus, who was wonderful at it, so light and springy on his feet it was a revelation. It was pleasant, anyway, to be partnered again by a handsome young man, even if it wasn't Angus, and before long she had forgotten her troubles and was dancing with exuberant energy.

But at the end of the set, Sir Gordon stalked over and, without a glance at Rachel, snapped to his son-in-law, 'You are neglecting your wife, Elrick. Come away.'

Maud, standing nearby, bristled. *Come away?* As if her daughter was something unpleasant he needed to be saved from! 'I *beg* your pardon?' she said, in her iciest tone.

Sir Gordon turned back, his face reddening ominously. 'If your daughter had any conduct, she would not display herself on the dance-floor in that shameless way.'

Rachel was white with shock at the words.

Maud seemed to her to swell to twice her size. 'How dare you speak like that about my daughter?'

'She has ruined one of my sons, and now seems determined to make a show of my son-in-law. Well, I won't allow it!'

'*You* won't allow it?' Maud's tone was low, but vibrated with outrage. This was not to be borne! 'It was *I* who forbade the match with your son. *You* would have been fortunate indeed to win a bride for him so far above his station, and well you know it.'

'His station? My son is a gentleman!' Tullamore snapped back.

'It's a pity the same can't be said of his father.' Even Maud thought she had gone too far with those words, but she was riding a flood of long-suppressed anger.

There was a sharp intake of breath from Sir Gordon. 'You forget who you are talking to, madam!'

'I know very well whom I am addressing – an industrialist,' Maud said, with furious scorn. 'Lady Rachel is the daughter of an earl and the granddaughter of earls on both sides. *She* may marry wherever she chooses.'

Eyes were turning on them now. Sir Gordon was about to retaliate. But Maud suddenly felt dizzy. Black spots swirled behind her eyes, she felt pressure in her ears and a wave of nausea as the floor seemed to rise towards her. A small, cold hand caught her outflung one, and someone guided her a step backwards to a chair. Seated, she leaned forward and took some deep breaths until the dizziness subsided.

She straightened up to find in front of her not Sir Gordon but their hostess – which did nothing to improve her feelings – and the concerned figure of the prince, stooping over her anxiously. And the cold hand that had stopped her sinking humiliatingly to the floor turned out to belong to Rachel, who was waiting beside her to be of help. Maud gave her a grateful look, probably the first she had ever given Rachel in her life, and allowed her and Paul to help her to her feet.

Giulia was asking what was wrong and what she could do to help, and Rachel it was who answered. 'My mother is tired,' she said, in a voice in which probably only Maud could detect the quiver. 'I will see her to her room. Please don't fuss.'

At the door Maud put Rachel's hand away from her and slipped her arm through her husband's, and Rachel accepted the hint and stepped back.

Fergus intercepted them. 'Are you all right, Maudie?'

'Just tired, dear,' Maud said. 'I'm going to bed. Don't stop the fun on my account.'

That was the advice Fergus really wanted to hear. He

beamed. 'Have a good rest, old dear. You'll feel better in the morning,' he said, and turned back to the dancing.

What a boy he was, Maud thought fondly.

In the bedroom, Miss Taylor was waiting. The prince bowed and kissed his wife's hand with a concerned look and asked, in German, 'May I return later? To see how you are?'

He must have hovered somewhere outside, because as soon as Miss Taylor left, he came back in. Maud was in her dressing-gown, sitting at the dressing-table, and he crossed the room and laid a hand on her forehead. 'You have no fever,' he observed. 'How do you feel? No pains anywhere?'

'Just tired,' she said. She gestured him to the nearest chair. She didn't like to be fussed, though in her vulnerable state, she found his tender concern rather touching.

'I think you are doing too much,' he said. 'Remember your condition.'

'I do remember it,' she said. He might have warned her not to risk his child's health, but he didn't, and she was grateful. And suddenly she realised how very tired she really was. 'I want to go home,' she said, and the words burst out of her almost without her volition.

Paul looked cautious. 'To Ashmore Castle?'

'No, to Usingerhof,' she said. 'To our home.'

Her reward was the surprised delight that rushed over his face. 'Yes, yes,' he said softly, in German, 'that is our home indeed. Oh, my heart's dearest, I wish more than anything to see you there, installed where you are queen of all, beloved and safe. Shall we go at once?'

'In the morning,' she said, smiling at his eagerness. Oh, she must be in a weakened state indeed to be smiling at him! 'Leave me now, my dear.'

In the morning she did not rise when Miss Taylor came in with her tea tray, but told her she would take breakfast in bed, and was glad that her maid was too well trained to show any surprise. As she went out, Rachel came in, dressed except for her hair, and with a shining morning face.

'Oh, Mama,' she cried, 'did you mean it? Really?'

Maud couldn't think what she was referring to. 'Please don't gush,' she extemporised. 'And speak quietly.'

'Have you a headache?' Rachel asked, in immediate concern, and a very quiet voice.

'What do you want?' Maud asked, instead of answering.

'I won't bother you, if you're not feeling well.'

'I am perfectly well, and we will be leaving this morning, so say what you have to say and go away. There is packing to do.'

Rachel wilted a little. 'I just wanted to know if you meant what you said last night – about my being able to marry anyone I want.'

Maud was about to explain that she had only meant Rachel might look as high as she pleased. But then she thought again. She was going to have a baby, and that was surely enough to be going on with. Did she really want to drag an unwilling daughter with her, suffer her sulks and complaints? She thought of all the time and effort she had put into bringing Rachel out; but she simply didn't have the energy to keep fighting now.

She said, 'The prince and I are going back to Usingerhof. You may come with us, or stay at Ashmore, whichever you prefer.'

Rachel did not rejoice yet. She looked at her mother cautiously. 'But – about marrying anyone?'

'Can the Tullamore boy support you?"

'He has a good position, and he's working hard and saving up. He says he will be able to in a year or so.'

Maud shook her head at the thought of 'saving up', and the sort of home Rachel would have, compared with what she was so blithely bent on giving up. But in 'a year or two', anything might happen. 'You have my permission to become engaged,' she said. 'And we shall see how it goes.'

Rachel's smile was as much astonishment as joy. 'Oh, Angus is very sensible! And hard-working! He'll look after me, truly! Oh, Mama, *thank* you!'

Maud allowed one grateful kiss on her cheek before pushing her back. 'I hope you won't regret it. But I've done my best for you. Go away now.'

She was up and dressed after her tray breakfast and preparing to go downstairs, so as to leave Taylor to pack, when Linda came in. Maud sighed in anticipation of a tirade, but Linda was subdued, almost gentle in her manner.

'Is it true that you are going back to the Usingerhof right away?'

'With a short stay in London on the way, yes.'

'Take me with you,' Linda said. Maud raised an eyebrow. 'Servants are all very well, *husbands* are all very well, but you need a woman to help you through the birth. And afterwards I can manage your nursery – you won't want to do that yourself. You need a companion, Mama, someone of equal rank, someone who speaks English.' She gave a tense smile. 'A friend.'

'A friend?' Maud was bemused. But, yes, she could see it. She spoke excellent German, but sometimes, wouldn't one want to converse in one's own tongue? German doctors were excellent, but a woman giving birth wanted someone closer to rely on. A companion . . . A princess should have a lady-in-waiting. And a daughter who remembered the same things and had the same references – a *grateful* daughter . . . And if in time she found a suitable husband among Usingen's friends for Linda, she would have her settled nearby, and that would be a comfort.

A thought came to her. 'What about your children?'

'Oh, they'll stay at Ashmore. No point in uprooting them.'

She relaxed. 'Very well, you can come,' she said.

After all, if it didn't work out, she could always send her back.

CHAPTER EIGHT

Sebastian had dressed with care in his most subdued clothes, but he still knew himself out of his place. The taxi-cab driver who had dropped him off in the reassuringly named Prince Albert Street had given him a curious look. When he'd received his fare he looked Sebastian over and said, 'I'd keep my hand on my ha'penny if I was you, sir. There's some funny coves about these alleys.'

'Thanks, I'll be careful,' Sebastian said. It was only when the cabby had driven off that he realised he should have asked directions. Although he had an address, he didn't know how to get there. With a shrug, he took a firm grip on his cane, and plunged in.

The alleys were narrow, and the overhanging houses made them dark, too; the cobbles were slimy from the recent rain, weeds grew in the cracks, and litter was lying about. The buildings had the unmistakable look of poverty – peeling paint, cracked rendering, patched panes, moss streaks on the walls from leaking downpipes. The shops were poor-looking and had faded, peeling signs. Dwelling-house windows had dirty and sagging curtains, or a bit of sacking nailed across. And there were few street signs: it was as if these alleys were too poor to merit a name.

He attracted some curious glances, but no-one offered him any insult, though he suspected a couple of boys in shabby clothes and patched boots too big for them were following him, either for the purposes of mockery or perhaps with more sinister intent.

It was no good, he would have to ask his way. For all he knew he was wandering further from his object with every step. He passed a low alehouse with several rough-looking men lounging outside with tankards in their hands, and felt their eyes following him. But he wouldn't ask them: this was not a place where you wanted to seem uncertain. He walked on, and saw a woman approaching, shabbily dressed but decent-looking, carrying a basket of folded clothes. Surely a washerwoman must be respectable? Forgetting himself, he touched his hat to her, and she stopped, staring.

'I beg your pardon,' he said, 'could you tell me where Hog Lane is?'

She continued to stare as if he had grown another head, while behind him he could hear the boys sniggering and trying to imitate him. At last she said, 'It's back a ways,' and jabbed her thumb over her shoulder. 'But you'll never find it. I'd show you, but I've got to get on.'

'Would a shilling help?' he said.

'A shilling?' She seemed struck. 'Here, mister, what are you up to? You don't want to flash your jingle round these parts. There's sorts here'd have it off you in two ticks.'

'Would you show me the way?'

'I'm in a hurry,' she said, 'but the kid'll show you. Here, you, Alfie Hedges!' she called to one of the boys behind him, then lowered her voice. 'Give him a penny. Don't go offering no shilling.' The boy sidled up, hands in his pockets, eyes slithering about so as not to look directly at Sebastian. The cap on his head was a man's and too big for him; the face under it was dirty and decorated with a runnel from one nostril, like a snail's trail. 'You show this gent to Hog Lane, and he'll give you a penny,' the woman said. 'And don't start getting any funny ideas or he'll clout you one with his stick, you hear me? Go on, then! Off you go.' The boy slouched past and started walking away, but stopped a few yards on and looked back. His friend scurried past Sebastian and joined him, and they both waited. 'If they give you any trouble, give 'em a clout,' the woman said, and went on her way.

The route seemed tortuous, and Sebastian wondered whether he was being led a dance. But the boys glanced back at him from time to time, and walked with confidence. At the end of a narrow, dirty alley, they stopped.

'Giss a penny, then,' the boy Alfie said. He shifted from foot to foot and didn't meet Sebastian's eyes.

'Is this Hog Lane?' he asked sternly.

The boy pointed to the lane that crossed the alley. 'Thass it,' he said, then held his hand out, palm cupped in an accustomed manner.

'Where's Jack Hubert's shop?' Sebastian asked.

The boy looked blank, but his companion whispered something into his ear, and he said, 'Wot, Shoddy Jack's? Thass down that way.' He gestured to the right.

So Sebastian felt in his pocket, identified a penny by feel – he didn't want to bring out a handful of change and tempt anybody – and handed it over. The grubby palm closed over it and the boys scuttled away like mice, leaving Sebastian alone.

He was relieved to see Hog Lane was wider, less dark, more decent-looking, with a narrow pavement on either side of the cobbled roadway. It even had an iron lamppost, positioned to give light to the junction with the alley. There were shops on either side – one had pots and pans, pails and brushes hanging up, another was selling second-hand furniture, a third was a pawn-shop – and there were people about who, though poorly dressed, seemed to be going about normal business.

A few doors along, a run-down and paint-bereft shop had old clothes hanging in the window. Walking past and looking in, he could see nothing in the dark interior, and there was no sign over the window to say who owned it, but if this was indeed Hog Lane – the address the aptly named Mr Bland had given him – then surely that must be it. He walked on to the next corner and stopped to light a cigarette to give himself time to think. He still had no idea what to say to Jack Hubert, or what outcome he hoped for. Yet he had expended a large sum to find him, and now had come all this way, so it would be feeble just to go away again. Perhaps something would occur to him when he actually saw the man.

He walked back slowly, and paused outside the shop, and after a moment a man emerged from the dark interior and stood in the doorway. 'Help you, guv'nor?' he asked, looking Sebastian up and down in a predatory manner.

'Are you Jack Hubert?' Sebastian asked.

The man scowled. He was as tall as Sebastian, though thinner, but he had the look of mean strength of an alley-dog. He wore no tie or shirt-collar, but the jacket and trousers, though old, were from the same suit and had once been decent. His chin was unshaven, his eyes bloodshot, and his face bore the unmistakable marks of a drinker, but it was possible to tell that he had once been handsome.

'And who might you be?' The eyes were fixed on Sebastian like those of a dog about to attack.

Sebastian shifted his grip on his cane and said, 'I want to talk to you about your wife.'

Hubert had been leaning against the door frame; now he pushed himself clear, and his hands clenched into fists. 'My wife's upstairs. What do *you* know about her?' he demanded dangerously.

A saving thought came to Sebastian. Bigamy was a crime, punishable by gaol. Could he perhaps put pressure on Hubert to promise never to seek out Dory, on pain of being reported to the police? 'Your name is Jack Hubert?' he persisted.

A few passers-by had paused in the hope of some entertainment, and one of them shouted, 'Don't tell him, Jack!'

There was laughter, and Hubert's face darkened. 'You look like a copper's nark to me. We know how to deal with copper's narks in these parts. You'd best be on your way.'

'Is your wife here?'

'What business is it of yours? You got some nerve, coming here asking about Mary.'

'So your wife's name is Mary, is it? I must make a note of that,' Sebastian said.

And Hubert said, 'I've had enough of this.' He surged forward, grabbed Sebastian by the lapels and shoved. Close to, Sebastian could smell the drink on him: not just on his breath but, in the manner of heavy drinkers, coming out of his pores. 'You clear out of here or I'm going to punch your lights out!'

Sebastian thrust him away, managing to break the grip on his jacket. 'Threats only mean you've got something to hide,' he said. 'I know things about you, Jack Hubert, that could get you a spell inside.'

Hubert's snarl showed missing teeth, but the blow from the bony fist at the end of the stringy arm was so quick it almost connected with Sebastian's face: he jerked his head back just in time to catch it on his collar bone. It was frighteningly hard, and his blood surged with fighting spirit, making him quick enough to dodge the second blow, though it grazed his ear.

Hubert paused, turned slightly away and back, and now something glinted in his hand. There was a short scream, and a woman's voice cried, 'He's got a knife!'

A man shouted, 'Watch out, guv'nor!'

Sebastian backed away, readying his stick, watching Hubert's eyes for the jump as he advanced. The ring of onlookers widened judiciously. Then from the shop a slatternly woman emerged and screamed, 'No, Jack! Don't stick a nob!'

In the instant that Sebastian's attention flickered towards her, Hubert sprang. Sebastian jumped back and felt a sharp burning, like a thin trail of fire, across his ribs; Hubert came at him again, the wicked-looking blade no longer concealed, his other hand raised to fend off any counter-attack. Sebastian feinted with his stick, sidestepped, caught Hubert's knife-hand by the wrist as it came at him – the forward and upward blow of the accustomed fighter – and managed, just, to keep it from his body. He brought his cane down on Hubert's arm, thrusting him backwards at the same time, and broke free. As Hubert came again, he swung and hit him hard with the cane between the shoulder and neck. Hubert swayed under the blow, lost his balance, took a half-step backwards to recover it, and caught his heel against the shallow kerb. He flailed and fell backwards, and there was a sickening sound as his head hit the iron lamppost.

A little sudden silence dropped, and Sebastian only then realised that there had been noise, the gathered crowd shouting, egging the fight on. He waited, panting, shifting his grip on his cane for the next attack, but Hubert, sprawled on his back, didn't get up. From the corner of his eye he saw that the slatternly woman – presumably the 'wife' Mary – had been caught by the arms by two onlookers to keep her from interfering. She had been struggling to be released, but was now still. 'Jack!' she yelled.

Close behind Sebastian there was the shrill sound of a police whistle, and he felt rather than saw the crowd starting to sidle away. Then a large, authoritative voice bellowed, 'All right, everybody, stand where you are! Stand still! You with the stick, don't you move!'

Sebastian was only too glad to obey. He didn't think he could have moved anyway.

Maud was standing when Angus was shown into Caroline's drawing-room: she wasn't prepared to have any young person loom over her. She had never really looked at him before – he was just one of the young cousins – but she saw now that he was a handsome boy, well set-up, and his smile, though suitably uncertain for this meeting, was attractive. She could see why Rachel had fancied him. Why she should want to give up everything for him was another matter.

'Aunt Maud,' he said cautiously. His eyes travelled to Caroline and Rachel, seated on the other side of the room and forbidden by Maud to speak. He nodded respectfully to them. 'Aunt Caroline. Rachel.'

'Sit down,' Maud said to him. She took the chair opposite, and studied him in silence to unnerve him.

He bore it well. 'Thank you for giving permission for us to become engaged.'

'Yes?' she said, to indicate that there was always time to withdraw the permission. Then, 'It is a great pity you managed to alienate your father and lose all your prospects.'

'But I have others now,' he said. 'I have a good position, and I've been told I'm giving satisfaction. When my trial period is over, I'll have a salaried place with excellent prospects for advancement. I intend to save hard and hope to be in a position to marry next year.'

Rachel drew breath as if to speak and Maud silenced her with a glance. 'You are an office clerk, I believe.'

'Something more than that, ma'am. I am to be Mr Cowling's general manager, a position of responsibility within his business empire.'

'Empire?' she queried witheringly. 'Is he a monarch?'

'It's an expression. His interests are wide, ma'am. He is a very wealthy man. He advises the King on financial matters.'

'My permission is only for you to become engaged. In a year's time, we will see how things lie. In the mean time, you may see each other under the normal rules of society, and you may correspond.'

'Thank you, Aunt Maud.'

'If there is the least impropriety—'

'I would never do anything to harm Rachel. I love her.'

'Hmm. Well, we shall see. When the time comes, if your application has been constant and your behaviour impeccable, I may find a dowry for Rachel commensurate with your financial position.'

'Thank you, Aunt Maud.'

Maud stood. 'You may have five minutes together,' she said. 'Caroline?'

The two dowagers went into the morning room, where Maud sat rather abruptly, and Caroline said, 'Are you feeling unwell, Maud dear?'

'Tired,' she said. 'This unnecessary situation wears me.'

'But he's such a nice boy, and they do seem very fond of each other. And don't forget, *I* was allowed to marry for love.'

'Sir James Manningtree was one of the richest men in London,' Maud observed.

'Well, perhaps Angus will make his fortune. It's very promising that Mr Cowling has taken him up.'

'You know this Mr Cowling well?'

'His London house is on the other side of the square. He's a shrewd businessman, and really rather a pet. I've taken a queer fancy to him. He moves in very good society, Maud – received everywhere. And you know he married Kitty's bosom friend Nina, the girl she was brought out with?'

Maud waved that away. 'I look to you, Caroline, to supervise their trysts.'

'Of course.'

'She will continue to live at Ashmore Castle, but may come up to Town, let us say, once a month.'

'They can meet here,' Caroline said. 'Or I can chaperone them to the theatre or a ball or suchlike.' She sounded pleased with the prospect.

'It is not necessary to entertain them,' Maud said. 'Or desirable.' Once the glamour of forbidden fruit was removed from Angus Tullamore, and Rachel realised what life as the wife of a clerk would mean, she might find her enthusiasm for him waning. A year was a long time when you were nineteen. He was a pretty boy, but nothing else. Maud wondered she had not thought of it before – allowing a tedious engagement to rub the gilt from the prize.

'When are you leaving for Germany?' Caroline was asking.

'The day after tomorrow. Then I shall stay at the Usingerhof until the baby is born.'

'But, Maud, what about Alice?'

'*What* about Alice?'

'You're happy for her to remain at the art school? You don't want to bring her out, or arrange a match for her?'

Maud made a gesture that was meant to be impatient, but in fact looked weary. 'Stainton can make those decisions, since he seems to have taken responsibility for her. I wash my hands of her.'

How did she come to have two such unnatural daughters as Rachel and Alice? Linda might be annoying in many ways, but her priorities had always been correct. Maud was quite glad she would have her at her side for the next few months. She thought briefly of the baby to come, but it was not yet real to her. Usingen wanted a son, of course, and she hoped it was, for his sake. Possibly for her own sake, too – girls were so much trouble! The thought of coping with another daughter's moods and fancies and then having to bring her out in seventeen years' time was exhausting.

In the drawing-room, Angus and Rachel sat close together on the settle, their hands interlinked. 'What did Mama mean about a dowry commensurate with something or other?' Rachel asked.

'My financial situation? I think she meant that whatever I managed to save, she would match, but nothing more.'

'Oh. Then you must save like mad.'

'I shall, but not for her sake. It's always nice to be given a sum of money, but I don't mean to depend on someone else ever again. I shall support you by my own efforts.'

Rachel glowed at such a manly statement. 'But,' she said timidly, 'aren't you a bit dependent on Mr Cowling?'

'Not dependent: he pays me for my work. And – I didn't mention it in front of your mother – he's already hinted that at some point in the future he'll allow me to purchase shares in his business, so I shall end up owning part of it. That will be something solid that can't be taken away, not like a wage that you lose if you lose your position.'

Rachel didn't understand the concept but was happy just to hear him talk. 'But suppose Mr Cowling has a son – won't he leave everything to him?'

'Why are we talking about Mr Cowling when we only have five minutes?' he said, drawing Rachel towards him.

The inspector had Dundreary whiskers, a look so old-fashioned it kept distracting Sebastian's attention. He was studying Sebastian's visiting card as if it might jump out of his hand and dance a jig.

'So you claim to be this Mr Sebastian Tallant, do you?'

'Not claim – I am,' Sebastian said.

'And your normal place of residence is Ashmore Castle in the county of Buckinghamshire?'

'Yes.'

'Which would make you – what? A lord of some kind?'

'My uncle was an earl. But the Castle belongs to my nephew, and I live there by his kindness.'

'And if I was to go to this castle and enquire after you, they'd know who you were, no doubt?' The irony was heavy.

'They would, but I wish you wouldn't do that.'

'Oh, and why not?'

'Because I don't want my private business bruited about. And – with all due respect to the forces of law and order – people like them don't care to receive visits from the police.'

'You've got the talk down pat, I'll give you that. You remind me of Smooth Cecil, the Gentleman Burglar. He got invited to grand houses by sounding like a nob, and then disappeared in the night with their bits and pieces.' He examined the card again. 'And what's this other address?'

'My club, in London.'

'And I suppose *they*'d know your name, if I was to enquire?'

'I've been a member for twenty years. They know me there. Ask for Stennings, the head porter.'

The inspector put the card down and leaned forward, clasping his hands on the desk, coming to business.

'So, Mr Sebastian Tallant, who lives in a castle and is not quite an earl, what were you doing in Hog Lane? Not your usual stamping ground, I'd say.'

Sebastian hesitated. 'It was idle curiosity,' he said. 'I'd heard about the area, I thought I'd go and have a look for myself.'

'Heard about it? Interested in slums, are we?'

'I'd heard that young bucks like to go there and carouse.'

'Carouse?' He tasted the word like an unusual potion. 'At eleven o'clock in the morning?'

Sebastian took the battle to him. 'Why am I being held here, Inspector?'

The inspector raised his eyebrows. They were very bushy and, what with the Dundrearies and a large moustache, didn't leave much of his face uncovered, except for his chin, which was like a knob of pumice. And his eyes, which were uncomfortably sharp. 'A man is dead, Mr Tallant, that's why. And you've got some explaining to do. How do you know Jack Hubert, or Hubbard as he's sometimes known?'

Sebastian had prepared for this question. 'I've never met him before in my life, and that's the truth.'

The inspector stared at him for a long time, and Sebastian stared back. His ribs ached. The knife that had been intended to stab him had, thanks to his jump backwards, only skittered across his front, but it was a long slash, and it hurt. It had ruined his shirt, of course, and he hated to sit here in cut and bloodstained linen, but they had not offered him a change. A doctor had been summoned to examine the cut, had put half a dozen stitches in the deeper end, and bound it up, after which Sebastian had had to resume the ruined shirt. And then there had been a long wait in this room until the inspector came in.

'But you killed him all the same,' the inspector said at last.

'I did not, sir. His death was an accident. And there were plenty of witnesses who saw him pull out the knife and try to stab me.'

'Yes, and that's the thing that's bothering me. Why would Jack Hubert, or Hubbard, want to stab Mr Sebastian Tallant, who he's never met before in his life?'

'The man was drunk,' Sebastian said. 'I could smell it on him. He just came at me like a madman. I had to defend myself.'

'Hmm,' the inspector said. As if in acknowledgement of his job title, he went on inspecting Sebastian in silence.

At last Sebastian said, 'Can I go now? I'm not feeling very well. And I need clean linen.'

The inspector seemed to come to a decision. 'You will have to remain in the area for the time being. There will be an inquest, and you'll be called as principal witness. Where are you staying in Brighton?'

'At the Grand.'

'Of course you are. Well, one of my constables will take you there and see you safe to your room.'

'There's no need.'

'Not for your sake, but for ours. So we know where you're stashed. And I do advise you, Mr Sebastian Tallant, to stay put, and not to think you can go wandering off before the inquest, because that would be a very bad idea, and put you in bad odour with – what did you call it? – the forces of law and order. Which at the moment is me. I'm a patient man, my wife tells me, but I don't take kindly to being messed around.'

'I have no intention of going anywhere.'

The inspector stood. 'Very well. Wait here and I'll send a constable to see you home.' He got to the door, and then turned quickly, as though wanting to catch Sebastian at something. 'One of the witnesses said they heard you asking Hubert about his wife, just before the fight started.'

'They must have been mistaken,' Sebastian said, keeping his gaze steady.

'How do you know Hubert's wife?'

'I don't. I didn't even know her name. I've never met her or heard of her before.'

'Really? Because she's known as a bit of a gay girl, if you get my drift. Free with her favours – or not exactly free but, say, for half a crown she'll be as friendly as you like. Are you sure you've not heard of her? Maybe you asked Jack Hubert for an introduction, not knowing he doesn't like her to engage in trade.'

'I've never met Hubert or his wife before. He was drunk and attacked me and I defended myself, that's all,' Sebastian said desperately.

The inspector stared in silence, then nodded and went out.

Sebastian held himself together a moment longer in case he popped back in to catch him out, then groaned and put his aching head into his hands. How much trouble was he in? Hubert's death had been an accident, but his blow was a contributory cause. Supposing witnesses said he was looking for him, supposing they said he started the fight, would that make it manslaughter? Would he go to gaol? Prison would kill him – he couldn't go to prison. Perhaps he should consult a lawyer. And, oh, God, what would the scandal do to the family?

He didn't allow himself to think about Dory. Not just then.

★ ★ ★

'Oh – Rose?' Mrs Webster called from her room as the head housemaid passed the door. She came in. 'I was thinking while Mr Sebastian's away we should give his room a good spring cleaning.'

'All right. I'll organise it.'

Mrs Webster saw Dory beyond the door, listening, and called her. 'Did you hear? I said we should thoroughly clean Mr Sebastian's room.'

'How long is he away for?' Dory asked.

'He said a few days. He didn't take Mr Crooks with him, so he probably went to London – he doesn't take a servant when he stays at his club. What I was going to say was that there's that worn place in the carpet in front of the wardrobe – do you think you can mend it? Otherwise we'll have to turn the carpet, and that means taking all the furniture out.'

'I can mend it,' Dory said. 'Did he *say* he was going to London?'

Mrs Webster frowned. 'He wouldn't tell *me* where he was going, would he?'

'No, of course not,' Dory said, and moved on out of sight.

'Strange thing to ask,' Mrs Webster said.

'If you ask me, she spends too much time alone,' Rose said, 'up in the sewing room or the upstairs linen room. You ought to tell her to do her work down here. It's not healthy to be alone all the time. Makes you go queer in the head.'

'She sees enough people at mealtimes,' Mrs Webster said. 'She's a sensible woman. I wouldn't interfere.'

Rose shrugged. 'The heavy laundry's come back, by the way.' They sent out the sheets to the Ideal Laundry in the village. 'I was just going to put it away, and then I'm going out.'

'Oh, it's your afternoon off, isn't it? Can you check the sheets as you put them away? The binding on one was torn last week. I don't want any torn sheets when we've got visitors.'

'They're only old friends of his lordship's. Arky-whatsits. They won't complain – if they even notice.'

'We have standards at Ashmore Castle,' said Mrs Webster. 'And a tear in a sheet only gets bigger. Someone *always* puts their foot through it. Besides, Lord and Lady Denham are coming, and it would be just my bad luck if the one torn sheet ended up on their bed.'

'How are they going to get on with the arkies?' Rose asked. 'Funny mix, isn't it?'

'Lord Denham has a herd of prize cattle, and Mr Richard wants to talk to him about them. And Lady Denham, apparently, is keen on gardens, so her ladyship can chat to her while his lordship talks about archaeology.'

'Arki-ology, that's the word,' Rose said. 'Why they can't just call it digging I don't know.' She turned to go.

'Going anywhere nice for your afternoon off?' Mrs Webster asked absently, going back to her ledgers.

'No,' said Rose, without turning.

A kindly chambermaid found Sebastian an aspirin, and he went to bed early and slept heavily. His first movement on waking caused him to wince as it jogged his wound, and brought the situation rushing back to him. He groaned at the thought of the trouble he was in. Was there no end to the pain Jack Hubert could cause?

His head felt stuffed with cotton-wool, and he thought longingly of the clean sea air outside. A walk along the front would do him good – he had some thinking to do. He got up, slipped along to the bathroom to wash and shave, came back and dressed. Putting on a clean shirt was painful – any move that required raising his arms pulled at the wound. When he slipped his watch into his fob pocket, he discovered it was after ten: he must have slept for twelve hours.

Down in the hotel lobby, an unremarkable character was propping up the desk talking to the clerk in the manner of a bosom friend. As Sebastian walked to the street door, the unremarkable character righted himself and followed.

Outside, Sebastian hesitated, looking left and right, then turned left, and a few yards along, as he paused to check if the road was clear to cross, he saw the character was still behind him. It was a breezy day, the air was full of the smell of salt and seaweed and the cries of gulls. He walked slowly along the promenade, breathing as deeply as was comfortable, and his shadow followed about ten paces behind him. So that was it. The inspector was making sure he did not abscond. For a moment he wondered what would happen if he broke into a run. Would there be a hue-and-cry? He imagined himself running to the station, jumping on the first available train and abandoning his luggage at the hotel. Would they physically stop him? But he couldn't have run in any case – his wound was too painful. And, besides, they knew where he lived. No, he would have to stay, face the inquest, and establish his innocence.

He *was* innocent, but the problem was that if the background were known about, he would not *look* innocent. He had asked the washerwoman the way to Hog Lane – but the police wouldn't know about her, unless she volunteered the information, and why would she do that? He had asked the boys about Jack Hubert, but he believed children could not be witnesses. As to his asking Hubert about his wife, if they brought that up he must say the witness was mistaken and keep saying it. To lie was bad, to lie in court was awful, but he had no choice. When it came down to it, he had done nothing wrong, had he?

A gull just above him screamed, making him jump. He stopped and leaned on the railings, staring out at the restless sea, billowing like a grey counterpane being vigorously shaken by a diligent maid. His shadow stopped too, and lit a cigarette. He realised he was hungry. He could go back to the hotel, but why make it easy for them? There was a café on the other side of the road. It would amuse him, just a little, to see how the shadow dealt with that. Would he follow him in and order a cup of tea, or lurk about outside? What if there was only one free table? Would he sit down with him and pretend he hadn't been following him?

It was not much of an amusement but, then, he hadn't much to be amused about.

When Rose turned in at the gate of Hundon's, she heard Jess bark from the barn. She would have expected Fly to come running out, warning Woodrow she had arrived: the dog's absence suggested he was not at home. She frowned. It was the right day and the right time. If he had forgotten, he'd get the sharp edge of her tongue. She would not tolerate being messed around.

She crossed the yard and rapped at the kitchen door, and it was opened by Martha, clutching a rolling-pin, letting out a gust of baking smell, and a glimpse of steam from the nose of a kettle on the range. But Martha herself was not welcoming. She scowled at Rose, and said, 'What do *you* want?'

'I've come to tea,' Rose said stiffly. 'He invited me.'

'He's not here. So you can go away.'

'What d'you mean, he's not here? He said Thursday at four, and it's Thursday, and it's four o'clock.'

'He's out with the cows. And he doesn't want to see you.'

Rose's eyes narrowed. 'He does too. You mean *you* don't want to see me.'

'I know your sort!' Martha said, glaring at her, folding her arms across her front. 'You and your wiles!'

'Wiles?' Rose was genuinely surprised. 'I haven't got wiles.'

'Luring men to the bad with your wanton ways! You want to take him away from me. Well, you can't have him! Clear off out of it, and don't come here again! He's not interested in you. He's a good man, and you're a bad sort, and I won't let you take him.' She unfolded her arms to wave the rolling-pin. 'Go on, clear off! Or I'll fetch you one upsides the head, you hussy!'

There was a bark from the gate, and Rose glanced round to see Fly running towards her, and Michael Woodrow coming in the gate behind him. 'Martha!' he said sharply.

Martha looked at him for a moment with her jaw jutting, then seemed to wilt. 'She's – she come here—'

'I know. I invited her,' he said, reaching them and gently removing the rolling-pin from Martha's hand.

Rose looked at him, uncertain and angry, a blush of chagrin warming her face. 'Your sister's threatening me. She's been saying shocking things about me,' she began.

He lifted a hand to stop her, but with a pleading look, and turned to Martha. 'Go in, Martha dear, and mash the tea. Everything's all right. Rose is a friend. Go on, now, all's well.'

Martha gave him an uncertain look, then went meekly in. Woodrow waited, then turned to Rose. 'I'm so sorry. I meant to be here when you arrived but one of the cows got her head stuck through a fence and I couldn't leave her. Please forgive me.'

Rose was not ready to let go of her anger yet. 'But what your sister said—'

'She doesn't mean those things. I told you she was a bit strange, ever since her mother died. Strangers unsettle her.'

'She should be locked up, threatening folks.'

'Oh, no,' he pleaded gently. 'She'd never do anything. It's just that she's frightened I'll go away and leave her. When a new person comes along, she thinks they'll take me away from her. Once she gets used to you, she'll be all right. She would never hurt you.'

Rose sniffed and tossed her head. 'I don't have to put up with that sort of thing.'

'Please,' he coaxed, 'won't you come in and have tea? You've come all this way. I promise she won't be difficult now.'

She allowed him to urge her through the door. 'Why d'you put up with it?' She gave a last retort.

'She's my sister.' He followed her in. 'Did you never have a sister?'

'Two brothers,' Rose said shortly. She looked warily at Martha, who was pouring boiling water into the teapot. The kitchen table was spread with a cloth with three places laid, and there was a plate of bread and butter, a dish of jam, and a cake stand at present unoccupied. All as nice as could be.

Woodrow pulled out a chair for her. 'Please sit. Guest of honour.'

Martha brought the teapot to the table and put it down gently, raised uncertain eyes to her brother's face, and seemed to be reassured by his smile. She didn't smile herself, but the fearsome scowl was gone.

'Is that your scones I can smell?' he asked her. 'Lovely! Martha makes the best scones in the whole of England,' he told Rose. 'So light you'd think they'd float off the plate.'

'Silly nonsense,' Martha snorted, but it was clear she was pleased. She went back to the range and brought out from the cool oven a plate of scones that were keeping warm there, and put it down with almost exaggerated care on the cake stand, then looked at her brother.

'Sit down, Martha dear,' he said, 'and pour the tea. How do you like it, Miss Hawkins?'

'Strong,' said Rose, still feeling uncertain. But the scones smelt delicious, and looked perfect, neat and round with shiny brown tops, and she felt a growl of hunger – it was a long time since dinner. Martha seemed as meek as a sheep now, and you wouldn't know from looking at her that she'd ever been otherwise. But if she could turn that quickly she could turn the other way as well, and Rose was wary.

Michael Woodrow seemed to know that, picked up the plate and offered it to her. 'Have a scone. You must be hungry. It's so nice of you to come and see us. A little tea party makes a nice change to routine, don't you think? Jam with your scone? Martha's own bramble jam.'

'Picked 'em myself last back end,' Martha said, her eyes on her plate. 'It were a good crop.'

Rose tried the scone, and it was delicious. She risked looking at Martha. 'Very nice,' she said. 'Nice scone, nice jam.'

The atmosphere seemed to relax. Martha didn't smile, but her shoulders went down.

'Tell me about your brothers,' Michael said. 'Older or younger?'

'Both younger,' Rose said. 'I had to be mother to 'em when I was a girl. Till they went out in the world.'

'Where are they now?'

'One's in the navy and one's in the army. That way they get their food and lodging. My dad always said—' She stopped, wary of being the only one to talk.

'Yes?' he encouraged.

'Get a job where your feet are under the table,' she concluded. 'That's why I went into service.'

'Yes, that's wise,' he said. 'When I went to work for Lord Denham, a cottage came with the job. And now there's this house.'

'D'you like it here?' Rose asked, finishing the scone.

Michael offered the plate again with admirable promptness. 'The house, or the job? I like both. Martha loves the house – don't you? – and the job is everything I've been working towards. To be dairyman in charge of my own herd!'

Rose wrinkled her nose. 'Cows! They're stupid, aren't they?'

'You'd be surprised,' he said. 'They're capable of learning and remembering. And they can be affectionate.'

'I wouldn't fancy one licking me, like a dog.'

He laughed. 'Well, they do that! And at Lord Denham's once, when I sat down in the cow field against a tree to have my lunch, one of them came and couched down beside me, and I thought she was going to try to get on my lap!'

'Lord and Lady Denham are coming to the Castle for

Easter,' Rose said. 'I've to get the Queen's Bedroom ready for them. That's the one his old lordship used to sleep in, but his present lordship didn't like it. Not one for being grand, Lord Stainton. He'd have taken one of the bachelor rooms when he came into the title, only his mother wouldn't let him.'

'Lord and Lady Denham are pretty grand,' said Michael, 'but I always had a good relationship with his lordship, because of the cows. I think they were the thing he loved most in the world.'

She wrinkled her nose. 'Not Lady Denham?'

'Well, you know what titled people are like. They don't generally marry for love.'

He happened to meet Rose's eyes as he said that, and there was a moment in which the world seemed to pause, its attention caught just for a second, before it rolled on. Martha lifted the teapot lid noisily and inserted a spoon to stir the contents.

'More tea?' Michael offered prosaically.

CHAPTER NINE

The coroner was a medical man, tall and bony, in the sort of good tweed suit that had been bought to last a lifetime. His thin hair was eked carefully over his scalp; his bony beak of a nose supported gold-rimmed pince-nez at the top and a drop of moisture at the bottom – the room in the back of the Mermaid Hotel, which had been requisitioned for the inquest, was clammily cold. His red, bony hands rested on top of his papers, except when they wielded a large white handkerchief, as he listened in attentive silence to the police constable's account, read out in a monotone from a notebook.

Then the police surgeon gave his account. 'Deceased had suffered a severe blow to the cranium causing a fracture of the right temporal bone and severe intracranial haemorrhage.'

'Would this blow have been fatal?'

'It would have led to unconsciousness and death,' the surgeon said, looking surprised. 'In my opinion.'

The coroner looked impatient. 'I am not questioning your expertise, sir. I am merely trying to establish whether there was some other or additional cause of death, or whether the blow itself was sufficient.'

'The blow was the cause of death. In my opinion.'

'And how was such a blow acquired?'

'That is beyond my knowledge, sir. I was at the scene only some time after death.'

More impatience. 'Was the damage to the cranium

consistent with deceased hitting his head on the lamppost by which he was lying?'

'Yes, sir. In my opinion.'

The coroner glanced at his watch, and instead of returning it to his pocket he placed it on the desk beside his glass of water. Sebastian thought this a good sign: he wanted to get the business done and perhaps would not ask too many questions.

The next witness, a large, red-faced man who gave his name as Bryson and his occupation as carter, said that he had just come out of the Three Tuns on the corner of Hog Lane and saw 'that posh gent over there' talking to Shoddy Jack outside his shop.

'By Shoddy Jack, you mean deceased? How do you know him?" the coroner asked.

'Bless you, sir, everybody at the Tuns knows him,' Bryson said. 'In there every day. I seen him a-dun-a-many times.'

The coroner looked as if he didn't much like being blessed by the likes of Bryson. 'What were you doing in a public house at that time of the morning?'

'Delivering beer, sir,' the carter replied smartly, with a look that said, *You don't catch me that way*.

The coroner sniffed. 'Continue,' he said. 'You saw them talking. What then?'

'I see Jack grab the gent by his coat, and the gent shoves him away. Then Jack gets out a knife. He goes for the gent, the gent shoves him back again, then he clouts him with his stick – the gent does – and Jack falls backwards and cracks his head on the lamppost. That musta done for him, for he doesn't get up again.'

'Very well. You may sit down.'

Then it was Sebastian's turn. There was a murmur of interest as he stood up. In steady tones he said he had paused outside the shop to look at the clothes in the window, and deceased had come to the door and demanded to know what he wanted. Then he had grabbed hold of him in a threatening manner. He had managed to disengage himself, and deceased had come at him with a knife, wounding him.

'You sustained a wound?' the coroner asked.

'Yes, sir. A long cut across my ribs and midriff. It required six stitches.'

'Very well. Continue.'

'He came at me again, and I struck at him with my cane. He staggered, took a step backwards, caught his heel on the kerb and fell, striking his head against the lamppost.'

'When you struck him, you believed he was intending to do you more harm?'

'I am certain of it.'

'So you struck him to defend yourself?'

'Yes, sir.'

'Did you strike him upon the head?'

'No, sir. The blow fell on his shoulder.'

'Very well. What was your relationship with deceased?'

'None, sir,' Sebastian said carefully and truthfully. 'I had never seen him before in my life.'

'If that is the case, why do you suppose he attacked you?'

This was trickier. 'I cannot explain it, sir, except to say that he was evidently drunk.'

The foreman of the jury stood up. 'We would like to know, if you please, what the gentleman and deceased talked about.'

The coroner sighed at the delay. He said to Sebastian, 'You hear. The jury wish to know what you talked about.'

Sebastian was on eggshells now. 'He asked me what I wanted. Then he demanded to know how I knew his wife. I said I didn't know her. Then he attacked me.'

'Did you, in fact, know his wife?"

'No, sir. I can only think he mistook me for someone else.'

'That sounds likely. You may sit down.'

A witness, a nervous older woman, gave testimony that Jack Hubbard was a 'great drinker' and 'often drunk out of his senses'. His wife Mary also was frequently drunk. She was 'a bad sort'.

The tapman from the Three Tuns said that he had sold a jug of flesh and blood to deceased's wife that morning about an hour before the incident. He further explained, on request, that flesh and blood was a popular local alcoholic beverage of porter mixed with gin. The coroner seemed to wince.

Another witness, a tiny old woman, very excited, shrill, and lacking teeth, said that Shoddy Jack was 'like a mad beast' in his cups, and used to beat his wife Mary when he'd 'had a few'. 'I see him pull his knife out,' she confided eagerly. 'It was me what shouted out and warned that feller – the gennleman there. Then Mary comes out and starts a-creatin', only some fellers held her back, or she'd likely have jined in.'

'What you think she might have done is not evidence,' the coroner said sternly. 'Is the wife present?'

The police inspector bobbed up to say that the woman, known variously as Mary Hughes, Mary or May Hubbard and Mary or Molly Welch, who lived with deceased as his wife, had been taken up dead drunk and disorderly in the early hours of that day and was still in the cells, not yet fit to be released.

'Very well,' said the coroner. 'Anyone else have anything more to say?'

The inspector rose again, and said, 'Sir, I feel Mr Tallant has not been sufficiently open about his presence in Hog Lane that morning. He has not accounted for why he was there at all. He claims he was wandering without any particular purpose, but I have a witness who says he asked the way to Hog Lane, and paid some boys a penny to guide him there.'

'Very well, we'll hear this witness.'

The inspector looked glum. 'I interviewed her, sir, but she was unwilling to appear in person unless subpoenaed. If I might request an adjournment . . .'

The coroner glanced at his watch again and said, with diminished patience, 'Oh, surely there's no need for that. The essentials of the business seem clear enough to me. Mr Tallant!' Sebastian stood up. 'Please state for the inspector's satisfaction what was your purpose in going to Hog Lane on the morning in question.'

'I confess it was idle curiosity, sir. I had heard of it as a place of ill repute and wanted to see it for myself.'

'A reprehensible curiosity, and no doubt you feel you have been sufficiently punished for it. Yes, what is it?'

A man in a worn suit had stood up, and said, 'My lord, I protest!'

'I am not a judge, and this is not a court of law. You address me as sir.'

'Well, sir, I protest about the gennleman calling it a place of ill repute. Us that live in Hog Lane are decent folk trying to make a honest living. I have an ironmongery shop, sir, and if people get to talking about ill repute and suchlike, what'll happen to my business? My wife's already in a state of nerves over having a dead body prac'ly right outside our premises.'

'What would you have me do?' the coroner barked impatiently.

'I would like it stated official, sir,' the ironmonger went on determinedly, 'that Hog Lane is a decent place.'

There was a murmur of agreement from several others in the room.

'Yes, yes, very well.' The coroner waved him to sit down. 'Mr Tallant, let us be clear, had you any knowledge of or dealings with deceased before that day?'

This was the moment Sebastian had dreaded, but he had his answer ready, and it was the truth. 'I had never met or seen the man before in my life,' he said, with all the sincerity he could muster.

'Well, Inspector?' said the coroner. 'That's plain enough for you, isn't it?'

The inspector rose again. 'Sir, I find it difficult to believe that deceased would attack a complete stranger at knifepoint for no reason at all.'

The coroner's patience snapped. 'I do not find it at all difficult to believe that an habitual drunk, known to be violent in his cups, should behave irrationally and violently. Those who engage in drunken brawls require only occasion, not provocation. Alcohol is rightly called "the demon drink" and its pernicious influence is the curse of the lower classes. It is quite clear that Mr Tallant was attacked with a knife – and wounded – and was merely defending himself, and that deceased tripped and fell and struck his head accidentally upon the lamppost. Does the jury need to retire?'

There was some shuffling, exchanged glances, and heads put together for some urgent whispering. Then the foreman stood up. 'No sir.'

'And what is your verdict?'

'That deceased came by his death by accident, sir, due to hitting his head on the lamppost.' He was given some strong, nudging looks. 'And we would like to add, sir, as there is too much drink taken around the Lanes and we should like to see the pubs closed earlier at night so as to cut it down.'

'That's not a matter within my competence,' the coroner said irritably, and closed the proceedings.

Sebastian held himself deliberately still, aware the inspector was looking at him and frowning. He should not see him slump with relief.

'I have to go to Portsmouth on business,' Mr Cowling said, sitting down at the breakfast table with a plate of kedgeree. 'Would you like to come with me? It would make a nice little change for you, before the London season starts.'

Nina heard the slightly wistful tone in his voice and before she looked up from her eggs and bacon was able to assemble her expression into something receptive.

'Portsmouth?' she queried.

'We could stay at the Queens – that's a nice hotel. And there are things for you to see while I'm busy. There's a cathedral, and the dockyard where you can walk along the ramparts – that's nice on a fine day. And there's Nelson's flagship, the *Victory* – she's moored there.'

'It would be interesting to see the very spot where Nelson fell,' Nina said. Like every English child she had learned about Nelson and Trafalgar at school, along with Wellington and Waterloo: the high points in all of history.

Mr Cowling shook his head. 'I'm not sure you can still go on board – she's in very poor condition. The King was talking about it when I saw him last. She's all but rotted away – the Admiralty won't fork out to maintain the poor old girl. They wanted to scrap her last year, but the King wouldn't allow it. He said it was a damned disgrace that she'd been let go so badly, especially with it being a hundred years this year since Trafalgar.'

'Of course – 1805,' Nina said. 'Will there be special celebrations?'

'The King's all for it.'

'With a special holiday for school children?' Nina suggested.

'I think the twenty-first of October is a Saturday this year. But still . . .' He ate some kedgeree. 'The King hopes a big celebration might raise some money for restoration, but she'd still need maintaining year by year, and where's that to come from? So you'd better have a look at her while she's still afloat.'

'But you haven't said why you're going to Portsmouth.'

'Oh, a business opportunity's come up.'

'Another glove factory?'

'A potted-meat company.'

'Potted meat?'

'And fish paste. They sell it in porcelain jars, sealed with butter. You might have seen it on the shelves in grocers' shops. Feltham's.'

'Oh, yes. I've never eaten it, though.'

'Well, it's a good little family business that's failing for lack of investment. The owner, James Feltham, is getting on and wants to retire, and he's two sons, neither of 'em very keen on meat and fish pastes. They'd like to sell the whole thing and share the money, and good luck to 'em. You can't run a business properly if your heart's not in it.'

'So what would you be buying?'

'They've a factory on the Camber in Portsmouth, and a shop in the town. They started up with fish paste and potted shrimps because it's right where the fishing fleet comes in, and then James Feltham's dad married a chicken farmer's daughter from the West Country and they went into potted chicken as well.' He looked to see if she was really interested, and she nodded encouragingly. 'What I'm thinking, you see, is that this is something we could export all over the world, same as we do the jam.'

'Oh, that's what caught your interest,' Nina said. 'I was wondering how fish paste fitted into your schemes.'

'Aye, well, it's a similar problem. We couldn't export the jam in glass jars, and in the same way, they couldn't export the paste in porcelain jars: too heavy, and sealing with butter wouldn't do on a long voyage to hot countries. So they never got the business any further. But if we were to put it into sterilised glass jars, with a sealed metal lid – well, the globe's the limit! It'd increase home sales too. It's nice for a picnic in a sandwich, or on toast for your tea. If we get the costs down, so it's in reach of ordinary working folk, we could have it on every table, in every larder. A household name.'

'Like Harvey's jam.'

'Exactly.' He looked pleased that she had understood. 'And the middling folk, too – they can't afford foie gras and caviar, but in a nice, dainty glass jar with a pretty label, they won't mind having potted chicken or sardine paste on their table instead.'

'You sound as if your mind is made up to buy it,' Nina said.

'Well, I have to look at the books first, see what condition it's in. I wish to God I had Decius with me for this, but I can't spare him from the London office yet.'

'But your new man,' she said.

He had taken on another factotum, a young man called Truman Smith, whom Nina had not met.

'Oh, he's fine as far as he goes. But Decius knows my mind better than I know it myself. Truman hasn't learned everything about me yet.'

'I don't suppose a lifetime would be enough to learn *everything* about you,' she said.

He looked pleased. 'Oh, I'm not so complicated,' he deflected modestly. 'I tell you what, if you come to Portsmouth with me, Truman can squire you around the sights.'

'You'll need him with you, surely?'

'Not all the time. Will you come, then?'

'Of course I will.' The hunting season was virtually over, and she had no important engagements ahead. It was a small enough thing to do to make him happy – and he had been as careful around her lately as if she had been an eggshell and likely to shatter. This might put them on a steadier footing.

Under the table, Trump sighed. 'Do you think I should take Trump, or should I ask Bobby to look after him?' she said.

'You'll be outside a lot,' he said. 'I think you could take him, if you wanted. He'd be company for you when I'm busy.'

'Trump and Truman. I'll be well looked-after,' she said.

Sebastian did not go home at once. He felt too wretched – not only still suffering from the shock of the incident, and the pain of his wound, but the unhappy reflection of how he had behaved at the inquest. He told himself that he had spoken only the truth and that there had been no injustice done: he *had* been defending himself against a murderous attack, and Jack Hubert's death *had* been an accident. Thus far the law of the land had been served. But the inspector had known there was more to it than that, and Sebastian had withheld a deeper truth. If the inspector cared to follow it up and he was found out, Sebastian could be charged with contempt of court.

The deeper truth, he told himself, was Dory's secret, and what she had told him in confidence he had no right to reveal. He'd had no choice but to dissemble. But he felt sullied by the whole experience, by having come here at all, by what he had seen of Shoddy Jack, by the horrible, ridiculous, lethal scuffle, by the unpleasant farce of the inquest. He had 'got off', and he felt the lesser man for it. So he stayed on at the Grand, and licked his wounds, and mourned his lost integrity.

There was no insouciant stranger lurking in the lobby when he went down, and when he ventured outside he did not find himself followed. The inspector, he concluded, had called off his dogs. So Sebastian was able to walk along the promenade and through the town unwatched. The weather was fine and breezy, sunny but cool, the sky high and veined with cloud, the sea restless. Exercise and fresh air gradually restored his equilibrium. The horrible memories retreated a step; the knife wound seemed to be healing cleanly.

He still had a problem to wrestle with: how would he tell Dory? His pulse quickened at the thought that she was now free, that if she wished she could accept his proposal of marriage, and he longed more than anything to see her and talk to her without subterfuge. In his more lyrical moments he imagined a golden future of companionship and conversation, trust and affection – all he had ever wanted. But the fact remained that he had indirectly been the cause of her husband's death, and what would her delicate conscience make of that? He knew her to be a principled woman. The idea that he could lose her over that sickened him. So he walked the streets of Brighton, stared unseeingly into shop windows and at the vista of the shore and the waves, and fretted at the problem, like a horse at a tether.

Archaeologists tended to be energetic people, and when Giles proposed a walk to look at the motte, there were no abstainers in their ranks. Lord Denham thought it would be too far for his lady, and Kitty suggested that Lady Denham might like a gentle stroll around the gardens, while Richard offered his lordship a mount to ride around the farms to look at the cattle and discuss his dairy plans. Thus everyone was suited and Giles was free to go off with his own friends – Max Wolski, John and Mabel Portwine, Talbot and Mary Arthur, and Andrew and Jane Lawrence.

With the dogs ranging about them, they walked up the hill and then along the crest, chatting about what was going on at Knossos in Crete. In 1894 Arthur Evans, the Keeper of the Ashmolean Museum and a keen archaeologist, had bought a quarter of the Knossos site with an option on the rest. The native owners would not sell to an individual, so he had set up the Cretan Exploration Fund, on the same lines as the Palestine Exploration Fund, without telling them that he was the only contributor. But in 1894 Crete had been part of the dying Ottoman Empire, rife with intersectional violence and religious purges, and it had not been possible to start excavating the site.

A stable government had finally been established in 1899, and Evans had then bought the rest of the site through the Fund – which by then had other contributors. In March 1900 he had started his excavations. Every year had brought news of the extraordinary things discovered, evidences of an ancient civilisation, which he had dubbed Minoan, after the Greek myth of Minos. There were so many wall paintings and mosaics of bulls and bull-leapers he concluded the myths were based on fact and the Minoans had worshipped the bull aspect of Poseidon, placating him with displays of bull-leaping.

But now, in 1905, he had announced the excavation finished, and he was having the walls of what he had called the Throne Room – because of a throne-like stone chair it contained – repainted by a father-and-son team of Swiss artists. Giles's friends were divided over the wisdom of the move.

'It's vandalism, plain and simple,' Talbot Arthur said, shaking his head. 'I think the poor fellow's brain must be touched.'

'But he's basing the paintings on archaeological evidence,' said Jane Lawrence.

'Which he himself provided,' said Talbot. 'With no oversight from his peers. And the man's a hopeless romantic. As well get Alma-Tadema to paint the whole thing.'

'Well, I for one love Alma-Tadema's paintings, and I find it very helpful to see what ancient sites may have looked like.'

'*May* have looked like.'

'Always with that caveat,' Jane said. 'You are such a purist, Tal!'

'How can one not be? Archaeology is a science. There's no room for interpretation.'

There was an outcry at that. 'Oh, come!' said Giles. 'When you only have a fragment of something you must interpret, or all you *have* is a fragment. Most of what we think we know about the ancient world is interpretation of one sort or another.'

'That's not our business,' said Talbot. 'As archaeologists we present the fragments for academic inspection. What academics do afterwards is their responsibility.'

'Arthur Evans never got over the death of his wife,' Mabel Portwine said, with a sigh. 'So tragic. He was terribly in love with her.'

Max Wolski raised his eyebrows. 'What on earth has that got to do with it?'

'Everything, I should think,' said Mabel.

'You think his brain was turned by tragedy, do you?' said Talbot. 'Well, I can believe that.'

'Don't be horrid, Tal,' his wife said. 'Arthur's a perfectly respectable archaeologist. We went out there in 1903, you know,' she reminded the company. 'There was nothing wrong with his methods.'

'Well, *I*'ve heard,' said John Portwine, 'that those painters have been given a free hand, and the frescoes are pure imagination.'

'I don't believe Arthur would allow that,' Jane Lawrence said. 'He cares too much about that site.'

'It's his child,' Mabel said. 'He has no other.'

'Who knows what he'll do next?' Talbot said. 'Will it stop at one room full of dubious frescoes? Will he start rebuilding the whole place according to his romantic fantasies?'

'I shouldn't think he'd have the money,' said Giles. 'And won't the Ashmolean expect him back at his desk some time?'

'They haven't yet,' said Talbot.

Max said, 'I'm more interested in the scripts he unearthed.' Evans had found more than three thousand clay tablets inscribed with what were clearly two different languages, one appearing to pre-date the other. 'Have you read his book, *Scripta Minoa*? He thinks the earlier one is the model for the Phoenician alphabet. I should think you'd have something to say about that, Giles, with your interest in ancient Etruscan.'

The conversation rambled on as they walked, and Giles spared a part of his brain to note how comfortable it was to be with his own people again, and to have intellectual conversation. This was where he belonged: his father's death had wrenched him out of his proper orbit.

The party stopped when they came in sight of the motte. It was the only part remaining of the original Ashmore Castle, which had been a simple motte-and-bailey built in 1080 and abandoned in 1202. Over the centuries the stones had been removed to create other buildings, and now there was nothing left of the above-ground works. It was just a green mound.

They walked around it, while Giles told them its history. When they came round the far side, several grazing rabbits were startled and dashed for cover. The dogs hurtled after them joyfully, and Tiger began scrabbling at one hole at the base of the motte, throwing out showers of dry soil and small stones.

Mary Arthur regarded the activity thoughtfully. 'You know, Giles,' she said, 'these old keeps almost always had underground rooms – dungeons and store cellars. Has anyone ever excavated the motte?'

'I shouldn't think so. I believe I'm the first and only archaeologist in the family,' Giles said, amused.

'Well, then – there's your next project,' she said.

Max gave a delighted crow. 'You've hit on it, Mary darling! Poor Giles is always complaining that he's not allowed to go on digs any more—'

'I never did!' Giles objected.

'The phraseology is immaterial. You can't come out to the Valley of the Kings – and you've missed the whole of the Knossos excavations – but here you are with a dig ready and waiting in your own back yard! I can't believe you've never thought of it.'

'But I never have,' Giles laughed.

'Well, think of it now. A proper, well-conducted, scientific excavation, documented all the way. Who knows what you'll find? We'll all come and help you – when we happen to be in England. It won't be often, of course. We'll be in Egypt and Palestine. Poor Giles!'

'You're baiting me,' Giles concluded, and Max grinned wickedly.

'No, too cruel, Maxie,' Mary said. 'Don't mind him, Giles dear. He hasn't got a wife, that's his whole problem. He's jealous of you, because no woman would take him.'

'Don't rub it in,' Max said, with mock ruefulness. 'After you went and married Talbot, what was I to do but bury my broken heart in some ancient ruins?'

'Is there a view from the top, Giles?' Andrew Lawrence asked, tiring of the nonsense. 'Shall we climb up?'

Mr Cowling was spending the day looking through Feltham's books, a task he said he preferred to do alone. But it was clear to Nina that Truman Smith did not want to be squiring her. *Not* a ladies' man, she thought. He was quite good-looking, in a cool, reserved, unsmiling sort of style, that made her think of Jane Eyre's cousin Mr Rivers. She was tempted to test him by saying that she wanted to go around the shops and look at hats; but she really wanted to see HMS *Victory*.

Probably he had been expecting this, because he had his answer ready. 'You can't go on board her any more. Her timbers are too rotten.'

'But I'd still like to see Nelson's ship,' Nina persisted.

He didn't actually sigh, but it was a close thing. 'There are boats that take visitors out to row around the hull. But it's a rough sort of ride for a lady. I'm afraid it might make you sick.'

'The sea looks quite calm to me,' Nina said. It sparkled under a bright April sky, deep blue and flickering with diamonds.

'I think you'll find it's different when you're out on it in a small boat.'

She gave him a pleasant smile. 'Are you refusing to accompany me, Mr Smith? Shall I have to go alone?'

A spot of vexation bloomed in his alabaster cheek, but he said calmly, 'I am instructed to take you wherever you want, ma'am. I merely warn you about the discomforts you risk.'

'Thank you. I am warned. Shall we go?'

Truman Smith called a cab and instructed it to take them

to Gunwharf Quays, where he left her with Trump to enjoy the view while he dickered with a weather-beaten type for a trip on a large four-oared wooden boat. When negotiations were complete, he escorted her to the steps and helped her down into it, and she smiled gaily at the two Guernsey-clad salts, with their caps and clay pipes, to show them she was not in the least afraid. Smith handed Trump to her, climbed down and seated himself beside her, and they pushed off.

As soon as they were clear of the wharf and out into the harbour, the movement of the boat picked up; and as a cloud crossed the sun at that moment, giving the sea a less gay look, Nina began to have misgivings, and wished she was on a much larger vessel, or better still back on dry land. After all, she'd seen pictures of *Victory*, hadn't she? She didn't *need* to go out there. It was on the tip of her tongue to say she'd changed her mind, but she wouldn't give Truman the satisfaction. And, indeed, she didn't feel seasick. It was only that the water was much closer to her than she liked, and the boat seemed more flimsy than it had looked from the wharf.

She sought to distract herself. 'Why do they row backwards?' she asked her companion.

'I believe they get more traction that way,' Truman said indifferently. 'Don't worry, they're quite used to it.'

'I can see that,' Nina said. She had observed how the one further from her, at the pointed end, looked over his shoulder from time to time and gave instructions to his partner: 'Pull starboard, Jed. Pull both.'

Jed shifted his pipe to the corner of his mouth to remark, 'Little feller's enjoying isself, miss.'

For an instant Nina thought he was talking about Truman, then realised he meant Trump, who had his forefeet up on the gunwale and was looking about with keen interest, whiskers bristling and nose twitching rapidly at the new smells. A small, graceful sailing boat went past them in the other direction, and he barked at it joyfully. He wriggled under the wooden plank seat on which she and Truman were sitting to get to the square end of the boat and bark at it some more.

'Why don't we have a sail?' she asked. 'Wouldn't it be quicker, and save these gentlemen some of the hard work?'

'Not with this wind. It's dead foul for the direction we're going,' Truman said tersely.

'You know a lot about boats,' she said, thinking flattery might unbend him a little.

'I grew up in Chichester,' he said – which, as she didn't know Chichester, was no answer at all.

'I've never been in one before,' she said. He gave her a look that said plainly, 'That doesn't surprise me,' and she lapsed into silence.

More clouds had blown up, cutting off the sunshine, and the sea was now a grey-green-brown colour that was much less jolly. The further they went the livelier the water became. She held on to the seat under her with both hands as a naughty wave went under them and nodded her back and forth; but she could tell that none of the three men with her was in the least concerned, so she concentrated on looking around at the harbour buildings and the other shipping. Seeing this, the lead oarsman kindly took to pointing out things to her, or at least to naming things he jerked his head towards, since he couldn't free a hand to point.

A much bigger ship was now coming towards them, one with a smokestack as well as a mast. It looked grim and black and businesslike – no pleasure craft, for sure. The lead oarsman looked over his shoulder and warned Jed, who said, '*Hero*. Used to be tender t'th' gunnery school. Gorn into dockyard reserve now.'

Truman Smith perked up. 'Oh, I've read a bit about her. She was one of the early ironclads. Supposed to be able to ram enemy ships without sustaining any damage, but they never tested the theory. What's she used for these days?'

'She bin in anchor trials, sir. Testin' stockless anchors for the navy.'

'What's a stockless anchor?' Nina asked absently, noticing the waves growing steeper as the ship approached and disturbed the water with its weight and speed. She had to hold on as they bounced violently up and down. She smelt the bitter reek of smoke, saw the dash past of the iron sides, saw men up on the ship's bridge, felt the beat of its engine. She was thrown vertically by one especially wild bounce, breaking her grip on the plank seat. Both oarsmen were looking over their shoulders now, gauging the movement of the waves and their response to it. She looked over her own shoulder to check that Trump was all right.

He wasn't there.

She ducked her head to look under the seats, thinking he'd taken shelter; twisted and peered more frantically, then clutched at Truman's hand and cried, 'My dog! My dog's gone! He must have gone overboard!' Truman repeated her actions. She cried to the oarsman, 'Stop! Oh, stop! We must go back!'

They were doing something to the oars, which meant they were not going forward any more, but holding more or less in one spot. The black steamship with her yellow superstructure and belching chimney churned on indifferently. Jed looked at Truman for instructions.

'Turn around!' Nina cried. 'Turn around! We must go back!'

'Pull starboard, Jed,' said the lead oarsman, and the boat began baulkily to turn.

Nina tried to stand up, the better to scan the water, but the boat rocked wildly and Jed made an inarticulate protest. Truman caught her wrist and pulled her back. 'Steady, you'll go over. Sit down. We're going back.'

Nina woke in the middle of the night to a feeling of heaviness and shock, and after an instant of blessed amnesia she remembered. The same image came to her that she had fallen asleep with, of her little dog struggling madly in the water.

The image came from her imagination only. There had been no sign of him. They had rowed up and down for almost an hour, long after it was clear the oarsmen thought it was pointless. Back on shore, Truman had parted with coins and handed out business cards to every boatman and idler on the wharf to look out for the dog, and to pass the word around, in case he was picked up or managed to swim to shore. Later, Mr Cowling had sent him out again to report the loss at the police station and to the harbour master, promising a reward for the dog's return, or for news.

Everything had been done that could be done. But Nina had heard Truman say to Cowling that the dog was probably overwhelmed by the churn as the steamship passed and would have drowned right away. Was it better to think that he died instantly than that he had struggled on, trying to find her, a tiny white head above the water in the vastness of the great harbour, until exhaustion overcame him? Probably. But dead was dead. Her little dog! Grief was compounded with guilt. She should have looked after him. She should not have taken him on the boat. She was to blame. It was bitter.

She had not cried – she would not allow herself to do so. Truman had not said so, but she believed he was thinking she should never have gone out on the boat in the first place, and certainly not have taken the dog with her. So she would not give him the satisfaction of dissolving like a weak and foolish woman. She held herself rigid, and buried everything deep inside.

Everything you loved was taken away from you. It was better not to love anything or anyone: it only ended in heartbreak.

She heard by the change of his breathing that Mr Cowling had awoken. He had tried to comfort her when they went to bed, tried to put his arms round her, but she had moved away from him to the very edge of the bed, hunched her shoulder against any touch of his. Now she lay rigid, so that he would not know she was awake and try to touch her again. Her grief was hers, not his; he would not understand it; and she would not let him have any part of it.

Cowling lay desolate in the darkness. What could he do to comfort her? He had said Trump probably didn't suffer. He had said he'd buy her another dog. But she had cried passionately that she didn't want another. It tore his heart to see her mute, white face. It was only a dog; but he knew it was more than that to her. It was the only thing she loved. She ought to have had a baby – that would have been the right and natural outlet for her emotions. He longed with every fibre of his being to give her a child, and could not.

In business he was a powerful, respected man, he was shrewd, capable, he created, he built, he achieved. But in his personal life he was helpless. What use all his wealth? He had taken this precious girl from her home, taken her into his keeping, with the unspoken contract that he would take care of her. But he could not make her happy. He could not even keep her from the ordinary pains of life.

The next morning he looked at her across the breakfast table, heavy-eyed, listless, and said, 'Do you want to go home?' She thought about it, but shook her head. 'London, then?' he said. He saw that London appealed more than Market Harborough in her present state, and elaborated. 'Now the Season's started there'll be plenty to do. You could visit your aunt. I expect your friend Kitty will come up at some point.'

'But what about you?' she said. 'Don't you have business to finish here?'

'I need a couple more days. But you could go up today and settle in and I could join you. I need to go up anyway, to see how young Tullamore's doing.'

'I don't have the right clothes with me,' she said doubtfully, but willing to be persuaded.

'Tina can pack everything and meet you in London.' She hadn't brought her maid with her to Portsmouth. 'I'll send a telegram. Moxton can pack for me and go up with her. And I'll send one to Berkeley Square, to open the house up ready for you. Truman can take you up on the train.'

'You needn't send him with me. I can travel on my own.'

'Without even a maid? Certainly not. I can do without him for another day – he can be back here by teatime. Would you like that, then?' He gazed at her yearningly. 'I just want you to be happy.'

She blenched as the word 'happy' brought up again the thought of Trump struggling in the water, and she forced her mind to reject it. She made herself smile for him. A feeble effort, but all she could manage just then. 'I know you do. You're very good to me.'

For once the reassurance didn't work. 'I try,' he said sadly.

CHAPTER TEN

The house party broke up in a flurry of thanks, farewells, promises to meet again, heaped luggage, waiting carriages, horses stamping in the chill late-April breeze under a sky of bowling clouds and fitful, watery sunshine.

Mary Arthur said, laughingly, 'Don't forget to let us know when you're starting your dig.'

And Talbot said, 'We promise to come for that!'

Walking back into the house, Kitty could feel Giles's attention slithering away from her. She said, 'Are you really going to have a dig at the motte?'

'Oh, that's just a joke,' he said absently, heading for the stairs.

She hurried to keep up with him. 'It sounded serious. You discussed it for hours at dinner.'

'It would be fun,' he admitted.

'There might be a lost treasure down there.'

'That only happens in stories. But it would be an excuse to invite my friends again.'

'Do you need an excuse?'

'They're busy people,' he said. He was busy too, but not at things he wanted to be doing.

They had reached the first floor, and he was turning away towards the library. 'Giles!' she said desperately, and he stopped.

'Did you want something?'

She summoned up her courage. She hadn't quite dared to mention it over the winter, with all the family problems that had besieged him, but she felt if she didn't say something now she never would. 'If you're going to have your dig, I want to have mine.'

'What does that mean?'

'My garden. You know I consulted Mr Blomfield last autumn. And he sent Mr Fenchurch to talk about what I wanted.'

'I remember. I thought nothing came of it.'

'They sent the preliminary plans in November, just before we went to Germany.'

'You didn't tell me.'

'I didn't want to bother you at such a busy time. But I do want my garden. I want to leave something behind me at Ashmore.'

He looked amused. 'Are you going somewhere?'

'Don't joke, Giles. I want this. I want my garden!'

He recoiled a little at the vehemence. 'I didn't know it was so important to you.'

She thought, You don't need me any more, now that you have two sons, and you certainly don't want me any more. I must have something of my own, something that will stand to my name. But she just said, 'It is.'

'All right, then,' he said, turning away again.

It sounded like a mere acknowledgement that she had spoken and she clenched her fists in frustration. It was like trying to pin down fog. 'Do you mean I can have it? I can go ahead with it?'

'I can't talk about it now, Kitty,' he said impatiently. 'You can show me the plans some time.' And he was gone.

Show me the plans some time. As if she could ever get his attention for long enough! And if he did look at them he'd say, *I'll have to think about it.* And when she reminded him it would be *Not now, Kitty, I'm busy* . . . But she had to start somewhere. She went straight to the Peacock Room, sat down at her desk, drew out a sheet of letter-paper, and started writing: *Dear Mr Fenchurch, I write with regard to the plans you sent me in November . . .*

It was difficult to find Dory at Ashmore Castle without asking where she was, and Sebastian couldn't – it simply wasn't done. He hovered about the corridors and stairs, hoping. Word would have gone around among the servants that he was back – Crooks would have talked about him, if for no other reason than the long, healing cut across his ribs. He had certainly stared, and had asked whether it required any unguent or dressings, probably wanting to hear the story. But if Sebastian had hoped that curiosity or simple gladness at his return would prompt Dory to seek him out, he was disappointed.

He returned to his piano and chose the C minor étude, the Revolutionary, as best expressing his frustration. His left hand, unused to doing so much work, grumbled, and his wound ached with some of the right-hand reach, but it worked. He did not see her, but he was aware of a shadow passing the door, and knew instinctively that she was standing just out of sight, listening.

He jumped up and got to the door before she could disappear. 'Come in,' he demanded. He reached for her arm and missed as she drew it back. 'Something has happened.' he said. 'I must talk to you.'

His urgency must have communicated itself to her, because she stepped into the room, looking nervous. She had someone's chemise folded over her arm. When he tried to close the door, however, she baulked, and would have retreated.

'Come over by the window, then,' he said impatiently, 'where we can't be seen by anyone passing the door.' As she still hesitated, he snatched the chemise from her and threw it on to a chair, and said, 'It's important.'

She walked over to the window, and stood, hands folded

before her. And now he couldn't think how to begin. In the end she said, 'I can't be long. I'll be missed.'

'*I* miss you,' he said.

And she turned her head away wearily and said, 'If that's all it is—'

'No,' he said. 'It's about your husband.'

Her eyes jerked back to him, and she stared in instant dread. 'Jack?'

'I found him,' he said.

Astonishment – and fear. 'What? Why would you do that? How?'

He took the last question. 'I employed an enquiry agent to look for him. He traced him to Brighton. He'd opened a second-hand clothes shop.'

'Is that where you've been? You saw him?'

'Yes. But, Dory—'

'Oh, God! Why did you do that? He'll follow you back here. He'll find me! I have to get out of here!' She was actually turning away towards the door. He could almost hear her feverish plans, to pack up the little she owned and get out of the house, to run and hide herself again.

He caught her arm to stop her, and she struggled, crying softly, 'Let me go!'

'Listen to me! Dory, be still, listen! You're safe. He can't hurt you any more.'

'You don't know, you don't know him – he'll never let me go!'

He gave the arm a little shake to get her attention. 'He's dead. That's what I had to tell you. He's dead.' She stared, uncomprehending. 'Jack Hubert is dead. He can't hurt you ever again. You're free.'

She was not sure yet. 'He's dead? How do you know? Is that what they told you? But he's cunning, he'll play dead, change his name, move somewhere else. You can't know for sure.'

'I do know.' Sebastian took a breath. 'I saw him die.'

She looked aghast. '*What do you say?*' Her voice was breathless.

'It was a wretched street, a mean little shop. He was drunk in the middle of the morning. He didn't know who I was. He attacked me, tried to kill me.'

'Mr Crooks said . . . A knife wound?'

'He tried to stab me with a knife. I defended myself, hit him with my cane. He fell over, and hit his head.' Her eyes widened. 'On a lamppost.'

'Oh, no, no, no!'

'He didn't get up.' He thought she might still be in doubt, and went on, 'The police came. There was an inquest. Dory, he's dead.'

'You killed him,' she said, in a terrible whisper.

'No! It was an accident. He was drunk. He stumbled and fell.'

He didn't think she heard him. Terror made her incapable of hearing.

'Oh, God, what have you done?' she moaned. 'Why couldn't you leave well alone? Now I'll have to go away again.'

'Didn't I tell you you're safe now? We can be together. It's all right – everything's all right. We can be married.'

But her eyes were wide, and she backed away from him. 'Marry? How can you think it? What sort of a woman do you think I am? No, don't touch me! I have to go. Oh, God, what did you do? What did you do?'

He called after her, not caring if anyone heard. 'It was an accident! I was defending myself! I didn't kill him. *It was an accident!*'

But she didn't stop.

Rose looked down the table at servants' dinner and said, 'Where's Dory?'

Mrs Webster said, 'It isn't her afternoon off. Has anyone seen her?'

Mildred spoke up. 'She's gorn.'

'Gone? What do you mean?'

'Went out a bit since. Kathleen in the kitchen told me. She had a bag with her.'

'Has she spoken to any of you?' Mrs Webster asked, looking down the line of faces. There were bemused expressions and shaken heads.

Then Eddie, the youngest house boy, said, 'She was a-talking to Mr Sebastian in the Small Drorin'-room.'

'When?' Mrs Webster demanded.

'Before.'

Afton looked up from his broth and said warningly, 'Don't make things up.'

'I ain't, sir. I went past the door and I heard of 'em talkin' in there. I was c'lectin' used candles from the bedrooms, like William tole me, and when I went past I heard of 'em, and I peeped in and she was a-talking to Mr Sebastian over by the winder.'

'What were they saying?' Daisy asked, inevitably.

'None of your business,' Rose snapped.

'I never heered anyway,' Eddie said. 'Only she looked upset.'

'There'll be no more discussion of this subject,' Afton decreed firmly. But his eyes met Mrs Webster's with a question and a doubt. To go out – with a bag – before dinner – on what was not her day off – smacked of trouble.

After dinner, Mrs Webster told Rose to go and check in Dory's room. She climbed to the top of the house, and reported back quietly to the housekeeper that the room was empty of Dory's few things. It looked as though she had left for good – without a word, without notice, without a reference.

Mrs Webster's lips tightened in vexation. It was not only the inconvenience of losing Dory's services, but the example it set to the other maids. People did not just quit their work on the instant, without due process.

'She was owed wages,' she said to Rose.

'P'r'aps she'll come back for them,' Rose said. She thought of the time she had found Dory in the small drawing-room listening to Mr Sebastian playing the piano. 'I wonder—' she began.

'Don't,' said Mrs Webster sharply, divining her thought. Their eyes met. 'Nothing good can come of that.'

Crooks, the old gossip, told Sebastian when he went up to dress him for dinner. Sebastian managed to control his features until Crooks bumbled out of the room. Then he sat down abruptly and put his face into his hands.

Truman Smith had no conversation, so Nina had time on the journey to think. Was going alone to London the right choice? Perhaps it would have been better to wait until Mr Cowling was ready to go up. At least she would have had his company in the evening. Instead, there would be an empty house in Berkeley Square and emptiness behind her where no dog pattered. She had remembered now that her aunt would not be at home: she had gone to an Easter retreat in Oxford to discuss Byzantine religious art.

But the die was cast. Truman saw her to the door of the house. She invited him in for refreshment but he declined coolly, saying he must go straight back. She felt snubbed, and miserably alone.

Mrs Banks, the housekeeper, was hovering in the hall. 'Has my maid come?' Nina asked.

'Yes, madam. She's in your room, unpacking.'

'Very well. I'll go up.'

Mrs Banks stayed her. 'Oh, madam, you have a visitor. Mr Blake is here. I showed him into the drawing-room.' She looked uncertain. 'He insisted on waiting, madam. I hope I did right.'

'Quite right,' Nina said, and ran up the stairs with a lifting heart.

He came out on to the landing to meet her. 'Nice surprise?'

'Oh, Decius!'

'I made your poor housekeeper admit me. She kept saying she didn't know when you'd arrive, but I knew which train you were on.'

'How?'

'A telegram this morning. I'm ordered to place myself at your disposal.' His expression changed. 'I'm so sorry about Trump. Poor little chap. Do you want to tell me about it?' She shook her head. He drew her hand through his arm and turned towards the drawing-room. 'Then we'll talk about other things. Tea will be up at any moment. I took the liberty of ordering it to be brought as soon as you arrived. It's early, but I thought you'd want it.'

'Poor Mrs Banks,' Nina said.

'She knows I'm Mr Cowling's proxy. I don't think it fractured her loyalty too badly.'

'Well, I'm very glad to see you,' Nina said. 'I'd got to the point of dreading being here alone.'

'Truman wouldn't even come in for tea?' He shook his head in wonder. 'He's a cold fish. Good at his job, so Mr Cowling tells me, but no time for the human dimension. With that classical Greek profile and the icy blue eyes, he puts me in mind of—'

'St John Rivers?' Nina finished for him.

'I was just going to say that!'

There was a fire lit in the drawing-room, but it hadn't been going for long, and the room smelt cold, unused.

'Aren't I taking you away from your work?' Nina asked. 'How is Mr Tullamore doing?'

'Astonishingly well. No, that sounds as though it's a surprise that he is. He's a very intelligent young man and, even better, he has a firm grasp of business.' He shook his head in wonder.

'What can his father have been thinking, to let him go? He'll be a severe loss to his enterprises.'

'But Mr Cowling's gain, so that's all to the good. Ah, tea.' Mrs Banks arrived with the tray, helped by Moxton, Mr Cowling's valet, who doubled as butler in Market Harborough and seemed now to be adding footman to his repertoire. 'Oh, and toasted teacakes too! I'm starving.'

'Didn't you have luncheon on the train?' Decius asked.

'Don't look indignant. Truman offered but I didn't want it then.'

Mrs Banks was hovering again. 'Did you want to give orders for dinner, madam?'

Before Nina could answer, Decius said, 'I already have plans for you. I'm dining at the Morrises', and naturally they want you too. Will you come?'

'I can't think of anything nicer,' Nina said. 'Thank you, Mrs Banks, I won't be dining at home.'

There was a low place in the day, between tea and dressing for the evening, when Decius had gone away and she was alone again. She mourned for her poor dog, and more generally for her confusion about her life. What was she to do? What was she *for*? She longed for the warmth and comfort of another person, for which Trump had been a substitute. When she'd set eyes on Decius that afternoon she had wanted to fling herself into his arms for sheer relief at his presence. She thought again, flinchingly, of her husband's suggestion. The idea of having a child was powerfully attractive. But – a lover? No, no, too dangerous, too difficult, too fraught with possible anguish on all sides. And yet . . . Her body ached as did her mind, both unfulfilled.

If there was to be no child, what then? What would she do with the long, long years to come? Something else that she did not want to think about directly was the possibility that she might one day find herself waiting for Mr Cowling to die, so that she could marry someone else. And she didn't, oh, she really didn't, want to be that person.

In the cab on the way to Kensington, Nina asked how come Decius had been invited to dinner that evening. 'I didn't realise you knew them particularly well,' she said.

Henry Mawes Morris, called Mawes by everyone, was an artist, illustrator and well-known cartoonist for *Harlequin*, the satirical magazine, also playwright and talented musician, had been a first-class cricketer in his youth, and was also a yachtsman. His many talents meant that he had acquaintances in almost every field. Nina had met him through her aunt, for he and his wife mixed in the same circle of intellectuals. She had discovered before their marriage that Mr Cowling also knew Mawes through the King, who adored his cartoons and often had him to dine.

'Mr Cowling asked me to take some papers round to Mr Morris, about an investment he had recommended,' said Decius. 'When he discovered I was living in lodgings, he invited me to dinner, and since then the whole family have had me on their conscience. I'm not allowed to be lonely or hungry or bored.' He grinned. 'I think they'd have the spare bedroom made up for me in an instant if I let them.'

'They are very generous,' Nina agreed. 'Lepida is my special friend.'

'I know. They all talk about you. What a remarkable young woman she is,' he added. 'I suppose with a polymath for a father she was bound to have an interesting mind.'

The Morrises lived in Stafford Terrace, in one of those tall houses, white stucco to the first floor and yellow brick above, that Nina thought of as 'very Kensington-y'. All three came into the hall to greet her, and she was enveloped in the motherly arms of Isabel, embraced by Lepida, and finally given a hearty handshake by Mawes, who said, 'You are looking more beautiful than ever, my dear. You must let me make another portrait of you.' A thoughtful expression crossed his face. 'D'you know, I think you would work quite nicely as my model for Emma Hamilton. I tried Lepida, but she's too thin in the face.'

Nina laughed, accustomed to his habit of using those around him as models for his cartoons – she had appeared in several of them in the past. 'I'm not sure I'm voluptuous enough. What's the occasion?'

'Oh, we're all Trafalgar-mad this year,' he said. 'Specifically, there's the Naval, Shipping and Fisheries Exhibition at Earl's Court. It's opening next week so I want to be ready. There's going to be a "scenic interpretation", whatever that may be, of the battle and Nelson's death. The King's going to open it, and I had an idea—'

'Not now, Mawes,' Isabel interrupted him before he could get into full flow. 'Let the poor child take her coat off at least! There, now. Decius, lead the way – we'll have sherry in the drawing-room first.'

Decius seemed very much at home. He had been welcomed like one of the family; and while Nina had been engaged with Mawes he and Lepida had been talking aside in low voices, like old friends. Over the sherry, she learned from Isabel that Decius and Lepida had been to several lectures together, and from Mawes that he had escorted the whole family to see *The Scarlet Pimpernel* at the New Theatre, and recently to a performance of the musical comedy *The Talk of the Town* at the Lyric. His feet, she thought in Mr Cowling's phrase, were well under the table.

Conversation over dinner ranged from the new Sherlock Holmes collection that had just come out – Holmes's explanation of how he had survived the Reichenbach Falls came in for some forensic dissection – to the plaster cast of the diplodocus skeleton, which was to be unveiled in May at the Natural History Museum.

'The King saw a sketch of the bones in Andrew Carnegie's

house in Scotland years ago,' Mawes said. 'He couldn't get the actual bones for the nation – they're in a museum in Pittsburgh – but he persuaded Carnegie to take a cast of the whole skeleton, and Carnegie's donated it to the British Museum. It will be just as good as the original to all intents and purposes. Who will know the difference? Eighty-five feet long, can you believe it?'

'How could anything so big ever walk the earth?' Isabel marvelled. 'You'd think it would collapse under its own weight.'

'Elephants don't,' Lepida pointed out.

'Elephants aren't eighty-five feet long.'

'When does it go on show?' Nina asked.

'The twelfth of May,' said Mawes. His face brightened. 'We should make up a party to go and see it. Nina, you and Mr Cowling would join us? I'm sure he'd be interested in it.'

The talk kept Nina's mind occupied, and eased the ache of her heart. In the drawing-room after dinner, Mawes insisted on taking some quick sketches of her, and though Isabel told her to 'refuse, he's being unreasonable', she didn't mind, especially as Isabel went to the piano and played to entertain her 'through your ordeal'. She was happy listening, and watching Lepida and Decius, side by side on another sofa, talking together. It seemed to be an earnest conversation – they didn't laugh or smile, and Nina guessed it was something intellectual. They were completely absorbed by it, as if they were alone in the room. She knew how clever Decius was, and thought Lepida would be a good match for his mind, but she didn't see any signs of romantic attachment. They might have been brother and sister.

Later, Decius was persuaded to join Mawes at the piano and sing some comic songs, and Nina took the opportunity to sit by Lepida. She was listening, her eyes fixed on the performers. Nina said, 'He has a nice voice, hasn't he?'

'Decius?' Lepida said, without taking her eyes from him. 'Very nice. But he does everything well.'

'Everything? I've never seen him dance.' Nina said provocatively.

'You can see from the way he moves that he would dance well,' Lepida said, unprovoked. 'In my experience, musicians usually make good dancers. They have the necessary sense of rhythm.' She looked at Nina at last. 'You look drawn. I'm sorry about Trump, but don't let yourself dwell on it. There must be proportion in all things.'

Nina shook her head, unable for the moment to answer.

Lepida went on, 'All things die. It is the natural end of life. We must cherish life while it lasts, and yield it, when the end comes, gracefully. There is no other rational course.'

'Love isn't generally known for being rational,' Nina said.

Lepida laid a cold hand over hers. 'That is why those of us gifted with a good intellect must make the effort,' she said.

'It's so good to see you again,' Nina said impulsively. 'I don't see you nearly as often as I'd like.'

'It is the lot of women to move in their husband's circle,' Lepida said.

'Well, we must make time for each other. And you must come and stay with me in Market Harborough when I go back. I'm sure the countryside would do you good.' She hesitated. She thought her friend had lost weight. 'You *are* all right, aren't you?' she asked on impulse.

'Don't I look all right?' Lepida said, smiling.

'Lepida!' Decius called from the piano at that moment. 'Come and sing "Very Suspicious" with me. It needs your voice.'

She got up obligingly and went.

Kitty had forgotten how nice Mr Fenchurch was, with his face that seemed always to be wanting to smile, and his gentle manners. And it was lovely to have the entire attention of someone, especially of a man. All the other men in her life were constantly busy, disappearing with a vague excuse as soon as she wanted to say something. They existed as a flicker at the corner of her vision, like a mouse when you enter a dark room with a candle. Her children loved her, of course, and were flatteringly excited to see her, but sometimes it was adult attention that one wanted.

So in the pleasant warmth of a May morning, with all the promise of the year burgeoning around them, they walked about with the initial plan open between them and talked about what was to be done. By the end of an hour his careful formality was softening and he seemed so much more relaxed that she found herself talking to him as a friend.

'You do understand,' he said, when they paused by the low wall of the rose garden, 'that it will make a very great mess? It will look like a battlefield for a very long time – nothing but mud and ruts and heaps of earth and stones – really very depressing.'

'Are you trying to dissuade me?' she said.

'Not a bit! But I want to prepare you for the process. I know you see the end result in your mind, but getting there requires endurance. Most of our clients,' he added, 'go and live somewhere else while we're working, and don't come back until it's done.'

'But we live here all the time,' Kitty said, 'except when we're in London.'

'You don't have another property that you can decamp to?'

'No. And even if we did, I don't think my husband would agree to it. Ashmore is everything to him.'

'Perhaps I ought to have a word with him,' Fenchurch said doubtfully. 'Make sure he understands how much disruption there will be.'

'Oh, he isn't the least interested in gardens,' Kitty said. 'He won't mind what you do.'

Fenchurch did not look convinced. 'Well, I shall make out a preliminary estimate and send it to you to show to him,' he said.

'Is that necessary? I do want to get on with it.'

He looked embarrassed. 'As the works are so extensive, I believe it is. But we can begin very quickly once he agrees. I should like to take advantage of the good weather for the earthworks. Will I be liaising with your head gardener? There should be someone to act as a go-between, to convey your wishes and receive progress reports.'

'I shall place my under gardener, Allsuch, at your disposal,' Kitty said, 'but you will report directly to me. I want to be involved in everything.'

He smiled. 'That will be my pleasure. As soon as your husband agrees the initial estimate, I'll make out a schedule of works and we can begin.'

On a fine May day a char-à-banc drawn by two strong horses pulled up outside the Blackwood School in Old Burlington Street and twelve girls in sensible serge skirts, neat blouses and straw hats climbed aboard, followed by three teachers. Servants loaded rugs and a picnic basket into the luggage space. Each girl carried a bag containing a sketching-pad, pencils and charcoals, and whatever else they deemed essential to a sketching party on Hampstead Heath. The twelve healthy young faces were wreathed in smiles, and they made a happy noise like a treeful of starlings as the driver cracked his whip and the vehicle jerked into motion.

Each row in the char-à-banc took three people, and Alice was seated with Bron and another girl she had become friendly with, a petite, cheerful redhead, Julia Stevens. As the char-à-banc made the awkward turn out onto Piccadilly a little shriek went up as all the girls were thrown against one another, and Julia cried, 'Emily Bronte Strachan, stop taking up all the room! And keep your elbows in! You tall girls ought to learn to squeeze yourselves up.'

'Am I squashing you, shrimp?' Bron replied. 'You're so small I simply didn't see you there.'

The three teachers, Miss Palgrave, Mr Wentworth and Miss Jukes – who specialised in landscapes – tried from time to time to quiet the excited chatter of the girls, invoking the honour of Blackwood School: 'Remember wherever you are, you are the school's ambassadors!' Or, rather, the two female teachers did. Once, when Alice looked back, she saw Mr Wentworth staring out at the street and smiling enigmatically, as though he was alone in a private carriage and enjoying the scenery. *He's a famous artist,* she reminded herself, *and far above us. I wonder he bothers with us at all.*

Once they reached a quiet spot on Hampstead Heath, the girls settled in groups to work, and the teachers moved around, helping and criticising. It was pleasant sitting on the rugs with their pads on their knees, sketching the panoramic views. It was warm, with a slight breeze, which created interesting clouds in the sky. Early bees murmured in the clover, and the soft sound of the girls' voices added to the background music. People passing by smiled indulgently at them; dogs on their walks broke away to investigate these strangers at their own level. One old gentleman actually came up to Bron, looked over her shoulder at her drawing, and tried to instruct her on how better to portray the perspective, until Miss Palgrave spotted him and hurried over to drive him, ever so politely, away.

Alice liked figures better than landscapes, and did some rapid sketches: people passing, a couple sitting on a bench not far off, a military-looking man scanning the horizon with a telescope. Then, turning a page, she saw that Mr Wentworth had sat down at a little distance to take his ease and smoke a cigarette, and she started surreptitiously drawing him. He was three-quarter-profile to her, her favourite aspect of a man's face. She finished a first quick sketch in charcoal and, as he had not moved, began another more carefully in pencil. Soon she was completely absorbed. Inevitably her mind went back to Castle Cottage, and Axe Brandom, whom she had drawn so often and so lovingly. She missed him sharply; but the action of drawing was soothing, and she felt oddly, perilously happy as she worked on Wentworth's profile and the way his hair grew – he had taken off his hat and the breeze was ruffling it interestingly.

She was working on the folds of his jacket when she realised that his profile had changed, and that he was looking at her. Her eyes met his for an instant, and she blushed and looked quickly away, pretending to be studying something else. When she dared to glance back, he had stood up, and for a moment she was afraid he was coming to see what she was up to, but it turned out to be time for the picnic luncheon, and everyone was putting their pads aside, standing up and stretching, while Miss Jukes was calling for volunteers to unpack the hampers.

Having been sitting for so long, the girls were happy to stand and walk about while eating the sandwiches and pasties the school kitchen had provided. Bron had made friends with a young golden retriever belonging to a strolling couple and was throwing a stick for it. Julia had asked Miss Palgrave about a small plant she had found growing in the grass, and Miss Palgrave told her it was self-heal, and was describing how it had been used in the past to stop bleeding, heal wounds and cure scrofula.

In another group Alice was discussing the exciting possibility that one of the senior girls might have something accepted for the Summer Exhibition at the Royal Academy. Then someone else said that Mr Wentworth was working on a painting of Cleopatra and Caesar, and if he finished it in time it would almost certainly be selected.

At the mention of his name, Alice instinctively looked round for him, and saw to her horror that he was standing by the rug where she had been sitting and was looking through her sketching-pad. She abandoned the group and hurried over, wondering if she dared snatch her book away.

But as she reached him she saw it was too late. He had folded it open at his own portrait. He looked up at her with a glinting smile.

'So, Miss Tallant, we bring you all the way out here to show you these wonderful views so that you may practise your landscape drawing, and you scorn the very idea!' She blushed, and tried to think what to say. He went on, subjecting her to a thorough examination, which did nothing to restore her equilibrium. 'Miss Tallant, I think, has an independent spirit.'

'I – I prefer figures to landscapes, sir,' she muttered awkwardly, wondering if she was in trouble. She couldn't tell from his voice, not knowing him well enough. He sounded mocking rather than angry, but of course that could change in an instant.

'So I see.' He looked at the drawing again. 'And I see from the style of the jacket and the hair that this is meant to be me.'

'I'm sorry, sir,' she mumbled.

'Don't be,' he said. 'It is quite good. You have a talent for figures. It is not very like, though.' He looked up at her quizzically. 'You have the folds of the jacket quite well – fabric is a whole skill of its own and we can work on that – and the hair is mine, but the face? No, not very like.'

Alice felt her blush increasing as she realised she had drifted without realising it into drawing the profile she knew best. She stared at the page, willing it to burst into flames, rather than meet Wentworth's eyes.

'And I do not think I have a neck like this,' he went on. 'Or such broad shoulders. No, it is not like me – but I think it is like someone?'

She felt him looking at her insistently, and suddenly rebelled. 'It's a fancy head,' she said defiantly. 'Just my imagination.'

'Hmm,' he said, keeping her gaze, and she made herself

meet it steadily, hands clasped behind her back, chin jutting just a little. What had she done, after all, that was so terrible?

Then he smiled, a dazzling smile that seemed to be minted just for her. 'No need to look like a startled fawn, Miss Tallant. If you drew this face from imagination – or was it memory?' He paused, but she was not tempted to answer. 'Either way, you have a promise that should be nurtured.' He put her sketching-pad into her unresisting hands and strolled away.

Bron and Julia, who had been drifting closer, wondering what was happening, hurried to her side. Alice explained.

Julia clapped a hand to her mouth. 'You *drew* him? I wouldn't have dared! He's *the* Ivor Wentworth!'

'Was he very angry?' Bron asked.

'No,' Alice said. 'I think he was laughing at me, really.'

'Show me the drawing,' Bron demanded.

Alice handed it over reluctantly, and the two bent their heads together over it. 'It doesn't look very like him,' Julia said after a moment.

'That's what he said,' said Alice.

'You haven't got the proportions right,' Bron said. 'But as a picture, it's very nice.' She looked up. 'You should think of specialising in portraits. A person can make a good living – rich people always want to have themselves done in oils and hung over the fireplace.'

'It sounds like a mediaeval torture,' Alice said, and the conversation ended in laughter.

Kitty had never needed to know anything about money. Before she married, everything had been bought for her; now she charged all purchases to account. And she had always known she was the heiress of a large estate, so that anything she had wanted, within reason, had been within her reach. So when Fenchurch's estimate arrived, she had no idea whether it was a shocking, impossible sum, or something reasonably affordable to the man who now owned her inheritance.

She was intending to pick the right moment to approach Giles, but seeing it all written down, suddenly so much closer to being real, she couldn't wait, and hurried along to the library where she knew he was alone.

He looked up when she came in, and his expression was not welcoming. 'What is it?' he asked.

'I've something to show you,' she said eagerly.

'I hope it's important. I'm rather busy.'

She was too happy to be put off. 'Oh, it's very important! It's the estimate from Mr Fenchurch! For my garden,' she added, seeing that the name didn't have the same glorious ring to him. 'Look!'

She laid it down on the desk in front of him, and with a sigh, he picked it up and began reading.

'He wants to start as soon as possible,' she said. 'And, oh, Giles, I can't wait! To see it all coming real at last – like magic! I wonder how long—'

He held up a hand to silence her while he read. She watched his frown of concentration harden into something grimmer as he turned the pages; when he reached the last page and the total, his eyebrows shot up. Even she could not convince herself it was in surprise at how small it was. She clasped her hands in front of her. 'Giles?'

He looked up at her. He put the pages down. 'No,' he said.

'No?' she faltered.

'Absolutely not! How could you even think for a moment—'

'No?' she said again, but in a harder voice. A flat denial? Was that all she was worth?

'It's an outrageous amount of money! I had no idea you were thinking of anything on this sort of scale.'

'You would have had an idea, if you'd ever bothered to talk to me about it,' she said.

'All these earthworks . . .' He was turning pages again. 'Moving half a mountain!'

'A hill,' she corrected.

'You want to take half the hill from the back of the house and move it to the front. Change the course of rivers. Plant what sounds like an entire forest of trees and shrubs. Engineering works, stone works, waterworks. And you expect me to pay for all this – this –' he sought words extreme enough for his outrage '– rampant folly?'

She flinched at them, but fought on. 'You know we haven't enough flat ground for a pleasure garden. It was almost the first thing you ever told me about the place, the first time I ever came here. You said there'd never been a proper garden because there was no flat ground.'

'And there are good reasons no-one has ever tried this before,' he said, flicking the pages with a dismissive finger. 'You could rebuild the Pyramids for less! No, Kitty, it's out of the question.'

She suddenly felt very cold and very still. 'Just like that? You dismiss it just like that?'

He was angry. 'You should never have let it get this far without consulting me.'

'You said that the jam business was doing very well. You said it was making lots of money.' Her voice came out higher than she'd meant it to.

'And I need every penny for the estate. You have no idea how much it costs just to keep this place going, let alone improve it. What do you think I work and worry about night and day? I can't throw money away on frivolities!'

Another word that hurt. 'But it's my money!' she cried.

That made him even angrier. He hated to be reminded that her inheritance had saved Ashmore's bacon. 'In point of law, my dear, it's my money now.'

Bringing the law into a private argument was unfair. And the 'my dear' was like a slap. She stared at him, quivering with emotion. 'Am I to have *nothing*, then?' she cried passionately.

He rose to his feet. 'Nothing? I have given you a home, a family, a title. A position in society. You call that nothing? And when have I ever questioned anything you buy for yourself? Let me tell you, some husbands in my position give their wives an allowance and check their receipts every month!'

'Oh, I am lucky indeed!' she said.

'Sarcasm is the resort of someone who knows they are in the wrong.'

'Yes, a female is always in the wrong! I think we were born wrong.'

'Don't talk such nonsense. You knew perfectly well that this garden scheme was out of the question. I don't know why you went on with it, unless it was to vex me.'

'Vex you?'

'When you know how much I have on my mind already – keeping a roof over your head, and your children's.'

'Oh, now they are *my* children, are they?'

'For Heaven's sake! I haven't time for this, Kitty,' he said tersely. 'Take your plans.' He folded the pages together and held them out to her. 'I'm sorry.'

She took them. 'Are you?' she said. 'Well, I am, too. Very sorry.' She turned to leave him.

'What do you mean by that?'

'I'm sorry I've taken up so much of your valuable time,' she said, without looking back. She went out, and closed the door quietly behind her.

Giles stared down at his cluttered desk for a moment, and then thumped it with a fist and said, 'Damn!'

CHAPTER ELEVEN

'This is very nice,' Michael Woodrow said.

The Three Corners Café in the village had a tiny garden, just big enough to take three small round tables, and for the first time that year it was warm enough to sit outside. Usually it was only the summer visitors who took tea in the garden: Rose felt self-conscious. She said, a little stiffly, 'I suppose it is.'

There were bright tulips in the beds, and the lilac bush was in flower, filling the air with the scent of childhood. The table had a nice white cloth – her housemaid's eye noted the tiny, neat darn at one corner – and the china was pretty. Michael Woodrow, sitting across the table from her, scrubbed to a shine and wearing a suit, was the most decorative of all. He was a nice-looking man, and he had gone to all this trouble for *her*. For plain, awkward Rose Hawkins. It made her a little tongue-tied.

'You're not cold?' he tried. 'We could have sat inside.'

'No, it's a nice change,' she said. 'I'm indoors all the time.'

'I suppose you have to be for your work. But I've always thought of you as an out-of-doors sort of person. You're such a good walker.'

'Am I?' She was surprised.

'Whenever I see you going past, you're always striding out.'

'I can't be doing with idling along, wasting time,' she said, unsure if it was a compliment. 'I want to get where I'm going.'

'But there's a place for idling, too – when you're just taking the air and enjoying the view.'

'I wouldn't know about that,' she said.

Mrs Henson came out from the kitchen with the teapot and the cake stand, placed them on the table and gave Rose a conspiratorial smirk that quite unsettled her. Rose took up the pot automatically and began to pour. Woodrow examined the cake stand. 'I don't suppose those scones are as good as Martha's,' he said, 'but they look nice enough. May I help you to one?'

She nodded, and passed him his tea. He resumed the conversation. 'Have you never been on a nature walk? We had them sometimes at school.'

'Not my school. What's a nature walk?'

'A teacher took us out into the fields or the woods to see what flowers and insects and birds we could find.'

'What's the point of that?' Rose asked, buttering her scone.

'Learning the names of things, their habits, how they grow. Sometimes we collected flowers and ferns, or birds' eggs, or we might find a caterpillar, or catch minnows. It's called nature study.'

'Nature?' She wrinkled her nose.

'It's all around us, and we're part of it,' he pointed out. 'Life is richer if you look with eyes that see.'

She was struck by the expression, and thought about it. 'My mother told us the names of things, when I was little,' she said. 'You know what's a sparrow and what's a robin redbreast, and what's a chestnut and what's an oak. How would you get on if you didn't?'

'But there's pleasure to be had, too. Just walking along, breathing in the scents, watching the birds and butterflies going about their work. Even better if you have an agreeable companion,' he added.

She met his eyes for a moment, then looked away. 'My brothers kept some tadpoles in a jam jar once,' she said. She hadn't thought about that for years. 'Most of 'em died, but a few of 'em turned into frogs. It was – interesting,' she admitted.

'I had a chrysalis, and watched it hatch to a butterfly. And we used to play with conkers, of course.'

'My brothers did. But Ma used them to keep moths out of the blankets.'

'I didn't know conkers did that.'

She was pleased to know something he didn't. 'And she made acorn flour, for baking. There's a lot of good eating in a wood.'

'Blackberries,' he said.

'Rosehips. And sloes.'

'And mushrooms.'

'You've got to know what you're doing with mushrooms,' she said. 'A kid along the row from us died from eating a toadstool by mistake. But we used to find poor man's beefsteak for my dad. That grows on oak trees.'

'Have you ever eaten young lime leaves? We used to call them bread-and-butter – I don't know why.'

They chatted on, about foraging, their childhoods, country lore: the conversation spread and flowed naturally like water finding new courses. Rose didn't notice that she was completely relaxed or that she was enjoying herself: she only realised it afterwards, when going home up the hill and contemplating the oddness of having accepted an invitation for a walk with Woodrow the following week.

'A nature walk,' she said to herself, with a snort of amusement.

When Grandmère summoned him, Richard went at once. The tiny, elegant *grande dame* was as gracious as always, and though he sensed an unusual tension about her, she made him sit and take tea and make light conversation first. It was the civilised way.

'And you, *mon petit*,' she said, when he had answered her queries about the rest of the family, 'how are the affairs of your heart progressing? When are you going to bring a prospective bride for me to interview?'

He laughed at her idea of how his courtship should be managed. 'Be sure when there is such a person you will meet her first.'

'At your age, you should be married. It will settle and improve you.'

'Like fine port? Dear Granny, how can I possibly marry?' he said, an edge of his frustration showing under the lightness of his tone. 'I have no income.'

She waved a hand at him. 'One sees that you eat and drink. You smoke – too much – you wear clothes. *Comment ça ce peut?*'

'I charge my necessities to the estate,' he said. 'But I have no money. Oh, I can draw a little cash for day-to-day things, but that's all.'

'But that is not *comme il faut*,' Grandmère said. 'You are a grown man. I shall speak to Giles.'

'Please don't. It would embarrass me.'

'*Pfui!*' She made a very French sound of dismissal. 'You cannot afford to be so nice. *Le travailleur est digne de son salaire.*' Her eyes narrowed. 'I suppose you *do* work hard?'

He changed the subject. 'What was it you summoned me here to say? I know it must be important.'

He saw her expression harden. 'It is Sir Thomas. Something very grave.'

'Is he unwell?'

'Oh, it is far worse than that. It is that girl, that girl! Oh, why did you bring her into our lives?'

'You mean Chloë Sands? I thought you said she was a brilliant artist?'

'What has that to do with it?' Grandmère cried in frustration. 'She will ruin Tommy. *C'est une catastrophe!*'

'But what has she done?' Richard asked in alarm. He had never seen her so upset.

Grandmère lifted her hands as if warding off an attack. 'He means to marry her!' she cried.

'*What?* But he's married already!'

'*Exactement!* This foolish, foolish man means to obtain – *un divorce.*'

She could obviously hardly bear to say the word. It sounded worse, somehow, in French.

'I can't believe it,' Richard said slowly.

'Believe! He means to divorce poor Violet and marry that child, and it will be the scandal of the year, of the decade. He will never be forgiven!'

'You mean *you* will never forgive him,' Richard suggested.

'That is entirely beside the point. He and I – we are what we are. *On n'y peut rien.* But his music is everything to him. His career. *Son éclat.* If he marries that girl he will lose everything.'

'I had no idea about this,' Richard said.

'*Had* you not?'

'Of course not, or I would have said something. Like you, I was worried that he might make her his mistress.'

'Oh, if it were only that!' Grandmère cried. 'No-one would care or even wonder.'

'*I* would care,' Richard said. 'But she told me, and I believed her, that she would never do that. And she said that she had the measure of him.'

'She is clever, I give you!' Grandmère said bitterly. 'To say no and no until in desperation he offers her marriage.' She shook her head. 'I never cared for Violet – I have no patience with those who use ill health to control others – but she and I, we knew our places. This girl – this terrible girl – seizes all for herself and cares for no-one else. She will ruin him.'

Richard sat forward urgently. 'I don't believe it's her idea at all. And I don't see how Sir Thomas can obtain a divorce anyway. Lady Burton will simply refuse, and that will be the end of it.'

'He will persuade her,' Grandmère said. 'He will talk and talk and exhaust her and she will agree for the sake of peace. And then there will be newspapers and scandal and shame.' She stiffened into an even more upright posture. 'You must stop it!' she declared.

'*Me?*' He looked appalled. 'What can I do?'

'Talk to the girl. It was you who brought her among us, I blame you for this. It must be stopped. He came to see me only yesterday, and said he was going to talk to Violet at the weekend, so there is just time for you to act. Make her tell him it will not be. You say she has influence over him. She must end it. *Il est hors de ses sens.*'

Richard looked grim. 'I will talk to her, for you. But I offer no hope. I have no sway with her.'

Grandmère rose from her chair, and he rose too perforce. 'Go now. Do not come to me and say that you have failed.' He bent towards her to kiss her cheek in farewell but she pulled back. 'No, I do not permit a salute from you until you bring me good news. Go!'

Molly Sands looked as anxious as Grandmère. 'She came to see me yesterday evening. I was shocked. I had no idea.'

'Grandmère is convinced it was all Chloë's idea.'

'That's not what Chloë said. She said that Sir Thomas is determined on it. She says he has never offered to make her his mistress. He honours her too much.'

'Honours her!' Richard exclaimed.

'She doesn't know how much damage a divorce would do. I tried to explain, but she said that as Lady Burton she would have security, power and influence.'

'Influence to do what? She would not be received in society.'

'She's not interested in society,' Molly said. 'It is only the music she cares about. She thinks he will use his fortune to advance her career.'

'He can do that anyway,' Richard said.

'But as an unmarried female she can't travel about with him freely.'

'Oh, she sees that, does she?' Richard said, with grim irony. 'The decencies must be observed, of course! *Miss Sands* can't be in close company with Sir Thomas Burton because there would be talk!'

Molly looked at him helplessly. 'I've used every argument I can think of. Richard, do you think you could do anything? Could you perhaps talk to *him*?'

He recoiled. 'I've no right. He would be outraged if I were to raise the subject.'

'Then speak to Chloë!'

'If you can't persuade her, how can I?'

'You know about society.' Her mouth trembled. 'You bought her a piano.'

'Oh, darling!' He took her hands. He couldn't bear the look on her face, the hope as much as the despair. 'I'll do my best. I'll talk to her like a Dutch uncle.'

Chloë was at home, in the flat behind the Royal Albert Hall owned by Sir Thomas, where she lived with the Scottish housekeeper, Mrs Mackie. She was at her practice when Richard arrived, but Mrs Mackie said she would announce him.

'Sir Thomas is not here?' he asked.

'No, sir, he is not. He was here last evening,' she added, with a significant nod that suggested she knew what the situation was. 'Customarily my young lady does not like to be disturbed when she is playing at the piano, but I think she will make an exception for you.'

She went away; Richard heard the piano stop, and a moment later she reappeared in the doorway of the drawing-room to say, 'Will you come away ben, sir? Miss Sands will see you.'

Chloë was just rising from the instrument. He had not been sure what her mood would be – defiant, perhaps, or elated? – but she gave him a calm, enquiring look. 'Richard,' she said. 'What brings you here? Would you like some coffee? Mrs Mackie, bring coffee, will you?'

When the door had closed behind the housekeeper, she said, 'Were you just passing or has something happened?'

'You ask me that?' he said. 'I come from your mother, and before that my grandmother, both of whom are devastated.'

She gestured him into a seat and took the one opposite. Her beauty, he thought, had only grown in the time he had known her – she had been a lovely girl, but had matured into a striking woman. It was wasted, he felt, on a musical performer, who could have looked like a mangold wurzel for all it mattered. If only David of Wales had been older, she was lovely enough to have been the future queen of England.

His words had not troubled her. 'Is this about Sir Thomas asking me to marry him?' she asked.

'What else?' he said. 'I can't believe you agreed.'

'Why not?' she said simply.

'Do you really not see? My grandmother is convinced it was all your idea.'

'Oh, no,' she said. 'I hadn't thought of it. But he has been growing more in love with me, and I could see the difference when he came back from the country after Christmas. Before, I think it was just a craze, the way men can be mad for a woman they have only seen and hardly know. Men have made themselves foolish over me before, because of my looks. But I told you, didn't I, that I knew how to handle it? You were afraid he would push me into being his mistress.'

'I wish now that he had,' he said. 'It would be better than this.'

She looked hurt. 'How can you say so? Marriage is honourable.'

'Marriage after a divorce is not,' Richard said. 'There would be a dreadful scandal. To many people it would not even *be* a marriage.'

'Oh, Mother said all those things,' she said. 'She doesn't understand.'

She broke off as Mrs Mackie came in with the tray. The housekeeper looked at Richard keenly and at Chloë frowningly as she placed the things, and went quietly out. 'She doesn't approve,' Chloë said calmly. 'She's been with him for years. Old servants don't like change.' She poured the coffee and handed Richard a cup. 'And now Mother's persuaded you to come and talk to me, hasn't she? But I promise you I know what I'm doing.'

'I honestly don't think you do. You don't understand that divorce can only be obtained after proof of adultery is presented—'

'There is no adultery,' Chloë said sharply. 'How can you think it?'

'I *don't* think it. But this is how it would work: Sir Thomas would have to persuade Lady Burton to submit a petition against him for adultery and cruelty – and how he can do that I have no idea. If she hasn't wanted to divorce him so far, I don't know why she would now. But if she did, he would have to go to an hotel with a woman and be found in bed with her by one of the hotel staff, who would give evidence in court about it. The woman and the member of staff, and probably the hotel manager as well, would be paid a fee for this – this chicanery. What evidence would be presented for cruelty I don't know and would rather not imagine.'

'Yes, I know. He explained it all to me.'

'Then how can you bear it? It's all so tawdry! How can you want to be part of it?'

'I won't be. He will arrange everything. And my name will never be mentioned.'

'It will be all over the newspapers when he marries you afterwards and everyone knows you were the reason for the divorce. And I promise you, you will be blamed far more than he is. The woman in the case always is. Your name will always be tainted.'

She made an impatient gesture. 'I will be Lady Burton. That will be my name.'

'It that why you're doing it? For the title? Or is it his fortune?'

She drew herself up and said coldly, 'You do not have the right to say that to me. I listened to you because I know you came from my mother, but I think you had better go now.'

He leaned forward. 'Chloë, I'm sorry, but I really don't know why you want to do this. You don't love him, you don't want his title – what on earth is the point in courting scandal in this way?'

'The music!' she said, suddenly blazing. 'No, you *don't* understand! Music is everything! As an unmarried female I would always be restricted, and he would not be able to give me what I need. As his wife, those barriers disappear. You need not worry about the scandal – Sir Thomas Burton will always be received. A very few strict hostesses might blank him for a time. But it will soon be forgotten.'

'I don't think you have any idea how bad it will be,' he said, in one last despairing attempt to get through.

But she smiled at him. 'Don't you understand yet, Richard? I *don't care*. If you want to do some good, go back and reassure my mother that everything will be all right. Look after her. I don't need you to look after me.'

'You told me not to come back and say I failed,' Richard began.

Grandmère waved a dismissive hand. 'You had to tell me. And I knew. The young are so sure of themselves. I hoped, but I knew. Tell me, what is she, this girl? Is it avarice? She does not love him.'

'Not Sir Thomas the man. But Sir Thomas the musician, the impresario, she does,' Richard said.

Grandmère stared angrily at the empty air. 'He came to tell me about it. As if I would be delighted for him. He was happy and excited, like a boy going to the circus. He is in love with her.' She spoke the last words in tones of disgust.

Richard sought for words to comfort her. 'I think they are both so determined to advance her career at any cost that they will hardly notice they are the object of scandal.'

She looked at him. 'Perhaps not. But I shall.'

Molly read his expression. 'She wouldn't listen?'

'I warned you I had no sway with her.'

She bit her lip. 'It's not just the scandal, Richard. I can't bear to think of her tied for life to an old man she does not love. She ought to have a proper marriage, love and companionship, children. I want that for her.'

'Grandmère says kisses don't last, music does,' he said, to comfort her.

She spread out her hands before him. 'In time they grow stiff and you can no longer play, and then you're all alone with nothing but the sadness of what you have lost, and what you never had.'

'*You* will not be alone as long as I live,' Richard said, stepping close, and she allowed him to take her in his arms. He held her close and kissed her hair.

After a pause she spoke into his chest. 'What will your brother think? His name may be connected with the scandal, since Sir Thomas met her through your family.'

'My brother does not care about anything he has not had to dig up from an old tomb.'

She laughed unwillingly. 'You say such foolish things. What would I do without you?'

'I don't mean you ever to find out,' he said.

'You're looking well, Mr Moss,' Rose said, as he conducted her into the kitchen at Weldon House. It was empty and clean, the freshly rinsed dishcloths hanging up to dry and the back door open to let in the fresh air, proving the cook, Mrs Grape, was having some time off. Cooks never allowed the kitchen door to stand open, because of flies.

'I'm feeling well,' said Moss. 'It's almost as if I never had that bit of trouble last year.' He had been the butler up at the Castle, until a heart attack laid him low. The doctor had said that the job was too onerous for him, and he had been grateful to be taken on by Miss Eddowes as general manservant, though it was a step down. The alternative was the workhouse.

'And you like it here?'

He hesitated a telling moment. 'My mistress is a lady, and very kind. But . . .' He didn't seem to want to finish.

'It's not the Castle?' she suggested.

He sighed. 'I never thought I would ever leave there. I'd reached, if you like, the pentacle of my career. How are things?'

'Oh, much the same. Mrs Webster runs a tight ship. Mr Afton's p'r'aps a bit less formal than you were.'

'Informality in a butler is not what I'd ever approve,' Moss said. 'A certain standard has to be maintained.'

'Well, we get along all right,' she said.

'And the family?'

'Her ladyship and Lady Rachel have gone to London for the Season. His lordship's busy about the estate. Mr Sebastian's at his own house. Mr Richard comes and goes.'

'His lordship didn't accompany her ladyship to London?' Moss said disapprovingly. It wasn't right for ladies to travel unaccompanied.

'I think it was said he might join them later,' Rose said, missing his point. 'They had a bit of a row, so I expect they're happy away from each other for a bit.'

Moss was torn between his disapproval of gossip and his desire to know everything about the Castle. When he was butler, he managed both by berating the other servants for gossiping, but only *after* he'd heard everything.

'I'm sure they did not conduct an altercation in front of the servants,' he said at last, forbiddingly.

Rose understood him pretty well after all those years. 'It was about her garden. She wants to have the hillside behind the house cut away and moved to the front to make two flat places, but it'd be very expensive, and his lordship said they couldn't afford it. She was upset because it was her money in the first place. Words were had, Mr Moss, and some people couldn't help hearing.'

'A wife's money belongs to her husband,' Moss said. 'Surely her ladyship understands that.'

'Knowing it and liking it is two different things,' Rose said.

She walked back the long way, by Hundon's, though she knew Michael Woodrow was not there. She had gone past the gate when she heard Martha calling. Looking back, she saw the tall, gaunt woman hurrying down from the kitchen with something in her hand. She went back to meet her at the gate, and thought at first there was something wrong with her face. She almost said, 'Have you got the toothache?' when she realised just in time that Martha was smiling, or at least trying to.

'I saw you go past earlier,' Martha said. 'I thought you'd come back this way, so I made you this.'

She handed over the cloth-wrapped thing she was holding. Rose lifted the edge: it was a small cake, still warm. 'That's very kind,' she said awkwardly. She didn't really want to accept presents from this woman. She didn't want to like her.

But for Michael's sake she took it and smiled back – almost as unnatural a smile as Martha's, but more practised.

'I was baking anyway,' Martha said. 'You liked my scones. Michael says I'm a good baker.'

'You are that,' Rose said stiffly. 'I'll have it with my tea.'

'Best eat it while it's still warm,' Martha said, and abruptly turned away, trudging back to the kitchen.

Rose walked on with the parcel in her hand. It smelt very strongly of cinnamon, and she wasn't over-fond of cinnamon. After some time she heard a whimper behind her, and turned to see a dog crawl out of the bushes, its nose working hard. It was skinny and had a large sore on its shoulder – obviously a stray. She gestured at it and said, 'Go on, get away!' and walked on. When she was nearing the back yard she looked back and saw it was still following her at a short distance, obviously attracted by the smell of the cake. It cowered when she turned, pressing itself to the ground, ears back, but it didn't run. Probably starving, she thought. Then she looked at the cake in her hand, and a hard smile came over her lips. A suitable end for Martha's famous baking! 'Here,' she said, unwrapping the cake. The dog looked at her hopefully. She broke it in half and threw one piece to the dog's feet, and it wolfed it down. She threw the other half, shook the crumbs out of the cloth and stowed it in her pocket. *That'll teach her to call me names*, she thought.

The dog continued to follow her hopefully, and she ignored it. It would get the message sooner or later. She was at the yard gate when she heard an odd noise from behind her, a strange, muted howl. She looked back, and saw the dog arch its back and vomit violently. 'Don't like cinnamon either, eh?' she said, and laughed inwardly that the great master cook's effort had been rejected even by a starving stray. The dog retched again, and then stuck its head up, howled again, and fell flat on its side, its front paws pedalling. 'Here,' she said to herself, 'that's not right.'

One of the stable boys passing the gate came out, stared, and said, 'What's wrong of it? It's having a fit.'

Now the dog was convulsing violently, head drawn back, a little foam oozing from its clenched jaws. Its paws reached and reached again; its back was so arched its head was almost touching its tail. 'Oh, good God,' Rose said. 'Can't you do something?' The boy looked at her, scared, and she snapped, 'Get a spade or something, put it out of its misery!'

He looked as though he'd sooner dig a hole in the ground and climb in it. But it was too late anyway. The dog gave one last convulsive spasm and was still. The boy crept nearer, goggling but afraid. 'It's dead,' he said in a kind of fascination.

'Get that shovel anyway,' Rose ordered him. 'Can't leave it there.'

'Poor thing,' the boy said. 'What was wrong of it, any road?'

'How should I know?' she said. 'Don't just stand there!'

And then the thought came over her. The cake. That could have been *her* lying there. Her lips felt cold. 'Oh, my good God,' she muttered. 'What now?'

Two fine-bred horses paced side by side along the tan in Hyde Park, one black, one bright chestnut. Their lady riders were neatly attired and followed at a respectful distance by their grooms. They were so engrossed in conversation they did not notice the glances they attracted from passers-by.

'Aunt Caroline says she's besieged,' Kitty was saying. 'Every acquaintance she's ever made – some of them she hasn't seen for years. She says she's thinking of taking the knocker off the door.'

'And all to talk about Sir Thomas Burton!' Nina marvelled.

'They know about him and Grandmère, so they think Aunt Caroline will know the details. She hates it.'

Nina didn't read the newspapers and was not yet so 'up' in society that she heard all the gossip, so she had only a vague idea about the story. 'It doesn't really affect your family, does it? It's not as if Sir Thomas is a relative.'

'No, but there's his connection with Grandmère and her patronage of the girl, and now it's got about that Richard was hoping to marry her – which is simply not true – but he's worried that at any moment the newspapers will discover that Mrs Sands lives in lodgings paid for by the estate. Giles sent him a livid letter because it was he who first got involved with them.'

'Well, I see that it's a scandal for a man to divorce his wife to marry a younger woman, but none of you are responsible, so why should the scandal touch you?'

Kitty sighed. 'I don't know, but somehow it does. And nobody likes to be talked about.' She decided to change the subject. 'Isn't it a lovely day? And isn't it nice to ride together?'

'It was a wonderful idea of yours to have our horses sent up. I wonder you didn't think of it before.'

'It isn't worth it when one's only up for a few days or a week. It's so expensive. But as we're staying for the whole Season . . .'

'Mr Cowling was fascinated by the process,' said Nina. 'He wanted to know every detail of how it would be arranged. He does love to know how things work.'

'Is he going to be staying in Town much?'

'Yes. Now Mr Tullamore has set up the London office, Mr Cowling can have Decius back, and he has Truman Smith as well, so he ought to be able to relax more.' She glanced sideways at Kitty. 'Is Giles coming up later? He didn't mind your coming alone?'

'Staying with Aunt Caroline is the opposite of being alone,' Kitty said. Nina noticed she hadn't answered the question. She wondered if something was wrong, but Kitty was a very private person. She supposed if she wanted to talk about it she would. 'Aunt Caroline says it's going to be a very good Season,' Kitty went on, 'and I'm so looking forward to it. I seem to have done nothing but have babies for years. We must make sure we see everything there is to see.'

'That's a large ambition.' Nina laughed.

'I shall have to chaperone Rachel for some of the time – I can't expect Aunt Caroline to do it all – but I don't mind. I had to bring her with me – it's so dull for her at Ashmore without Alice, and it's hard for her seeing Angus only once a month.'

'Don't you have to stop her seeing him?' Nina asked.

'No, only stop them being alone together. At least, that's how I interpret it. I think my mother-in-law is too tired to be strict. It must be hard to be having another baby at her age.'

'Have you heard anything from her?'

'From Linda. She writes mostly about herself – she seems to have managed to get invited to some parties – but she says her mother is in reasonable health. The baby's due in August.'

Nina didn't comment. Kitty glanced at her and saw her inward-looking expression. Nearly three years of marriage and no sign of a baby. Kitty adored her own two sons, and felt compassion for her friend. Every woman needed something to love. 'I was so sorry to hear about your little dog,' she said tentatively. Nina didn't answer. 'Will you get another?'

'No,' said Nina. Not even to Kitty did she want to talk about Trump. And it had not been about her dog she had been thinking. Mentioning the dowager's pregnancy had made her remember the way, every time she met Mr Cowling after an absence, he looked at her with an intent, questioning expression and she *knew* – though he never mentioned it – that he was wondering if she had settled on someone to father a baby for him. It was like a maddening itch that she could not reach. She wanted love, she wanted physical love, she wanted a child, and half the time she thought it would be the best thing for both of them if she did have an affair. The other half of the time she was horrified by the whole idea. And she knew that if she did come to him to tell him she was with child, he would be delighted and at the same time heartbroken because he loved her. And he would never stop wondering who the father was.

Her aunt would say, *I warned you not to marry an older man you didn't love.* Nina shook away the thoughts, and looked around her at the lovely parkland, intensely green with new grass, the trees decked in soft young leaves, the lovely horse beneath her. If she had not married Mr Cowling she would have been a teacher in a small school in Yorkshire, living in lodgings, with a restricted life that did not include horses, dogs, Seasons in London, and she would have been unmarried and just as childless. She had so much to be grateful for.

Kitty was looking at her curiously. 'Shall we canter?' she said.

CHAPTER TWELVE

Rose brooded over the dog incident as she went about her work. A stray dog, of course, could have been dying anyway. It might have been chance that it keeled over at that particular moment. But it seemed a strange coincidence. And the boy she had once seen die of toadstool poisoning had gone the same way – vomiting and convulsing.

On the other hand, she was loath to believe that Martha, however much she resented her, would go that far. It was chilling to think even for a moment that anyone could hate her enough to want to kill her. And if it was true – what then? What should she – could she – do? What about Michael? Should she tell him? Would he believe her? And what could *he* do about it?

She slept badly, dreaming fitfully about people shouting at her, some shapeless creature pursuing her, a dead dog writhing with maggots crawling out of the ditch and dragging itself towards her. She woke with a jerk and a shudder, glad for once to be waking early.

As she reached the foot of the back stairs, she met Afton coming out of the plate room. He looked at her, concerned. 'Are you ill? You look pale.'

She brushed him off. 'I'm all right.'

'I noticed you looked a bit under the weather yesterday,' he persisted. 'What's wrong? Maybe I can help.'

She would never have unburdened herself to Mr Moss –

and Mr Moss would never have asked. But Mr Afton was a different sort of butler. Perhaps he could give her advice. 'I've got a bit of a problem,' she admitted at last.

'Come and tell me about it, and we'll see what we can do,' he said comfortably. He led the way to the butler's room and she followed, half reluctantly. No-one else was down yet, apart from the scullery maid scrubbing the kitchen floor. She wondered why Mr Afton was about so early, but it wasn't for her to ask.

In his room, she hesitated, wondering about the wisdom of it, then plunged in. 'I think someone tried to poison me.'

He didn't waste time with useless exclamations. He said, 'Why do you think that?'

Her liking for him rose a notch. She explained. 'I saw a kid die of eating a toadstool once. It looked like that,' she concluded.

'Hmm. But strychnine could cause the same symptoms,' he said, 'and there's rat poison lying about in most barns. A stray could easily eat some while it was sniffing about for food. You said it seemed starving?'

'It gobbled up the cake in a second. It seems queer, just after it ate it . . . And she ran after me to give it me. Why should she bake me a cake when she doesn't like me?'

'It's a delicate business,' he said, drumming his fingers on the desk in thought. 'A person would have to be unbalanced to do such a thing.'

'You mean queer in the head? Well, I think she is. Michael – Mr Woodrow – said she's always been a bit strange.'

'But strange enough to attempt murder?'

'Murder?'

'That's what it is, if the cake was poisoned.'

It was what she'd been wondering, but it was a shock hearing the word. 'The thing is,' she went on after a pause, 'what should I do? If it *was* her, I don't want her having another go at me.'

'A cook certainly has opportunities,' he mused. 'But I don't think you've got enough evidence to go to the police.'

'The police?' She was shocked. 'No! But what I'm wondering is, should I tell Michael? It'd cause ructions.' She gave him an appealing look, not having the words to spell out all the scenes she could imagine.

'Yes,' said Afton. He saw well enough.

'Or should I say nothing and just not see him any more?'

As she said it, she realised she didn't like that option. She had grown fond of him in a particular way – a fluttery and yet sharp-edged feeling, perilously hopeful, warm and comfortable and more than half amazed. No-one had ever shown that sort of interest in her, and she had never thought anyone would. She didn't want to lose it.

Afton said slowly, 'I don't see how you can say nothing. You have to put him on his guard. If she did try to poison you, she might try to poison him.'

'Why would she want to kill him? I don't understand,' Rose said, frowning.

'She doesn't want to share him with anyone. She wants to keep him all to herself. And if he was dead, no-one could ever take him away from her, could they?'

She was silent. She thought at first that was stupid, but then it made a kind of sense. 'You really think that?' she said at last.

He lifted his hands. 'I don't know these people, only what you've told me about them. I'm just saying it's possible, given what you've said.'

'You think I should tell him what happened?'

'It's only fair. Apart from saving your own skin, think how you'd feel if anything happened to him.'

She shook her head doubtfully.

He said, 'When I lived in New York, there were some friends of my master, a married couple – he was a wealthy businessman, she was the daughter of a railroad baron, with a lot of money of her own that she'd inherited. She was supposed to have a delicate stomach – every now and then she'd have vomiting fits, and take to her bed, and live on boiled water for a few days. She recovered each time, but it was taking its toll. She was gradually getting more frail. The doctor put her on different diets but still these attacks came back. Then one day she had really bad one, and died. It was very sad. But I remember my master saying to me one day a few months later, when I was shaving him – gentlemen often unburden themselves when they're being shaved – that this businessman had been in trouble. He'd borrowed unwisely and from the wrong people, and his wife's death had saved him. They didn't have any children, so all her money went to him.'

He looked at Rose, and she said, 'You thought . . . ?'

'I didn't think anything, it wasn't my place. But my master dropped the acquaintance after that. And I often think about that poor woman, maybe being poisoned just a bit, over a long time, getting sick and getting better for a while, so as to prepare everybody for the big one when the time came. Arsenic, I believe, is the thing, if you get the dose right. A weak stomach . . . Lots of people suffer from that, don't they? Who's to know?'

Rose looked at him, head up and neck stiff, like a frightened horse. 'You've got a very dark mind, Mr Afton, if you don't mind me saying.'

Michael Woodrow seemed a fit and healthy man. But if his food did disagree with him now and then, no-one would think anything of it. And lots of people died of violent stomach pains, and no-one thought anything of *that*. Not if they weren't important people. Your insides were full of all kinds of tripes, and things could go wrong with any of them, any time.

'I think I'd better talk to him,' she said unhappily.

* * *

Mr Cowling was still away a great deal, with Portsmouth and Nottingham added to his usual rounds, and he apologised to Nina.

'It'll get better as things settle down. I've got Decius back now, and Truman, and Tullamore is proving himself a real find – worth his weight in gold, that young feller. He really knows his stuff. His father must be kicking himself for letting him go! He's going to need a Decius of his own before long. He's well worth the big salary I'm going to give him – don't want anyone else poaching him away from me! And if he marries that nice girl, all the better, because marriage settles a young chap down, there's no doubt about it. What was I saying?'

'You were apologising for leaving me alone – in London, during the Season, when of course there is no-one around and simply nothing to do,' said Nina.

'Aye, you're roasting me now, Mrs Cowling!' he said, laughing. 'Are you really all right?'

'I'm not all alone, you know. I have Kitty, and Lepida Morris, not to mention Lady Manningtree and Lady Rachel. And there's Richard to keep an eye on me when he's up. And my aunt.'

'Aye, that Miss Lepida is a very clever young woman! Though I think Mawes and Mrs Morris have brought her up a bit *too* clever, because who will marry her?'

'*You* married *me*,' Nina pointed out. 'Of course, I'm not as clever as Lepida, but you always gave me to understand you thought I was cleverer than the average girl.'

'Roasting me again! I'm just a butt of fun to you, aren't I? How is your aunt, by the way?'

'Just exactly the same as she always is. She never changes the slightest bit.'

'Well, give her my respects when you see her. Now, to what I was saying: when the Season's over, I thought maybe you'd like to go away somewhere – to the Continent, if you like: France, Italy? Think about it, any road. And while you're in

London, why don't we throw a grand dinner party? I'll be coming and going, so if you arrange it, I'll make sure to keep the date free.'

'How grand?' she asked.

'As grand as you like. Go all out. You never *do* spend enough of my money to please me. I've told you again and again.'

'Yes, you have. You'd like me to be dripping in diamonds like a chandelier.'

He looked at her fondly. 'You'd suit 'em better than all the old duchesses who wear 'em. Let me buy you something now, this week. Just to show you what I feel about you.'

'If you really want to please me . . .' she began beguilingly.

'You know I do.'

'Then be here for dinner on Friday.'

'A party?'

'No, just close friends, but it would be nice to have you there.'

He glowed at the thought that she wanted his company, and she was pleased to have pleased him.

'I'll make sure to be there. Decius must get me out of anything that's in the diary.'

'Oh, Decius is invited too,' she said. 'And Lepida Morris. It's to be a very *talking* dinner.'

Apart from Decius and Lepida, the guests at the Cowlings' were Kitty and Richard, and Lord and Lady Stavesacre, who had a large estate, Holm Abbey near Watlington, and were keen franchisists. So the talk was naturally about the Women's Enfranchisement Bill, which had come up for its second reading in the Commons on the 12th of May and had been defeated by a filibuster: talked out of time with long, rambling speeches.

'It's no more than we've come to expect after the Bills of 1870, 1886, and 1897 were defeated,' Lord Stavesacre said.

'But it's a particularly bitter blow,' his wife continued, 'because this was by a length the best Bill that's been presented. It had the beauty of simplicity – to give the franchise to women on exactly equal terms to men. All the others have had qualifications.'

'What does that mean?' Kitty asked.

Lepida explained. 'Oh, they said that only single women and widows should have the vote, for instance, or only women who owned property, or were leaseholders, or were over a certain age – that sort of thing.'

'Exactly,' said Lavinia Stavesacre, 'and that was the beauty of this Bill. It didn't create some new-fangled fancy franchise. It simply extended all existing franchises to women, making it the easiest thing in the world to vote for. All it did was abolish the electoral disqualification of sex.'

'A pretty big "all", if you don't mind my saying,' said Mr Cowling, mildly.

'You think so? But half of all human beings on earth are female! Fifty-three years ago Herbert Spencer wrote, "Equity knows no difference of sex. It manifestly applies to the whole race, female as well as male."'

'If I'm not mistaken, Herbert Spencer believed the human mind was subject to natural law,' said Mr Cowling. He saw Lord Stavesacre's eyebrow rise, and said, 'Aye, I've read a bit in my time. And in every species the females and the males are different from each other. They have different functions.'

'That's true,' said Richard.

'Women can't be soldiers. Or policemen. Where strength is wanted to protect the realm, where are women then?'

'That's exactly what Mr Labouchère argued,' said Decius. 'I've read the account in Hansard. He said that order and liberty rested ultimately on force, and the fact that women couldn't contribute to that force was a limitation of citizenship.'

Lepida looked at him in astonishment. 'Mr Blake, I thought you were one of us!'

'It is an argument,' Decius said mildly. 'I didn't say I agree with it. For instance, on that argument a weak, sickly or crippled man should be denied the vote too.'

'Women can't be solicitors, barristers or judges,' Lavinia said, 'and they're barred from serving on juries. Yet they are prosecuted, tried and judged by men under laws enacted by men. It's unconstitutional!'

'Not to say inexpedient, mischievous, and unjust,' her husband added.

'Fine words butter no parsnips,' Mr Cowling said impatiently. 'Think about this: there are more women than men in the country, so you'd have more people elected to Parliament on women's votes than on men's. And what if they passed a law against men's interests, or one that men didn't go along with? How could you force men to obey it? You'd have riot and revolution.'

'But if women are the majority,' Nina asked, 'why shouldn't laws favour them, as they favour men now?'

Richard gave her a humorous look. 'I don't think that's the right question to ask,' he said. 'I imagine the franchisists are promoting the idea of a more just society, not one that's biased in the opposite direction.'

Stavesacre gave him an approving nod. 'It is equity and freedom under the law that we seek. Women suffer great injustice, prejudice and hardship. Give them the vote and the greatest of their grievances would be assuaged, because they would have a voice in the constitution.'

'Who are those women who made the fuss and bother outside Parliament?' Mr Cowling asked.

A group of women had protested against the filibuster outside the Houses of Parliament until they'd been driven away by the police. They'd been allowed to regroup by the gates to Westminster Abbey and had held a rally demanding the government intervene to secure passage of the Bill.

'It's an organisation called the Women's Social and Political

Union,' Lady Stavesacre answered. 'The leading lights are a Mrs Pankhurst and her daughters.'

'Political, is it? I suppose they were put up to it by this new Labour Party, then?'

'The Pankhursts *were* affiliated with the Independent Labour Party, but they broke with them. They want the WSPU to be a political party in its own right, because none of the others will focus on the issue.'

'They're right there,' said Mr Cowling. 'With everything else there is to put right!'

'I shouldn't think many women really *want* the vote, do they?' Kitty said tentatively. 'It's not something you hear discussed.'

'We're discussing it now,' Nina pointed out.

'Yes, but you are all especially clever people who talk about that sort of thing all the time,' Kitty said, blushing at having to explain what she only vaguely perceived. 'I mean that you don't hear ordinary ladies talking about it. Politics are so confusing,' she sighed.

Mr Cowling smiled at her. 'That's right, Lady Stainton. Much better leave that sort of thing to the men. And there's a point!' he added, to the rest of the company. 'If the ladies had the vote, the married ones would vote the way their husbands told them, so a married man would end up with two votes, while a single man'd only have one. Where's the fairness there? I'd have thought you wouldn't be in favour of that, Decius – and Mr Tallant.'

Richard grinned. 'Oh, sir, questions begged right and left! Kettles of fish all over the place! I think we should change the subject.'

Decius obliged. 'How is your new milk venture coming along? I've been so busy helping with the London office I haven't kept up.'

'Doing nicely, thank you,' Richard answered. 'Another farm has come in, and I'm making slow progress with Lord

Shacklock. At any rate, I thought it worth investing in a second motor-lorry.'

'Motor vehicles seem to be taking over from horses everywhere,' said Lady Stavesacre. 'It's rather a shame. A carriage is much more elegant.'

'It makes crossing the street in London more pleasant, though,' Nina remarked. 'Especially in wet weather.'

'I always feel so sorry for those poor cab horses,' Kitty said, 'standing for hours at the ranks in the rain and the cold.'

Cowling gave her an approving look for this proper, feminine comment. 'Motor-cabs make a lot more sense, given all the waiting,' he said.

'Oh, I grant the *convenience* of the motor vehicle,' Lady Stavesacre said, 'but I mourn the decline in civilisation. We'll see ever more furious driving on the road, and more deaths.'

'There have always been furious drivers of horses,' Decius pointed out. 'And the 1903 Act limited motor vehicles to twenty miles an hour.'

'I don't recommend being struck by a motor vehicle at twenty miles an hour,' Richard said, with a wry smile.

'Quite so!' said Lady Stavesacre. 'You never see a horse running at that speed.'

'Except if it bolts,' Nina pointed out.

'But a horse will always try to avoid you. A motor vehicle is insensate,' she concluded.

'Where do you buy your motor spirit from?' Lord Stavesacre asked Richard. 'Is it hard to get hold of?'

'We used to get it from Bolliard's, the hardware shop in Canons Ashmore, but they didn't carry very much and sometimes ran out. But now Tim Tucker has opened a garage in the village, and sells petrol as well. And since it's more in his line of trade, he's keeping a larger stock, so we should be all right from now on.'

'We ought to start manufacturing it in this country,' Decius said. 'Most of our benzene comes from Russia, and with all the unrest over there, the supply shouldn't be relied on.'

Richard looked amused. 'Is there anything you don't know?'

Decius smiled. 'I keep up with the news. And import and export have been rather my concern for the last couple of months.'

'I should like to drive a motor-car,' Nina said, out of her own train of thought.

'Heaven forbid!' Mr Cowling said, startled.

'I'm sure driving a motor-car must be easier than driving horses,' she objected.

'As the only person here who has come a cropper in a motor-car, I wouldn't recommend it for the nerves,' Richard said.

Lepida judiciously changed the subject. 'Father tells me George Bernard Shaw has a new play opening on Tuesday at the Royal Court: *Man and Superman*.'

Mr Cowling nodded. 'Aye, your pa told me he's getting up a party to go to the opening night. I've enjoyed some of Shaw's plays.'

Decius said, 'I've heard it's based on Nietzsche's philosophy of the *Übermensch*.'

'Father told me he asked Shaw about that, and he denied it,' Lepida said. 'He said he's exploring his own idea that it's woman who advances natural selection, because it's women who force men to marry them, rather than men taking the initiative.'

'It sounds like a tremendous romp,' Richard said gravely, and Nina laughed.

'We can't get away from the woman question this evening, can we?' she said. 'Rescue us, Richard!'

Richard bowed. 'With pleasure! Tell me, Mrs Cowling, what do you think of this summer's hats? Isn't it rather like wearing a fruit bowl on your head?'

★ ★ ★

Sebastian was in miserable seclusion at Wisteria House, his place in Henley. He had no guests, and was not at home to callers. He went for long walks along the riverside, his expression deterring those who might have passed the time of day with him.

The early-summer weather was fair, mocking him; the willows were filling out with pale green leaves, reaching down to the water, the oaks thick with olive-yellow flower. The river was peopled with pleasure boats, rowers and idle paddlers: under a sky of tender robin's-egg blue, the constant ripples laid their flèches of light and shadow on the surface, rocking the ducks and moorhens as they dabbled along the banks. And everywhere the hawthorn hedges were in starry bloom, filling the air with their sweet, maddening scent.

Sebastian brooded as he walked. When he had been a young man, he had wanted to marry a girl named Phyllis. He had delayed asking her because of family disapproval, and in the delay she had caught the fever and died. How could he have lost his love again? He went over and over the few phrases he had exchanged with Dory before she ran away. What should he have said instead? What combination of words would have cut through her panic and won her over? He was a clumsy fool to have bungled it.

Where was she now? He tortured himself with imagining her suffering. At best, she would have got a position, but it would be a lowly one without a reference. She might be scrubbing doorsteps, or toiling in a laundry, dragging wet heavy sheets from boiler to mangle for fourteen hours a day. Or a drudge in a house where they kept no other help and pitilessly drove the maid-of-all-work from dawn to midnight with scolds, abuse and contempt.

Around him the days lengthened and new life was everywhere, the fields greening, insects busy in the campion and rattle, the cranesbill and loosestrife, the red clover and the bugle. The first swifts screamed overhead, glorying in their own speed; ducklings and moorchicks followed the adults in neat, sagittal flotillas. Mrs May, his housekeeper, tried to tempt his appetite with lamb and spring greens; even Crooks dared to murmur something about a new straw hat for summer wear, as if that might lift the winter in his heart. He did not play the piano. He could only mourn in silence.

And then one day as he exited the garden wicket onto the path leading down to the river, he saw a figure in the shadow of the trees at the end. An undefined female figure, any-woman-shaped, in drab skirt, jacket and felt hat. She was almost indistinguishable in the bosky darkness, but he knew who it was, and his heart contracted so sharply it hurt him. He started forward, almost tripping over his own feet in his haste. 'Dory! Dory!' he cried. The figure hurried from him, darting away out of the tree-shadow, turning onto the river-side and out of sight. 'Wait! Dory, wait!'

The river path was narrow where the gardens of the houses came down to it, and it was thronged. He glimpsed the small, dark-clad figure some way ahead, but he was too bulky to slip through the crowd as she did, and she was getting away. At the end of this section was a cattle gate, which further slowed him down, after which the way opened out into meadows and he could move freely. But where was she? In the wide open space there were couples and groups dotted about, sitting on rugs, one set playing a game of cricket with their children, others strolling. He twisted about, searching for her. And then he spotted her hurrying to the top of the meadow where it joined the road.

Gentlemen of his age and condition did not run. He probably had not run since the last time he had played cricket for the village team, years ago. He attracted stares of disapproval, suspicion and, in the case of a group of young men, derision; but the road led back into town and he'd never find her there. He ran, clutching his hat and his stick, until he was close enough to cry out, breathlessly, 'Dory! Wait! Wait! Talk to me!'

She had gained the road. She turned her head to look, and for a moment he thought she would hurry on and leave him behind. But she hesitated, and he cried, with the last of his breath, 'Please!'

And she stopped.

He reached her, hot, breathless, feeling dishevelled, ridiculous. She looked so small in her practical dark-brown stuff coat and skirt, just a working woman no-one would give a second glance to; but to him she was limned in light.

There was a bench a little way along, and they sat in silence while he got his breath back and his heartbeat slowed. He took off his hat and laid it on the bench beside him, and felt the fingers of air cooling his head. She sat with her hands folded in her lap and everything about her quiet, but he felt her tense unhappiness as though she were radiating it.

When he could talk normally, he said, 'How long have you been in Henley?' It seemed as good a question to start with as any.

'Some days. A week, perhaps,' she said. 'I lose track of the time.'

'But why didn't you come to see me?'

'I didn't know you were there. I thought you were at the Castle.'

'Then – why did you come to Henley?'

She didn't answer for a moment. Then she said, 'Because it was your place. I've stood and looked at your house. Just because it was your house.' She stopped.

'How have you been living?' he asked. 'I've been so afraid that you – were destitute.'

'I had some money saved. And I've had odd jobs. Scrubbing, mostly. I earned a shilling here and there. I couldn't get a proper job because I had to keep moving.'

Now he turned to look at her. 'But *why*?' he cried in anguish. 'Why did you run away?'

She began to speak, and stopped, and made a useless gesture with her hand. 'It all seemed—' She stopped again, and looked away from him, as if she was ashamed. 'I don't know,' she muttered.

'Dory!' he protested.

'It was such a shock,' she said. 'All these years I've lived with the fear. Always looking over my shoulder. Never able to settle. Not really a person at all. And then there was you.' She stopped again, at the worst moment for him.

'Did I make it harder for you?' he asked.

'You did,' she said.

His heart hurt. 'I never wanted that. I never meant to add to your burden.'

'But it was good. A good pain, like the pins-and-needles when numbness wears off. Only – there was no future to it. I knew that. So I couldn't let myself . . .' She shook her head. 'It would have been wrong to enjoy it. And then you came and said you'd killed him. What was I to do? I couldn't let myself be that person. All I had left was my self-respect. It was all that kept me breathing. If I lost that I might as well be dead.'

He had winced at the word. 'But I didn't kill him! I never said that. If you'd only let me explain – but you ran away. And what did I feel when I realised you'd gone, not just from me but from Ashmore, from everything, all alone again when I wanted only to look after you and make you happy?'

She sighed deeply. 'Tell me it again, then. It was such a horror, I don't think I really took it in properly. Tell me everything and I promise I'll listen.'

He could hear from the tone of her voice that she still thought it was hopeless, but he was determined not to waste this one chance Fate had given. One last chance of life.

Quietly, unemotionally, he told her everything, in detail, of his dealings with Mr Bland, his visit to Brighton, how he had found Jack Hubert, and exactly what had been said and done between them. He described the inquest, and then the days when he had wandered about the seaside town, too shocked and debilitated to go home straight away. And then he stopped.

She was silent for a long time, staring in the direction of the river. At last she said, quietly, 'His death was caused by you. You were the reason of it.'

'He was trying to kill me,' Sebastian said. 'I had to defend myself. I would not willingly have killed him. He was the villain of the piece, not me. You must see that.'

She sighed again. 'How could I ever lie easy—' she began, almost too quiet to hear.

His patience broke. 'No!' he said, and, startled, she looked up at him. 'He was a bad man. You told me yourself he would have killed *you* if he'd found you. He tried to kill me, for no reason except that he was drunk and mad. You ask how you could lie easy? There is no trial of conscience here! Not mine and not yours. An accident has freed you, not of your causing and not of mine, either. The only question you have to answer is, do you love me?'

He was so afraid of the answer that he could hardly bear to wait for it. He was an ordinary, middle-aged man of no particular beauty, and he had fallen in love with a woman of strange courage and luminous integrity, who could have married him for his money and never mentioned the previous husband – who would ever have known? – but instead had held fast by her self-respect, and would die for it if she had to. After a lifetime of loneliness he had found the one person he wanted to be with, and the idea of losing her was terrible.

He made himself look steadily down into her face; and she scanned his, as though hoping to see some holy script written there.

'Do you love me?' he asked again, when she didn't answer. It might have been the bravest thing he ever did.

'Yes,' she said at last, as if it was an irrelevance, and not what was really being asked at all. 'How could I help loving you? You are so kind and good and clever and – and everything a woman could want. But—'

He almost laughed with relief. He grabbed both her hands. 'There's no "but",' he said. 'You love me! And you know I love you. That's all that matters. We are both free to marry now. Will you marry me?'

Now a faint smile passed across her pale, drawn face like a gleam of sunshine on a winter's day. 'What would people say? What would your family say?'

'You can have no idea,' he said, 'of the depth of indifference there is towards me and my affairs.'

'I don't believe that for a minute. Can you really imagine me entering the main door of Ashmore Castle as your wife, when I've always gone in by the kitchen yard as a servant?'

He hunched his shoulders a little. '*My wife* can enter by any door she pleases. But we needn't bother much with Ashmore Castle. I have a house of my own, and no-one in Henley knows you.'

'Your servants do,' she pointed out.

'I'll get new servants,' he said largely, 'if you can't deal with them. But if you're half the woman I think you are, you'll manage them all right. So? You haven't given me an answer. Will you marry me?'

'I *want* to—'

'Then do!' He lifted her hands to his lips, one after the other, and kissed them. 'Say yes!'

The rigidness went out of her. 'Yes,' she said, on an outgoing breath.

'With all your heart?' he insisted.

'With all my heart. I don't know what I've done to deserve you, but if you really want me—'

'You know I do.' He couldn't kiss her in this public space, so he kissed her hands again.

They looked at each other for a little while. Then she said, 'What happens now?'

He thought for a moment. 'Where have you been staying?'

'The last two nights at the Ship, across the river.'

'I don't know it.'

'It's a common alehouse.'

He frowned. 'That won't do. We must—'

'You're thinking of moving me into the best hotel in Henley, aren't you?'

He was startled. 'How did you know?'

'If you take me there, tongues will wag. And I don't have the right clothes.'

He thought again. 'We'll take the train to Wallingford. No-one knows me there. The Coach and Horses is a decent place, not too fine. And there are shops in Wallingford. You can buy yourself new clothes, just enough for now, until we can get you fitted out properly.'

'And where will we marry?'

'In London. The most anonymous place of all. And then you must decide where you would like to go for your honeymoon.'

She looked startled. 'Honeymoon? You mean like a holiday? I've never had a holiday.'

He blinked back tears. 'Oh, Dory, there's so much I want to give you.'

'Well, you can. But not all at once, or I shall be overwhelmed.'

CHAPTER THIRTEEN

Rose was just passing Harriot's feed and seed store when Michael Woodrow came out and almost bumped into her. He pulled off his hat and said, 'Good afternoon, Miss Hawkins. And where are you heading this fine day?'

'Poining's. For some tape and thread.' She looked at the roll of baling twine he was carrying and didn't return the question. 'Well, I must get on,' she said.

'Why the hurry? Come and have a cup of tea and talk to me,' he said.

'I haven't got time,' she said. 'I've got to get back.'

'Then I'll walk with you.' She said nothing, looking at him with a frown. He lowered his voice. 'Rose,' he said, 'what's wrong?'

She thought of Afton's advice and sighed. 'I've got something to tell you. Meet me by the Pack Bridge in a quarter of an hour.'

He looked about to argue, then nodded, and walked away in the opposite direction.

He was there at the bridge when she came along, sitting on the low parapet, hat in hand, and her heart gave an unruly flutter at the sight of him, so familiar and male, comfortable and exciting at the same time. *What would it be like to . . . ?* She cancelled the thought. After this conversation he would probably want nothing to do with her.

He stood up as she approached. 'I was afraid you wouldn't

come,' he said. He examined her expression. 'What have I done? You didn't want to be seen walking along the high street with me?'

'It wasn't that,' she said. 'But when I tell you . . . you might be angry. I didn't want . . . People are so nosy.'

'This is not like you,' he said. 'You're always so direct. Tell me what's wrong, and we'll see if we can't make it right.'

She felt it would be easier to talk while moving, so she turned along the path beside the river, and he fell in beside her. And she told him about Martha's cake, and the dog's death.

'Wait, wait,' he said. He stopped, turning to face her. 'Are you suggesting that Martha deliberately put poison in a cake and gave it to you?'

Rose looked at him steadily. 'It's what it seemed like to me.'

'But – that's madness! That dog could have died of anything at all!'

'It was poison all right. I know what that looks like,' she said.

'And simply from that you conclude that my sister – *my sister* – tried to do away with you? Are you out of your senses?'

'She hates me. You saw how she was when I came for tea that time.'

'She takes time to get used to people, that's all. It's hard for her to cope with new faces. Once she knows you, she'll be all right.'

'You didn't see her face when she gave it me.'

He ran a wild hand backwards through his hair. 'Martha's a bit strange, I admit, but to jump to the conclusion that she's trying to kill you . . . All she's done is show a bit of friendship in her own, odd way. You must have a warped view of humanity, that's all I can say.' He looked at her with a mixture of anger and perplexity. 'What must you think of me, then? When I raise my hat to you, you must think I'm about to bludgeon you to death.'

'I was afraid of this,' she said. 'I thought you might react this way.'

'How else can I react, when you accuse my sister of murder!'

'I wasn't going to tell you, but I thought I'd better put you on your guard, in case.'

'In case she murders me as well?'

'All right, you think there's nothing in it, but I've warned you, that's all. I can't do any more.'

'I think you've done quite enough. And if you're so sure that you can't trust me and mine not to do away with you, I shan't ask you to tea again. And I'll be sure to cross the road when I see you coming in future.' And he walked away, back towards the bridge, with angry, jerky steps, kicking a stone into the river when it happened to lie in his path.

Rose watched him go, then turned in the other direction to walk down to the Old Toll Bridge and go home that way. Her heart was sore, and she wondered if she had, after all, jumped to a mad conclusion. To an outsider it must look like that, but she had been there, she had seen Martha's expression. If it was merely a peace offering why not offer her a slice of a larger cake, invite her inside to eat it with a cup of tea? Why bake her a whole small cake to take away with her? And she had seen the dog die, so soon after eating it. Rat poison worked quickly, she knew that, and there were no barns near the place where it had come out of the hedgerow.

Perhaps she shouldn't have said anything to Michael – kept her suspicions to herself. Mr Afton's idea that Martha might poison *him* did seem far-fetched. On the other hand, she could never have gone to the house again or eaten anything there, and how would she have explained that to Michael?

She walked on, with her usual brisk, head-up walk, as though she hadn't a care in the world. But inside she grieved. She had lost Michael Woodrow, the only man ever to pay her that sort of attention. Long before she met him she had accepted that she would die a spinster, and now she cursed herself for having let down her guard and allowed herself to grow fond of him. She should have known no good could come of it.

Lady Marlow leaned so far forward in her enthusiasm, the lace of her much tucked and puffed blouse was in danger of dipping into her tea. 'You must be so thrilled that your dear brother is back in Town! And with his delightful new wife! One quite longs to meet her.'

There was an element of question in the statement. The fashionable world had long ago decided that Lord Leake would never marry, and now he had burst back onto the scene with a young, handsome, *foreign* wife. There was some comfort in her foreignness. It would have been intolerable to have him prefer one locally grown daughter over another.

Caroline Manningtree merely smiled and sipped. She was grateful to Fergus and Giulia for driving the Sir Thomas Burton scandal, at least temporarily, from everyone's minds.

'Do they make much stay?' Lady Marlow asked.

'I believe a month or six weeks. Giulia wants to enjoy the Season before they go to Italy.'

'One hears she is *quite* the intellectual. Almost a bluestocking?' Lady Marlow was not sure whether to suggest any disapproval of this unfeminine tendency.

Lady Manningtree said, 'She's frighteningly clever to someone like me who has no brains at all, but not at all *outrée*. She loves the theatre and the opera and so on, but she loves to dance as well.'

'I'm so glad to hear it,' Lady Marlow said, seeming relieved.

Forbes opened the door at that moment and announced, 'Lady Beaminster, my lady.'

Lady Beaminster rushed in. 'My *dear* Lady Manningtree! I've just come from Lady Vane's, and all the talk is of your dear brother and Lady Leake. She is *quite* the sensation! So beautiful, so vivacious, so – Italian! And her style of dressing so new and interesting! You will laugh at me, but I quite *rave* about Lady Leake.'

'I had no idea you had met her,' Lady Marlow said, with a hint of jealousy.

Lady Beaminster sat, her pouter-pigeon front even more tucked and lacy than Lady Marlow's, her upper sleeves even fuller and more beribboned, her tilted-forward boat-shaped hat, filled to the brim with artificial flowers and berries, the very apogee of fashion.

'Oh, I haven't, but I hope to *very* soon! They have taken the Rylance house in Grosvenor Square, I understand – so charming! Edith Warminster had it for Pamela's come-out in oh-three. They had the floor of the ballroom completely re-laid for her ball because it was shockingly warped. I remember the year before *that*, poor Georgie Sargent's girl tripped and fell on it, and that was the end of their hopes of the Macclesfield boy for her, because it had to be said that she was a *large* girl and she did not fall gracefully. She *wallowed*, poor child, and it's the sort of image that sticks in the mind. He married an American girl in the end – though I suppose he might have done that anyway, because Georgie told me, in strictest confidence, that Sir Harold had been unlucky with some Russian stocks and needed to recoup. What was I saying?'

Lady Marlow picked it up. 'I do hope Lady Leake will give a ball. I suppose that is why they took Rylance House?'

'Yes, you are right,' Caroline said. 'Giulia is set on a ball—'

'Such a pretty name!' Lady Beaminster interjected. 'My dear papa favoured it for me, but there were expectations from a great-aunt, so I was named Mabel for her. And in the end nothing came of it, and she left her fortune to a hospital – such a mistake! Family must come first, don't you think? The sick we have always with us – isn't that in the Bible? I've never liked the name Mabel. But Julia – I'm surprised they have such an English name in Italy.'

'Spelled differently, I believe,' Lady Marlow said, catching at the narrative as it sped by. She had her own agenda, and carried on determinedly. 'Now, Caroline dear, I hope you will put in a word for me and persuade them to come to my little soirée next week.'

'No, no, I've come specifically to ask you to bring them to *my* card evening,' Lady Beaminster interrupted. 'It's too bad of you, Marjorie!'

Lady Marlow ignored the outburst. 'The Argylls said they might drop in, and you know how artistic they are. Princess Louise is so clever. I think it would be nice for them to meet someone of superior intellect for a change.'

Lady Beaminster felt there was an insult somewhere in there, and was silent while she ferreted it out.

Caroline Manningtree was firm. 'I'm afraid I have no influence over their diary. Giulia is very strong-minded and Fergus, of course, wants nothing but to please her.'

'Quite proper,' said Lady Marlow. Lord Marlow, who would always sooner have sat in his own study with the newspaper in the evening than venture into someone else's house, nevertheless put on full fig and meekly followed his wife wherever she decreed they should be seen.

'But I'll mention that the Argylls will be there,' Caroline went on. 'I expect Fergus would like Giulia to meet them.'

'Thank you, dear,' said Lady Marlow.

Lady Beaminster reached the end of her thought process. 'I do think *too much* intellect is a mistake in a female. A gentleman does not like to be shown up in front of others.'

'Indeed,' said Lady Marlow. 'No *real* lady would ever be contentious in company. But it is quite possible to have intellect and be graceful about it.'

Lady Beaminster was baffled again.

Giles had plenty of work to do: the farms to ride around; agent, bailiff, gamekeeper, woodsman and tenants to interview; neighbours and village worthies to keep in touch with. And in the evenings there were letters to answer, agricultural matters to study, books and articles to read. But the fact was that as the days accumulated he found himself noticing that he was alone in the house. When it was full, he was constantly seeking escape. But it was one thing to want solitude, another to have it thrust upon him.

His appetite, never very robust, quailed at eating alone at a large table: he felt he might drown in that lake of polished mahogany. He took to having his meals on a tray in the library; but still he had to endure being consulted about them every day. When Kitty was there, she gave orders to Mrs Webster every morning, choosing things she knew he would like. He appreciated now what a burden that took from his shoulders. Early summer's fresh vegetables and soft fruits were coming in, the things you longed for all through winter and spring, but it took the joy away to have to make decisions. Talking about food was the worst possible prelude to eating it.

He had forgotten about the only other occupants of the house – his niece and nephew, Linda's children – because he never saw them. Then one day when he came in from a farm visit, Afton intercepted him in the hall. 'I beg your pardon, my lord. We seem to have a crisis.'

'What sort of crisis?' he asked tersely. He noticed the governess, Miss Kettel, lurking behind Afton; and behind her, Arabella.

'Young Lord Cordwell seems to have gone missing, my lord,' said Afton. He beckoned Miss Kettel forward.

'We were having a lesson in astronomy,' she explained. 'I was only absent for a moment, to get a ball out of the cupboard to represent the planet Mars, and when I returned, he had gone.'

'We searched the house, my lord,' Afton said, 'in case he was hiding, but one of the stable boys, Bobby, thought he saw him on the track going out towards Crown Woods.'

'Have you sent anyone out to look for him?' Giles asked.

'Not yet, my lord. I've only just heard.'

Giles cursed very softly, then called Arabella forward. She had just turned ten, and was a plain child, with a nose too big for her face, and freckles, and impossible mouse-coloured hair that never looked smooth. Her stout, undeveloped body was packed into an unbecoming dress of dull red-brown stuff. She had a look of her mother about her. Her late father had been quite a handsome man, but unluckily she hadn't taken after him.

'What's all this about?' he asked her. Her eyes slid about. 'Where is Arthur? I know you know something.' He grabbed her shoulders, not roughly, but with intent. 'Where has he gone? You must tell me. He's only a little boy. He could get into trouble, he could be hurt. You're older than him, you're supposed to look after him.'

'I told him not to,' she said, defending herself.

'Arabella!' Miss Kettel said in shocked tones. 'You told me you knew nothing about it.'

She wriggled out of Giles's grip. 'Can I go out riding now?'

'There'll be no more riding for you if you don't tell me everything,' Giles said. 'Where has he gone?'

She sighed, then said, in a mutter, 'He's run away.'

It took patient questioning to prise the story out of her. They had been reading the story of Dick Whittington, and he had decided to emulate the hero and run away to London, where the streets were paved with gold, to seek his fortune. 'Only he didn't have a cat,' Arabella said. 'So he was going to take Goosebumps.'

Giles looked at Afton.

'The boy Bobby saw was on foot,' Afton said. 'I'll check with the stables if Goosebumps is missing.'

Giles turned back to Arabella. 'London's a long way. What did he take with him?'

'He wanted to make a bundle on a stick like in the picture,

but he couldn't make it stay on, so he put things in his pockets. His pen-knife and catapult and some biscuits and Pepper.'

'He took pepper with him?' Giles was, baffled. 'What on earth for?'

Miss Kettel intervened. 'It's a toy pig made of felt. He's never parted from it.'

'We must organise a search,' Giles said, with a sigh. 'Probably he hasn't got far. If he was heading for Crown Woods he was going in the wrong direction anyway.'

'I'm so sorry, my lord,' Miss Kettel said, twisting her hands together. 'I really only turned my back for a moment.'

'I've heard he's getting too much for you to handle,' Giles said.

'He's a good boy really,' she said. 'But restless. They lead such confined lives,' she added, in a low voice so that Arabella, who was patting the dogs, wouldn't hear.

Giles's nostrils flared as he detected a criticism. 'Let's concentrate on finding the boy first. Then we can look into the children's situation. And your role in all this.'

He saw her blanch as he turned away, and was not sorry. This was her fault entirely.

The pony, Goosebumps, was not missing: evidently Arthur had been unable to extract him from the busy stable yard. Every horse was now utilised with all the grooms and boys riding, while the footmen and house boys went out on foot. Everyone they passed was to be put on alert, all the farmers told to keep an eye out for the boy, especially as it started to get dark – he would probably seek shelter somewhere.

Giles went out on Vipsania, his road horse, and passed from a state of annoyance to a state of worry. Arthur was a very small boy, not yet nine years old, and had never been out on his own, as far as Giles knew. Miss Kettel was right: the children were too much confined. A boy ought to be roaming the fields and exploring with his dog at his heels, as he had been at Arthur's age with his spaniel Buffy. But Arthur, of course, was not on his own estate, which had been sold when his bankrupt father died. There was no reason for him to learn every inch of Ashmore, which would never be his.

He rode out past Crown Woods and towards Motte Woods, calling in at Hillbrow Farm to pass the word and ask if anyone had seen him. Then, reaching Motte Woods, he thought to call on Axe Brandom, his woodsman, who had a cottage there.

A small terrier ran out and barked as he rode into the beaten-earth yard, and the woodsman came out from his saw-pit, sawdust on his shoulders and leather apron.

'Afternoon, my lord,' he said, and stood and waited for Giles to explain his visit. He was, Giles thought, the most extraordinarily *still* man he'd ever known. There was never any unnecessary movement, no wasted words: most people chattered and fidgeted, but Axe listened and observed, then acted, neatly and efficiently. It was no wonder animals loved him: Giles had observed him sometimes when he had worked at the village smithy, and had seen the most skittish horse grow quiet in his hands.

'My nephew has gone missing, Brandom,' Giles explained. 'Told his sister he was running away to London to seek his fortune, but he was seen heading this way. He's only eight years old and not country wise.'

Axe said, 'I haven't seen him, my lord. But I'll keep an eye out. Or would you like me to search the area?'

'Yes, if you will. I've got everyone I can out, on foot and on horseback. He was last seen by Crown Woods heading in this direction.'

'I don't think he's in my woods. I've heard no disturbance,' said Axe. 'A tired boy would likely head downhill.' He looked at the sky. 'Some showers coming over. He'll try and shelter.'

'Yes, check any outbuildings.'

'I'll go out on my horse, my lord, cover more ground.'

'Thanks,' said Giles, and turned Vipsania. He felt oddly comforted that Axe Brandom was going to look – as though that made all the difference! It was the quality of the man, he thought, to reassure.

When Vipsania was tired he headed back to the Castle, hoping he would find a tear-stained and chastened boy being simultaneously comforted and scolded by the females of the house. But Giddins, the head man, took Vipsania's rein from him as he dismounted and said there was no news yet. When he went into the hall, Afton confirmed the negative. 'Should I send down to the village, my lord, and inform the police?'

'Might be as well,' Giles said. It was a very big world out there, and it would start to get dark soon. Inwardly he cursed his sister for abandoning her children to him. Hadn't he enough unwanted responsibility with the estate? Afton was looking at him with sympathy, but he felt suddenly lonely. There was no-one to share the burden with him. Even Kitty had gone off to London to enjoy herself.

'We'll find him, my lord,' Afton said.

'Will we? How many trees are there in Buckinghamshire, do you think? How many miles of hedges, acres of field?'

Afton had no answer to that. He said, 'Shall I have water sent up for a bath, my lord? You've been in the saddle for a long time.'

This was about the time of day when Giles usually paid a visit to the nursery. But Kitty had taken the boys with her to London. No comfort there. 'I suppose a bath is the next best thing,' he said wearily.

In the morning Giles woke to no news. He began really to worry. Not just a lost boy, now, but possibly an injured or dead boy. There were so many hazards out there for an unwary small child – quarries and bogs and rivers – and he'd been without food and shelter through the night. He felt a twinge of conscience that he resented but could not ignore. When Afton came to wake him he said he would take his breakfast upstairs with Arabella and Miss Kettel.

When he had addressed the staff and arranged for the search parties to go out again, he climbed to the top of the house, expecting to find Arabella frightened and tearful. But she seemed unaffected by her brother's absence – perhaps she hadn't the imagination to think him in danger. She was excited by the novelty of Giles sitting down to breakfast with them, not to mention the dogs, and prattled away to him, once she had got over her tongue-tied shyness. But he could see that Miss Kettel appreciated the gesture. Apart from natural anxiety for her charge, she must be thinking she was sure to be dismissed for losing him.

Giles spent another day in the saddle, wearyingly unproductive. Flocks of small clouds like floating sheep passed across the sky, clustering together now and then to drop brief showers of thin rain, making Vipsania lay back her ears and fidget. The paths became slippery, but quickly dried when the sun came out again. Everything smelt wet, green and fertile. The Ashmore bull, Roderick, was out in a field with some of his wives, and turned to face Giles as he passed. He stamped a warning hoof, but the grass was too delicious to waste time being bullish, and he soon returned to it.

Up at the top of the hill, on Topheath land, real sheep scampered away from him, with the ability of their kind to be startled today by the same thing that had startled them yesterday. He stopped and dismounted to give Vipsania a breather. From the crest he could look down the Ash Valley one way and the Wye valley the other. He could barely see a man-made structure, only the top of a distant church spire poking above the treeline, and a thread of smoke from someone's chimney. He saw only miles and miles of rolling, thickly wooded hills, looking much as they must have in every century past since the ice retreated: intensely green, so green they almost hurt the eye; silent, massively indifferent to man's petty concerns. How would you ever find one small child in all that?

Home again, and little as he wanted to, he was working out in his mind how to phrase a letter to Linda and his mother. But as he turned in at the stable yard he sensed the atmosphere even before Giddins hurried up to catch Vipsania's rein.

'News, my lord!' he cried.

'He's been found?' Giles said, heart lifting as he swung his leg over the cantle and jumped down.

'A message come in just now, my lord, a boy sent by Axe Brandom. Says he's found young Lord Cordwell, but he needs help, and to bring shovels and rope.'

'What on earth for?'

Giddens looked anxious. 'I couldn't rightly say, my lord. The boy wasn't clear about it – too young to carry a message right, but I s'pose he was all Axe could find.'

'And where are we to send ropes and shovels to?' Giles asked, patience fraying.

'The motte, my lord. I've got the pony harnessed to one of the carts and we're loading what we think might be needed, but I'm at a bit of a loss, my lord, not knowing what to expect.'

'Very well, I'll go with it myself. Throw in some forks and a mallet as well, and an axe. And get some blankets from the house, and a flask of brandy – ask Mr Afton. I'll take six men – whoever you think best.'

Giddins selected five of the grooms, and a stable boy, Oscar. Afton came out himself with the blankets and brandy, and was also carrying a canvas bag and a first-aid box from below stairs. Giles eyed it and said, 'Good thought, though I hope to God we don't need it. What's in the bag?'

'Food and water, my lord. He's been out for some time. And I'll come too, if I may, my lord.' Giles looked a query, and he said, 'I have some knowledge of first aid. In case it's needed.'

'Come, if you like.' Giles turned away, preparing to mount his tired horse.

The day was declining, but the sky had cleared. To the west, the last of the sheep-clouds, their fleeces now edged with rose and gold, were streaming away towards a plum-indigo bar that floated like a distant island in a transparent sea. Giles kept his mind away from useless speculation about what they might find that required shovels and ropes. The grooms trudged along beside the cart, hardly talking – they had been on horseback all day, but walking was at least a change of exercise. Now and then there was the scratch of a lucifer and the sneeze-sharp tang of first-lit tobacco. Someone coughed. Someone cursed softly when he tripped on a tussock. The harness creaked rhythmically as the pony Biscuit plodded along; now and then a horseshoe rang on a stone, a wheel rattled as it jolted over it.

The motte reared up, the top black against the pale, clean sky. Axe Brandom had been sitting at the foot of it, and now stood – a lesser man would have waved in relief. His eyes checked the men, the cart, and what he could see of its contents. Giles halted Vipsania and Axe came to her; she sighed and rested her nose against his chest. Over her ears he addressed Giles.

''Twas my bitch found him, my lord. I wondered what she was after, scrabbling at a rabbit hole, then I heard him cry out.'

'Rabbit hole?' Arthur was a small child, but too big for any rabbit hole.

'There's something deeper below,' Axe said. 'Reckon it might be the dungeons of the old castle. The lad must have tried to get under the bush to shelter for the night, and the earth gave way, and down he went. The roots've probably loosened it enough and it's fallen in. I could just see him before the light got worse. He's down a good six feet. Reckon he's hurt himself. Can't climb out on his own, so someone'll have to go down there.'

'Hence the rope,' Giles said out loud.

'And the hole needs to be made bigger.'

'Is he conscious?'

'I've been talking to him, trying to jolly him along,' said Axe. 'He's scared, o' course. I can't make out from him how bad he's hurt.'

'Let's get to work,' Giles said.

CHAPTER FOURTEEN

It was awkward to get at the place and they had to chop down and then pull the bush out entirely, which caused an alarming-sounding fall of earth and stones inside the hole. Once that was out of the way, it was clear enough to see what had happened. Much activity by rabbits plus the roots of the bushes had loosened the earth, and whatever had formed the ceiling of the space below had collapsed. It didn't take long to enlarge the hole, and Giles knelt down carefully and peered in. The light was failing, and it was hard to see much, but there was a stone-flagged floor below, and he could see a glimpse of stone walls as well. Definitely some kind of ancient chamber. His archaeological senses shivered at the thought of exploring what had not been entered in hundreds of years.

Arthur was a huddled shape, and a white face turning upwards. 'Arthur, it's Uncle Giles,' he called. 'We're going to get you out. Don't be afraid. I'm coming down to get you.'

The boy only made a whimpering noise. God knew how long he had been down there. He had probably feared he would never be found. It was not surprising that speech had abandoned him.

They tied the end of the rope to the cart's axle, with two men to take the strain of the descent. He didn't want to put too much pull on the axle – it was an old cart, and they'd need it to get the boy home.

Afton said, 'I'll go down, if you'll permit me, my lord.'
'Why you?'

'I'm smaller than you, my lord, and lighter to pull up. And,' he added, when Giles was about to argue, 'I know a bit about first aid.'

Giles locked eyes with him, then his shoulders went down. 'I suppose that makes sense. Go on, then.'

Afton lowered himself carefully through the hole, hand over hand down the rope. There was an anxious wait with nothing but small noises and a murmuring voice down below. Then he appeared under the hole, face turned up, and called quietly. 'I think we've got a broken leg down here. I'll need to splint it before we move him. Can you find some stout lengths of wood?'

Giles sent two men to cut some branches, glad they'd brought an axe. 'How is he otherwise?' he called down to Afton.

'Very cold, frightened out of his wits. I'll have the blankets and the brandy now, please.'

Dusk came on while the quiet endeavours went on around the hole. In the woods a tawny owl called, and was answered from another stand of trees, the sound haunting on the chilly darkling air. Biscuit sighed and eased his weight, and blew at Vipsania, who was standing nose-to-nose with him. Giles threw one of the blankets over the mare's back. One of the men offered him a cigarette but he refused.

Then Afton called up that he was ready. The problem was how to get the boy up without hurting him. Afton said the best way was for him to hold the child and for them to be pulled up together.

Axe said, 'We got six men. And horse power.'

So they unhitched Biscuit and Axe fixed the rope to his collar. Afton tied his end round himself, clasped the child tightly against his body. All of them took a place on the rope as if they were about to play tug-of-war, Oscar at Biscuit's head clicked and led him forward, and slowly but without much difficulty they hauled Afton up. The trickiest bit was at the top. While the pony and three of the men kept the rope taut, the others knelt by the hole and got hold of Arthur to manoeuvre him out. A shrill cry told them it had hurt him, but then Axe was rising to his feet with the blanket-wrapped bundle safe in his arms. They lowered Afton again to collect the first-aid box, and then got him out.

'How did you manage to see down there?' Giles asked.

'It seems darker when you're outside looking in than when you're inside looking out,' Afton said, brushing loose soil from his sleeves. 'The poor little lad's very shocked, but I don't think too badly hurt. Someone should go ahead and prepare them at the house, and have the doctor sent for.'

'Yes,' said Giles. He put the stable boy up on Vipsania and sent him off at a trot. Afton got into the cart and held Arthur, and the little procession set off again. The path was only visible as a whitish line between what were now the black stretches of the grass.

Dr Welkes had set the leg and administered a draught, and Arthur was sleeping heavily, with hot-water bottles and extra blankets.

'One or two scratches and bruises. Luckily children tend to fall easily. It was bad luck about the leg, but it could have been much worse – you say the drop was about six feet?'

'More like ten. Afton couldn't reach the hole at full stretch. Did the child say anything to you while you were treating him, about what happened?'

'He didn't speak at all. Shock, I think. He must have been very frightened, quite apart from the pain. The leg should heal normally. Your man did a good job of splinting it. I wish everyone understood first aid. The times I've attended accidents where well-meaning people have made things worse. What I'm more worried about is that he got so cold, and was without food for so long. I'm afraid he might take a fever. Better have someone sit up with him tonight.'

Afton and Mrs Webster went to the nursery after locking up, and found Miss Kettel anxious. 'He woke screaming a little while ago. Didn't know where he was – thought he was still in the hole.'

'He looks feverish,' Mrs Webster said. The little face was flushed, and he moved restlessly. As they watched, he opened his eyes, glassy with fever, and made a hoarse sound, before closing them again.

'Dr Welkes left a draught to give him. Can you help me?' said Miss Kettel.

'I will,' said Afton. He raised the boy and Miss Kettel managed to get some of it down the unwilling throat. Then he laid him down again and drew the covers over him.

'You're very good at that,' Mrs Webster remarked.

'Oh, I like children,' he said. 'I used to help with the little ones at the workhouse.'

Miss Kettel threw him a curious glance – no-one but Mrs Webster knew about his origins – but had no thoughts to spare just then. They watched as the child slipped into a heavier sleep. 'I won't leave him tonight,' the governess said, as if to herself.

Arabella appeared in the doorway in her nightgown. 'Is he all right?' she asked, in a small, plaintive voice.

'Go back to bed, Arabella,' Miss Kettel said automatically.

'Is he going to die?'

'No, of course not.'

She stared past the governess at the small shape in the bed. 'He said nobody wanted him. It's true, isn't it?' Her eyes filled with tears. 'Daddy's dead, and Mother's gone away. She never wants to see us. One of the boys called him a beggar. We're both beggars, aren't we?'

'Take her back to bed,' Afton said quietly to Miss Kettel. 'I'll stay with the boy.'

When they were gone, he said to Mrs Webster, 'It's true. Nobody wants them, poor creatures. I know a bit about not being wanted. How can their mother abandon them like that? I suppose my mother was destitute, but Lady Linda—'

Mrs Webster put a warning hand on his arm. 'Not our business to wonder. And I have warned you about mentioning the workhouse.'

He sighed angrily. 'I think I was better off, when all's said and done, than this scrap. Lord Cordwell, indeed! At least I knew what I was from the start.'

Mrs Webster did not want to discuss imponderables. 'It's a nuisance, Lady Stainton taking the nursery staff to London. There's no-one in the house used to looking after children. Miss Kettel oughtn't to do it alone.'

'I'll sit up with him,' Afton said. 'Miss Kettel and I can relieve each other.' Mrs Webster hesitated, as if wondering whether she should volunteer as well, but he said, 'You need your sleep. Go along. A valet gets used to sitting up – all those late nights waiting for the master to come home.'

Having taken the earliest train, Richard arrived the next day while the doctor was still upstairs. He was talking to Giles in the hall when Welkes came down.

'How is he?' Giles asked.

'He's very ill,' Welkes said. 'His fever is increasing and he's not aware of his surroundings. The governess says he woke crying out several times in the night. I'm afraid it may turn into pneumonia. He got so cold and damp down in the cellar that it opened his body to extreme infections.'

'Infections?' Giles said. 'Should he be isolated?'

'I don't think he's a danger to anyone but himself,' said Welkes.

'What's the treatment?'

'There's nothing that can be done, except for expert

nursing. The governess has no medical training, and she has the little girl to look after.'

'Should I hire a trained nurse?'

'You would need a day nurse *and* a night nurse,' Welkes said. 'He must be watched twenty-four hours a day. It will be expensive.'

Giles flushed slightly. 'The expense does not signify,' he snapped. 'Please put it in hand at once.'

'Very well,' said Welkes. 'He's sleeping now, and I've given Miss Kettel another draught for him for later. I'll come back this afternoon.'

When he had gone, Richard turned to Giles. 'What was that about?'

'What?'

'The irritation at the mention of expense?'

Giles stared at the floor for a moment, then said in a low voice, 'Afton told me something when he came to wake me this morning. Looking like hell, by the way, having sat up with the boy all night.'

'Noble fellow! What did he tell you?'

'That the reason Arthur ran away was that he felt nobody wanted him.'

Richard raised his eyebrows. 'Well, I suppose he's right. Our dear sister never had any time for them. It's very sad, but hardly your fault. You've given them a home.'

'Much against my will. And I don't have any time for them, either. I've been alone in the house since everyone went to London, and forgot entirely that they were upstairs.'

'All the same,' Richard said, 'I don't see why it's your responsibility. You feed and house them, what more could anyone ask?'

Giles shook his head, then said, 'Do you know why Afton sat up all night with Arthur?'

'I did wonder. Not a butler-valet's job.'

'It's because he was a foundling. Left on the steps of the workhouse.'

'I didn't know.'

'Don't spread it about. I shouldn't like it to be the subject of gossip. His mother abandoned him presumably because she couldn't feed him and one has to assume his father would never own him, if he ever knew about him. Abandoned as an infant nobody wanted. He was fed and housed by a beneficent state. He knows the difference between charity and being given a home.'

Richard clapped a hand on his shoulder. 'I see you've got a bad case of conscience, but I don't see what you can do about it, beyond what you already do. You've two sons of your own to raise and provide for. You can't adopt Linda's brat.'

'He's my nephew.'

'Mine too, but he's not haunting my dreams.'

Giles scowled. 'What are you doing here, anyway?'

'I came to see how you're coping, of course. Then it's back to Town for Uncle Fergus's ball on Saturday.'

'But you're staying tonight?'

'I was thinking of it. By the way, why did your butler ask me *where* I wanted to eat this evening, rather than *whether* I did?'

'I've been taking my meals on a tray.'

'Letting standards slide in your misery?'

'I'm not miserable,' Giles said impatiently. 'There doesn't seem any point in laying the dining-room for one, that's all.'

'Just because one is *en garçon* it doesn't mean one has to live like a hermit. Whatever next? Will you grow a great beard and fingernails like bird's claws and mutter to yourself and keep the shutters closed all day? You had better come back to Town with me when I go.'

'I can't leave while Arthur is ill.'

'You're not a trained nurse, what can you do? Children

have these ups and downs, he'll be better in a day or two, you'll see. Don't make a drama of it. And you can't miss Uncle's ball.'

'I can't think of anything I'd sooner miss.'

'It would look like a snub. Now I'm off to see a few people. I won't be here for luncheon but I'll be back in time to dress.'

'Dress?'

'I am not prepared to eat on a tray, even for my nearest and dearest. We shall have a proper dinner, at a proper dinner table, properly dressed, like civilised men. And I want a good bottle of wine, too – tell Afton. I promise you'll feel much better afterwards. You're too inclined to brood.'

'Brood? I'm not a hen!'

'You're all too prone to think yourself hard-done-by and sink into impenetrable gloom. You don't have my cheerful, outgoing character that leaps over obstacles like a particularly lighthearted mountain goat.'

'I can't think about food when that poor child—'

'Will your not eating do him the slightest good? No. It's pure self-indulgence on your part. A proper dinner – and you will come up to Town, if not with me then at least for the ball. It's your duty, and we know what a whale you are on duty.'

Giles turned his head and looked instinctively towards the staircase, thinking of the troubles at the top of the house. But it only made him aware of how large and how empty it was – and it would seem even emptier when Richard had departed. 'I also have a duty to my nephew,' he said stiffly. 'But I will come if he's better by then.'

'I could ask no more,' said Richard.

'He is a lot better,' Afton said, opening the wardrobe. 'The Lovat tweed, my lord? He's sitting up, though he's very weak, and he's taken some nourishment.'

'The fever's gone?'

'It comes and goes. And he has a troublesome cough. But, on the whole, Dr Welkes is quite pleased with his progress.' He frowned to himself, remembering that Sister Sturgeon had not seemed so sanguine. She'd said, after the doctor had gone, that she didn't like the look of that young man at all. But she seemed like someone naturally inclined to pessimism. Plump Sister Ogden, the night nurse, was more cheerful, cooed over the boy, stroked his hair, said what a good little soldier he was and promised him he'd be out of bed in no time. The good little soldier liked her much better than his unsmiling day nurse.

Giles, getting out of bed, did not see the brief frown. He said, 'If he's going on satisfactorily, I think I might go up to Town. I ought really to pay my uncle the attention. It will be expected.'

'Very good, my lord.' He smiled. 'It will be pleasant for you to see her ladyship again. And the children.'

Giles smiled too. 'Louis will certainly be glad to see *you*.'

'The pleasure will be mutual, my lord.'

Kitty was sitting in the low nursing chair with Alexander in her lap, watching Louis play on the floor with his Noah's Ark. Nanny Pawley was pottering about in the background and the maid Jessie was sitting sewing. Giles paused in the doorway a moment to take in the scene. The nursery at Aunt Caroline's house was much smaller than that at the Castle, but was very pleasant, with a skylight as well as windows, making it light and sunny, fresh cream paint on the walls and pretty apple-green curtains. And Kitty was smiling contentedly, looking absurdly young to be the mother of two.

She glanced up and saw him. The smile faded and she eyed him cautiously for a moment, then said neutrally, 'I didn't know you were here.'

'I've only just arrived,' he said.

Louis saw his father, and his face lit. 'Daddy!' he shouted.

'Hello, my boy.' Giles stooped to ruffle his hair.

But he was more interested in his toy than endearments. 'Look, Daddy, I've got a nelephant, and a camble, and a draff!'

'Only one of each?' Giles murmured. 'Rather a miscalculation, surely?'

'And a stripy horse, too.'

While Louis happily displayed his treasures, his parents carried on a conversation over his head. 'I wasn't sure you would come,' Kitty said. 'Uncle Fergus was asking yesterday and I had to say I didn't know.'

'You saw him yesterday?'

'We all went to the theatre. To see *The Scarlet Pimpernel*.'

'Did you enjoy it?'

'*I* did, very much. Uncle Fergus dozed through quite a bit of it.'

'It is hard to stay awake in a theatre. Particularly when one has dined well.'

'He applauded loudly at the end.' She hesitated. 'Giulia was very critical. She said the story was unbelievable, that it was impossible for Lady Blakeney not to recognise her own husband.'

'It was a long time ago,' Giles offered. 'Perhaps people of rank led very separate lives back then.'

'Oh, have you seen it?'

'I've read the book.'

'I didn't know there was a book.'

'There is.'

Conversation stuttered to a halt. Nanny, perhaps sensing something, came and took Alexander out of Kitty's arms. Louis was deeply involved with the Flood, mumbling a narrative as he moved the animals and figures about – 'They went up here and round there and down there and he went smack smack with his stick and the camble ran away and they all ran after him . . .'

Kitty stood up and moved to the window and Giles followed her. 'I didn't think you'd come,' she said, in a low voice, staring out at the tops of the trees.

'I couldn't let Uncle down.'

'Oh, you couldn't let *Uncle* down,' she said bitterly.

'Kitty—'

'After all these weeks, that's what you decided. You didn't even want to know how the children were.'

'I knew they were all right. They were with you,' he said. She looked up at the tone of his voice, doubtful. 'They were lucky.'

She didn't speak, waiting for more.

'I missed you,' he said.

'But not enough,' she said.

He gathered himself. It had to be done. 'Kitty, I'm sorry. I behaved like a fool, and a brute. I said things I shouldn't have said.'

'But you meant them,' she said, and it was only half a question; half an epitaph.

He ran a frustrated hand through his hair. 'How can I explain? It's such a responsibility, such a burden, I sometimes feel as if I'm shackled to a great weight and I can't get free. It makes me angry. But I shouldn't show my anger to you.'

'You don't show me anything,' she said very quietly. 'I thought married people were supposed to share their feelings. But, then, I'm middle-class, I know. Perhaps it's different for people like us.'

He winced. 'Don't. I never thought that. Please forgive me, Kitty. I was worried and I overreacted and there's no excuse, but forgive me anyway. And you can have your garden.' She looked up quickly, and he added, 'Not all of it. Not the earth-moving part. That really is more than I can afford. There's so much still to do to get the estate on a sure footing. But you can make a start. When you come home we'll look at the costs, perhaps have your garden man back, and decide which parts we can afford. We'll decide *together*. And when Richard's milk scheme is running at a profit, we'll see about the rest.'

She regarded him for a long, searching minute. But by 'the rest' she realised he meant the rest of the garden plan. He was not referring to married people sharing their feelings. When she went home, nothing would really have changed.

'I see,' she said in a flat voice.

'Will you forgive me?' he pressed.

'There's nothing to forgive,' she said, and it was true, in the sense that he was who he was, and she couldn't change that.

He seemed to realise that a harmonic was missing from the absolution, and was about to say something more when Afton came in and the dressing bell sounded at the same moment.

'Time to change, my lord,' Afton said. There was no need for him to come and announce it, but the real reason for his presence was made clear when Louis jumped up and ran to him with a glad greeting, grabbed his hand and tugged him towards the Ark to have him join the play.

He didn't jump up when I came in, Giles noted. And for some reason thought of poor little Arthur.

So that the visit to Town should not be entirely wasted, Giles went out early on Saturday morning and was able to have an interview with Vogel, his man of business, about the state of his finances. They were in better health even than he had hoped, and Vogel expressed himself cautiously pleased. Giles raised the matter of Kitty's garden plan, and when he mentioned the cost, Vogel shook his head.

'Those sorts of schemes were all very well a hundred years ago, or a hundred and fifty. The landed peers of those times were blessed with vast amounts of capital, and labour was cheap. But the world is a different place now. I venture to suggest that the great gardens like Stowe and Blenheim and Highclere could not be replicated today without the sort of fortune that only American railway barons amass.'

'That's what I thought,' Giles said.

Vogel cocked his head, and the light glinted off his gold-rimmed spectacles, which he wore at the end of his nose. 'Lady Stainton's ambitions for Ashmore Castle are laudable, and were they carried out, they would create something magnificent that would stand for ever, like Chatsworth, perhaps, on a smaller scale. But . . .'

'I am not a duke,' Giles finished for him.

'The great gardens at Chatsworth have been developed over hundreds of years. And the present duke, I believe, employs forty or fifty gardeners. I am sorry to say the Ashmore estate is not, if I may put it so, in that class.'

Giles smiled. 'I wish her ladyship had heard all that from you. It might have softened the blow.'

Back at Aunt Caroline's house he became aware that he was following another visitor up the stairs, and arrived in the drawing-room to see Kitty, Aunt Caroline and Grandmère staring at Uncle Sebastian.

'You've been away a long time,' Giles said, when they were all settled. 'I can't remember exactly when it was that you left. Have you been in Henley all that time?'

'Most of it,' Sebastian said.

'You're looking very well,' Aunt Caroline interrupted. 'And your suit . . .' She circled a hand to indicate the *tout ensemble*. 'Is it new? Not your usual style, but very becoming.'

'Oh, I thought a change was overdue,' Sebastian said.

Grandmère gave him a suspicious look. 'A gentleman settles his mode on reaching maturity. There is no purpose in "a change" . . .' her tone mocked the expression. '. . . unless he has a change of audience.'

'Audience?' Aunt Caroline said. 'What can you mean? He is not an actor.'

'All men are actors,' Grandmère said. 'Some are charlatans and mountebanks.'

'I say, steady on,' Sebastian objected.

'But I think what we have here is an illusionist.'

Sebastian remained composed. 'No illusion, I promise you. The change goes all the way through.'

'What is her name?' Grandmère demanded.

'Which "her" are we referring to?' Aunt Caroline asked, not keeping up at all. 'Oh dear, I wish everyone would speak plainly.'

'There is a woman in the case,' Grandmère said, her eyes not shifting a fraction from Sebastian's face. 'Note the new necktie. The hair, cut recently and to a new style.'

'I *thought* there was something different, apart from the suit,' Aunt Caroline exclaimed, as though the riddle was now untangled.

'And an odour of Muelhens entered the room with him,' Grandmère concluded. '*Il ne lui manque qu'un gardénia à la boutonnière!*'

'But how exciting,' Aunt Caroline exclaimed, catching Grandmère's meaning at last. 'Is there really someone, Sebastian? Is that what you've come to tell us? Oh, who is she? When may we meet her?'

'Yes, there is someone,' Sebastian said, massively patient before the inquisition. 'And you may meet her as soon as you wish.'

'But how sly you have been!' Aunt Caroline said. 'We never knew a thing about it until now. She must be very special to have won your heart, a bachelor all these years – and an eligible bachelor into the bargain. I've known several very nice females who would have been glad to have you. What is her name, the dear creature?'

'Dory,' said Sebastian.

Giles frowned. 'That's an odd name. Is she a foreigner?'

'It's short for Dorcas.'

'That is not a lady's name,' Grandmère decreed.

Kitty looked up. 'We had a maid called Dory. The sewing maid. She left us quite suddenly.' She stopped abruptly, with a startled look, and could not go on.

'Obviously it's not the same person,' Giles told her impatiently, then saw Sebastian's expression. 'You can't have come to tell us that you are romancing a housemaid?'

'No, I've come to tell you I am to be married to a woman whom I love very much.'

'Married?' cried Aunt Caroline. 'But surely not to— She's surely not a—'

'*Mon dieu, quelle farce,*' Grandmère muttered.

'Oh, Uncle, how lovely!' Kitty said bravely, remembering how kind he had always been, and how she had not been deemed worthy of Giles by her mother-in-law.

Giles said slowly, 'Let me be clear. You want to *marry* one of my servants? Why on earth would you do that?' His eyebrows went up. 'Were you interfering with her? In my house?'

Sebastian rose to his feet. 'I am very fond of you, Giles, and I believe you have had a hard row to hoe in many ways, but if you ever speak in that way again, I shall strike you.'

Aunt Caroline said anxiously, 'No, no, we don't mean to be unkind, Sebastian dear, but are you really going to *marry* her? When? How?'

'On Monday at eleven o'clock, at St Luke's Church in Chelsea. She's been staying in a hotel in Sydney Street for the three weeks while the banns were read. I've been at my club,' he added, with a hard look at Giles.

'But – but why all the secrecy?' Aunt Caroline asked.

He spread his hands. 'Because I anticipated exactly the sort of reception you've just given me.'

'Well, what do you expect?' Giles said roughly.

'I hoped that you might be happy for me. She is the daughter of a respectable tradesperson, and only undeserved ill fortune forced her to go into service. She makes me very happy, and I hope to use my own position to make her happy in return. And I will bring her to visit you if you can be trusted to treat her as a lady should be treated.'

Kitty said, 'I am very happy for you, Uncle, and I would really like to meet her. Well, I mean, I've met her, of course. At Ashmore. Obviously. She seemed . . . seems . . . She does wonderful work! Invisible stitches. And she was very kind to me when I tripped on that hole in the carpet—' She stopped, confused, afraid she had not helped matters.

'Which she subsequently mended, if I'm not mistaken,' Giles concluded. 'Really, Uncle, can you honestly propose bringing her as your wife to Ashmore, where she was a servant?'

'That's up to you,' Sebastian said. 'I have no need of you, or Ashmore. I have my own house, my own fortune. You need never see either of us again. I only wanted to give you the opportunity to behave graciously. Any one of you who wishes may come to the wedding. We will go away on honeymoon directly afterwards. When we come back, you may acknowledge us, or not, as you please.' He turned to leave, then turned back. 'Has none of you ever been in love? When you love someone, it doesn't matter who they are. You ought to know that. Shame on you, all of you. I'll see myself out.'

He left a silence behind. Kitty was tearful, Aunt Caroline uncomfortable, Giles grimly thoughtful.

Grandmère said, 'I suppose it cannot signify a great deal who Sebastian marries. He is not in society.'

Kitty looked hopeful. 'So you will receive her? Be nice to her?'

She wrinkled her nose. 'Nice? Oh, that word! Perhaps one day it might be possible. Giles is right, you cannot walk out of the back door as a servant and come straight in at the front. There must be time for edges to be worn smooth. Timing is everything.'

Richard came in, followed by Forbes.

'Luncheon is served, my lady,' Forbes announced to Aunt Caroline.

'Was that Uncle Sebastian I saw leaving?' Richard asked.

'I'll tell you everything over luncheon,' Kitty promised.

'I suppose we must be grateful he did not propose to bring her to the ball this evening,' Grandmère said.

'Bring who?' Richard asked.

'Oh, that ball!' Giles exclaimed, rolling his eyes in despair. 'For one comfortable moment I'd forgotten about it.'

'I'm looking forward to it,' Kitty said, in a small voice. 'And I know the girls are.'

Dory was waiting on a bench in Berkeley Square's central garden. She stood up, seeing his expression as he approached. She put her hands into his. 'No good?'

'I'm afraid it will be just you and me at our wedding.'

'I'm sorry to be the cause of a rift with your family,' she said.

'You're not the cause. It's their bone-headed stupidity that's to blame. I should apologise to you.'

She shrugged a little. 'I have no family, I have nothing to lose. I don't want you to lose anything by marrying me. There's still time to call it off if you want. I'd understand.'

'I don't think you do understand,' he said gruffly. 'I've been lonely all my life, even though I had a family. Now I'm not lonely any more. So don't talk nonsense about calling it off. I have you, and if they want to behave decently I'll have them too, but otherwise I'll do without them. *You* I cannot do without.'

He drew her hand under his arm and they started walking.

'I don't understand what you see in me,' she said, with a contented smile, 'but I'm very glad you do.'

'I could say the same. I think I have the best of the bargain.'

'How can you say that? I'm a servant girl marrying a rich gentleman.'

'Ah, it was my money you were after, was it? Well, that's a relief – at least I won't disappoint you in *that* department!'

'You won't disappoint me in *any* department,' she said softly, looking up at him with warm and longing eyes.

He felt his insides melt. 'I love you so much,' he said. 'I wish I could kiss you right this minute.'

'I'm so glad there's only another two days to wait,' she said.

A child rushed past them with a clatter of boots, and a nursemaid's shrill cry followed him. 'Master Percy! Come back at once! You'll dirty your nankins!'

'Bathos in knickers and an Eton jacket,' Sebastian said ruefully. 'Shall we go and find some tea?'

CHAPTER FIFTEEN

The house was as rented houses are, the deficiencies covered by ranks and banks of fresh flowers – fortunately, June provided them in masses. The ballroom had evidently been added at a later date because there was a separate grand staircase up which to process, and a wide landing at the top for the receiving line – in this case, just Lord and Lady Leake.

Marriage had changed Uncle Fergus, Giles thought. He looked leaner in the face, tauter in the figure; his evening clothes were cut slightly more youthfully; like Sebastian he sported a new haircut. He held himself more alertly: gone was the slothful, indolent, soft-bodied Stuffy of old. Giles was put in mind of a gun dog quivering with contained excitement as it waited for the shot to be fired.

But if there was less of Fergus, there was more of Giulia. Her figure had filled out, the planes of her face were softened. Her gown of peacock blue silk had an overdress of chiffon encrusted with silver lace; she wore a heavy-looking sapphire and diamond necklace with matching earrings, and a diamond tiara sparkled in her high-piled hair. She looked – it came to him with a slight shock – matronly. The passionate, unconventional girl who had sat under a desert moon with him and talked of Plotinus and Philo, Akhenaten and Hatshepsut, had been subsumed into a married woman. She looked exactly as someone called Lady Leake ought to look.

The smile she gave him and Kitty was a conventional, social smile, and she murmured, 'So good of you to come,' as she had to everyone, her eyes already sliding on to the next person in line. He felt oddly disconcerted, as though he had gone up a step that wasn't there.

Uncle Fergus gripped his hand in a firm shake, and said, 'Giles, my dear boy! Haven't seen you for ages. Hope everything's all right?'

'Yes, thank you,' Giles said. He felt the same sense of unreality about the contact as his hand was given back to him without ceremony. The invisible pressure moved him and Kitty along and they passed into the anteroom. In the ballroom beyond, the orchestra was playing quietly, waiting for the company to come through.

Kitty said, 'She's changed.'

'He has, too,' Giles said. He was trying to analyse it. It came to him that his uncle was a very rich man, and an earl, but had never really acted the part before. Now he was like Giles's father, a public figure, playing the part that was expected of him. And Giulia had caught the trick from him. She was officially, remotely, publicly charming. The passionate girl was gone. He felt a sadness at her passing.

'But they look happy,' he said tentatively, in valediction.

'Yes,' Kitty said. 'They seem like a married couple. I never thought they would – it was such an odd match – but now they seem to fit together.' Giles grunted assent, and she looked up at him with suppressed amusement. 'Will you really call her Aunt Giulia?'

'If the occasion calls for it,' he said. They moved forward, impelled by the newcomers entering behind. Against the magpie black and white of the gentlemen, the ladies glittered with jewels and sequins and spars. Quick gestures and turning heads as they chattered made a constant sparkle, like the sun glinting on a gently moving sea. It was, he thought, what might truly be called 'a glittering occasion'. 'What a pity my mother and Linda couldn't be here,' he said. 'They would love all this.'

Rachel and Alice stood out of the way against the anteroom wall, getting their bearings. 'There are a lot of old people,' Rachel observed. 'I hope there'll be enough young men to dance with. Oh, I think your flower's come loose,' she noticed. 'Let me fix it for you.' She attended to the artificial rose in Alice's hair. 'You're awfully quiet. Are you all right?'

'Of course I am,' Alice said.

'You've been brooding. Is it the art school? Have you realised you don't like it after all? You could give it up. I don't think anyone would mind – they all think it's mad anyway.'

'It isn't mad. I love it there. I don't want to give it up.'

'Well, what is it, then?' Enlightenment flashed over her face. 'Don't tell me!' she breathed. 'You've fallen in love!'

'Don't be silly,' Alice said, trying not to show she was put out. She had been thinking about Axe, and wondering what he would look like in evening dress.

'I'm right, aren't I? You're always looking as if you're miles away. Who is it? You never go anywhere, so it must be someone at the school.'

'I'm just wishing I was back at the Castle instead of here. I'd sooner be riding than dancing. Oh, look!' she said quickly, glad of the distraction. 'Isn't that David Latham? Wasn't he one of your beaux last year? He's quite handsome, isn't he?'

Rachel was distracted. 'He's *very* handsome! But he's a terrible rattle. I might dance with him, though, if he asks me – he's amusing. And there's Adam Massingberd.'

'I can see quite a few young men. You needn't have worried.'

Fergus came up beside Giles. 'I think we should begin,' he said. 'I'd like to lead off with Kitty. And, Giles, as head of your family, will you take Giulia?'

The crowds parted before them as they walked into the

ballroom, then fell in behind, with a scramble for partners. Giulia's hand rested on Giles's arm. He could smell her perfume – that at least had not changed: a chypre mixture of the light, the floral and the earthy. The three conditions of a woman, he had once said to her when it came up in conversation. He wasn't sure he would dare say anything like that to the new Giulia. They reached the centre of the floor and turned to face each other. She put her gloved hand into his, he placed his other hand behind her shoulder, feeling the harsh silver lace even through his glove, and a rigidness of corset beneath that. Once, she had been as supple as nature.

The music struck up, and they moved. Her head was slightly tilted, she seemed to observe the company as though conscious that everyone was watching her.

One circuit, and then the other couples flooded onto the floor. He found that she was looking up at him, with her social smile.

'How nice to see so many people here,' she said. 'It is gratifying that all our invitations were accepted.'

'It must be,' he said blankly.

'The band is very good, don't you think?'

'Very good.'

'It was recommended by Lady Vane. She is a charming woman.'

'I don't really know her,' Giles said. It came to him uncomfortably that this really was like dancing with an aunt. If inane conversation was the order of the day, he had to contribute. 'The flower arrangements are very nice. Did you use Atkins?'

'No, Williams.' Suddenly her smile disappeared, and disconcertingly it was Giulia who was looking at him, not Lady Leake. 'Giles,' she said, 'I am glad of this dance. I wish to talk to you seriously.'

'Giulia, I—'

'No, let me speak. It may be the last chance I have.

I behaved very badly. I made a craziness, and I am sorry for it. You must forgive.'

'I think it is I who need forgiveness,' he said awkwardly. 'I never meant to—'

'I know you did not,' she said, and there was an infinity of sadness in her dark eyes. 'When I was a child you were my big brother. You were tall and kind and listened to me. Then in the Valley of the Kings, suddenly it was different.'

'Please don't,' he begged. He was afraid she would say it all again, perhaps in Italian, and in her own language her voice was like liquid honey.

'It was wrong of me,' she said gravely. 'I knew you were married. *No, non dire niente! Lasciami finire*. I made a craziness. And afterwards I blamed you for it. I wanted to punish you. It was very wrong of me. But now the craziness is all gone away. All is well. So I apologise.'

He didn't know what to say. 'Are you happy?' he asked at last.

'Of course,' she said. 'I have everything that I want. To travel! To learn! To be comfortable. Never to be afraid for money. To take care of my mama and papa when they are old.'

'But are you *happy*?'

'He loves me and takes care of me. What more could I want? And I make him happy too, so it is fair.'

He didn't know what to say. They danced in silence until the music ended. He released her and bowed.

'We may never dance together again,' she said. Then, just as suddenly, Lady Leake was back. Her eyes were as impenetrable to him as the glass eyes of a stuffed animal. 'We will live mostly in Italy, I think,' she observed unemotionally, 'so I shall not often meet you.'

He led her towards where he could see Fergus waiting for her. 'Thank you,' she said formally. 'It was pleasant.'

'Thank you for the dance, Lady Leake,' he said, in like manner.

'But you may call me Zia Giulia,' she said graciously.

He had no idea whether she meant it as a joke or not. There was nothing in her face to suggest it. He could only bow again and hand her back, and was quite glad to do it.

Her latest partner led Rachel off the floor, and Angus was there to catch her. 'This is *my* dance,' he said firmly. 'I've hardly seen you all evening.'

She fanned herself vigorously. 'I didn't realise so many people would want to dance with me,' she said modestly.

He took the fan from her and plied it, and as the music started again he said, 'Would you like to walk outside instead of dancing? I want to talk to you.' She seemed to hesitate and he said impatiently, 'It's quite proper – we *are* engaged.'

'Mama never let us go outside at a ball. She said we'd catch a chill.'

Angus took her hand and pulled it under his arm. 'If you feel chilly I'll put my jacket round you.'

She glanced at him as they slipped out through the French windows onto the terrace. 'You look awfully grim. Has something happened?"

There were a few other people on the terrace, walking up and down, or standing at the parapet looking out on the dark garden, talking quietly. He led her to the far end where they could be alone. Was he going to kiss her? she wondered. Or tell her off?

He stopped and turned to face her, leaning one elbow on the stone balustrade. He looked very handsome in evening dress, she thought. The light from the ballroom silhouetted him against the darkness beyond. She hoped it was going to be kissing. 'What did you want to talk about?' she asked, in what she hoped were seductive tones.

'You've danced with an awful lot of people tonight.'

'That's what balls are for,' she said reasonably. 'Besides, if people ask one, it looks so *particular* to refuse.'

Angus sighed. 'I'm worried that you're enjoying all this too much – all the parties and balls and everything.'

She laid a hand on his arm. 'I wish you would come to everything with us. I don't think Mama would mind, as long as we're chaperoned.'

'I couldn't – I have work to do. But I worry you have the wrong expectations of how life will be. I don't want you to be disappointed.'

She tilted her head. 'What do you mean?'

'By the time you're of age and we can marry, I shall be able to afford a house for us, but it won't be a large one. And we won't be able to afford to go to entertainments like this.'

She thought for a moment. 'Well, all the more reason to enjoy them while we can,' she said uncertainly.

'But I think you should be spending your time preparing for marriage,' he said. 'Learning how to run a household. You should learn how things are cleaned, how to cook, how to lay a fire, how to keep a budget.'

'But we'll have servants,' she objected.

'One or two. But how will you know if they're doing their job properly if you don't know how it *ought* to be done? How will you manage them?'

'Aunt Caroline just gives her orders. I don't expect she knows how things are done. That's what Mrs Wells is for.'

'Is that her housekeeper? But we won't be able to afford a housekeeper. Just talk to Mrs Wells, get her to explain how a house is run.' He took her unwilling hand. 'I thought you understood that things would be different for us. You said you'd be happy to live in a hovel, as long as we could be married.'

'But I didn't mean it!' she cried, then opened her eyes in horror at what she had said.

Angus let her hand go. 'I was afraid of that,' he said quietly. 'Perhaps you should release me from our engagement.'

She reached for his hand again. 'No, no, I don't want to!

Don't look like that! Of course I want to marry you. It's just that . . . We won't be so *very* poor, will we?'

'We won't be poor at all. But we won't be rich, like these people. It worries me that the contrast will be too great for you. Your clothes, for instance: you won't be able to have new things all the time.'

'Well, I've loads of things from my come-out last year. They'll last for ages. Especially if – if we don't go out very much.' Her tone, which had started reassuring, faltered at the end of the sentence. 'We will go out sometimes, won't we?' she asked, in a small voice.

'Yes, of course,' he said sadly. 'We'll go out sometimes. But we'll have a different set of friends, you know. People like me, not people like you.'

'But you *are* people like me,' she said. 'I love you. I do!'

'I know. But perhaps love isn't enough on its own.'

'Of course it is!' She felt he was slipping away from her.

'I love you, too,' he said. 'I just want you to be happy.'

'I *am* happy! Terribly happy! Shall we go inside and dance? I'm starting to feel cold.'

'Of course,' he said, and led her back down the terrace towards the bright lights.

The telegram came in the morning, when everyone was still abed after the exertions of the ball. Afton took it in to Giles with his morning tea.

Giles sipped while he opened it. 'Damn,' he said.

'Not bad news I hope, my lord?'

It was from Mrs Webster. LORD CORDWELL WORSE + DOCTOR SAYS IT IS PNEUMONIA + OUTLOOK CONCERNING++

Giles gave it to Afton to read. 'She wouldn't have sent it unless Dr Welkes was really worried,' Afton said.

'It isn't right to leave her alone with the responsibility. I had better go back. Fetch me some hot water right away, will you. And bring me some toast and marmalade on a tray, and I'll eat it while I'm dressing. Can you pack in time to come with me?'

'There isn't much to pack, my lord. I'll be ready.'

Giles went to Kitty's room to find her sitting up in bed with her tea and bread-and-butter tray, while Hatto pottered about tidying.

'Oh dear, I'm so sorry,' she said, when she had read the telegram. 'Poor little soul. Are you going back? There won't be anything you can do that isn't being done already.'

'But I think I should be there. For morale, and to make decisions.'

'Will you come back here?' she asked.

'It depends what happens. But I was only intending to be here for a few days anyway. There's a lot to do at home.'

'I see,' she said, with a very small sigh. He hadn't asked her to come with him. She could simply assume he wanted her and go, of course, but it would be a huge upheaval to get everything packed and ready, for her and the children, and they had engagements for the whole week ahead. And she didn't want to risk another rejection. She wasn't sure her heart could stand it.

Sebastian and Dory arrived at the church together, to find Richard standing outside. He grinned at Sebastian's surprised expression.

'Couldn't let you put your head in the noose all alone!' he said. 'I am here to be your supporter, if you'll allow?'

'I'd be delighted!' Sebastian shook his hand with vigorous gratitude. 'May I present—' he began.

'We have met,' Richard interrupted. He bowed over her hand with a smile and said, 'I give you joy, madam. And may I say you are looking very beautiful on this happiest of days?'

Dory smiled uncertainly, unsure how to take him. She had

mended his nightshirt and sewed on his buttons without being his wife, and the situation ought to have been awkward. But he seemed quite relaxed. And she did think, in all modesty, that she looked well, though she would never have said beautiful. Sebastian had approved her wedding outfit. It was a ready-made, but her neat figure was not hard to fit. It was a two-piece in dusky pink crêpe de Chine, and the high-necked, finely tucked blouse underneath had real Alençon lace on it, while her new hat of forward-tilted ivory glazed straw was filled with an extravagance of pink and white artificial roses.

'You may,' Sebastian said, 'and she does. Shall we go in?'

Above them, the church clock began to strike as they walked together down the aisle, and the priest came out of the vestry, with the clerk beside him for a witness. Crooks was already there, sitting modestly in the rearmost pew. The priest looked at the assembly doubtfully, as if wondering whether a marriage like this, with no family or friends attending, was really quite the thing.

'Shall we begin? Are you quite ready?' he said, and then his eyes went past them to the door of the church, which had been left open on such a lovely day. All of them looked round.

Grandmère was walking slowly towards them, with the absolute air of a monarch approaching the throne, wearing a black-beaded magenta dress and jacket and a terrifyingly fashionable black hat filled with birds' wings, and carrying an umbrella, which she tapped at each step so that the metal ferrule made a sound like the knocking of Fate on the door. Reaching them, she gave them a raised-eyebrowed look that dared them to question her on any point.

Sebastian took her hand, and said simply, 'Thank you, Victoire.'

Richard bent to kiss her cheek, in order to say, for her ears only, 'You steal the show, as always, *ma chère*. What changed your mind?'

'I have been the lover for twenty years of another woman's

husband,' she murmured into his ear. 'I know a little about *mésalliance*.'

Then as he straightened, she lifted the umbrella imperiously and said to the priest, 'You may proceed.'

The priest knew quality when he saw it – and in fact he recognised her from the illustrated papers his wife enjoyed. He suddenly felt much better about the whole business.

'Dearly beloved,' he began, in his most sonorous tones.

Mr Moss had always insisted on the proper ceremony when a senior member of the family or an honoured guest arrived, and Mr Afton had inherited the arrangement. So the servants were lined up outside when the carriage arrived back from the station; and Giles stood at the centre of the chevron of welcome. Behind him, Arabella tightly held the hand of Miss Kettel.

William went to open the near carriage door and hand Kitty down, while on the far side Alice jumped out in her usual way without waiting for Sam.

They reached Giles at the same time, and he kissed them in turn. 'I'm so glad you came,' he said.

'Poor little boy,' Kitty said. 'It's so very sad.'

'No Rachel?' he asked.

'She didn't want to come,' Alice said. 'She had engagements.' And she left them to go to Arabella, who received her embrace woodenly. Alice had always had more to do with Linda's children: Rachel had been away for most of her come-out year, while Alice, sorry for them, had taken them out riding and played with them. She took Arabella's free hand and she and Miss Kettel walked her back into the house.

Kitty and Giles went in together. 'She looks different, poor child,' Kitty said. 'Thinner. Is she eating?'

'Not well, according to Miss Kettel. I've tried talking to her, but she's hard to reach. Understandably, I suppose. They must have been very close, having so little attention from anyone else.'

'Is Linda really not coming?'

'I'll show you the letter. She said she wouldn't be able to get back in time. And we can't delay the funeral any longer in this weather. She said to continue without her.'

'But she'll come afterwards?'

'There was no suggestion of that in her letter. She said she couldn't leave our mother at the moment.' He shrugged. 'I don't think she has a maternal bone in her body. Even as a child, she never played with dolls.'

'I can't understand it,' Kitty said. 'I don't even like leaving the boys in London for a few days.'

'You're going back?'

'The day after tomorrow, to supervise the packing, and I'll bring them home on Friday. The Season's almost over now, and I don't mind missing the last few events.'

'I'm glad,' he said. 'The house isn't the same without you.'

She would sooner he had said he had missed her, but it was something.

'Good to have you back, Miss Hatto,' Mrs Webster said.

Kitty's maid paused to strip off her gloves and said, 'A sad occasion.'

'They thought he was getting better,' Rose said, 'but then the pneumonia came on. Struggling for breath at the end. I never liked the brat, but it wasn't a nice way to go.'

'Lady Rachel didn't come, then?' Mrs Webster said.

It wasn't enough of a question for Miss Hatto, who never spoke much anyway, to make an answer. Children died all the time, you had to expect it, and though it was sad for the mother, and possibly the father, it meant little to the rest of the world. The loss of an unformed child was not like the loss of an adult, a unique and irreplaceable personality, whose character had been years in the making. The proper obsequies had to be observed for a viscount, even though he had been a minor, but it was no use pretending that anyone had cared about Arthur. 'I'd better get my lady's blacks unpacked,' she said.

'I have a spare black armband for you, if you need it,' Mrs Webster said, as the neat little figure went past her towards the stairs.

'Thank you, I've already sewn mine on,' Miss Hatto replied.

'She's a funny one,' Rose remarked, when she was out of hearing. 'A lady's maid who won't gossip? Makes you miss old Taylor sometimes.'

'Miss Taylor didn't gossip,' said Mrs Webster.

'She wouldn't have called it that, but she had ways of letting you know what was going on,' said Rose. 'Not that I needed it when Lady Linda was here. She always told me everything.'

'It's a surprise, her not coming for the funeral.'

'Not to me. She never wanted Arabella, and once the estate was gone and there was nothing for Arthur to inherit, she had no use for him either.'

'Speaking of which, what do you know about the heir – the new Lord Cordwell?'

'No more than you, that he's coming tonight. I don't suppose anyone ever thought he'd be needed, once Lady Linda had a boy.' Afton appeared, coming down from the hall, and Rose asked, 'What time is Lord Cordwell arriving, Mr Afton?'

'Not until half past six,' Afton said. 'If the train's late, he'll have to go straight up to dress. You've put him in the Tapestry Room?'

'It's all ready for him.'

'He's not bringing a manservant?' Mrs Webster queried.

'Probably hasn't got one,' said Rose. 'He's only a country solicitor.'

'He might have one and not bother to bring him for such a short stay,' Afton said, with a hint of rebuke.

'And no Mr Crooks to fill the gap. Will you give him William?'

'I'll need William to be down here while I'm dressing his lordship,' said Afton, feeling a little distracted. Combining butler and valet was all very well, as long as there were no guests. 'Sam can take care of him as well as Mr Richard.'

The new Viscount Cordwell stepped down from the carriage to a greeting party of Giles and Richard – who had been out on business when Kitty and Alice arrived – and two footmen. Even this modest honour seemed to overpower him. He stopped and looked around, then up at the façade of the house, before advancing uncertainly towards the two men. 'The name's Cordwell,' he said. 'I'm afraid the train was late. I'm sorry to have kept your horses standing.'

'Welcome to Ashmore Castle,' said Richard. 'I'm Richard Tallant and this is Lord Stainton. Only cousins by marriage, but please call us Cousin Richard and Cousin Giles.'

'Thank you,' he said blankly. He was a well-favoured young man, who looked about thirty, and was wearing a light grey suit with a black armband, and a soft hat. He had stepped down with a leather holdall in his hand. Sam, the second footman, was hovering at his elbow, trying to take it from him. Cordwell noticed at last and relinquished it, slightly reluctantly.

'Is that all your luggage?' Giles asked.

'Er – yes. What time is the funeral tomorrow?'

'At eleven. And Mr Fossey, of Fossey, Gleeson and Tuke, will be here just after breakfast, to have a word, if that's all right.'

'I did have a letter from them,' said Cordwell. He had a very slight accent, no more than a modest West Country roundness of the vowels, but it was noticeable next to the clipped voices of the brothers. 'I'm not sure what there is to discuss, though.'

'Just tidying things up,' Giles said. 'I'm afraid we have to go straight up to change.'

'Sam, here, will attend to you,' said Richard, extending a hand towards the door to get him moving. 'We've put you in the Tapestry Room.'

'Very well,' he said, and followed Sam inside.

Richard and Giles lingered a little behind to exchange a glance. 'Charm personified,' said Richard.

'It can't be easy for him,' Giles offered in excuse.

'But can he possibly have evening clothes *and* a frock coat in that bag?' Richard said with a suppressed grin.

'And where has he hidden his silk hat?' Giles murmured.

'Perhaps he has a gibus,' Richard said. 'I wish Crooks was here to sort him out.'

Mr Fossey was the grandson of the original Fossey of Fossey, Gleeson and Tuke, and was young enough not to be too stately with the new viscount, even though his job was to tell him that no money or property whatsoever came with the title.

'I hope you don't mind my staying for the meeting,' Giles said to Cordwell. 'I would like to be sure that you understand the arrangements that had to be made when my brother-in-law Gerald died.'

'I believe there was considerable debt,' said Cordwell.

Giles nodded. 'So much so that the entire estate was taken up with discharging it.'

'And you took the widow and children into your own house?' He had a flat way of talking that gave no hint as to his approval or otherwise.

'I really had no choice,' Giles said. 'I could not leave them destitute.'

'I knew nothing of all this,' said Cordwell.

Mr Fossey spoke up. 'Naturally, at the time there was no thought that it would be necessary to inform you of how matters stood.'

Cordwell looked at Giles. 'I did not mean any criticism. I see that you did the best you could in the circumstances.'

It sounded less than generous to Giles, but he hoped it was just Cordwell's manner. 'Holme Manor was sold?'

'The house and what little land was left. The rest of the land had already been sold over the years. The finances had been suffering for a long time.'

'I see.'

'Were you acquainted with my brother-in-law?' Giles asked, hoping to get a little more out of him.

'Not at all,' said Cordwell. 'My grandfather was his grandfather's cousin, so Heaven knows what relation that made me. Third cousin, possibly? Something very remote, anyway. My father told me when I was a child that we had a distant relation who was a lord, but naturally we never thought anything of it. We never met any of them. I made my own way in the world. My father was a solicitor before me, but it was a small country practice when I joined it. I'm the one who built it up to what it is today.' He frowned. 'I'm not sure I care for being "Viscount Cordwell". I don't know how it will affect my business. I don't want people to think I'm getting above myself.'

'There is no necessity for you to use the title if you don't want to, but I don't imagine it will do you any harm with your clients,' said Fossey. 'You might even win one or two new ones.'

'And your wife may enjoy being *Lady* Cordwell,' Giles added. 'Ladies generally set more store by that sort of thing.'

'Oh, I'm not married,' Cordwell said bluntly. 'I've never had time – too busy building up the business.'

That, Giles thought, might explain a certain roughness-around-the-edges. 'Well, there's plenty of time,' he said, smiling.

Cordwell only looked at him blankly.

Fossey cleared his throat. 'Perhaps I may go through the formalities with you, my lord, for the transfer of the title, show you the coat of arms and mention the benefits and duties associated with it?'

When that was done, Giles insisted on Fossey showing him

the accounts concerning the winding-up of the estate. He listened to and looked at everything in silence, not even responding to Fossey's courteous interjections of 'As a man of the law you will know, of course . . .'

They had come to a natural pause when the dressing bell was rung downstairs. 'We must go up and change,' Giles said. 'Thank you, Mr Fossey, for explaining everything so clearly.'

Fossey bowed, and said to Cordwell, 'I hope you feel you are in possession of all the necessary information now, my lord. Is there anything further you wish to ask me?'

'No,' said Cordwell. 'There's not much to it.' As Fossey was gathering together his papers, Giles walked with Cordwell to the library door; and the viscount said suddenly, 'There were *two* children, weren't there? A girl as well? What happened to her?'

'She's living here, at Ashmore Castle. Arabella. She's ten years old.'

Cordwell gave him a cautious look. 'What happens to her now?'

'Um – nothing in particular. She'll remain here.' He wasn't sure what was being asked. 'We have a governess for her.'

'As long as I won't be expected to take her on, along with the title,' Cordwell said.

Giles felt a little offended. 'She's my sister's child,' he said. 'Of course I will take care of her.'

Cordwell gave a curt nod of satisfaction. 'As long as that's understood.'

Sam was hovering near Giles's bedroom door. 'My lord,' he said, in an urgent undertone, his eyes frantic with appeal, 'Lord Cordwell doesn't have any blacks with him, nor a silk hat, and I don't know what to do.'

When Giles had come back for his father's funeral, he hadn't owned a mourning suit either, and Crooks had taken in a coat of his father's and stuffed the lining of one of the late earl's hats for him. But the case now was rather different. He didn't feel they owed anything in particular to the new Lord Cordwell.

'I don't see that you can do anything,' Giles said. 'He knew he was coming to a funeral, and if he didn't care to bring the appropriate clothing, he must go as he is.'

Sam bit his lips in anxiety. 'In a lounge suit, my lord? And a soft hat!'

'You'll put a black band around it – you can do that, can't you? And a black band on his sleeve.'

'Um – yes, my lord, I think I can manage that.'

Afton appeared during the last exchange. 'Off you go, Sam,' he said firmly, and the footman hurried away, still looking anxious. 'He thinks he's going to get into trouble if his lordship appears in public improperly dressed,' Afton said, following Giles into his room. Seeing Giles's amused quirk of the lips, he went on, 'Poor Sam! He came to me last night when you'd all gone in to dinner to say that Lord Cordwell wouldn't let him dress him. He kept taking the things out of his hands and putting them on himself.'

'Shocking!' Giles said, and exchanged a grin with his manservant.

Alice travelled to the church in the second carriage with Arabella and Miss Kettel. Arabella held her hand, and unexpectedly fell asleep on the short journey with her head on Alice's shoulder. In her other hand she clutched the felt pig, Pepper. Her face showed new planes, making her look older than her years – twelve or thirteen, past the first stage of childhood – and the black dress did nothing for her. Alice wondered what would happen to her in the coming years, a penniless girl without a title.

Miss Kettel leaned forward and spoke to Alice over the sleeping child's head. 'They blame me, you know,' she whispered. Alice was startled to be confided in. 'And I blame myself,' Miss Kettel went on. 'I should have taken better care of him. I'll never forgive myself. I don't know why they've kept me on. I expected to be dismissed straight away.'

'But Arabella needs you,' Alice said.

The carriage stopped outside St Peter's Church, and the child woke, sat up and looked bewildered. 'Is it over?' she asked.

'No, it hasn't started yet,' Alice answered her.

Arabella looked at her with dread. 'I don't have to see him, do I? They won't make me look at him?'

'No,' said Alice, kindly. 'He's asleep in his nice cosy box now.'

'Like a dormouse,' said Arabella. 'He always wanted a pet mouse.'

The door was opened and the step let down. 'Come along,' said Miss Kettel, briskly. 'Mustn't keep people waiting.'

Arabella climbed out obediently, and took Alice's hand again. 'Can we go riding this afternoon?' she asked.

'Not this afternoon. Tomorrow, perhaps.'

'I never let him ride Biscuit,' she said. 'I wish I had now.'

'He was better off on Goosebumps. Biscuit would have had him off,' Alice reassured her.

Arabella sighed. 'I suppose it doesn't matter now.'

Lord Cordwell excused himself straight after luncheon. 'If you'll forgive me I'll go up and pack. And would you be kind enough to order the carriage for me, to take me to the station?'

'But – you'll stay the night, surely?' Kitty said.

He bowed slightly to her. 'I don't see any purpose. We come from such different worlds – I don't think any of us enjoyed dinner last night, and to repeat the experiment would be folly. I'd like to get back home tonight if possible. I have clients to see tomorrow.'

'You're a busy man,' Richard said, with faint irony.

Cordwell looked at him seriously. 'I am. And I don't see how this title with no estate attached to it changes anything.

So I must be about my business. Thank you for your hospitality, Lady Stainton. I don't suppose we will meet again.'

Richard waited until he was well out of earshot before laughing. 'One can't fault his logic – but oh dear! "Thank you for your hospitality," in a tone that said, as clear as day, "This whole visit was a waste of my valuable time."'

'I suppose it was,' Giles said. 'We could have had the funeral without him. It was only courtesy to include him.'

'And to think I told him to call us Cousin Richard and Cousin Giles!' Richard chortled.

Giles gave an unwilling half-smile. 'I did think at the time you were rather going overboard.'

When Kitty and Alice arrived back at Aunt Caroline's house, they were met by Rachel in a state of agitation. 'A letter's come from Mama,' she said. 'Linda wants Arabella to go to Usingen. Miss Kettel's to take her.'

'It's proper that she should want to see her,' Kitty said, almost in relief. It troubled her to think of anyone having so little care for their children.

'Yes, but you don't understand. Mama says that since Miss Kettel will be going, she can chaperone us on the journey as well. She's ordered Alice and me to go. She wants us to stay all summer.'

'I don't want to go,' Alice said. 'I don't want to miss school.'

'It's worse for me,' Rachel said wildly. 'She'll try to stop me marrying Angus, I know she will.'

'She's given her permission,' Kitty said. 'She's allowed you to become engaged.'

'But it wasn't announced anywhere, so she can change her mind,' Rachel said. 'I'll bet she's got someone else lined up for me – some dreadful old relation of the prince's that she'll try to force me to marry.'

'You only have to stick it out,' Alice said.

'You needn't sound so smug,' Rachel said, irritated. 'If

she's asked for you to go, it's because she's found someone for you as well.'

Alice paled. 'You don't really think so?'

'You are heartless girls,' Aunt Caroline said. 'This is your mother you're talking about. She wants to see you, that's all. She wants to spend some time with you.'

Two pairs of eyes turned on her. 'She's never wanted to spend time with us before,' Alice said frankly.

'You're grown-up now, you're able to be proper company,' Aunt Caroline said. 'And she's having a baby, so she won't have been able to visit or have visitors for some time.'

'That's true,' said Kitty. 'She must be terribly bored. Having you there will cheer her up.'

'Besides,' said Aunt Caroline, 'I'm closing up the house at the end of next week.'

'Are you going to Usingen?' Kitty asked.

'The South of France first, to stay with Vicky and Bobo. But I expect we'll all go to Usingen after the baby's born. One ought to pay one's respects,' she added, with a vague look. It was hard to think of her older sister being involved in childbirth again, at her advanced age, with her youngest children on the brink of adulthood. The whole thing smacked of the bizarre – and Aunt Caroline had a dislike of anything *outré*.

'I wish I could go with you,' Angus said, 'but I can't possibly leave the office for that long. You ought to have a man to look after you on the journey. It isn't right for ladies to travel alone, especially abroad.'

'I wish you were going too,' Rachel said. 'Then you could stand up to Mama if she tries to separate us.'

'I can't believe she'd go back on her word. Why would she, after all this time?'

'You don't know her. If she wants to do something, she does it. But Kitty and Aunt Caroline both say we must go.

I thought Kitty would be on my side, but she says it's the proper thing to do.'

'I suppose it is,' Angus said. 'Perhaps you'll enjoy it when you get there.'

'I don't suppose they'll be having any parties until the baby is born, so it will be deadly dull.' She brightened slightly. 'It will be nice to see Aunt Vicky again, though, if she comes. She took me about when I was over there before my come-out. Parties every day, and balls, and hunting, and military reviews. Aunt Vicky makes such fun! She's not a bit like Mama. And Uncle Bobo's terribly nice, too. He bought me the prettiest coral set for my birthday. It will be my birthday again while we're there,' she added, with a thoughtful look. 'They might take Alice and me away with them after the baby's born, to the summer palace, or the South of France. You meet everyone there.'

'I hope you *do* have a nice time,' Angus said, 'but don't get carried away, will you? All this talk of balls and parties . . .'

'I know,' Rachel said impatiently. 'There won't be any after we're married. You said so.'

'I didn't say there won't be *any*. But we won't be mixing with dukes and princes. And you ought to take the opportunity of studying how a house is run in Germany. They might do things differently, and it would be interesting to compare and see which way is better.'

Rachel looked astonished at his idea of what was interesting, and said quickly, 'Oh, I don't think Mama would like me to question the prince's housekeeper. I'm sure it wouldn't be proper at all.'

Angus opened his mouth and closed it again. It wasn't in his nature to nag, but if Rachel had been less absorbed with her own thoughts she'd have seen that he was worried.

CHAPTER SIXTEEN

'It's almost too hot to ride,' Kitty said, checking Apollo as he objected to a carriage and pair coming the other way. The two ladies in the open landau were wearing light summer dresses and shading themselves with frilly parasols. 'Riding habits are so heavy.'

'It's a good thing you're going down to the country, then,' said Nina. She glanced back. 'I can see our grooms disapprove of our being here. Yours looks quite thunderous.'

'Oh, that's just Josh's way. He always looks cross. And he hates London. He won't have to suffer much longer, anyway. This will be my last ride. He's taking the horses down this afternoon, and I'll be leaving with the children tomorrow.'

'Hm. I suppose I might as well send mine back tomorrow. Without you to ride with, it won't be as much fun. And you're right about riding habits. I feel like a pudding wrapped up for boiling!'

'I wish you would come down to Ashmore with me. It's been lovely seeing so much of you, but it's never enough.'

'Dear Kitty! But I've engagements all week, and then we're invited to the Isle of Wight. My friend Bobby Wharfedale's father has taken the house there again for the summer for the whole family, and they've asked us. I had such a lovely time last year.'

'And Mr Cowling's going too?' Kitty asked.

'He'll come and go, as business allows.'

'Doesn't business let up even in August?'

'Hardly at all,' Nina said. 'People still want to buy things in August. Your housekeeper wouldn't be happy if there was suddenly no jam.'

'The Castle makes its own,' Kitty said.

Nina smiled at her literalness. 'Not your housekeeper, then, but other housekeepers and housewives. And what about all the picnics that would have to be called off if there was no fish paste for the sandwiches?'

Kitty was about to say Mrs Webster didn't buy fish paste either, but changed it at the last moment to 'It seems a strange sort of life, seeing so little of your husband.'

'You said you didn't see very much of yours,' Nina said. 'Isn't he always busy?'

'Yes, but he's *there*. At the Castle. I see him at dinner and up in the nursery before the dressing bell. And we'll be entertaining once I'm back, Saturday-to-Monday parties, so I'll see a lot more of him.' Always with other people around. But perhaps that was best, having guests as a buffer between them. She was still not certain where she stood with him after their quarrel, though he had apologised. And she had the boys – poor Nina didn't have a child to fill her life. 'You are happy, aren't you?' she concluded wistfully. 'I worry that—'

'Don't,' Nina said. She turned to look at Kitty. 'I don't suppose marriage is the way either of us expected, but we can't change things. And I have a lot to be thankful for, so let's leave it at that.'

'I wish you would come to Ashmore instead of the Isle of Wight,' Kitty said.

Nina was afraid there was some hurt there, but it was best if she didn't spend too much time in close quarters with Giles. 'Perhaps later in the summer?' she said lightly.

'We go to Scotland in September,' Kitty said.

'Well, later in the year, then. For the shooting. Or perhaps you could come to Market Harborough for the hunting. Don't worry, darling, we'll catch up with each other,' Nina said. 'Shall we canter? The breeze might cool us down.'

As Richard walked along Bruton Street, he saw two shabby figures leaning against the railings opposite Grandmère's house. He might have taken them for burglars reconnoitring, except that one was obviously a photographer – a camera was too large an object to conceal – which made the other one a reporter. His temper rose. He pulled his hat low over his face and sauntered innocently, and managed to creep up close enough to leap forward and make a grab for the camera before they realised what was happening.

'Give me that, you sneaking dog!'

'Oy! Leggo! You'll break it!' The camera's owner tightened his grip and tried to wrest it away.

'What the hell d'you think you're doing?' the reporter shouted, joining the fray. He grabbed Richard's shoulder; Richard had seized the photographer's collar with his spare hand, his other hand on the camera strap; they writhed to and fro in a bunch.

'You mangy sneaks! I'll see you taken up!' Richard panted. His hat had come off and bowled into the gutter.

'Just – doing – our – job, guv'nor!' the photographer gasped.

'What's got into you? Let him go, I warn you!' the reporter panted. He had Richard by both shoulders and Richard felt his coat coming off. One or two passers-by had stopped, an elderly lady was tutting, while a smart man was murmuring a dismayed 'Oh, I say!' over and over. A passing carter had pulled up his horse and was shouting with interest, 'Go it, Jack! Black his eye! Draw his cork!' though it was not clear which side he was encouraging.

Richard let go of the photographer in mid-yank and the man went over backwards, sprawling on the pavement, desperately holding up his camera to protect it. In the same movement Richard let his arms slip out of his coat, causing the other man to stagger, spun on his heels and threw a punch at his face. He misjudged the distance and his fist only grazed the reporter's cheek; the reporter regained his balance and came forward and hit out at Richard, catching the end of his nose. Richard yelled with pain and felt a wet trickle of blood.

And then there was another figure in the mêlée, the large, blue-black, reassuring presence of a policeman, who caught the reporter by his collar and almost lifted him off the ground, took in Richard's quality by a glance at his clothes, and boomed, 'That's enough of that! Stand still, the lot of you! What's going on here? Stand still, I said,' he added to the reporter, giving him a shake like a large dog with a rat. 'Are you hurt, sir?' he asked Richard, who had taken out a handkerchief and was staunching his nose. 'What is it, a robbery? You, on the ground, stay still! I'll tell you when to get up.'

'I'm all right,' Richard said. 'I'm Richard Tallant – that's my grandmother's house, and these two've been hanging about watching it. They're up to no good.'

'We're reporters,' cried the man, his voice slightly strangled by the upward pull on his collar. 'We're with the *Bugle*. We're just doing our job.'

'And I'm just doing mine,' the policeman said. 'D'you want to press charges, sir? Common assault?' He gave the collar another shake. 'Blood has been drawn. The magistrate will take a serious view of that.'

Richard considered quickly. His grandmother wouldn't like it – and at the moment, her whole purpose was to avoid publicity. 'No, Constable,' he said, 'as long as these two make off and don't come back.'

'Just as you like, sir,' the policeman said, releasing the reporter. 'Go on, then, clear off! Before I change my mind. And don't let me catch you round here again.'

Muttering angrily, brushing themselves down, the two moved away, while the policeman watched them with the massive indifference of a stone wall. The rest of the onlookers drifted away. Richard put his coat back on, picked up his misshapen hat, and said, 'Thank you, officer.'

'Next time,' the policeman said, looking down at him kindly, 'send for the police. Don't try and deal with it yourself. You might have taken a pasting, sir. And I don't think Lady Stainton would have liked that.'

Richard raised an eyebrow. 'You know?'

'This is my beat, sir. I know everyone on it. And I collared a burglar here once many years ago. She was nice enough to commend me. A very fine lady, Lady Stainton – one of the old school.'

'She is.'

'Give her ladyship my respects, if you please. And tell her I'll keep an eye on the house for the next few days, to make sure they don't come back.'

Grandmère sipped her linden tea, and looked at Richard over the rim of the cup as he soothed his nerves with a brandy and soda. 'You are not a fit sight for a drawing-room,' she mentioned.

'I'm sorry,' he said, a little shakily. 'But I couldn't ignore them.'

She made a graceful gesture of her hand. 'It is good to have a champion. But we had better rely on the police in future. There will be more of them, I am sure. The case comes on in the Court for Divorce today. It creates . . . an interest.'

'In Sir Thomas, not in you,' Richard said. '*He* should be the one to be hounded. Why should you suffer?'

'Someone at the newspaper has discovered our long association,' said Grandmère, who despite her calm voice was not as unmoved by the situation as she wished to appear. 'And perhaps they have found also that I took up the girl, encouraged her. It is *une histoire*. They all want that. *Une histoire de coeurs brisés.*'

He was upset. 'Yours is not broken, surely? I thought it was the *dérangement* that you disliked.'

She shrugged. 'I dislike every part of it. But the newspapers will want a broken heart somewhere. They are looking in the wrong place, however. Did I tell you I went to see Violet Burton?'

'No, you didn't. Was that wise?'

'She is an old friend. One felt one should show her some attention in all of this.'

'Not a friend, surely – an acquaintance at best.'

'*Nous nous sommes toujours entendues,*' she said, evading the question. 'We had much in common.'

'Yes, her husband,' Richard said wryly. 'Come, Granny, you detested her, admit it!'

'Not at all. She was necessary to our relationship. You do not understand. And don't call me Granny.'

'But what were you hoping to achieve by visiting her?'

'She was the only one who could stop the madness. And I did not believe she understood what she was doing. I wondered, was she being pressed to do it? She is not *une femme d'esprit fort*. And he can be hard to resist.'

'And what did you discover?'

Now Grandmère looked angry. 'She would not stir herself! Lying on her *chaise longue*, with a silk shawl of hideous Oriental style over her legs, and a *carafe*, positively, of madeira at her elbow. Sip, sip, sip, *mon dieu*!'

'You didn't know? Or is it a recent habit, do you think?'

She shrugged in her most French manner. '*Qu'importe?*'

'But what did she say about the divorce?'

She winced at the word, but answered, 'She said that they had discussed it in a most civilised manner and that she had agreed to it.'

'She didn't *mind*?'

'Of course she *minds*, but she will not admit it. She said she wanted him to be happy. *Pah! Quelle bêtise!* I tried to persuade her of the horrors of the scandal. I tried to awaken in her some indignation. But she sipped, and smiled, and said she would do very well, with the house and a pension and her circle of friends – and the magician in the bottle, *bien sûr,*' she added sourly. There was a moment of silence. She resumed. 'So nothing can stop it now. There will be a decree nisi today, and it will be absolute in January. The newspapers and magazines will be filled with gossip, and scandal, and all their foul glee, and who will care but me?'

'I will,' said Richard.

'Well, I go at the end of the week with Caroline to the South of France, and perhaps *there* one may find a little perspective.'

He had never seen her look unhappy, and it struck him to the core. He reached across and took one of her thin, cold hands, feeling how fragile it was. 'He does not deserve you,' he said.

She came back abruptly from her reverie, raised her eyebrows at him, snatched her hand away impatiently. 'Of course he does not,' she said briskly. 'He never did. What has that to do with it?'

'I would have thought everything.'

'Don't talk nonsense. My tea is cold, ring the bell.'

'Thank God, there have been no reporters here. I suppose they don't know about me yet,' Molly said. 'Or I'm not important enough.'

'Chloë's name won't be mentioned in court,' Richard said. 'Even the professional co-respondent isn't named when the petitioner is a woman.' It was thin comfort. There would be few in the *ton* who would not soon know the real reason for the divorce, if they hadn't guessed it already. And the press would easily trace Chloë back to her mother.

Molly knew it too. 'Well, when they do work it out and come here, they will find me gone.'

He felt a prickle along his scalp. 'What do you mean?'

'I met her yesterday at an hotel – she didn't want to come here, in case it drew attention to me – and she told me their plans. They're going abroad at once, to do a concert tour.

France, Germany and the Low Countries to begin with. Then Italy. Christmas in Vienna. He is taking a string quartet as well, and he'll hire other musicians locally as they're needed. Apparently he has been working on the details for months. All the bookings are in place. Chloë will have a dresser with her, but he insisted she must have a chaperone as well. He wants no breath of scandal to touch her, so he said.'

'But that's a good thing, isn't it? That he's being careful?'

'Oh, Richard!'

He knew what that exasperated cry meant: *It would have been better if he had left her alone!* But he believed that the business had been driven as much by Chloë as by Sir Thomas. She knew what she wanted, and in pursuit of her career she was ruthless. Sir Thomas, though ruthless in his own way, was the one who was helplessly in love: the trembling dragon in the clutches of a fire-breathing maiden.

'So, what has all this to do with your leaving this house?' he asked.

She met his eyes steadily, in the way that told him he was not going to like the next part. 'He was going to hire a chaperone, but Chloë asked me, and he reinforced the request, strenuously. Oh, don't look like that! It makes sense, you know it does! A young artist travelling in the company of her mother: what could be more respectable? A chaperone might be suspected by those determined to look for scandal, but never a girl's own mother.'

'So you will be gone for four or five months?' he said, carefully controlling his voice.

Now her eyes moved away. 'The decree will be made absolute in January, and they intend to marry immediately, or as soon as it can be arranged.'

'So you will see them married? And then you will come home?'

'They are going to marry in New York,' she said. 'The east coast of America is very strong for music. Boston, New York,

Philadelphia, Washington all have rich patrons and enthusiastic audiences. He thinks of building his own concert hall – in Manhattan first, but perhaps later a string of them. A Burton Hall in every big city. And then there are phonograph records. Musical artists are becoming known over there by their recordings, quite independently of actual concerts. Fortunes can be made that way. There's a new business, the Victor Talking Machine Company, in New Jersey – Caruso has a recording contract with them. Imagine if they took up Chloë—'

'Stop, stop!' Richard begged. 'They are going to live there, permanently?'

She gave a nervous smile. 'Divorce is not frowned on in America in the same way. They can make a life over there without shadow. Once they are established, I expect they may come to Europe on tours. But the American market is so big, they would not need to.'

'And you? You still have not answered my question. You will come home?"

'No, my dear,' she said steadily. 'I will make my home with them. Chloë will need me to keep her feet on the ground, especially if her career takes wings. And if there are children, *they* will need me – dedicated artists do not make good parents.'

'But what about me? *I* need you.'

She reached out and took his hand. 'It's better this way. You know that you and I can never marry.'

'I don't accept that! Just because—'

'Yes, just *because*. It would be wrong. You know that. Society forbids it, God forbids it. It's in the Bible. Leviticus: thou shalt not uncover thy father's nakedness. Cursèd be he—'

'Oh stop!' Richard cried. 'The *Bible*? I love you. Don't you understand? I love you, and if you love me, that's all that matters.'

'I do love you. But it's never all that matters,' she said sadly. 'I've had to deal with Chloë's situation, and it almost destroys me. I've thought about you and me, night after sleepless night, longing for you, wishing we could . . . But we can't, we just can't. This is for the best. To be here, always tempted, always struggling, is more than I can bear. And you – when I'm gone, you can make a proper life for yourself. You're young. One day there will be someone else.'

He was holding her hand so tightly it was hurting her. There were tears on his face. 'This is the end? You're leaving me?' She didn't answer, only looked at him with immense sadness. 'How can I live without you?' he cried.

'Don't make it harder for me,' she said. 'Try to understand.'

'I want it to be hard for you,' he said passionately. 'I hope your heart will break.'

She stood up, and he had to stand too. 'It's breaking now,' she said.

'Kiss me,' he demanded. 'One last kiss.'

But she pulled her hand free and shook her head, turning her face away. 'You must go now. I can't bear any more.'

He gave her one long, searching look, then turned away.

'God bless you,' she said softly, as he reached the door. 'Richard, I will never . . . There will never – *be* anyone else. You understand? If that comforts you.'

'It doesn't,' he said harshly, without turning round. And then he was gone.

For the last big dinner of the Season, the Morrises had pulled out all the stops. Every leaf had been put into the dining table, and straying dining chairs had been gathered from the places they had been put to temporary use. The best double-damask cloth had been ironed in situ to eliminate the fold marks; the best silver and crystal glittered. And Mawes had borrowed two footmen from the obliging Lord and Lady Leven to wait at table, to make sure nothing hindered the free flow of pleasure.

Mr Cowling and Decius had just come back to London

from Cambridgeshire. Nina was glad to be going to a dinner party on her husband's arm, for a change. Decius had been invited too, as had Nina's Aunt Schofield. The other guests were a typical Morris mix: the music publisher John Benson; two sisters, Sylvia and Evelyn Partridge, who were both writers of popular and slightly steamy novels; Dame Myra Lang, the opera singer; Mannox Launde, the Irish playwright and poet; an immensely rich Russian Jewish furrier, Ilia Malkin; and the well-known painter Ivor Wentworth.

In such variously talented company, Nina worried that someone might ask her, 'And what do *you* do?' to which she would have had to answer, 'Nothing at all.' She had Launde on her left, so was obliged to speak to him first, but fortunately he was not at all inclined to ask her anything about herself. He was tall and lean, with slightly over-long hair brushed straight back from his brow, the better to emphasise the hooded eyes and the bony beak of a nose, which made him look like a supercilious predator. He was famous for his acerbic tongue, and for his 'difficult' plays which satirised the leading characters and mores of society.

She felt that out of politeness she ought to let him know that she knew who he was, so she began with, 'I must tell you that I saw your play *Tiberius* last month, and enjoyed it very much.'

He aimed the eagle's beak at her and said, 'If you enjoyed it, you cannot have understood it.' He proceeded to explain the play, and his own inner workings, at great length, and since he didn't seem to require anything from her in return, she was free to enjoy her soup and fish while covertly watching the rest of the table.

She was interested to see that Dame Myra Lang and Mr Cowling were engrossed in conversation. The diva was a vividly dark, very round person in black-beaded garnet-coloured velvet, and she moved her fingers constantly to emphasise her words, which made the diamonds in her many rings catch the light. When Mr Cowling spoke, she nodded in eager agreement, and the diamonds in her tiara flashed instead. It was good for Nina to see her husband in a different environment: here he was not just her Mr Cowling, he was the powerful businessman and shrewd investor, adviser to the King and acquainted with almost everyone you cared to name. And Dame Myra Lang, who had starred opposite Caruso and Zenatello, and who had sung Norma at the Met, found Nina's husband worth talking to!

She noted that her aunt was getting just as good value out of Mawes Morris. He was regaling her with some of his many anecdotes, and Nina actually saw her laugh at one point: Aunt Schofield was in no way bad-tempered or sullen, but she was serious-minded and rarely laughed in company. Lepida and Decius were talking together in low tones, though their serious expressions prevented anyone from imagining that there was flirtation going on. Lepida, Nina thought, was looking very handsome that evening in midnight-blue silk, with Indian enamelled ornaments in her hair, and wearing the sapphire-drop pendant that had been Mr Cowling's bridesmaid's gift to her when he married Nina.

When Isabel turned after the fish, Nina got the Russian as a pleasant relief from Mr Launde. He had large dark eyes and a melancholy, fleshy face that made her think of a sad dog and want to be kind to him. He began by talking to her about the Russian war with Japan, which had recently ended with the disastrous battle of Tsushima, in which all eleven Russian heavy battleships had been lost – seven sunk and four captured – forcing Russia to sue for peace. It seemed very much on his mind. Trying to be intelligent, Nina brought up the Dogger Bank incident from the previous autumn, the only detail of the conflict she knew about because it had been in all the papers and caused a diplomatic incident. The Russian fleet, coming into the North Sea via the Sound, had fired on a group of British trawlers out night-fishing, mistaking them for Japanese warships. One had been sunk and six damaged, and only the inaccuracy of Russian gunnery had avoided greater loss. In the dark, they had even fired on two of their own flotilla.

Mr Malkin's melancholy increased with this topic, and Nina, feeling guilty, asked him instead about furs, on which he was able to wax enthusiastic. He told her that he was hoping to use some of his fortune to open a department store in London, perhaps in Oxford Street, along the lines of Harrod's, in which he would establish the largest fur sales, alteration and storage facility in the country – perhaps in Europe.

'As ladies go automatically to Paris to buy gowns, they will come to London to buy furs,' he told her. 'You will come and see us, dear Madam Cowling, and I will find you the perfect fur, the very one that will most enhance your beauty.'

Nina was glad that with the next turn, the conversation became general. Mr Cowling began it by saying, to the table at large during a lull, 'We have a lot of artistic people here, from different fields. I would like to know whether the thing that makes you artistic – the artistic germ, if you like – is the same, regardless of what form of art you practise. Or is it different for a writer, say, rather than a painter?'

Mr Launde looked contemptuous of the question and lowered his eyelids still further, muttering, *Artistic germ*, as though someone had offered him pigs' trotters to eat.

Mawes Morris said, 'Interesting! Well, in so far as I am an artist at all, I write, draw, and play and compose music, so I am a jack of all trades. Do I feel differently when I practise these different genres? I don't think so.'

'Perhaps the question should be answered by a serious artist,' Launde said, with a world-weary air. 'I think you would not deny that your abilities are modest at best.'

Mawes said, with a straight face but a gleam of laughter in his eyes, 'By all means, answer it yourself, my dear fellow. No-one could accuse you of being modest.'

Launde didn't know how to take the remark, and while he hesitated, Mr Cowling spoke again. 'Well, shall I put it a different way? Does the artist start with a certain skill – say, a talent for drawing – which forces him to be artistic, or is there a sort of artistic drive that comes first, and it finds its way out through whatever he has a bent for, like water bubbling up through the cracks in the rock, following the line of least resistance?'

'I'd have loved to be a concert pianist,' said Miss Sylvia Partridge. 'I play the piano, but not awfully well. And Evelyn draws very nicely, don't you, dear?'

'Thank you, dear,' her sister answered, 'but drawing is only a hobby. I only truly get inspiration when I write.'

'Is inspiration necessary?' Aunt Schofield asked. 'Is it real? Or is it a meaningless word deployed to keep the non-artistic at arm's length?'

'Good point, ma'am. Well, then, what is inspiration?' Cowling asked. 'What inspires all you fine people?'

'I must say,' Mawes Morris said gravely, 'that the coal bill gives me the greatest possible inspiration. One glance at the "demned total", and I find myself beavering away like anything!'

Everyone laughed, except Mr Launde, who curled his lip and said, 'Inspiration comes from outside one. As it has divine origins, it cannot be explained.'

Mr Wentworth looked at him indulgently and said, 'I've heard Launde before on this subject many times – haven't I, Mannox? – and he's not the only one of us to promote the idea that artists exist on a more exalted plane than the rest of humanity. And why not? If anyone could do it, we wouldn't be valued – at least, not sufficiently.'

Launde looked at him with distaste. 'Are you suggesting that anyone *can* do it? That artistic talent is not an extraordinary gift bestowed on the very few?'

'In my experience,' Wentworth answered, 'artists are earthy creatures. Art is toil.'

'Toil?' Launde cried in outrage.

'Surely there is more to it than that?' Decius asked.

Wentworth shrugged. 'You've heard people like Launde say you must suffer for your art. What you suffer mostly is dirty hands, sweat, sometimes an aching back. Art is a great deal of hard work allied to a modicum of skill.'

There was a general protest at this, and Mr Cowling said, 'But aren't there some folk – your great names – who are different? Like – er – your Michelangelo and your Rembrandt. Otherwise, how did they get to be so great?'

'Simply, they worked very much harder at it,' said Wentworth.

'I think Mr Wentworth is trying to be mischievous,' said Aunt Schofield. 'You surely don't suggest that anyone can be taught to be a Michelangelo?'

He bowed to her. 'I confess I exaggerate a little for effect. But this idea that the artist is some rarefied fellow with ichor in his veins, who sips nectar from the flower of inspiration and sustains himself on manna from the gods . . .' He shrugged. 'It gets in the way. I teach in an art school, and the first thing I have to do with any pupil who shows promise is to break down their internal prohibitions, the barriers to thought and expression they've learned from their parents and society. They must dig their fingers deep into the soil. They must get grubby. They must be willing to try anything, *do* anything for their art.'

'That sounds dangerous,' Decius said.

'Yes,' said Lepida, 'and aren't you by that measure still preaching that the artist is different from the ordinary man? Aren't you, in fact, agreeing with Mr Launde, even if your sustenance is bread and cheese rather than manna from the gods?'

Mawes Morris said gleefully, 'You have him, my darling! Well said! But I am going to expose your secret, Wentworth, my dear fellow. This dangerous man, this bohemian free spirit, this cocker of snooks at convention, goes home when term ends to Surrey, to a dear little cottage with roses round the door where he keeps a dear little wife and six dear little children with roses in their cheeks!'

'Not six! You exaggerate,' said Wentworth, with high good humour. 'Only four at the last count.'

'Well, I don't pretend to know much about art,' said Mr Cowling, 'but a cottage and a wife and a quiver of children sounds like a fine outcome, and if Mr Wentworth can get there by painting his pictures, good luck to him!'

John Benson spoke up. 'We seem to have concentrated on painting, which, with writing, is something we all practise to an extent, but surely we must all agree that music is different.'

The conversation took off in a new direction, and Nina sat quietly and watched the ball being lobbed back and forth with great pleasure. She rather missed this in her ordinary life.

Rose had to flatten herself against the wall to avoid being barged into by the delivery boy from Bowden's, the grocers, staggering under the weight of a box of dry goods and big with news.

'There's such a to-do at Hundon's!' he exclaimed, as he erupted into the kitchen and thumped the box down on the long table. 'I saw when I went past on me bike! There's been police there and all sorts!'

Rose followed him to the kitchen door, a cold feeling in her stomach.

Mrs Terry said crossly, 'Don't put it down there! I'm just about to roll out pastry. Over there on the side table.'

Ivy, one of the kitchen maids, was a better audience. 'What d'you mean, police?'

'I saw the police wagon going down the hill. And the cows was making a hullabaloo, like they'd not been milked, and I saw Mr Ogg in the yard talking to that yard boy with the hare lip, and he was wringing his hands like he was ever so upset about something. D'you think Mr Woodrow has been arrested?'

'Of course he's not, and don't you go spreading rumours about,' Mrs Terry berated him. Rose didn't hear any more. She ran out of the back door without even putting on her hat and coat.

She half ran, half walked to Hundon's, consumed with dread. She could hear the cows before she came in sight of the yard. Ogg, the yard man, seemed to be arguing with Beattie Gale, one of the milkmaids, while the other milkers huddled in the doorway, watching. Ogg looked at Rose with hope as she came through the gate. 'Have you come with a message?' he asked. 'From up the house?'

'No, I've not. What's up with the cows?'

'Mr Woodrow's been took away,' Ogg cried, wringing his hands. 'And his sister. All over blood, he was, and no orders given. I don't know what to do.'

'Milk the cows for a start,' Rose said impatiently. 'What are you waiting for?'

'But we'll have missed the collection,' Ogg said helplessly.

'Milk 'em anyway! They're suffering!'

'That's what I said,' Beattie Gale cried, 'but Mr Ogg's hanging back.'

'Get on and milk 'em, for God's sake!' Rose snapped. 'I can't stand that noise.' She had no authority there, but a sure demeanour and a sharp voice went a long way.

'But what'll we do with the milk?' Ogg asked feebly.

'How do I know? Better out than in, that's all I know.' Beattie scuttled off in satisfaction. Rose stopped Ogg as he was about to follow. 'What happened in the house?'

'I don't know. All I know, Mr Woodrow came out of the kitchen all over blood and told me to send a boy to get the police, urgent. And they come and took Mr Woodrow and Miss Woodrow away. Oh, thank God, there's Mr Richard!'

Rose turned to see Richard coming in at the gate almost

at a run. His eye brushed over Rose without taking her in, such was his urgency. 'For God's sake, get those bloody cows milked!' he shouted at Ogg. 'I can hear 'em half a mile away.'

Rose backed carefully out of his line of sight and left, hurrying back to the house, hoping she hadn't been missed. She chewed over the meagre information she had. No doubt word of what had happened would reach the below-stairs community soon – exciting stories always had wings – but until then she could only torment herself with questions.

'It seems she tried to kill him with a knife. He managed to overcome her, and tied her up with her own apron,' Afton said to Mrs Webster. 'I don't know how seriously he was wounded, but he was able to send someone for the police, and apparently got into the police wagon under his own steam, so perhaps not too badly.'

Mrs Webster stopped him with a look as Rose passed the door, and he turned, and said, 'Ah, Rose.' He beckoned her in. 'A job for you, if you're willing. It's not a very nice one, but it needs to be someone we can trust not to have hysterics. And not to talk about it, either.' He paused. 'Are you all right? You look a bit pale.'

'I'm always pale,' Rose said curtly. It wasn't true. She had *felt* pale ever since the grocer's boy burst in. 'What's this job?'

'There's been an incident at Hundon's,' Mrs Webster said.

'I heard. Something about Mr Woodrow being wounded.'

'Yes,' said Afton. 'There was some kind of – a fight, or struggle, between him and his sister. We don't know all the details, but Mr Richard says the kitchen is in a mess, and he'd like it cleaned up before Mr Woodrow comes back. He thinks very highly of him, you know.'

Mrs Webster took it up. 'It seems there was some blood spilled, and he says it wouldn't be good for Mr Woodrow to come back to it, after such a shock. So would you go and see to it? I can't force you to, but I'm asking nicely.'

Rose said, 'Now?'

'Yes, right away, if you will. Here's the key. Mr Richard locked the kitchen door when he left. Don't let anyone else in, will you? Rumours will have got about and there are always some gawkers.'

There was no-one in the yard when she arrived for the second time that day, and the cows must have been let out, because there was no bovine sound. The dogs had been tied up, and barked as she appeared. She went across to talk to them, and they looked at her anxiously, wondering if she had come to restore order to their disrupted world.

Fly stood up and wagged his tail. 'I don't know what's come of him,' she said, as she petted him. Jess, lying down chin on paws, twitched her eyebrows. 'Good dogs. It'll be all right,' she said.

She unlocked the kitchen door, and stood just inside for a moment, taking it in. The evidence of a struggle was clear. Two chairs had been overturned. The cloth had been half pulled off the table, and what had been on it had mostly ended up on the floor. The teapot remained balanced on the edge like a clifftop house that had narrowly survived a landslip. Some of the crockery was broken. The heel of the loaf of bread had been kicked across the room. A jam jar was smashed in a mess of raspberry jam, which had been trodden about. There was also a broken glass by the sink, and some kind of brownish liquid, presumably its contents. The kitchen range had gone out, and the kettle that had been left on it had boiled dry – she could smell the tang of burned metal. And there was blood – splashes and drips of it all over the place, and a blood-soaked dish-towel lying on the draining-board, as if it had been used to staunch the wound. Or wounds?

Mr Afton was right to send her, she thought. Any of the housemaids was physically capable of the job, but which of them would not be overcome with horror, or at least want to rush out and find someone to babble to? She shut her lips tightly, and started methodically to restore order. She collected the broken glass and crockery into a box she found in the larder, scraped up the jam and put it, with the bread, into the pig bucket. She raked out the range, re-laid and lit it, scoured out the kettle – it hadn't burned through, luckily – and went to refill it, to find no water in the tap. She went into the scullery to prime the pump and pump it up, then filled the kettle and put it on to boil.

She cleared the table and put the four chairs upside down on it, put the tablecloth in to soak with the dish-towel, and when the kettle was hot, got a bucket and cloths from under the sink and began to wash the floor. When that was done, she got a fresh bucket and cloth, and went round eliminating all the smears and splashes. She had just refilled the kettle and put it back on when the dogs barked, and she turned to see Michael Woodrow coming across the yard, his face white and drawn, his arm in a sling.

She avoided his eyes, embarrassed after their last meeting to be found in his house. 'Mr Richard asked me to come in and clean the kitchen. He gave me the key,' she said.

'That was . . . kind,' he said. He put a hand to his head and rubbed vaguely.

'Are you all right? You look as if you ought to sit down,' Rose said. He stepped across the threshold and looked around the kitchen with the air of not really knowing where he was. She pulled out a chair, and said, 'Sit down. I'll make you a cup of tea before I go.'

'You did all this?' he said hoarsely. 'You're very kind.'

She went about making tea without answering. When she put the teapot on the table and was turning away to find a cup, he said, 'Rose – Miss Hawkins. Please. I want to apologise.'

'What for?' she said, her back to him.

He waited until she brought the cup to the table, and said, 'Please sit down. I must talk to you.'

She sat, but still avoided his eyes, busying herself with stirring the pot and pouring.

'You won't look at me. You're angry with me. I don't blame you. I should have listened to you.'

She shrugged.

'She's my sister,' he said. 'I didn't want to believe she'd . . . How could I?'

'It's nothing to me,' she said.

'I kept thinking about it. I was angry that you'd suggested it. But then yesterday I went up to her room while she was out – she sleeps in the attic, right under the roof. I thought there was a wasp's nest under the tiles just above. I moved the small cupboard away from the window so I could reach it and I heard something fall over. So I looked inside, to make sure I hadn't broken anything. It was a bottle of brown liquid. No label. It smelt like mould or mushrooms.'

Now she looked up.

'I took it away to my room. I thought she'd say something about it being missing, but she didn't say a word. This morning, at breakfast, I brought it out, I asked her what it was. She said it was medicine. So I – I pushed it into her hand, I said, "Let me see you take some, then." I was rough with her – I was afraid, you see. Afraid of what I might find out. Then she said it was rat poison. I asked where she'd got it, with no label on it, and she said she made it herself. I asked where she was planning to use it, and she said, "I'll poison any rats that come in this house." She said, 'They'll not take you away from me."'

Rose let out a breath that sounded like a sigh. His face looked so worn she felt sorry for him.

He rubbed his eyes wearily and went on: 'So I asked her if she'd put the stuff in the cake she made for you. I asked her quite quietly. I still couldn't believe . . . She didn't answer, but she gave me such a hard look, I knew then. I said, "Martha, don't you realise what you've done?

Something like that is a matter for the police." And that's when she went wild. She screamed at me. She threw the bottle at me. I ducked and it hit the floor and smashed. I tried to grab hold of her to quiet her and she fought me off. We struggled. Chairs fell over. The tablecloth got dragged off and everything smashed on the floor. I tried to subdue her but she's tall and strong and – well, I was trying not to hurt her, which didn't help. Then I trod on something sharp and lost my balance and fell. Cut my hand on a piece of glass as I tried to save myself. It was while I was trying to get up that she – she stabbed me with the big kitchen knife.' He put a shaky hand up to his shoulder. 'Back here. Twice. I managed to get up. She kept on coming. I – I couldn't hit her. Not a woman. Not my sister. I had to try and grapple with her. I was bleeding and I couldn't use my right arm properly. I—'

He stopped. Rose said gruffly, 'I'm sorry you got hurt.'

He shook his head. 'She kept saying, "I won't let you leave me." She said, "I'll not let her take you."'

'You don't have to tell me,' Rose said, feeling uncomfortable. *Mr Afton – he was a very clever man, wasn't he?*

'I got the knife away from her. I held onto her in the end, and suddenly she gave up, stopped struggling. She was weeping. I – I didn't dare let her go. I tied her apron round her, round her arms so she couldn't move them, tied her to a chair. But she didn't struggle, just sat there, weeping. I was bleeding and feeling faint. I went outside to call for help.'

'I know. The police came.'

He raised haunted eyes to her. 'What could I do? She'd tried to kill me. She might do it again. How could I trust her? She has to be—' He didn't want to say it.

'Locked up.' The words were flat as the smell of stagnant water.

He was silent, drawing on his reserves. 'Down at the station, the doctor came, gave her something to make her drowsy.

Looked at my wound. He said I was lucky, half an inch and it would have struck an artery and I'd be dead.'

He stopped. She waited, but he didn't seem to be going to continue. She said, 'Where is she now?'

'They took her to Asham Bois,' he said starkly.

She'd expected that. It was where the insane asylum was.

He looked at her as if she had accused him. 'What else could I do? I couldn't have her here, never knowing if she'd poison me, or stab me in my sleep. But she's my *sister*!' He shook his head miserably. 'She's always been a bit strange, but she was never a danger, not to me, not to anybody.'

Rose said, 'You're blaming me.'

'I'm not!' he protested.

'Yes, you are. You think it's you and me walking out that tipped her over. She thought I was taking you away from her. Well, I could have set her right on that score.'

'Rose, don't!'

She got up. 'I'll get out of your way now. I won't bother you again. You can have her back here for all it matters to me. I'll make sure to keep out of the way.'

'Please don't be angry. Please—'

'I'm not angry,' she said curtly. 'You and me – that was always daft. We're from different worlds. What do I want with a man, anyway? They're nothing but trouble.'

She took her coat from the nail on the back of the door. He said, 'Please don't go,' but she made no answer. She went out and closed the door quietly behind her.

Fly stood with a rattle of his chain and looked up at her hopefully, swinging his tail. 'I don't know what you're laughing at,' she addressed him. 'Clown face.' And she walked off. She felt scoured inside, with the raw satisfaction of one who expects the worst and is proved right.

CHAPTER SEVENTEEN

'He's moved back in with the Gales for the time being,' Richard said. 'He can't use his right arm properly, so he needs help with washing and dressing. And he can't cook for himself.'

'It's a grim business,' Giles said, fiddling with a letter-opener on his desk. Richard walked restlessly over to the library window, then back. The dogs, lying in a patch of sunshine in front of the desk, watched him both ways, turning their heads in unison. 'And there was no indication before?'

'Evidently not, or he'd have had some other living arrangement,' said Richard. 'But the point is now, what's to be done about him? Even when his arm is sound again—'

'The damage isn't permanent, then?'

'Apparently not. But he'll still need a housekeeper of some sort, and he has no more relatives.'

'Pity he's not married,' Giles grunted. 'He's not a bad-looking fellow.'

'In the mean time, there's only Ogg to run the farm, and he's a good worker when he's told what to do, but no use when it comes to making decisions. So I shall have to go down there every day and keep things running until Woodrow's sound again and decides what to do. He seems to have had the stuffing beaten out of him.'

Giles looked up. 'You think he might give it up?'

'I don't know,' Richard said, sounding harassed by the

question. 'I certainly hope not. I was pleased to have found someone so perfectly qualified for our purposes. I can hardly hope to find another.'

'Perhaps we'd better start looking for an assistant stockman. Even if Woodrow comes back, what with the increase in the herd . . . And, as you say, Ogg's no deputy, if something happens when Woodrow's out somewhere.'

'I'll ask around,' Richard said. He walked back to the window. Tiger sighed gustily and laid his head on his paws, ginger eyebrows twitching. Silence settled, the book-lined, leather-scented, ancient silence of the library.

Giles looked up from what he was reading, at last. 'I wonder if Bexley knows of a good stockman who might want a change of place,' he said. He stood up. The dogs stood too, and stretched fore-and-aft, expectantly. 'I have to ride over to see him about those poachers in Crown Woods.' Lord Bexley, of the Grange, was the local magistrate. 'Why don't you come with me? The ride and the fresh air would do you good. You look as though you have the cares of the world on your shoulders.'

'Not the whole world. Just a hemisphere, perhaps,' Richard said.

Maud Stainton had always had a sternly repressive policy towards ill health, and ill health had always been too cowed to defy her, so Alice had been shocked at the sight of her mother recumbent on a *chaise longue* with a counterpane over her, her face puffy and pallid, dark circles under her eyes.

Her hair was done differently, in what Alice supposed was a German style – tonged into thick horizontal rolls that seemed to gather and twist above her ears, like complicated bread products. Alice thought it looked strange and wrong – but no-one likes their mother to change.

She found Linda changed, too. She seemed to have put on some weight, which suited her, as did the fat roll hairstyle, which she had also adopted. She was nervously, fidgetily pleased to see Arabella. She talked in a rapid, high voice about her grief for her son and her determination never to be parted from her daughter again, but to Alice it seemed as though Linda was saying what she thought a mother should. She didn't sense any real feeling in it. And Arabella didn't cling and cry prettily and lisp of childish love. Withdrawn and uncommunicative, still clutching Pepper tightly in one hand, she endured Linda's embraces, and got away from her as soon as possible. Since her brother's death, Arabella seemed to have grown taller, and with the weight she had lost she was becoming bony and looking even more like her mother.

Though there was no entertaining in the Usingerhof, there were parties at other houses in the neighbourhood, to which Linda went on her mother's behalf. She spoke about this as a duty, but Alice did not sense any real reluctance to go. Sometimes Paul accompanied her. Alice wondered how he could abandon his wife in her condition to go to parties. But one day when all three sisters were out riding together, Linda gave away the reason.

She was talking about the dinner she was going to that evening at the Anhalt-Saales' summer house, and said, with what was almost a girlish smile, 'Cousin Pippi will be there again. He had to go back to his own estate because of some business, but Anna Anhalt-Saale says he's returned at the *earliest possible* opportunity, when they hadn't expected him back at all this summer.'

'Who is Cousin Pippi?' Alice asked.

'You can't have been paying attention,' Linda said sharply. 'Paul was talking about him at dinner only two days ago. He's his third cousin – Landgrave Philip of Plotzkau-Zeitz. He has a *Schloss* on the White Elster – not very pretty, but large and quite modern – and another in Thuringia. He has a coal mine in the Saar and an ore mine in Württemberg – cobalt, I think Paul said, whatever that is. And he's distantly related to the Hesse family. Hesse used to be part of Thuringia some time or other,' she concluded vaguely.

This recital of his possessions brought a suspicion to Alice's mind. 'Is he married?' she asked casually.

'He's a widower. What has that to do with anything?'

'I'd have thought it had everything to do with everything,' Alice said.

Linda coloured a little. 'You've become very sharp since I last saw you. It must be that school you're going to. I told Mama it was a mistake. It has coarsened you.'

But Rachel's interest had been engaged now, and she said, 'Do you like him?'

'Pippi Plotzkau-Zeitz is a well-born person with perfect manners,' Linda said loftily.

'Yes, but do you *like* him?' Rachel persisted. 'And does he like you?'

She hesitated. 'Paul says he's spoken of me to him in very warm terms.'

'Are you going to marry him?' Rachel asked.

'Goodness, what a question! He hasn't even asked me yet. I think we should canter along here.' And she kicked her horse on, ending the conversation. Alice fell in behind Rachel, thinking that it was not like Linda to be reticent, which suggested that the matter was not yet settled. If Cousin Pippi was indeed a suitor, Linda was anxious that nothing should put him off. It appeared also that stepfather Paul was keen to promote the match. Perhaps having Linda under his roof for a prolonged visit had made him fear he would never get rid of her.

That afternoon Alice took Arabella out in the donkey-cart to give her and Miss Kettel a rest from each other. They took sketching materials with them and settled before a fine view, where Alice passed on what she had learned of landscape drawing. It was wonderfully peaceful, with the wind stirring gently in the pine trees behind them, and the bees working in the wild thyme at their feet, and no person or building in sight – nothing moving, indeed, but the occasional cloud-shadow over the valley, and an eagle gliding on an air current far above them in the intensely blue sky.

She watched Arabella wielding her pencil, and thought that she looked happy for the first time since Arthur's death. She knew from her own experience that art could take over your mind and leave no room for unhappy thoughts. She wondered what would happen if Linda did marry Pippi Plotzkau-Zeitz. Would she have Arabella to live with her, and would the new stepfather be kind? Poor child. Alice was glad for once to have a mother who had no interest in her. There was obviously no plot going on to marry her off.

And then an unwelcome thought arrived: was she to remain unmarried in order to be her mother's attendant in Linda's place? Was she marked out as the spinster daughter-at-home, meek fetcher and carrier and possibly useful 'aunt' to the new baby? When the summer ended and Mama was out of childbed, would she be allowed to go home?

I have to! I have to go! She thought of the school, her friends, and she longed fiercely to be back there. If she tries to keep me here I'll run away, she thought. But as Rachel had before her, she realised deep down that without money she could not get from the depths of Germany back to England. She would not get further than the Usingerdorf railway station.

The train beat its hypnotic rhythm on the rails, swaying like a dancer as the suburbs of London were left behind and it picked up speed. The smiling countryside, fat and dark green with August, rolled by the windows. The air was warm inside the compartment and smelt of dusty upholstery; the sunlight slanted in, with a shadow-flick from each telegraph pole it passed.

Sebastian looked down at his wife and said, 'Are you all right? You're very quiet. You're not nervous, are you?'

'Of course I am.' She gave him the smile that said, *I know more about the world than you, even though you're older and much more clever.*

'There's no need. You saw the letter – it couldn't have been nicer.'

When they got back to England, he had written from their hotel to say that he would like to bring his wife to Ashmore on their way home to Henley, provided they would be welcome, and had received a reply inviting them in warm and civil terms.

'What people say in letters and what you see in their eyes is not always the same thing,' Dory said. 'I don't doubt they'll put a good face on it.'

He took her hand. 'I promise you this, if you're at all uncomfortable we won't stay.'

But it's your home, Dory thought. *I can't be the reason you have to stay away.* She smiled. 'You're very kind to me.'

'Don't start that again,' he said, with mock sternness. 'I'm not kind – *you*'re the kind one, to marry an old man and make him happy.'

'Don't *you* start that again! You're not an old man.'

'I don't feel it when I'm with you. Are *you* happy, my love?'

'So very happy,' she said. 'It's hard to get used to, after all those years. I keep catching myself out, thinking I ought to be worrying, and then realising I don't have to any more.'

'No shadows?' he asked.

She knew he meant about his part in Jack Hubert's death. It was a question he asked now and then because, loving her so much, he sensed, or perhaps just feared, that it still troubled her. 'No shadows,' she said, and then, to change the subject, 'You'll have to begin playing the piano again when we get home. You've hardly touched one in months. You'll be getting out of practice.'

He noticed that she had called it 'home'. 'Would you like me to teach *you* to play?'

She hadn't expected that. 'Aren't I too old to learn?'

'Not a bit. It's just a matter of practice. You'll soon get the hang of it. Then we could play duets.'

'We do already,' she said, giving him the look that made him long for bedtime.

The carriage was waiting for them at the station, with two greys harnessed, John Manley and Joe Green on the box. The porters carried out their valises: just overnight things – their big trunks had been sent straight to Henley. Joe Green jumped down, opened the carriage door and put down the step. John Manley was exchanging a greeting with Sebastian. He said, 'Welcome home, sir.'

'The horses look well,' Sebastian said.

'Thank you, sir.'

Dory thought he was going to ignore her existence as an unfortunate mistake, but then he said, 'If I might be permitted, sir, to offer my congratulations? And my felicitations to your good lady.'

'Thank you, Manley,' Sebastian said. He bent to murmur in her ear, 'There, you see? Nothing to worry about.'

Dory thought, *Coachman is one thing. He doesn't work in the house. He barely knew me when I was a servant.*

With Crooks occupying the forward seat, they could not talk on the ride up to the Castle. The carriage and horses were well known in the village, and several people stopped to look as it went past. Dory felt absurdly that she should wave, like Queen Alexandra. They crossed the river by the stone bridge, passed through the gateposts, and then John Manley chirruped to the horses and they threw their weight into the collar for the pull up the hill. Dory remembered when she had walked up there for the first time, carrying her suitcase, on her way to a new job. She had been passed by two grooms exercising carriage horses and they had ignored her, as grooms in high-up stables usually ignored lower servants. And now she was riding behind those same horses, and would be transported to the front door. Life was strange.

As they swung round in front of the house, she saw there was a reception line waiting for them: his lordship and her ladyship and Mr Richard on one side, and on the other Mr Afton, William and Ellen. Dory knew how great houses worked. The full line-up was only for the master or mistress coming home after an absence, or for royalty. The servants here now were only the ones required: Mr Afton to open the carriage door, William to carry the luggage, and Ellen because Dory had no lady's maid of her own, and one would have been assigned to her. On their long honeymoon holiday, she'd had to get used to being attended by a maid, but a hotel chambermaid, especially one who spoke little English, was a much lower hurdle than an English housemaid with all the proper notions, let alone one she had sat down with in the servants' hall at mealtimes.

But for now there was the family to navigate. Her ladyship came straight to Dory, offered her hand, and said, with a shy smile, 'I'm so pleased to welcome you to Ashmore Castle.'

Don't call her 'my lady'. Don't call her 'my lady'. 'Thank you,' Dory managed to say.

Her ladyship seemed to understand the difficulty. 'You must call me Kitty – won't you? How was the journey? Are you terribly tired?'

'We only came from London today,' Dory reminded her. 'But we seem to have been travelling for months.'

'That's because you have.' This was Mr Richard, taking her hand and bowing over it with a parade of gallantry that was intended to amuse. 'I was at your wedding, remember, so I know exactly how long you've been gone. Was Italy glorious?'

'Yes, but getting too hot by the time we left. Sebastian—' She caught herself up, embarrassed to have called him by his first name in front of them, then realised that 'Mr Sebastian' would have been a far worse *faux pas*. 'Sebastian was rather suffering in Rome, and we were glad to head north. The lakes were lovely.'

'The lakes! How lucky you are. I mean to go myself one day,' Richard said, with kindly ease. He was so nice, and Kitty (*Kitty*!) was kind, but now his lordship had finished with Sebastian and was ready to greet her. He didn't smile, but then she knew from hearing the other servants talk that smiling was not his way. He was the serious one where Richard was the joker, and everyone was a little wary of him.

He shook her hand and said, 'Welcome to the Castle. Come in and have some tea.'

There was nothing in what he said or the way he said it to upset her. But he didn't ask her to call him Giles. And it was just as well because she never, never could have.

'Well, I'm not curtsying to her,' Daisy announced to the table, round which the servants had gathered for their tea – thick slices of bread, and a vast fruit cake. 'Not a servant who's sat at this very table.' She liked the sound of that, and repeated it. 'At this very table!'

Mrs Webster was quick to squash her. 'Nobody's asking you to curtsy to her. So don't talk nonsense, and pass the bread down.'

Daisy automatically passed the plate, but carried on with her complaint. 'She's only a sewing maid when all's said and done.' She was resentful because she had expected to be asked to maid Dory, since she had maided the two young ladies, and had been intending to refuse. This glorious act of rebellion would have conferred distinction and have been talked of in the servants' hall with hushed admiration for weeks. But Mrs Webster had asked Ellen instead.

'I never trusted her,' Daisy went on. 'The way she used to hang about the small drawing-room when Mr Sebastian was playing the piano. She had her eye on him right from the start, the sly—'

'Be quiet, Daisy,' Mrs Webster stopped her before the word 'baggage' could tumble from her lips. 'That's quite enough from you. If that's the quality of your opinions you had better keep them to yourself.'

Daisy looked black, and took a savage bite out of her slice of bread.

Cyril said, 'But what Daisy says: why should we wait on her when she's just a servant?'

Afton spoke up. 'Mrs Sebastian Tallant is entitled to every courtesy we offer to a guest in this house, and anyone who thinks differently can come straight to me after tea and give me his notice.'

Mrs Webster built on that. 'Quite right, Mr Afton. Furthermore, the wife of a member of the family is entitled to an extra level of consideration, and don't you forget it.'

Ellen said, 'I don't mind maiding her. I've done guests before, and I bet there were some rum characters among 'em. They're not all saints. It don't matter to me. The work's the same, whoever you do it for.'

'Well, I don't agree,' said Daisy. 'It's – it's demeaning, that's what it is, when they're not real ladies.'

'Mr Sebastian wouldn't marry anyone that wasn't a real lady,' Ellen said. 'It's what's inside that counts.'

'That's the proper attitude,' Mrs Webster said.

Ellen gave a satisfied smirk over her bread-and-jam.

Mabel, slow of thinking as of speaking, caught up. 'I think it's romantic. It's just like one of them stories, when the chimney-sweep turns out to be a prince in disguise, who's trying to find out if a woman can truly love him when he's not wearing his crown and that.'

There was a pause as people untangled the syntax.

Then Rose said, 'You're an utter fool. Mr Sebastian isn't in disguise.'

'Well, but you know what I mean,' Mabel said, bewildered herself now.

'I think she was always a cut above us,' said Milly. 'I mean, she liked that high-up music Mr Sebastian played.'

'I like music,' said Wilfrid, cheekily. 'D'you think I could get a posh lady to marry me?'

'No-one will marry you until you learn to scrub your nails before you sit down at the table,' said Afton. 'Go and do it now, you heathen.'

The reluctant scraping of Wilfrid's chair accompanied his departure; and the pause extended as Mr Crooks came in, and everyone had to inspect the next thing they were going to say for appropriateness.

Afton indicated the seat beside him. 'Did you find everything to your satisfaction, Mr Crooks?'

'Thank you, yes,' Crooks said, sitting down.

'It's a shame you're only staying one night,' Mrs Webster said, from the other end.

'My master and mistress are eager to get home,' he said.

'Well, perhaps they'll favour us with a longer visit later in the year.'

'I have no information about that.' Crooks looked around the table, at the staring eyes and the averted eyes, and noted the unusual silence. 'What were you all talking about when I came in?' he asked.

No-one could remember. Then Rose said, 'Music, wasn't it?'

There was a pause, before Sam said bravely, 'I like music all right if it's something you can jig about to. Like that barrel organ that went through the village last week – did you hear it?'

'There's going to be a band at the fair,' Doris said, 'and dancing!' The servants all got time off to go to the Canons Ashmore annual fair on Poor's Field, in the village. She threw a sly glance at Sam. 'You can dance with me, if you like. Show me how you jig about.'

The dam broke and they all started talking about the fair,

which would have rides, and booths, and races, and plenty to eat and drink.

'It's a pity we can't have it here,' Mr Afton said to Mrs Webster.

'We don't have the space outside,' said Mrs Webster. 'If only we had a park, like at the Grange. But Miss Taylor once told me that they used to have a flower show here. I wonder if her ladyship would revive it.'

'It'd be something,' Afton said. 'Miss Hatto, perhaps you could mention it to her ladyship. When the moment seems right?'

Miss Hatto only gave her mysterious smile and didn't say yes or no.

And Mr Crooks ate bread and butter and let the noise wash over him, reflecting on the changes of fortune life brought. Once he had been valet to the old earl, the most consequential person below stairs after the butler; now he was just a visiting valet. But Mr Sebastian was a kind master and a true gentleman, and Crooks was gradually raising his sartorial standards to match Crooks's own.

The long sojourn abroad had taught him that his master and the new mistress were truly devoted to each other, an attachment that deserved his respect. Furthermore, Mrs Sebastian had displayed an evenness of temper at all times, which boded well for the household. Travel, especially abroad, involved inconveniences that could bring out the worst in people of the bluest blood. To bear patiently with delays, lost items, unhelpful officials, and incomprehensible foreigners made the former sewing-maid a true lady in Crooks's eyes. He only hoped the other Wisteria House servants would see it the same way.

'This is very fine, madam,' Ellen said, approaching with the evening gown. 'Is it Paris?'

'Yes,' Dory said. 'Paquin.'

Ellen committed the name to memory. 'Beautiful embroidery. And the colour's lovely.'

Dory was emboldened to ask, 'Are they all very upset, downstairs?'

Ellen didn't answer at once, lifting the dress over Dory's head. Then, from behind her, starting on the hooks, she said, 'You know what some of them are like, madam. Mr Afton says, "Dogs bark when the caravan goes by."'

Dory met her eyes in the mirror. 'Do you know what that means?'

'Sort of,' Ellen said. 'Not the words, exactly, but the sense of it. I like Mr Afton. He's always got a twinkle in his eye.' There was silence until she'd fastened the last hook, and twitched the shoulders into place. 'This is such a lovely gown, madam. Even her ladyship hasn't got one as nice. If you'll excuse the liberty, your hair's not quite right at the back.'

'I did it myself,' Dory admitted, slightly embarrassed.

'Can I fix it for you?' She pulled out a few pins and began re-coiling the chignon. Then, feeling the moment was right, she said, 'Will you be hiring a lady's maid, madam, if I may ask?'

'I haven't really thought about it,' Dory said.

'Because, if you don't mind me saying, you ought to have one. Fine lady's gowns always have hooks in hard places. And they need the hair to be just so.'

'I expect you're right. I don't know whether Mr Sebastian—'

'I bet Mr Sebastian will want you to have everything you ought. He's such a kind gentleman. And, madam, if you *were* to be thinking about engaging a lady's maid – well, it's what I've always wanted to be. I've maided lots of ladies who've come without their maids so I know what to do, and everyone says I've got a light hand with hair. There, that's done.' She pushed in a last pin and stepped back. She gave Dory a cocked, hopeful look. 'I promise I'd give satisfaction.'

'We're only staying one night,' Dory said doubtfully. It would be a rushed decision.

'I know, madam. I could be ready to come tomorrow. I'm sure her ladyship wouldn't mind if it was what Mr Sebastian wanted. I know she thinks the world of him.'

Dory looked at her reflection while she pondered. Probably Ellen was right, and Sebastian would want her to have a maid. And probably she needed one. Would it be better or worse to be maided by someone who knew her from the old days? But a stranger might learn what she had been and take offence. That would be painful.

She thought of arriving home in Henley without a maid, and having to call on Olive the housemaid to hook her up, the only other choice being Mrs May. Ellen was ambitious to be a lady's maid, which meant she would insist that the person she maided was treated with respect. She would be . . . an ally, perhaps? Dory had witnessed the closeness that sometimes developed between mistress and maid. She had never had a friend – it would be nice to have someone on her side, perhaps to confide in.

'I should like you to be my maid,' she said, and saw Ellen beam with genuine pleasure. 'I will ask Mr Sebastian, and send a message to you.'

Ellen handed her the long silk gloves. She knew what an opportunity this was. It was hard to make the jump from housemaid to lady's maid. Another chance like this might not come for years, if ever. 'Thank you, madam,' she said.

'Thank *you*, Ellen,' said Dory.

Prince Usingen's English, carefully instilled in him in childhood by a tutor with the aid of a whippy cane, had abandoned him entirely. It didn't matter very much as the doctor, of course, was German, as was the brick-faced nurse; and, in any case, once labour started he was banished from his wife's presence and confined to the ground floor. Linda, who spoke excellent German, had established herself in the lying-in chamber before anyone could question whether she should be there. Miss

Kettel was giving Arabella lessons in the old schoolroom to keep her mind off things. Which left only the two young ladies to comfort and reassure him through the ordeal.

Rachel and Alice hadn't sufficient grasp of the language to cope with such a delicate task. So the three of them sat exuding silent goodwill, except when Paul leaped to his feet as though driven by a hot spike and walked up and down the room, while the two girls held hands and whispered to each other.

'Why is it taking so long?' Alice whispered, when the prince was at the window, his unquiet hands clasped behind his back. 'Linda told me that the more babies you have, the quicker it should be.'

'I don't know,' Rachel whispered back. 'Linda's only had two, perhaps she doesn't really know.'

'Mama's much older than Linda. Perhaps that makes a difference.'

Rachel's eyes were beginning to fill with tears. 'You don't think . . . She won't *die*, will she?'

'No, of course not,' Alice said automatically, not sure at all, and forgetting to whisper.

The prince turned and said, '*Bitte?*'

She had to say something. 'You must be tired, sir. And you had nothing at breakfast. Shall I ring for coffee?' she tried. He stared at her blankly. She racked her brain for the German. '*Möchten sie Kaffee? Soll ich klingeln?*'

He mustered a scrap of English. 'Sank you, no.' He turned his eyes towards the ceiling. '*Ich frage mich* . . . Is all *in ordnung*? Why is it to be so long?'

Alice was embarrassed by his emotion. Mothers and fathers should be remote figures, not human beings made of flesh. 'The doctor knows what he is doing,' she said, trying to sound confident. 'Everything will be all right.'

He resumed his tormented pacing.

'Did you really mean it?' Rachel asked. 'That Mama will be all right?'

'Of course.' Alice wondered why it was left to her to reassure people. Shouldn't someone be comforting *her*? She thought of Axe, his big, quiet, powerful presence. He would not pace about and wring his hands. She would not be afraid or uncertain if he were there.

Rachel blotted her eyes. 'Did I hear you say something about coffee? Could we have some? And cake? Breakfast was so long ago, I'm starving.'

'I'll ring,' Alice said, and got up. It gave her something to do.

'It's not right, Mr Crooks,' said Mrs May. 'Whichever way you look at it, she's been a servant in this house. I don't see how we're supposed to forget that.'

'Forget it you will, and you shall,' Crooks said.

The maid Olive had moved to Mrs May's side as if seconding her opinion, and Crooks guessed that this argument had been rehearsed many times in the past weeks. Joe, the handyman, who had come into the kitchen for the mid-morning bait, only stared from one face to another with his mouth open.

'But it seems to me—' Mrs May began, settling in for the fight.

Crooks interrupted her: 'Tell me, when you applied for your position here, did Mr Sebastian promise he would consult you if he ever decided to take a wife?'

Mrs May paused a moment before answering. 'You're an educated man, Mr Crooks. You've got all the words, which I haven't, and you can twist things round so they sound right when you say them. But it doesn't make it so.'

'Then I'll make it simple for you, Mrs May. Suppose you went to the master, and said to him, "I don't like your choice of wife. Get rid of her, or I'm handing in my notice." What do you suppose he would say?'

Mrs May's lips tightened. 'There's no need to be sarcastic, Mr Crooks.'

'Isn't there?'

'I'm sure I never meant—'

'It seems to me that's exactly what you meant. I'll tell you plainly – and this goes for you, Olive, and Joe, as well – the master has waited all his life to meet the woman who could win his heart. And if you don't care for him enough to welcome her, you had better find another place.'

Olive stared anxiously at Mrs May for her reaction. It was a good place. She didn't want to give it up. She looked at Crooks. 'I s'pose if the master really loves her . . .'

From the drawing-room, the sound of the piano started up – a halting scale going up then, even less certainly, down.

'He's teaching her to play the piano,' Crooks said. He saw that the significance was beyond two-thirds of them at least. 'The master has chosen a wife and he loves her with all his heart. You'll treat her as you treat him, or he'll have your hide.'

There was a brief, thoughtful silence, then Joe said, 'I think she's really pretty. The mistress, I mean.'

Crooks smiled at him. 'One person, at least, who understands his own interests.'

Joe, who had meant it simply and literally, didn't understand the implication of the words, but he accepted the smile.

'It's hard,' Dory said, working her way again up the scale of C with hands that had quite other ideas.

'Everything worthwhile is hard,' Sebastian said. 'Except being married to you, which is as easy as breathing.'

'For you, perhaps,' she said, then looked up quickly and said, 'Oh, I didn't mean—'

'I know what you meant. Didn't you have servants when you were a girl? When you lived with your papa?'

'Only Mrs Higgins, who came in to scrub and do the heavy wash.'

'And did Mrs Higgins ever say, "I'm not taking orders from you"?'

Dory smiled. 'I was only a child. I didn't give orders.'

'Very well,' Sebastian said patiently. 'When you go into Poining's to buy some thread, Mrs Poining greets you with a smile and waits on you. She doesn't scowl and say, "It's over there, get it yourself," does she?'

'That's different,' Dory began.

'It isn't, though. You are the customer and it's her job to serve you. This house is my shop, and my servants are paid to wait on you.'

'Easy for you to say.' She stood up. 'My hands are aching, I must rest a moment. Will you play for me?' He took her place on the piano stool, and let out a ripple of scales like running water. 'Oh, now you're humiliating me,' she said, with a laugh.

He looked up at her with a fondness that made her catch her breath. 'I can't cut out, hem, sew a seam, darn or embroider. Your skills are far more useful than mine. You are a more worthwhile human being than me, as well as being a hundred times better to look at.'

She laid a hand on his shoulder, and it still gave her a little jolt of pleasure that she was entitled to do so. 'Just tell me how I should behave to them,' she said, going to the meaning behind his compliment.

'Be pleasant and firm, just as you would be to Mrs Poining, or any other shop assistant. They will soon get used to your altered status, I promise you. And you will, too – Mrs Tallant.'

'When it comes to playing the piano, Mrs No-talent-at-all.'

'Mrs Far-too-impatient! One lesson is all you've had. You must stick at it.'

'I shall, but play something for me now. The Chopin I like.'

He obeyed, and grinned up at her as his fingers coaxed out the familiar notes. 'I wonder if they'll think this is you, and be in awe of you?'

'I doubt it,' she laughed.

'I don't see why not. I am,' he said.

CHAPTER EIGHTEEN

Linda came down at last, with the doctor scurrying behind her, feeling it should be his privilege to announce the news.

'A boy,' Linda said, at the same time as the doctor squeezed past her and addressed the prince in their own language. Paul put his own immediate, anxious question in German, and Linda answered it in English for the girls' sake. 'She's very tired, but she'll be all right.'

The doctor's exposition went on for a lot longer, and Alice asked, 'What's he saying? I can't catch it. He looks serious. Is Mama really all right?'

Linda fidgeted. 'It was a long labour and it went hard with her, at her age. She *will* be all right, but it will take time. And he says she must never have another. Well, I don't suppose she'd want another anyway, after that. It's a good job she got a boy.'

The prince was looking more bemused than delighted as he listened to the doctor, but gradually realisation seemed to spread over his face. '*Ich habe einen Sohn,*' he said in wonder. He shook the doctor's hand. The doctor said a lot more, and went out of the room.

'I must get back,' Linda said 'He's going to make sure Mother's fit to be seen by the prince, but she won't see either of you just yet, so you needn't wait. Why don't you go out for a walk or something?' And she hurried away to secure her place.

The prince stared after her for a few minutes, then seemed to remember the girls, came over and shook their hands in turn. 'A son,' he said, with a smile that looked slightly shocked. 'I have a son.' He rummaged through his brain for more English words. 'You have *ein Bruder* – a little brother. You will be happy for that, I think?'

Then distractedly he walked out of the room. Alice and Rachel looked at each other.

'Our brother,' Rachel said. 'It feels very queer.'

Alice thought, *Giles, Richard – and a little Usingen baby*. 'It does,' she agreed.

The priest came up to the house that evening to baptise the baby. It was done privately with only the parents present. Miss Kettel explained to the girls that it was a precautionary exercise: it was done as early as possible so that if the baby should not survive it would still go to Heaven – a full christening in church would follow at a later date.

'Heinrich Adelbert Leopold von Usingen,' Rachel marvelled. 'What a lot of names for one small baby.'

'Linda said he'll probably get called Heinz. Or Heiko,' Alice said. 'Germans love pet names.'

Linda had also told them that Heinrich meant 'master of the house'. 'The prince thought it was appropriate for his heir. He's waited so long for one,' she added. 'He's terribly excited.'

The next day there was a grand celebration party, starting in the afternoon with much eating and drinking, and going on through the evening with music and dancing. The baby was brought down several times to be shown to the guests, though the mother was still in confinement. Alice and Rachel had not seen her, and were told not to expect to for some days. They did, however, get to see the fabled Cousin Pippi, the Landgrave Philip of Plotzkau-Zeitz, who came in the evening with another crowd of well-wishers and, as soon as the music struck up, invited Linda to dance.

Alice had expected an old man, perhaps a foolish or ugly one. The fact that he was a widower had suggested the first to her; the second was her rather guilty supposition, given that Linda was without dowry or beauty. But Cousin Pippi turned out to be only about fifty and was perfectly presentable. What alchemy had gone on Alice couldn't imagine, but there seemed no doubt that Pippi was trying to fix his interest with Linda. Watching them dance, Alice thought that Linda looked different when she was twirling with him: his attentions seemed to have softened her sharp edges. She looked almost pretty. It was sad, Alice thought, that poor Gerald Cordwell had had to die for Linda to be happy. She wondered whether it was the years of financial anxiety that had made her so disagreeable before, and whether, had Cordwell been rich, she might have been a nicer person.

Among the guests were an English MP, Sir Jocelyn Farocean, with two of his sons, Jervis and Bentham, who had been staying with the Pfaffenheims, Usingen's nearest neighbours, on their way home from a summer tour of Italy. Alice had not expected to be dancing at all, unless it was to do a duty circuit with some elderly gentleman, so she was pleased, after Jervis had hurried to claim Rachel's hand, to be asked by Bentham.

He was not entirely clear what the party was in celebration of, and asked politely to be enlightened. 'We only arrived last night and, to be fair, my German is not as good as my Italian.'

Alice told him about her baby brother, and mentioned his names.

'Golly, that's a mouthful!' her partner exclaimed. He was not as tall as his brother, and was stockier, and while Jervis was out-of-the-common handsome, Bentham was only pleasant-looking. But she thought she had the better deal: he was easy company and inclined to chat. Rachel and Jervis seemed too painfully aware of the need to impress each other. 'Parents really ought to be fined when they give their children challenging names,' Bentham went on. 'It's not they who suffer for it!'

'Is yours challenging?' Alice asked.

'I don't mind the Bentham part so much. Everyone calls me "Ben" anyway. Named after Jeremy Bentham, of course, and he was a pretty decent old cove, after all. Not someone to be ashamed of. It could have been much worse.'

'How so?' Alice asked.

'Well, Jervis was named after Johnny Jervis – Admiral St Vincent, you know? – and there's no way to shorten it except "Jarvey". Who wants to be called a cab-driver?' Alice laughed, and he looked pleased to have amused her. 'And I have another brother named after Admiral Cornwallis, who gets called "Corny".'

'Two admirals?' Alice queried.

'Well, the pater made his fortune in shipping, so the sea is rather on his mind, y'know. Apparently I was going to be named after Cuthbert Collingwood, only Mama objected that it should be her turn to choose. She was very keen on utilitarianism, so the Royal Navy was given a rest. Good thing, too. Our surname is enough to be going on with. No-one who only sees it written down knows how to pronounce it. I had a master at school who called me "Farrow-seen". I tried to tell him different and he gave me a very beady look. Not wise to correct a beak. They don't like it, y'know. So I had to leave it go, and was "Farrow-seen" to him for the whole five years. It grated. Don't know why it is, but one gets sensitive about one's handle.'

'Far Ocean,' Alice said, tasting the name. 'I get it now. Very appropriate for a shipping family.'

'Which came first, the chicken or the egg?' Bentham said. 'I imagine if your name was Butcher you'd be hard pressed to go in for haberdashery. It'd confuse people no end.'

'My surname is Tallant, and I haven't any.'

'I'm sure that's not true. You are an excellent dancer, for one thing. And good at conversation, which is unusual in a girl.'

'That doesn't sound like a compliment.'

'Oh, Lord! It was meant as one. I'm sure girls are naturally just as capable of conversing, only they get told not to, don't they? They're made to simper and languish instead. Girls' mamas all seem to think that men prefer empty heads and won't propose if there's any danger of thought going on under the golden tresses.'

'Was there a glance at my sister accompanying that obliging observation?'

He laughed. 'I say, you are jolly! And a very decent sort. I confess I was thinking of our esteemed elder siblings, but in my defence, just look at 'em! Both being fascinating, following the guidebook line by line, the "Mrs Beeton's" of courtship. I'm positive you and I are enjoying ourselves more. I know I am.'

Alice looked across at the other couple, and frowned. 'Do you think she's flirting?'

'I wouldn't go that far,' he said, 'but there is definitely hard work going on on both sides. Do you disapprove of flirting?'

'I don't really have an opinion one way or the other, except that Rachel's supposed to be engaged.'

'Supposed to be?'

Alice found herself explaining, briefly, the circumstances. 'Is your brother looking for a wife?'

'Yes, a rich one,' said Bentham.

'Well, Rachel should be safe, then. She hasn't any dowry.'

'I'm sorry to hear it,' Bentham said kindly. 'But she is so very pretty, I'm not surprised this fellow Angus has been eager to secure her.'

'Yes. It's lucky, really, that I don't want to get married, because I haven't any money either, and I haven't Rachel's looks.'

'I'm afraid you are fishing for compliments, ma'am, which your governess ought to have told you is a very bad habit,' he said, with mock sternness.

'I didn't have a governess. My vices are all self-taught,' said Alice.

'You must be aware that you are very pretty too,' he said lightly. 'Or, rather, I wouldn't say pretty, which is a commonplace word, while your beauty is quite *un*common.'

Alice looked awkward, and blushed slightly. 'I didn't mean—'

'Ah, but I did,' he said quickly. 'An uncommon beauty, if anyone was to ask me.'

'I'm sure no-one will,' Alice said, and hurried on, changing the subject lest he think she was fishing again. 'Do you make much stay with the Pfaffenheims?'

'Alas, no, we are leaving tomorrow. It was really only an overnight stay to break the journey. More's the pity.'

Alice agreed – it had crossed her mind to see if Mr Farocean could be invited to go riding the next day.

'The moment must satisfy us, I'm afraid,' he went on. '"Present mirth hath present laughter; what's to come is still unsure".'

Alice could supply the next line for herself: *Then come kiss me, Sweet-and-twenty*. She blushed. He was watching her face, and seemed to enjoy it.

'But perhaps we shall meet again in England,' he said. 'Do you make much stay in Usingen, Lady Alice?'

'I hardly know,' she said. 'It depends on my mother. But I hope not. I want to be back in London when the new term starts.'

'New term? You intrigue me, madam. Surely you cannot still be at school.'

So she told him about her studies, and the topic lasted to the end of the dance. When the music ended he bowed, and said, 'At least now I know how to find you when next we're in London. Thank you for the dance, *bella signorina*. I'm enjoying myself much more than I had any expectation of.'

Rachel hurried to join her as soon as her partner released her, and said, very flushed, 'What a charming boy Mr Farocean is! You danced with his brother, didn't you? What a pity they're going away tomorrow. Everyone else in the neighbourhood is so old and dull. I wonder if Aunt Caroline knows Sir Jocelyn.'

'Aunt Caroline knows everybody, but that's not the same as receiving them,' Alice said. 'I don't think you ought to have flirted when you're an engaged woman.'

'I wasn't flirting, I was being civil,' Rachel said automatically. 'But, oh dear, we shall be so dull tomorrow!'

But when tomorrow came, it brought news that Aunt Vicky and Uncle Bobo would be with them by dinner time, and everything grew cheerful again.

'It really is quite a sweet little thing,' Aunt Vicky said, with slight surprise – unflattering, but understandable. 'But goodness! I don't envy poor Maud. At her age!'

Everything was nicer when Aunt Vicky was there, for she had an irrepressible charm and cheerfulness. The difference in the prince was remarkable: he stood up straighter, looked and spoke like a proud papa, and remembered much more of his English. The servants vied with each other to please her, and everyone reaped the benefit. Even the cook served up more interesting food, ransacking seldom-consulted recipe books for un-German fancy dishes.

One morning Rachel was summoned to her mother's chamber for the first time. Alice was giving Arabella a drawing lesson, sitting in one of the windows and sketching the view outside. Arabella seemed to be settling down from the shock of her brother's death. Though she was quiet, she did not seem to be unhappy, was learning German both from Miss Kettel and from the housemaids, and had been taken on one or two visits to neighbours with suitably aged children to play with.

As Alice was helping her with a difficult fir tree, she said suddenly, 'Kettel said Grandmama's new baby is my uncle, even though I'm ten years older than him. Isn't that queer?'

'It is,' Alice said. 'But I believe it quite often happens, when people marry a second time.'

'I hope I'm let to see him soon. I'd like a little baby to play with.'

'A baby isn't a toy,' Alice said. 'Put more shading on that side. See how the light is coming all from the other side?'

'I think Mother means to stay here – don't you?'

'I really don't know. Would you mind? Do you like it here?'

'It's all right,' Arabella said. She frowned over her sketch for a moment, drawing more branches on the tree. 'It wasn't very nice at home in Dorset. It was always cold and I was always hungry. But Papa was alive then. And at the Castle there was enough to eat, but no-one liked me. But Arthur was alive then.' She sighed. 'I don't really belong anywhere, do I?'

Alice felt a pang of pity. 'You belong where your mother is,' she said awkwardly.

'Mother doesn't really like me. She's never bothered with me.'

Alice knew that was true. And if Linda married again – if Cousin Pippi came up to scratch – what were Arabella's chances then?

The little girl looked up. 'But I like Kettel. She can be strict, but she's always there. And new grandpapa Paul is very rich, so perhaps I can have a pony. I miss Biscuit and Goosebumps. Don't you miss Pharaoh?'

'Very much,' Alice said. At that moment a servant came in and told her she was wanted at once in her highness's room above. 'I must go,' she said to Arabella.

'I know.'

'Perhaps you could add Biscuit to your picture – have him waiting for you beside the tree.'

'But he isn't there.'

'Use your imagination.'

★ ★ ★

Alice had expected to find Rachel still there, but her mother was alone. 'Your sister is with Aunt Vicky,' Maud said. 'Sit there and let me look at you.'

Alice took the seat indicated at the bedside, and sat up straight, hands folded in her lap, as she had been taught. She was shocked at the sight of her mother, lying propped up on half a dozen pillows, in a lace and chiffon bedjacket with a lace-and-ribbon cap over her hair. The extravagant lingerie did nothing to mitigate her worn and frail look. She was as pale as milk, with blue shadows under her eyes, her face more gaunt than ever.

'You look just the same,' Maud said at last, and it was not a compliment. Alice said nothing – what was there to say? She was used to being a disappointment. 'You've seen the baby?'

'Yes, Mama. He's very sweet.'

'Well, I have done my duty. The prince is pleased. And the child is healthy.' She broke off and was silent. Alice thought she could supply the thought. Every man with a title wanted an heir and a spare, just in case. She had heard her brother Richard talk about it often enough – joking that he would never have been born except for the need for insurance. But would little Heiko ever have a brother? In marrying her mother, would the prince even have hoped for one child?

Maud came to the end of a train of thought and a shudder went through her. She drew a handkerchief out from her sleeve and coughed into it, eyes closed, and Alice half rose and said, 'Are you all right, Mama? Shall I ring for someone?'

Maud emerged from the handkerchief looking annoyed and therefore much more like herself, and snapped, 'Don't fuss. Sit down. I wish to talk to you.'

Alice sat, reassured by the sharp tone. But her mother leaned back on the pillows and closed her eyes again, looking exhausted, and it was a while before she went on.

'Your aunt Vicky is taking Rachel away to the Summer

Palace,' she said. The sharp tone was gone. She sounded only weary. 'She will stay with Vicky and Bobo until October, when they will be going to England and will take Rachel with them.'

So Rachel was to be drowned in pleasure, Alice thought, and if that did not convince her of the folly of her present engagement, the attentions of dozens of eligible young men surely would. *Oh, Mama!* Alice thought reproachfully. And *Poor Angus!*

'The question is, what is to be done with you?' Maud went on. 'Linda stays here. She has expectations of Cousin Pippi.' Maud closed her eyes. 'It would be the best outcome for her,' she murmured. 'For me, too. We do not deal comfortably together. Although she is much improved lately . . . He seems in earnest . . . I must do all I can to foster the match. I have already . . .' She opened her eyes abruptly and looked at Alice with a touch of confusion. 'What was I talking of?'

'You wondered what to do with me,' Alice said.

'Alice. Always such a disappointment,' Maud said, as if she hadn't spoken. 'Well, Vicky must do what she can for you. She says she's willing to take you as well, and I hope you will do your best to attract a husband, because I don't know what else to contrive. I can't have you here. As soon as I am well, Paul and I will be travelling. To Venice first to see Fergus and that woman – his bride, I should say. Linda, I hope will stay here, if she is not already married. But you?'

'Oh, Mama, please let me go home!' Alice said urgently.

'Home? To the Castle?'

'To London, to Aunt Caroline's. I must be back before the new term starts.'

'What new term?'

'At the art school. Don't you remember? You gave me permission to study there and, oh, I do love it so. I'm good at it, all the teachers say so. You *must* let me go back!'

It was the wrong word to say to her mother, even in her present weakened state. Maud frowned. 'There is no "must" about it. I don't know what I was thinking. You haven't your sister's looks, but you are well enough, or will be once Vicky has worked on you. And if Linda can attract an offer, so can you. I won't have you disgrace me.'

'I shan't, Mama, but I don't want to be married. I want to be an artist. Oh, please, *please* let me go back! I'm not like Rachel, I couldn't bear that sort of life. If I'm in London, you won't see me or hear about me so you won't be able to be disappointed. It's the only thing I want. Oh, *please*!'

'Stop talking! You exhaust me.' Maud closed her eyes and waved Alice away, like a troublesome moth. 'Go away now, I can't bear any more. Ring the bell for my maid on the way out.'

Maud drifted . . .

She was back in her childhood home, Cawburn Castle. There was a new baby in the crib, the longed-for heir, her brother Fergus. Her father, a cold and autocratic man, had made his disapproval manifest at the arrival of three daughters, and his oppressed and miserable wife had died as soon as Fergus was born. So Maud had become mother to the baby, and mistress of the castle, to atone for her unwelcome existence. Plump little Fergus, her darling baby, had thrived, but she had never won her father's love. She had done her duty, but he had never given her a word of approval.

Nor had Willie Stainton, her husband, a cold and autocratic man. Another castle, another baby – a girl! How furious he had been at Linda's birth! How racked with anxiety she had been all through her second pregnancy, how fearful while giving birth. A hard birth – old Nanny, who had come with her from Cawburn, had said second births were always hard. She had been quite ill afterwards, and perhaps because of that had never been able to rejoice much in Giles's birth, or feel affection for him. But she'd had a boy, and bearing a second boy had completed her duty. If she did not secure an approving word from her husband, she did at least deflect his wrath.

And gain relief from his bedroom attentions. There followed a period of comparative peace.

Then his infidelities came to light. She writhed at the memory. Men had mistresses, it was understood, but he was not discreet. Or discriminating. His tastes were low. No servant was safe from him. Oh, those girls! The ones who gave her sly, sidelong glances; the ones who flounced and tossed their heads; the ones who came weeping and snivelling for sympathy! Those who became pregnant. The furious quarrels, the humiliations . . .

She had built a carapace around herself, within which she could feel no hurt. She did her duty, and spared neither herself nor anyone else. It was not love or even lust that had brought him back to her bed and forced her into another series of pregnancies. He had done it to spite her. Two daughters and several miscarriages she should never have had to endure.

Willie Stainton. She had not loved him. When he was brought in on a hurdle like a dead stag, she had felt only fury that he had used her up and discarded her . . .

She drifted in the cold fog of desolate memories . . .

There was the sound of a baby crying. A new baby, the longed-for, the precious son and heir. Not Fergus, her loved, her adored, the first of her babies. It was Paul's son. The realisation jerked her for a moment back to reality. How strange it was that Paul had wanted to marry her. He had known she had no money; and she had never been under any illusion that she was handsome. She had supposed he wanted her for an efficient chatelaine, a suitably blue-blooded consort. She had thought she had done with the tiresome bedroom activity, but he had proved uxorious. And then had come the shock of another pregnancy.

He had been so pleased, it had been almost touching . . .

He loved her. There was no other conclusion. No-one had ever loved her. Not her father, not Willie, not her children. But Paul loved her. His face when the baby had been put into his arms for the first time! His expression as he leaned over her and asked – oh, so tenderly – how she did . . .

Pain. Exhaustion. There was always a price to pay. They used you. Men used you up, for their own purposes. But what else could you do? Boys went into the army, the Church, the law. Girls went into marriage. It was their career, their only option. It was that, or dwindle into 'daughter-at-home', no better than an unpaid servant; or 'companion' to some elderly widow, at her beck and call for nothing more than bed and board. Better marriage than that . . . Better cold-hearted Willie Stainton . . . Better a title, a position. She was a countess . . .

No, she was a princess, wasn't she? Paul . . . ?

A baby was crying somewhere. She stirred in her half-sleep. The baby needed her, her little brother. She must be a mother to him. Their mother was dead. It was her responsibility now. She must be mother to them all, run the castle, somehow please her father. It was all on her shoulders, always had been, always would be. The burden, the responsibility . . .

Maud drifted . . .

Linda found Alice down in the little conservatory. 'Why are you sulking in here?' she asked briskly.

'I'm not sulking,' Alice defended herself. 'I'm thinking.'

'Drawing again,' Linda remarked. Alice closed the cover of her sketching-pad to hide what she had been doing. 'Some rubbish, I suppose. I don't know why you are so set on it.'

'It makes me happy,' Alice said.

'Happy! What has that to do with anything?'

'Don't you want to be happy?'

'I shall be happy when I do the right thing. That's the only happiness that matters.'

'Is marrying Cousin Pippi the right thing?' Alice asked, a little crossly.

'Of course. It's what Mama wants. It's what Papa would have wanted.'

'Papa never cared a jot about any of us,' Alice said.

'That's a shocking thing to say, and shows you have a very bad character. And, by the way, your sulks have been noted. Aunt Vicky has been asking about you. Personally, I think it's far too good of her to want to take you in hand and find you a husband.'

Alice grasped at that. 'Yes, far too good. I wish she wouldn't. It would cost a great deal of money, and for what? I'll never "take".'

'Not with that attitude.' Linda hesitated, and it came to Alice that she was not here merely to harangue. 'Mother said you want to go back to London, and go on with that silly school.'

'I do. It's the only thing I want,' Alice sighed.

'Well, I think you should go,' said Linda.

Alice looked up in amazement. 'You do?'

'You're not needed here. I can look after Mother until she's out of bed. And I don't want you hanging around with your miserable face and bad temper.'

'I'm not bad-tempered,' Alice protested.

Linda wasn't listening. 'And you won't do Rachel's prospects any good if you tag along with Aunt Vicky.'

'Rachel's engaged to Angus. She doesn't need any more prospects.'

Linda ignored that, as well. 'So the best thing is for you to go back to school until you come to your senses and realise it will get you nowhere in life. Then you'll come begging for another chance, and perhaps some clergyman might be found willing to take you. Don't expect anyone better, because it will be too late.'

Now it was Alice's turn to ignore what to her was as meaningless as a sparrow's chirping. 'Will you help me go home? Will you persuade Mother? Oh, thank you! You don't know what it means to me. But how can it be managed? She'll never let me travel on my own.'

'Of course not,' said Linda, 'but as it happens, it fits in with my own plans. Miss Kettel shall take you back.'

'Miss Kettel?'

'I've only been keeping her on until I could find a new governess. Now the Pfaffenheims have recommended someone. A Fräulein Schneider. She comes tomorrow. So as soon as you've packed, you can be off.'

'You're getting rid of Miss Kettel?' Alice said slowly.

Linda looked scornful. 'Did you think I would keep her after her appalling negligence cost the life of my son? I needed her to bring Arabella to me. I intended to punish her by turning her off to fend for herself in Germany. But as it is, she can accompany you back to England. She should be grateful for the opportunity, which she doesn't in the least deserve.'

'But what will happen to her then?'

'I neither know nor care. Why on earth do you? My little boy is dead.'

Alice had never understood Linda, who had always seemed only to want to be rid of the bother of her children. But perhaps she had a mother's heart underneath all the crossness. And, in fairness, the crossness was not much in evidence these days. She couldn't help asking, 'If you marry Cousin Pippi, will you take Arabella with you?'

Linda frowned. 'Of course I will. What a strange question! He has two daughters of his own, just about her age, as well as two older sons. One more won't be noticed in the nursery. Fräulein Schneider can teach them all.'

'I see,' Alice said. She was wondering whether that was Linda's attraction for Cousin Pippi – he wanted her as a stepmother for his brood. A suitable woman of rank to run his house and supervise his children.

Then Linda said, looking rather conscious, 'Of course we may well have children of our own.'

'I suppose so,' Alice said blankly.

Linda turned away. 'If Mother can manage it, at her age . . .' she added, under her breath.

The journey was long and slow and tiring, and by the time Alice and Miss Kettel were on the final train to London, they were weary and grubby.

Alice was worried about what would happen to her companion.

'There are agencies,' Miss Kettel said, in a leaden voice. 'But without a reference . . .'

'Didn't Lady Cordwell give you one?' Alice said, uncomfortably.

'One could hardly expect it, after the death of her son.'

'But it wasn't your fault!' Alice cried. 'He ran away and got in an accident. There was nothing you could have done. He was always running away. You couldn't watch him every moment of every day.'

'It was my responsibility,' said Miss Kettel. 'He was in my charge.'

'But what will you do?'

'I doubt I shall be able to get another position as a governess. I can teach at a school, however. Not at a good school, of course, with no reference. But there are lesser schools that are not so particular.'

Alice looked at her in silent sympathy, not knowing what to say. She looked so worn and uncomfortable. 'I'm sorry,' she said at last.

Miss Kettel roused herself. 'Let me be a lesson to you, my dear. For a woman, reputation is everything. Once lose it, and you are lost indeed. Take care of your reputation, Lady Alice. When one is young and full of passion, one is too likely to undervalue it.'

Alice was not sure what she was being put on guard against, but there was no doubt Miss Kettel was sincere in her warning.

★ ★ ★

The brake had been brought round into the back yard, so that the luggage could be carried out that way. There was a great bustle, laden servants trotting to and fro and dodging each other in doorways, as the handsome leather cases and trunks were piled up ready to load. Miss Hatto was supervising her ladyship's with a sharp eye, one hand tightly gripping the jewel case. Afton should have been doing the same for his lordship's, but he had got sidetracked, handing over the butler's responsibilities to William, who could be slow in his responses.

Sam came up to him. 'Excuse me, Mr Afton, but I don't see his lordship's gun case anywhere.'

'Gun case?' Afton said blankly.

'And his rods.'

Afton snapped his fingers in annoyance. He had been thinking only about deer-stalking, which meant rifles, which his lordship didn't own. But of course there would be game birds as well. And fishing? The Tay was all about fishing. How could he have forgotten? 'I haven't packed them yet,' he admitted.

'I can do it,' Sam said. 'I know how.'

'Thank you, Sam. William, go and help him. You know which rods?'

'Yes, Mr Afton.'

He turned and bumped into Rose. 'Mr Afton, are the dogs going with them, or staying here?' she asked. 'If they're going, you know they have to have separate tickets?'

Afton shook his head. 'I don't know. I didn't ask.' He hurried indoors and found Mrs Webster standing like a monument in Piccadilly, where she could keep an eye on everyone at once.

'You look harried, Mr Afton,' she said.

'I forgot to ask his lordship if they're taking the dogs.'

'They're not,' she said. 'Since Mr Richard is staying, it was thought better to spare them that long train journey.'

'Oh. Thank you. How did you know?'

'Mabel overheard them discussing it when she was tending the fire.' She eyed him closely. 'If you'll forgive me, you're looking rather worn, Mr Afton. Are you quite well?'

'Just tired,' Afton said. 'It's been a busy few weeks, with all the house parties.'

'Well, you'll get a bit of a rest in Scotland. Just valeting duties. Though there'll be enough of those, with all the mud to get off every day.'

'There are always enough valeting duties,' Afton said. He hesitated. 'I've been thinking lately . . .'

Mrs Webster gave him an intelligent look. 'That combining valet and butler is too much, in a house like this?'

'When I agreed to it, I didn't know they'd be doing so much entertaining,' he said.

'You should tell his lordship,' Mrs Webster said.

They exchanged a long look. It was never a good idea to tell your master you couldn't do the job. It might all too easily lead to his kindly relieving you of it. 'I don't want to let him down,' Afton said at last.

'Hiring a new butler always brings disruption below stairs,' Mrs Webster said. 'I don't relish having to get used to a new man, I can tell you. But on the other hand, things have to be done right, and if combining is too much, better you tell him *before* something goes wrong.'

Afton sighed. 'You think I'm pretty feeble, don't you?'

She looked surprised. 'Not at all. *I* couldn't combine housekeeping with maiding her ladyship. I'm surprised you've stuck it this long.'

'Thank you,' Afton said. 'I'll think about it while we're away.' He would have to work out a tactful way of saying it that would not get him dismissed.

Cyril appeared with the small overnight valise. 'Mr Afton, are you putting his lordship's studs and links in here, or carrying a separate box?'

Afton made an annoyed tut. 'I haven't finished packing that one. Take it back upstairs. No, wait, go and help with the loading. I'll take it myself.' And, with a nod to Mrs Webster, he hurried off.

'I wish you would come,' Giles said. 'You can still change your mind, you know.'

'Oh, I've plenty to do here,' Richard said. 'I'll have Alice for company, and someone's got to look after the dogs. I'm not in the right frame of mind for Scotland, anyway.'

'You've been looking glum lately,' Giles said. 'Not your usual cheery self. Is anything wrong?'

Richard hesitated. He had always maintained an air of devil-may-careity in all circumstances, preferring always to be envied rather than pitied, but since Molly had gone he had found it hard to keep it up. If Giles, not the most noticing of brothers, had finally registered his gloom, there was perhaps some need of explanation.

'Someone I cared about – er – very much . . .' He began awkwardly. 'In short, she turned me down.'

'I didn't know,' Giles said. 'You've kept it awfully quiet. But surely you won't give up. Have another go at her – women always succumb to your charm sooner or later, don't they?'

Richard could hardly blame Giles for taking it lightly, when he had always spoken lightly of himself. 'It's different this time,' he said. 'I thought I had met the one woman for me. But there were – obstacles. And she's gone away now. Abroad. So it's definitely over.'

'My dear chap, I'm so sorry,' Giles said. 'I had no idea.' He couldn't think what else to say. He saw, now, by the lines in Richard's face that it had been serious, that his brother was really suffering. 'Is there anything I can do? I know it's foolish to ask that when you're obviously broken-hearted, but I do care about you.'

'Thanks. There's nothing you can do about my personal tragedy. But there is something in general.'

'Fire away, then,' Giles said.

'I've never wanted to marry before. But when I discovered that I did want to at last, I realised I didn't have an establishment to offer her. If she had accepted me, I'd have had to have it out with you. And even as it is, the situation needs to be resolved. Not that I expect there'll ever be a next time, but for my pride alone, if nothing else.'

Giles frowned. 'I'm sorry, I'm not following you. What sort of establishment?'

'A salary, for the work I do for the estate. A position, so that if anyone asks me what I do, I can tell them. And a house of my own.'

'But you have your expenses paid by the estate. And you live here.'

'Damn your parsimony, Giles! The estate is no longer bankrupt. It's doing rather well, in fact, and when my milk scheme is running full speed, it will do even better. I have big plans, you know. Ashmore may be my childhood home, but the estate belongs to you, and eventually to your son, so I am working for your benefit and getting nothing out of it myself. The labourer is worthy of his hire, so put aside this penny-pinching habit you've got into, and recognise what you have in me.'

Giles raised his hand. 'Pax, old man! Don't bite my head off. I know you do a lot for the estate—'

'I don't think you *do* know – not consciously. You're so used to having a little brother to order about—'

'Now you're being absurd. I've never ordered you about. We've hardly lived in the same house for most of our lives.'

'There you go again, laughing at me!' Richard cried, running a hand backwards through his hair. 'Why can't you take me seriously?'

'I do. I am. Please, don't fly off the handle,' Giles said. He had never seen Richard upset about anything. 'Tell me what it is you want.'

'Make me your estate agent. Yes, I know Markham is called your agent, but he can still go on doing what he does. He's your secretary, factotum, deals with the day-to-day. You can give him a different title – managing agent, perhaps. I will go on doing what I'm doing – being in charge of the overall strategy, the larger scheme of things. Where we overlap, you'll find we can work together – we're both reasonable people.'

'Estate agent,' Giles mused.

'It's a respectable job for a younger son.'

'And a salary?'

Richard named a sum, and Giles raised his eyebrows, then hastily lowered them as Richard scowled. 'Very well. I suppose we can afford it.'

'You'd damn well better, or I'll take my considerable abilities elsewhere. Good estate agents are hotly sought.'

'And what else was it? A house?'

'I'll still live here when I'm in the country – it would be foolish not to – but I want a place of my own in Town. I don't want always to have to lodge with Aunt Caroline or go to the club. Just a small house somewhere convenient – Dover Street, Bolton Street, somewhere like that,' he concluded defiantly.

'Anything else?' Giles asked, with a touch of irony.

'That'll do for now.' He gave Giles a look under his eyebrows. 'You could stay there too, when you came up to Town *en garçon* instead of at Aunt Caroline's. If you wanted to. So it wouldn't be all for me.'

Giles smiled. 'Stay with you. And I suppose we'd go out on the town like two gay bachelors?'

Richard shrugged. 'We could strap on the nosebag together, yes. Perhaps take in a show. If you felt like it.'

'That would be nice,' Giles said, feeling oddly shy. 'We haven't spent much time together, one way or another.'

'So you agree? I can have what I asked for?'

'If Vogel says it's all right—'

'No, Giles. You *tell* Vogel what's all right.'

'Of course I do. Consider it done, then.' He held out his hand and the brothers shook. 'So will you come to Scotland now?'

Richard smiled. It was not quite his old grin, but it lightened the gloom of his face a little. 'Not a chance. I have to go house-hunting.'

CHAPTER NINETEEN

When the carriages had been waved off, Rose said to Mrs Webster, 'I want to go down to the village. I need some elastic.'

'All right. You can take a message for me to Trapper's. I'd like to get the chimneys swept while they're away.'

'Mr Richard and Lady Alice are still here,' Rose pointed out.

'We can work around them. I can't leave it any longer in case the weather changes. Oh, if you're going to Poining's, can you get me some plain shirt buttons? I'll give you one to match.'

Rose went down the back way, round Mop End and Cherry Lane, as she always did now to avoid passing Hundon's. There was more shade that way, anyway, and it was a hot day. The village basked in shimmering heat. None of the trees was yet turning: it was more like August than September. As she passed the post office Michael Woodrow came out. She would have walked on, but he stepped in front of her. 'Please stop a moment and talk to me,' he said.

She stopped, rather than make a scene. 'How's the shoulder?' she asked coldly.

'Better, thank you. Still a bit stiff, but I can use it all right. How are you?'

'Me? I'm always well,' she said, in a conversation-ending tone.

But he didn't move aside, looking at her earnestly. 'You

look well,' he said. He chewed his lip, then gestured towards the post office. 'I was putting in an advertisement for a maid.'

'I heard you were back at Hundon's.'

'I can't really manage without someone there – being out all day, I don't have time for—'

'Women's work.'

'I didn't mean—'

'How's your sister?'

He looked miserable. 'Settling in, I think. She's – she's never come back, you see.'

'Come back?'

'To herself. She's not really Martha any more. Not like she was. I can't bring her home.'

Rose looked away. 'I suppose not.'

He put his hand on her arm. 'Rose – Miss Hawkins – please. Forgive me. Be friends again.'

'Friends?' she enquired, as though it were a foreign word.

'I was upset and scared, and spoke hastily. You were right and I was wrong, but I didn't know then and – well – I had to stand by her, didn't I, my sister? Isn't loyalty a good thing?'

'I wouldn't know.'

'I mean, if you and I—'

She crushed the opening briskly. 'I must be off. I hope you find a suitable maid.'

But he didn't let her past. 'I don't want a maid. I want a wife.'

She gave him a mirthless grin. 'Comes cheaper, don't it, a wife? And you don't have to give a wife a day off, ever.'

Now he seemed just a little riled, and she liked him better for it. 'You're deliberately misunderstanding me. I spoke clumsily, but you know what I'm trying to say. Let us go back to what we were before all this. Let me court you. You deserve to be courted properly. Walk out with me, Rose – please!'

She considered him for a long moment. He was handsome and nice, and she had enjoyed talking to him. But she knew what marriage meant. She'd seen enough of men and their nonsense over the years, and what it cost. You were better off without them, if you had a home and a job, and she did. It had been pleasant to have a man admire her, but it all ended up the same, didn't it? You cleaned up their messes and waited on them hand and foot, and either you got paid to do it – or you married them.

'I'm too busy to be walking out with anybody. Let me past, please.'

He stood back to let her go, but as she passed he said, low and urgent, 'I won't give up, you know.'

Good, she thought, heading down the street. *It'll be exercise for you.*

Chaplin showed Richard into the drawing-room and announced him. Richard crossed the room to take his grandmother's hands and kiss her cheek. She looked, he thought, somehow diminished, and it affected him: she had always been so robust.

'You have only just caught me,' she said, gesturing him to a chair. 'I go away again tomorrow, to stay with the Levens.'

'Yes, I know,' said Richard. 'Quite the gadabout you've become lately.'

The joke fell flat. She looked at him with real pain. 'A great part of my life is over,' she said. 'I was still a young woman when I met him. What is there for me now?'

He became serious. 'I understand. Believe me, I do.'

'You?' she queried, and her gaze sharpened. 'Do not say it! You assured me you had no feelings for her.'

'For Chloë? No.'

Her eyes widened. '*Bon dieu!*' she said faintly. 'The mother? *O, mon pauvre petit!* You must forgive me. I did not see it.'

He was uncomfortable with her sympathy. 'You weren't meant to.' She was looking at him penetratingly, stripping away layers. 'Please don't pity me.'

'I do not,' she said at last. 'One ought to feel a great love once, or one is not truly alive. Well, well. We are the wounded, we two, *n'est-ce pas?* Life will go on, *mon cher*, but differently, and we will adapt.'

He shook his head. 'I shall never love again.'

She did not argue with him, but continued with her own thoughts. Eventually she roused herself to say, 'He came to see me, you know. At the end.'

'*Vraiment?*'

'Oh, yes,' she said, with a spark of anger. 'He came to say goodbye to me. Can you imagine it? To say goodbye – to *me!* – as if it was merely a *congé* visit, a commonplace courtesy, like leaving one's card when one quits Town. After all we had been to each other!' There was a colour of indignation now in her cheeks.

'I'm sorry,' he said.

'She has changed him, that one. And not for the better.' There was a silence, and then she roused herself to say, 'Tell me some news to distract me. What of your mother?'

'Still at the Usingerhof. She wrote to Aunt Vicky, who wrote to me. They were to have gone to Venice to see Uncle Fergus, but she is still convalescent.'

'That does not surprise me,' said Grandmère. 'A baby, at her age? What of your sister?'

'Which one?'

'*N'importe.*'

Richard smiled at that. 'Well, Rachel is having a fine time, I believe.'

'Yes, we heard something of her frolics, Caroline and I, when we were in France. Vicky means only to be kind, I believe, but Maud is hoping the silly child will fall in love and break her engagement to the unsatisfactory man.'

'Is that a bad thing? Except for the unsatisfactory man, of course.'

'But will she fall in love with someone suitable? And will

he offer for her without a dowry? There are too many imponderables.'

'Better the bird in the hand? Well, you may be right.'

'I am always right. And you, what goes on with you? Why did you not go to Scotland?'

'I have been looking for a house, and I have found one. I came to tell you. In Bolton Street, so I shall be handy to come and visit you. Just a little place, but neat and convenient.'

'What need have you of a house?'

'To stay in when I come to London, which will be more often in future. I don't want to keep bothering Aunt Caroline.' The rooms Molly had occupied had been given up. He had seen to that. There were too many memories there.

'She does not mind being bothered. Which you know. So it must be that you wish for a house to be private in. Which means you are contemplating some *grivoiserie*.'

'Grandmère! As if I would! There are other reasons for wanting to be private, you know.'

'Such as nursing a broken heart – yes, I know. But that is not good for you. You are a young man, you must go out and attack life. Ever onwards and upwards!'

'You exhaust me,' Richard said, smiling. 'Can a fellow not have a moment to lick his wounds?'

'Certainly not,' said Grandmère.

Nina arrived at the familiar house in Stafford Street to find everything in disarray, the air full of dust, the incontinent sound of hammering, and sundry extraneous persons blocking the passages and doing incomprehensible things to the walls.

'Oh, my dear! Come in,' said Isabel Morris, 'but do be careful where you step. There are nails and snips of wire and I don't know what underfoot. We are having the electric light put in. Mawes is upstairs somewhere, making a nuisance of himself. It was all his idea, of course. He is such a one for new-fangled inventions!'

'Shall I be in the way?' Nina said. 'You know Lepida and I are going to the lecture later, and I thought we could have a comfortable chat beforehand. But I can go away and come back.'

'No, no, do stay, if you don't mind the mess. But, my dear, Lepida won't be going to the lecture. She is laid down on the *chaise longue* in her room, quite prostrate. I'm so angry with Mawes that the men have come today to do the electricity, when she's so poorly, but he says they are quite booked up, and if they don't come today it will be a month or six weeks until they can come again.'

'What's wrong with Lepida?' Nina asked anxiously. They were treading upstairs now.

'It's another of those turns she's been having. It starts with a fever, and pains in the joints, but then she becomes exhausted and can't do more than lie on the sofa. It goes away after a few days, but it worries me terribly. The doctors can't decide what's wrong. Gillespie thought it was a kind of influenza because of the fever, but Conroy is now inclined to think it must be a disorder of the liver. But Mawes says people with livers turn yellow, and poor Lepida is just as pale as milk.'

'I'm so sorry. I ought not to disturb her, perhaps.'

'No, do come and see her and talk to her. It's all she can bear, poor child, a little conversation. And I know she's been longing to see you.'

They picked their way down the passage, where the workmen had chipped the plaster away in places and now seemed to be trying to thread electric wires through the gas brackets. 'We've not long had the incandescent mantles put in,' Isabel mourned, 'and they gave such a lovely bright, clean light. A neighbour of ours has had electric light for a couple of years, and really, you know, it's more like electric *dark* – not nearly as good! I notice every time we visit them. And she says the electric globes are so fragile, the servants are always breaking them. And sometimes they simply blow themselves out for no reason.'

'Why have it, then?' Nina couldn't help asking.

'Oh, Mawes is all for novelty. And he says it will be convenient simply to turn a switch. It is the future, he says, and gas is the past. That's reason enough for him,' she added, 'but it's never the man of the house who has to cope with the inconvenience. Here we are. Lepida, darling, do you feel well enough for a visitor?'

'Oh, Nina – the lecture! I'm so sorry. I ought to have put you off but it slipped my mind.'

'I'm not surprised it did. Shall I go away, or would you like to chat for a little while?'

'Please come and talk to me. This wretched thing has me completely flattened, but I'm bored to tears as well. You must go to the lecture for both of us, and come and tell me about it tomorrow. Sit, and tell me what you've been up to.'

Even so much talk seemed to have exhausted her. She lay back against the pillows, looking pale and thin, her cheeks hollow and her eyes blue-shadowed. Her hands rested limply on the shawl that covered her from the waist down.

'Oh, Lepida,' Nina said softly, in distress. 'I didn't know about this.'

Lepida moved her fingers, as if pushing the subject away. 'I don't like to talk of sickness. I get these attacks now and then, and they go away. I haven't seen you for two months. Tell me everything.'

So Nina obliged, telling her about the Isle of Wight, sea-bathing, family fun with the Wharfedales, picnics and boat trips, games, and lots of quiet reading under the shade of the trees in the garden. 'The weather was perfect,' she said. 'They tell me the Island, as they call it, has better weather than anywhere else – some geographical quirk or other. And Mr Cowling was able to be there quite a lot of the time. It was good to see him rest and relax a little. He works so hard.'

'Yes, I know,' Lepida said.

'Of course, Decius will have told you,' Nina said. 'Did you see anything of him while Mr Cowling was with us?'

'He went north to visit his family for the first break, but he came to London the second time, and we saw quite a bit of him,' said Lepida.

Nina wanted to ask whether he had declared himself, but Lepida looked so weary she didn't like to make her talk too much.

She went on. 'Then after the Isle of Wight we went to stay with Lord and Lady Latham for a Saturday-to-Monday. They wanted us to come with them to Drumcorbie – they hold Mr Cowling in high esteem, since he helped them with a financial problem – but it turned out he had other plans.'

'Decius told me. You went to Paris.'

'Yes, Paris,' Nina said. 'We never did have a honeymoon, and Mr Cowling has always been promising me one. He had to see to some business over there, so it was an opportunity for me to go with him.'

'Was it wonderful?'

Nina hesitated. 'It was interesting,' she said judiciously. 'He's exporting his shoes now, so he had to see the distributor and then visit the shops. After that, we did see some of the sights. But I'd like to go back when there is more time.'

She told Lepida about the things they had seen, and did not mention the oddness of being on 'honeymoon' with a man who seemed more like her father than her husband. He took her to restaurants, but did not want to go on anywhere afterwards. He did not like late nights. He was always tired and preoccupied. He did not care for dancing, there seemed no point in going to the theatre when neither of them spoke good enough French, and when she suggested that the ballet did not require a knowledge of the language, he looked so dismayed that she didn't press it. The thing he liked best was a boat trip along the Seine, and he held her hand and said it was very romantic. But their suite at the Meurice had two bedrooms, and he didn't visit hers at all while they were there.

'Is Mr Cowling in London now?' Lepida asked, when she had finished. 'Papa would love to see him.'

'No, he's had to go to Leicester,' Nina said. 'I shall be going back on Saturday – I only waited for this lecture. I'm so sorry you can't come to it. But when you're better, you must come and stay. I'd like to show you the countryside. I'll borrow a horse for you – it's fine riding country. And you'll be able to see something of Decius while you're there.'

Lepida gave a faint smile. 'You don't need to tempt me with Mr Blake. Your company is enough. I would love to come – if I'm well enough.'

She looked suddenly so exhausted that Nina was alarmed. 'I've worn you out – I'm so sorry. I'll go now and leave you in peace.' Lepida did not beg her to stay. She leaned over and kissed the thin cheek. 'Please get better soon,' she whispered.

Lepida laid a cold hand over hers. 'I must rest now. But come again before you go north and tell me about the lecture.'

Mawes came in at that moment. 'Nina! I didn't know you were here. You look radiant! Are you staying to dinner? I've come to move Lepida into another room so that the electrical men can come in. I would really like to photograph you, my dear – I have a wonderful new camera. It's a Rietzschel. It has a superb lens. If I can get you into my studio later— Yes, yes, my dear,' he broke off, as Isabel appeared in the doorway, 'I'm just taking her now. What, not staying, Nina? What a pity. But come again soon. Our poor girl is bored to sobs, being confined to the sofa. All this mess and noise will be done with today, and then you shall see a sort of miracle – instant illumination at the turning of a switch! I don't know why we didn't have it long ago.'

★ ★ ★

Nina would have preferred not to go alone, but the lecture hall was on Piccadilly, convenient for home, and she didn't want to miss it, because the subject sounded so interesting.

Two scientists from University College London, Ernest Starling and his brother-in-law William Bayliss, had been investigating pancreatic secretion. They had discovered that whenever food was put into the duodenum, a substance was immediately released into the bloodstream that stimulated the pancreas to secrete. Now they proposed that the body had many other similar systems, and had named the various catalysing substances 'hormones', from the Greek meaning 'setting in motion'. The idea that a chemical signal could be sent from one part of the body to another to control the functions of the distant part was quite novel, and suggested a fascinating new area of biology.

Nina found a good seat halfway back, and one seat in from the aisle. She was reading the programme notes when she noticed from the corner of her eye that someone in the aisle was conducting a sotto-voce conversation with her neighbour, which resulted in his getting up and yielding his seat to the newcomer. She glanced, and then stared, her stomach contracting and the hair rising on her scalp.

Giles gave her a nervous smile. 'That gentleman most obligingly agreed to move elsewhere.'

'What are you doing here?' she managed to say. 'I thought you were in Scotland.'

'No, we've been back a week. I had to come up on business. I saw you at the entrance, but there were so many people between us I couldn't get to you. What are *you* doing here? And alone, moreover.'

'I was to have come with Lepida Morris. She and I go to lectures together now and then. But she's not well, and I didn't want to miss it. Are you interested in pancreatic secretions?'

'When you put it like that,' he said, with a smile that made her stomach clench again, 'not more than in any other subject.

But I was in Town and at a loose end, and it sounded interesting.'

'Aren't you—' she began, but at that moment someone on the platform stood up and called for silence, and they had to settle down and listen.

The lecture was absorbing, though Nina found some of the scientific terms difficult, but while she listened with all her intellect, her body was acutely aware of Giles's presence beside her. He seemed to radiate some magnetism that was as obvious to her as the heat from a furnace when the door is opened. She felt happy, shaken into life, excited as a child on Christmas morning just to be near him. She would not allow herself to think beyond that.

When the lecture ended questions were invited, and since many of the audience seemed to be either medical students, physicians or scientists, the questions were erudite and abstruse. And after that there was a vote of thanks, hearty applause, and finally everyone began to stir and rise and gather their belongings.

Nina, pressed close to Giles as they were carried by the crowd towards the exit, assumed that he would now bid her a polite and regretful farewell and that this exquisite interlude would be over. But when they emerged onto the street, they found that a light but blustery rain had started, and that neither of them had an umbrella.

'How improvident we are,' he said, as they edged sideways under the hall's entrance canopy to allow others behind them to exit.

'It wasn't raining before,' she said indignantly.

'So I noticed. But have we not learned that English weather is changeable?'

'Obviously not. Oh dear, it seems wrong to take a cab for such a short journey.'

'You'd never get one, anyway,' Giles said, looking at the crowds lining the pavement.

'At least we can walk together,' she said hopefully. 'I suppose you're staying at your aunt's house?'

'No, at Richard's new place in Bolton Street. He has rented a *pied-à-terre*, though he's not there now – he's at Ashmore. Are you going back directly to Berkeley Square? I suppose you are waited for.'

'No, Mr Cowling has gone to Leicester on business. He goes home from there, and I join him on Saturday. I had one or two things to do in Town tomorrow.'

They stood in silence for a moment, as occupied cabs swished past, and the few unoccupied ones were snapped up by those nearer the kerb. Then he said, 'Look here, the rain's blowing in on us and we're getting wet anyway. We might as well take the plunge, don't you think?'

'I'm resigned to getting wet,' she said. She only wanted to prolong this moment with a short walk – he would surely escort her to Berkeley Square.

But he was looking at her keenly, if uncertainly. 'I'm starving – are you?' he said. 'What do you say to a little supper? I know a nice little restaurant on Dover Street. If we walk quickly, we might make it there without drowning.'

Her heart lifted with joy. 'I'm hungry too,' she said.

He took her hand and pulled it through his arm. 'Stick close and I'll keep the worst off you,' he said, and, huddled together, they stepped out into the rain. They hurried across the road, dodging between the wet horses and rain-slicked motors. As they crossed Albemarle Street a gust threw a hatful of drops straight into their faces, but they only laughed, like children on a lark, and Giles tore open his overcoat and wrapped it round her, so that she was pressed against him inside its warmth. The intensity of her feelings was almost more than she could bear. They turned into Dover Street and stopped outside Pinotti's, where she removed herself from inside his fine tweed, they straightened themselves, and entered the welcome light and warmth with a modicum of dignity. It was a small place, and obviously popular, but the genial Italian *patron* who greeted them gave them a comprehensive once-over and escorted them to a tiny table in a rear corner, seating them catty-corner to each other so that their knees were almost touching under the table.

'Pinotti's is known for good food at reasonable prices,' Giles told her. 'Not that price is an issue for me now, but I used to come here when I was a student. I hope you like Italian food.'

'I hardly know, but it smells delicious,' Nina said. In truth, she would have eaten matchboxes for the chance of being with him a little longer. She was determined to enjoy every moment, shutting her mind to any other consideration. This fragment of joy had been vouchsafed to her by Fate, and who was she to reject it?

The food was simple and delicious, with bright, honest flavours, and they ate heartily, drank red wine and, after a little awkwardness to begin with, relaxed and warmed into a freedom of thought and expression that seemed utterly natural. They talked and talked, ranging from subject to subject with the ease of old friends. There was laughter, and when at one stage he put his hand over hers and squeezed it to emphasise a point, that seemed natural too. When they had finished their main course, the waiter came to propose *dolci*, and when that was finished, there was coffee, and Signor Pinotti brought them a *digestivo* and placed the glasses with an exaggerated gesture and an indulgent look. He murmured and gave Giles something that was almost a wink.

'What did he say?' Nina asked, when he had gone.

'Something in Italian. I didn't understand,' Giles said, stirring his coffee.

She frowned. 'But you speak very good Italian. I know that for a fact.'

Now he met her eye. 'He said, all the world loves a lover,' he told her.

Time seemed to hold its breath. Nina's chest felt tight, as though she had taken a big breath of cold air.

He laid his hand over hers, folded the fingers under it. It was warm, and strong, and it gave her such a feeling of safety, it was as if it had conferred invulnerability on her. Perhaps there was another world, parallel to this one, where another Nina was licensed to hold the hand of another Giles, and was with him whenever she wanted to be, was not exiled from the all-encompassing happiness of his presence.

It was almost over, this magical interlude.

How was it that he read her unspoken thought? 'Not yet,' he said. 'It's not over yet.'

She met his eyes, and everything was said without words.

They were silent then, but it was a silence of warmth and closeness. Some time later they went out into the evening street, lamplight and wet pavements. The rain had stopped. They walked, not hurrying now, further along Piccadilly. Bolton Street was the third turning along, no distance at all. At the street door she waited behind him while he fished in his pocket. 'You have a key?' she said.

'There's no live-in staff. Richard and I both use it when we're in Town.'

The house was in darkness. She shivered. He opened the door and she stepped inside, and he followed her. But then he paused and said carefully, 'Do you want me to take you home?'

To take the offered escape, the safe way out, or to jump into the void? But it was long past the moment of choice for her. She had to have this. She stepped forward into his arms. 'You are my home,' she said.

He closed the door, shutting them together in the dark. Just enough street glow came in through the fanlight for them to find their way upstairs.

In the bedroom he said, 'I think we're owed this. Life owes us this.'

She said, 'Just this one time.'

It was not a stipulation but an understanding of reality. Such chances did not come twice. This was time out of Time; a different story they might have lived – but the ending would be the same.

'Can it be enough? Can we make this one time pay for everything?'

'No,' he said. 'But we can try.'

Afterwards he held her tenderly. She understood now. The poems, the novels, the paintings, all the great passionate and tragic outpourings of art in all its forms that had puzzled her. She had been standing outside a closed door, hearing faintly the music from inside. Now she had stepped through the door, and she knew.

'You've never—' he began to ask.

'No,' she said. Not properly, she thought. Not like this.

'Thank God,' he murmured, kissing her hair, holding her a little tighter, as though someone were about to snatch her away.

'But you have,' she suggested, in a small voice.

'Not like this,' he said. But that was all.

No more *could* be said, without betrayal. But she wouldn't think about that. She sighed and pressed closer, feeling the great warm wash of contentment that was as powerful as sexual passion and, she guessed, would be more enduring, for those lucky enough to be able to know it. They lay entwined without speaking, and slept a little, the best sleep of all.

She woke in the dark and felt him wake too, and joy surged in her as she realised where she was. Giles, she was with Giles. She felt his skin against hers, smelt the scent that belonged to him alone out of all the creatures in the world. She would know it, even if she was never with him again until the end of her life. He drew her against him, his mouth to her ear. 'I love you,' he whispered. 'Only you.'

But words were not their friend. Words were sentinels of Time, and Time was not their friend. She nuzzled closer, and felt his body respond. It was so natural, this fitting together, such a miracle the sensations, the satisfaction. They made love again, and slept again, tumbled together like puppies, utterly content.

The curtains were undrawn, and she woke to a lightening of the sky over the chimneys. 'What time is it?' she said.

He separated himself from her and searched for his watch. 'Nearly half past six,' he said.

It was almost over.

He took her in his arms again. They were silent, her head on his chest, his chin resting on her hair. He said, 'Will they have worried about you?'

'It's only the servants. They'll think I've stayed with friends.' The staff at the house in Berkeley Square were not old family retainers, concerned for her well-being. But the question had started up a train of thought. She felt it in his body, that he was thinking too.

'You mustn't feel guilty,' he said at last.

'No. You mustn't either,' she said.

'It wasn't wrong. It was . . .' He didn't seem to be able to finish.

She thought. It was wrong, of course. They had always taken such care that no-one else was hurt. They must go on doing so. It was wrong, but it was also right. 'It was a balancing of the books,' she said.

'Oh, my love,' he said brokenly. 'My only love.' He kissed her wildly, and she responded, and thought, There it is, the grief that always, in art, seems to come coupled with love. The lovers are separated, the loved one dies, it all ends in tragedy and a mighty crashing chord of desolation.

She held him tightly, and said, 'We had this. No-one can take that away. We will always remember this.'

'I love you,' he said.

'I love you too,' she said. And that seemed to be all of it.

The *monde* was not about, only people going to work, heads down and hurrying in the damp October air. The postman in his red collar and peaked cap was working his way up the street. Two doors down, the milkman's horse stood with its forefeet on the kerb, fragments of its breakfast chaff still caught in its whiskers, contemplating eternity. A dog trotted busily by, and glanced up at them without interest. Reality going about its business, as if no earth-shattering event had taken place. Nothing had changed, and everything had.

A café was open on the corner of Hay Hill, and they went in and had coffee and toast, drawing no curiosity from the proprietor or the other customers. Ladies and gentlemen breakfasting after a night out were not uncommon. They sat close and did not talk, too aware of the approaching end, savouring these last drops from the bottom of the cup.

Berkeley Square was just round the corner. When they quit the café, he said, 'I'll walk you to your door.'

But 'Better not,' she said. They might be spotted and recognised. And she needed a few moments to compose herself before she reached the house. Her husband's house.

'So, then – goodbye?' he said. He held out his hand.

She took it, and felt the warmth, the shape of his palm and his fingers that she would know for ever. 'Goodbye,' she said.

She walked away, and forced herself not to look back. There was such a pain in her throat she could not swallow.

CHAPTER TWENTY

'Might I have a word, my lord?' Afton said. His lordship had been looking more than usually grim since his return from London, but Afton knew he should not put things off any longer. There was a full diary of shooting events, and then in November the hunting would start. He ought to have said something in Scotland, but somehow or other the right moment hadn't arisen.

'Can't it wait?' Giles said impatiently. When a servant said *Might I have a word, my lord* it always meant trouble, and he had enough on his mind at the moment.

'If you would be so kind,' Afton insisted.

'Very well. Out with it, man,' he added, as Afton hesitated.

Afton cleared his throat. 'When you were so good as to appoint me butler as well as valet, I thought the two roles could be combined. But I have been finding it difficult as the Castle has done so much more entertaining. In short, my lord,' he hurried on, as Giles's scowl spurred him, 'I would be grateful if I could return to being your lordship's valet, without the other duties.'

'The dickens!' Giles exploded. 'You're telling me you want me to find a new butler?'

It was a nervous moment. 'I don't feel I can give satisfaction in both roles, my lord.'

Giles glared at him. 'But you want to remain valet?'

'It is my natural calling, my lord.' He coughed again. 'I was never entirely comfortable as butler.'

There was a silence, and Afton made himself stand still, though he was longing to insert a finger and ease his collar.

'Well,' said Giles at last, and Afton held his breath, 'I don't want to lose you as valet, so I suppose I must find another butler.' Relief washed over Afton. 'But it's a damned nuisance. And a damned expense!'

This last struck Giles as ungenerous even as he said it – actually Afton combining the roles was not the norm and had saved him money.

'Very well,' he said, before Afton could apologise and make him feel worse. 'I'll put it in hand. I assume you'll continue as you are until a replacement can be found?'

'Of course, my lord. And I'm very grateful.'

Moss paused at the door to the kitchen until the cook looked up, then greeted her with a large and genial smile. 'Ah, Mrs Terry.'

'Mr Moss. How nice to see you here again. What do we owe the pleasure to?'

'Mrs Webster invited me to tea. Something smells delicious.'

'A beefsteak pie for upstairs dinner. It's only his lordship and her ladyship and Mr Richard tonight, but we shall be getting busy again on Saturday, with a whole party coming for the shooting.'

'Yes, so I understand,' said Moss.

Mrs Webster appeared at his elbow in the catlike way she had. 'We'll have tea in my room, Mr Moss. Will you come? You may send it in, Mrs Terry.'

Moss looked about him keenly as he followed her to the housekeeper's room. 'It's good to see that nothing has changed,' he remarked. 'Except the pictures on your mantelpiece,' he added, as he entered behind her. 'You have them the other way around.'

'A remarkable power of noticing you have, Mr Moss,' Mrs Webster commented coolly.

'Essential for a butler, I believe,' Moss said, pleased with what had not been meant as a compliment. The round table was pulled out and laid for tea. 'And is that a new tea set?'

'Different, not new. It was in the very top of the cupboard.'

'Ah, yes, I remember now. Your predecessor used it sometimes. It came from upstairs originally, when breakages rendered it unusable for the family.'

'So I supposed. There isn't much of it left, but enough for my purposes. It's pretty, isn't it, with the bluebells and primroses?'

'More suitable for spring, perhaps,' he said, taking the seat to which she had gestured. 'And laid for three, I see.'

'Mr Afton is joining us. Ah, here he is now.'

Moss rose again. Greetings were exchanged. Ivy followed Afton in with the tea tray, everything was set out, and Mrs Webster began to pour. 'You like it strong, I believe, Mr Moss? And do have a scone while they're hot.'

There was Mrs Terry's latest batch of blackcurrant jam to go with them, and a cake. 'Cherry, one of my favourites,' Moss remarked, eyeing it.

'Mrs Terry remembered,' said Mrs Webster.

'You're looking well, Mr Moss,' said Afton.

'I'm feeling well, thank you,' said Moss.

'No recurrence of the trouble?' Mrs Webster asked delicately.

'No, indeed. That unhappy episode is all behind me and quite forgotten. I am as fit as I have ever been – fitter, in fact. I walked up the hill just now without stopping.'

'I expect working in a quiet household has given you a nice rest,' said Mrs Webster.

'It *is* quiet,' Moss said. 'In fact, it is rather too quiet for me. Miss Eddowes is a true lady and I could not ask for a better mistress. But with only a cook and one girl under me, and very little in the way of entertaining, I must confess it is no challenge for someone of my experience. I was accustomed to commanding a large staff and running a great house. I frequently have too little to do.' He sipped his tea. 'Whereas you, Mr Afton, must be very busy. It is good to hear that the Castle is entertaining again. An earl's house ought to set the example of hospitality for the whole neighbourhood.' He looked up in time to intercept the quick glance that passed between Afton and Mrs Webster. 'Just the family upstairs at the moment, I understand? And no young ladies?'

'Lady Alice has gone back to London,' said Mrs Webster. 'Her classes have started again. Wonderfully keen not to miss any, she is.'

'It's an odd business,' Moss said judiciously, 'but I suppose there's no real harm in it. There *have* been gently born female artists in the past,' he added, 'like, er . . .' He couldn't recall any names and covered the moment with a cough. 'And Lady Rachel?' he began again.

'We haven't seen her all summer,' said Mrs Webster. 'She went with the Prince and Princess Wittenstein-Glücksberg straight to Scotland. They're staying with the Strathmores.'

'Ah, then there may be an invitation to Balmoral,' said Moss, pleased with the thought. 'That would be a great thing for her.'

'Lord and Lady Leake are in Scotland as well,' Mrs Webster went on, 'staying at Kincraig, of course, but I dare say there'll be visits back and forth.'

'Are they expected here?'

'Nothing's been said to me,' said Mrs Webster.

'But I did hear his lordship say that they might call in on their way south,' Afton said. 'I believe Lady Leake wants to spend a few days in London before they go back to Venice.'

'Quite the vagabond life they are leading,' Moss remarked. 'But then, Lord Leake always was one for travelling. I remember her ladyship – her dowager ladyship, I mean – her highness as she now is – saying that she hoped he would settle down once he was married and stay in one place.' Mrs Webster had refreshed his tea, and he sipped again. 'I must say it is good to have news of the family. I often wonder how you are all doing up here. Any news below stairs?' He looked at them keenly.

'Only that Cyril is leaving to better himself,' said Mrs Webster. 'He's got a position as first footman at Loughton Manor.'

'Oh, the Massingberds,' Moss said. 'You will be left short-handed.'

'Wilfrid will be promoted to third footman,' Afton said. 'He's ready. But we really need a fourth, in a house this size, and with all the extra work of entertaining.'

'It must be especially difficult for you, Mr Afton,' Moss said, 'given that you have valeting duties as well.'

Mrs Webster exchanged another glance with Afton. She'd suspected Moss knew why he was here.

Afton abandoned pretence. 'You've obviously heard that I am giving up the role of butler, as soon as we've found a replacement.'

'Rose told me,' Moss admitted. 'She calls in when she's in the village. And I *did* wonder,' he coughed discreetly, 'when I received your kind invitation to tea this afternoon . . .'

'We don't want a stranger,' Mrs Webster said bluntly. 'You never know what you're going to get. And the disruption of teaching a newcomer how we do things, and possibly having him make changes, is more than I can contemplate. So Mr Afton and I have been wondering whether you might consider coming back. If you're well enough for the extra work.'

Moss beamed. 'I would like it beyond anything. It's what I have dreamed of, ever since I went to Weldon House, though of course I didn't know in the beginning if I would ever . . .' He stopped, overcome, and took out a handkerchief. 'His lordship knows you're asking me, of course?' he said, when he emerged from it. 'And her ladyship?'

'I wouldn't have put it to you without their approval,' said Afton. 'His lordship would much prefer it, if you really are able for it, rather than find a new man. In fact, the idea of having you back is the only thing that softens his disappointment in me.'

'I would have to put it to Miss Eddowes very carefully,' Moss said. 'I wouldn't want her to think I was ungrateful. I don't know what would have happened to me if she hadn't given me a place.'

'I'm sure the details can be managed to everyone's satisfaction,' Mrs Webster said. 'This would be a pleasant solution all around. Ashmore Castle and Mr Moss, united again!'

'And Mr Afton once more a valet only,' said Afton.

'I don't wish to cause offence, Mr Afton,' Moss said, already regaining some of his magnificence, 'but I never thought you to be cut out for a butler.'

Afton grinned. 'Now why should I take offence at that? But would it trouble you to tell me why? I don't think I did too badly, all in all.'

'Of course you didn't,' said Mrs Webster, sharply. 'Why did you not think him cut out for it, Mr Moss?'

'I'm afraid he's not tall enough,' said Moss.

'Moss back at the Castle,' said Aunt Caroline, looking up from her letter. 'How splendid! There's something properly grand about the old fellow. Sets the right tone.'

'But is his heart strong enough?' Alice asked.

'It seems so. Kitty says Giles talked to Dr Arbogast and had him run the rule over him, and apparently he's in good shape. He's quite a bit trimmer, which helps – I suppose working in a smaller household he had more tasks to perform.'

'And less port to finish up,' said Alice. 'Poor Miss Eddowes, though. Isn't it hard on her to have her butler stolen away?'

'Oh, Kitty says she didn't mind at all. She didn't really

need a butler in the first place and there wasn't enough for him to do. She only took him on out of charity.'

'That is *very* kind,' said Alice, struck.

'Yes, one doesn't often come across genuine philanthropy,' said Aunt Caroline. She went back to the letter, and turned the sheet over. 'Oh, they're having a visit from Sebastian and his wife. Just a Saturday-to-Monday, with other guests, for the shooting.' She put the letter down. 'All very well for Sebastian, because he'll be out with the guns all day, but what about that poor woman? I must say, I shouldn't like to be in her shoes.'

Alice thought about it. 'But probably the other guests won't know she was once a servant there.'

'Yes, that's true. And Kitty will be kind and try to make her feel at home. Very different from your mother's day.'

'Goodness, yes,' Alice said. 'I don't suppose Uncle Sebastian would ever go back if Mama was in charge.'

'I must write to her – your mama,' Aunt Caroline said. 'I haven't heard anything for an age. Linda used to be a good correspondent but lately she seems to have lost the habit.'

'I expect she has other things on her mind,' Alice said. 'Like Cousin Pippi. I wonder how things are going with him.'

'Cousin Pippi?' Aunt Caroline said vaguely and, without waiting for Alice to elaborate, went on, 'I wonder if she's going to come back to England when Maud is up and about, or whether she means to stay in Germany permanently.'

'I think it depends on Cousin Pippi,' Alice said wisely.

Ellen was pleased about the visit to Ashmore Castle. She couldn't wait to sport herself in front of her former colleagues in her black lady's-maid dress, and sit at the important end of the table. And life at Wisteria House was rather dull. Jealous of her new status, she felt she had to keep aloof from the cook and the housemaid, which left only Mr Crooks, and he was poor company for a modern young woman. At the Castle, on a shooting weekend, there would be visiting lady's maids to talk to – and perhaps a handsome visiting valet . . .

She was heartened by the bustle of arrival below stairs as she strutted in with Crooks behind her. It was clear that Mr Moss was in charge after the more relaxed era of Mr Afton, for Mrs Webster addressed her as Miss Tallant and Crooks as Mr Tallant.

'You'll be sharing with Miss Bayfield, Miss Tallant. And you'll be in with Mr Ravenscar,' she told Crooks, and gave him a considering look. 'Lord Denham hasn't brought a man with him – I wonder if I could ask you to look after him as well.'

Crooks blinked. 'I will do my best,' he said.

'Thank you. Mr Sebastian doesn't usually need much valeting, does he? And Mr Afton has his lordship and Mr Richard to look after.' One might ask a 'family' valet to double.

Ellen had managed a squint at the guest list in Mrs Webster's hand. 'Bayfield,' she said, as she and Crooks started up the stairs. 'That's her ladyship's mother and father, isn't it? Quite elderly company, then, what with Lord and Lady Denham.'

'As long as the gentlemen can shoot,' Crooks said. 'Nothing worse on these occasions than a poor gun. Spoils the sport for everyone.'

'I don't see much sport in shooting a poor, helpless little bird,' Ellen said.

'You don't mind eating them, though, do you?'

'Give me a nice bit of pork with crackling any time. What are the Ravenscars like? I don't remember them.'

'Youngish couple, about the same age as his lordship and her ladyship. Halton Manor, near Wendover. Lady Ravenscar's sister lives with them, a Miss Rowsham. She was engaged to be married but her fiancé died just before the wedding, a tragic story. I wonder if she'll be here.'

Another lady's maid coming up fast behind them overheard him and said, 'She *is* here, and I have to maid both of them, Lady Ravenscar *and* Miss Adeline. I don't mind at home, but in a strange house when you don't know where anything is . . .' She gave a tut of annoyance.

'If I can be of any help, Miss Ravenscar,' Crooks began courteously.

But she said tersely, 'Excuse me, I'm in a hurry,' and pushed past him. He flattened himself to let her by. She paused a few steps higher to look back. 'Are you Mr Tallant?'

'I have that honour, yes,' said Crooks, who disapproved of hurrying on principle.

'You're sharing with Gaston. Watch out for him.'

'Who is Gaston?'

'Lord Ravenscar's valet,' she said. 'French – and he *hates* sharing.' And she was gone.

Ellen suppressed a snigger. 'Looks like you're in for some fun, Mr Crooks.'

'We are all God's creatures, Miss Hatching. And our duty is to our masters and mistresses. If we have to put up with a bit of inconvenience, so be it.'

'If you say so,' she said, reaching the landing. 'I'll see you later.' And she turned off to the women's side.

Crooks's philosophy was tested by reality. In truth, he didn't like sharing either, but now he was no longer resident he could hardly expect to have his old room back. The room he was sharing was lacking all the little comforts he had collected over the years, and when he stepped in, the other valet had not only chosen a bed, but had put his suitcase and a valise on the other to unpack them. He gave Crooks a furious look when asked to move them, and answered with a flood of French, which sounded irascible and rude, and was clearly a refusal of some kind.

'This is my bed, Mr Ravenscar. I need to unpack my

things,' Crooks said, trying to sound firm. He did not like confrontation – it made him shake.

The man glared at him. 'My name is Gaston,' he said, heavily accented, 'and I do not share. Go away!'

Crooks drew himself upright, his cheeks quivering. 'In this house, a visiting valet takes his master's name. As a valet of many years' experience, I am accustomed to following the rules of the house where I am serving, however temporarily.'

'Bah!' said Gaston, barking the word into his face and went back to his unpacking.

Crooks recoiled. 'Perhaps in France you have different ways. But the saying is, when in Rome, do as the Romans do.'

Gaston whirled round, made a gesture with his hand imitating the quacking of a duck, and shouted, 'Cease your noise, barnyard!' Followed by a few more obviously disobliging things in French.

Crooks flushed, and felt his eyes grow moist. This was too much! A gentleman's *gentleman* – note the second word – should not be slighted and insulted. Barnyard indeed!

'I insist that you move your baggage, sir,' he cried, his voice distressingly reedy with emotion. 'And that you address me with proper respect.'

'*Allez-vous en!*' Gaston said deliberately, leaning towards him with an air of menace. 'Go away, old man. *Silly* old man! *J'en ai assez de votre bavardage bête!*'

'What did you call me?' Crooks gasped.

'*Bête! Niais! Stupide!*' hissed the valet, who evidently understood some English, if he chose not to speak it.

'How dare you, sir? How dare you?' was all Crooks could manage in his outrage. He had never been spoken to thus in his life.

Gaston said nothing, but picked up Crooks's case, threw it out into the passage, shoved Crooks roughly after it, and slammed the door. Before Crooks could gather his wits, he heard the key turning from the inside. Near to tears, he stood staring at the impenetrable barrier, wondering what to do. He would not thump on it and shout and make a show of himself – even if there were any likelihood that it would help. He had been insulted, abused – and locked out of his legitimate room. He had no bed for the night, nowhere to change. He would have to go ignominiously downstairs and ask either Mr Moss or Mrs Webster for help, like a child reporting to Nanny that his brother had stolen his toy. It was humiliating. It was undignified. It was *not right*!

He plodded back to the landing where, as he started down the stairs, he was overtaken again by the Ravenscar maid, with a gown over her arm and a pair of shoes in her hand. She gave him an amused glance as she passed and said, 'Chucked you out, did he? Yes, that's his favourite trick. I told them downstairs that he doesn't like to share but they didn't listen to me.'

'He called me a— He called me names!' Crooks quavered.

She dashed on. 'You've only got him for the weekend. I have to live with it.'

'Really, Mr Crooks, I'm surprised at you,' Moss said, at his most monumental. 'Quarrelling with a visiting valet? It's not what I would have expected of a man of your experience.'

'*I* am a visiting valet,' Crooks pointed out, hot with chagrin.

'But you're also family,' said Moss. 'I expect you to show an example to the younger servants.'

'I did nothing to provoke it!' Crooks cried. 'He started to abuse me as soon as I appeared.'

'I can't take sides. You'll just have to apologise and find some way to get along,' said Moss. He wasn't really listening. There was so much to do. He had forgotten in the fallow fields of Weldon House how much there was to do when the Castle entertained.

'But he's locked me out!' Crooks said desperately. 'Where am I supposed to sleep?'

Mrs Webster, passing the door, looked in. 'Is there a problem, Mr Crooks?'

'Mr Tallant,' Moss corrected her with a frown.

'When I went up to the room, Mr Ravenscar shouted at me in the French language, pushed me out and locked the door,' said Crooks.

'Have you tried to get back in?' Moss asked vaguely, running a finger down the cellar book. 'Have we a spare key, Mrs Webster?'

She took Crooks's arm and drew him out into the passage. 'Lady Ravenscar's maid did say he could be trouble, but we had no idea he'd go this far.' She tapped her lips with a forefinger in thought. 'You'd better have your old room. The bed's not made up, but I'll send one of the girls up while you're dressing Lord Denham.'

'Thank you,' Crooks said, comforted. Mrs Webster had taken his part. And he'd end up with a better room, which was snooks to the rude Frenchman!

'There, that wasn't too bad, was it?' Sebastian said to Dory when they got back to their room that night. Before his marriage he had always had the Gainsborough Room at the Castle, but the Waterloo Room had a small dressing-room attached, making it more suited to a married couple. It was a rather masculine chamber, with red flock wallpaper and heavy mahogany furniture, and over the mantelpiece a large reproduction of *The Forming of the Squares at Quatre Bras*.

'The dinner was very good,' Dory said.

'You know that's not what I meant.'

Hatching was waiting to undress her, and she didn't want to say too much in front of the maid. She was getting more used to being on the wrong side of the service when they had company or went out, but she managed mostly by saying very little, which made people think her dull. The company for this weekend was composed of people who did not know her past, which helped; but she always went in fear of the wrong question being asked. There had been a moment, for instance, when Lady Bayfield had asked her where she had got her gown. It was one she had made herself, and she hesitated and then said Paris. Lady Bayfield, who by her appearance knew a great deal about fashion, had given her a long, cool look, then turned away to speak to someone else. Dory decided to wear the Paquin at dinner tomorrow, so her ladyship might think she was merely confused, rather than a pitiful liar.

'The Ravenscars seemed pleasant people,' Dory said. 'And I like the sister – Miss Rowsham.'

'Seems a nice girl. Invited for Richard, obviously,' Sebastian said. 'Perhaps rather too obviously,' he added, with a rumble of a laugh. 'Richard tends to be perverse. Expect him to do something and he'll do the opposite.'

'But he was very attentive to her,' Dory noted. 'Perhaps he was smitten.'

'He has engaging manners,' Sebastian said. 'But I hope he does take to her. It's time he got married.'

'You think everyone should be married,' Dory said fondly.

'I would like everyone to be as happy as I am. And now I suppose I must leave you with Hatching,' he said. He met her eyes, and a message passed between them. For decency's sake he had to let Crooks put him to bed in the dressing-room, but he would not stay there once the servants had gone.

The trouble started at breakfast. Dory was down early to spend as much time with Sebastian as possible before the men went out. Miss Rowsham was the only other lady down, and Dory, accustomed to observing the gentry and analysing them, guessed she was hoping to further her cause with Richard. He, however, having helped her at the sideboard, went and sat down on the other side of the table and talked to Lord Ravenscar. Dory helped herself to eggs and sausages and, looking round to see where Sebastian was sitting, encountered a very frosty glance from Sir John Bayfield, instantly withdrawn. She supposed he merely objected to females coming down early to breakfast on a shooting morning and paid no attention, sitting down beside her husband.

But then Lady Bayfield came in, scanned the room, and said, in a penetrating voice, 'Oh, Mrs Tallant, how early you must have risen. But I suppose it is old habit with you.'

Dory, startled, didn't know what to say. Miss Rowsham, across the table from her, gave her a puzzled look, but said nothing. But then Lady Bayfield sat down next to Sir John, stared straight at Dory with a brittle and glittering smile, and said, 'By the way, I happened to tear the hem of my gown just a little last night. I wonder if I might ask you to mend it for me.'

Beside her, Dory felt Sebastian draw a sharp breath, and Richard's head flicked round to look at her.

Lady Bayfield went on without pausing: 'I would ask my own maid, but she is not skilled with the needle. I'm persuaded it would be nothing to one of *your* experience.'

Kitty had come in, and from the door she said, in a high, tense voice, 'Mama, Mrs Tallant is *my guest.*'

'To be sure, dear,' Lady Bayfield answered, still staring at Dory. 'You always were a little too liberal in your ideas.'

Dory felt Sebastian about to explode, but she knew that would only make things worse – a horrible scene at breakfast, news of which would spread through the house and thence to how many other houses? She caught his hand under the table and squeezed it hard in warning, and said lightly, 'I would oblige you, Lady Bayfield, but I don't ply the needle any more.'

'Indeed?' said Lady Bayfield archly. 'But I am reliably informed you made the gown you had on last night.'

Kitty had moved to Dory's shoulder and was about to speak, but Richard intervened in a light, quick voice. 'It always amazes me you ladies have the time to learn so many accomplishments. My sisters used to paint screens, and Kitty embroiders prettily – you made all the baby's shirts, didn't you, Pusscat? Smocking, now – how ever you do that I can't think, it looks so complicated. And my mother used to do tapestry-work. You are in the Tapestry Room, aren't you, Lady Bayfield? The chair seats there are some of her work – Princess Usingen as she now is.'

It was, in fact, a lie – his mother had despised needlework of all sorts, but it silenced Lady Bayfield and deflected the company, and Sebastian started up a conversation with Lord Ravenscar about the day's prospects, so the moment passed. Soon afterwards he rose to leave the room, and invited Dory by a crooked arm to go with him.

Out in the hall, he felt her trembling slightly and wanted to go back into the breakfast room and wring Lady Bayfield's scrawny neck. 'She's just one horrible old woman,' he forestalled her.

'Her maid must have got it from someone in the servants' hall and told her,' Dory said, in a flat voice. 'It won't stop there. She'll tell Lady Denham and Lady Ravenscar.'

'To hell with them,' Sebastian said robustly.

'That's all very well, but it will keep happening,' she said. 'This is what I was afraid of.'

'Who cares what a few superannuated hags think?'

'Do you mean to avoid all company for the rest of our lives? And what if they dig up worse things?'

'Darling, we are what we are,' he said, looking down at her. 'Have courage. They'll soon forget about it. It's a five-minute wonder.'

'Yes, but it's *my* five minutes,' she said, trying to hold on to her sense of humour. 'You'll be out with the men – I'll have to sit in the drawing-room all morning being insulted or ignored.'

'Don't sit there, then. Come out with me.'

'Is it allowed? I thought shooting was for men only.'

'Ladies shooting is rather frowned on, though one or two do it. But quite a few ladies go out and stand behind the guns. Particularly if they're conducting an affair with one of them. Or hoping to. I remember in earlier days Sibella Bissell used to go out and stand behind her husband – she even used to load for him. And I'll bet Miss Rowsham would love to go out and further her cause with Richard. She won't like to be the only one, though, so if you tell her you're going she'll be your friend for life.'

'But won't it just prove to – certain people that I'm not a lady?'

'Not a bit. You're a newly married lady, so your wanting to be with me won't surprise anyone.'

'Will it *please* anyone, though?' she asked.

He gave her a tender smile. 'It will please one of the guns immensely,' he said.

'It was that fool Daisy told Lady Bayfield's woman,' Mrs Webster reported to Afton. 'I don't *think* she meant any harm by it. She just mentioned it as a cause for wonder. But Higgins has a swollen idea of her own importance, considering Sir John is only a baronet, and decided to take offence.'

'His lordship said her ladyship had a sharp word with her mother,' Afton said, 'so let's hope that's the end of it.'

'It won't change feelings,' Mrs Webster said. It still felt more natural to exchange thoughts with Afton than with Mr Moss – and in any case, Moss had always been an advocate for people remembering their place. Afton, with a past of his own, was more flexible of mind.

'As long as nobody talks about it,' Afton said, 'they can think what they like. And they will. Life is a stew-pot,

Mrs Webster. Bits of carrot come up to the top, jostle with the peas, and sink again.'

She looked at him with raised eyebrows. 'And who, in this case, is the carrot and who the pea?'

He merely smiled. 'It's very pretty to see them together, Mr Sebastian and his bride. It's nice when a gentleman well up in years finds true love, don't you think?'

'Surprising, I'd call it, in this case. Well, it's just for the weekend, and I don't suppose they'll be going into society a great deal. Ellen said they're happy in their own company.'

Afton smiled. 'I'll bet she said that as a complaint. She's ambitious. Not much chance to shine if her master and mistress dine alone at home every night. I give it six months.'

'If she's sensible she'll stay a year and make sure of a good reference before she moves on. Nobody wants a flighty lady's maid.'

Moss appeared in the doorway. 'I'm just going to ring the dressing bell,' he said, looking curiously from her to Afton.

'We were discussing Lord Ravenscar's man,' Mrs Webster lied smoothly.

'Ah, yes,' said Moss, grandly. 'I shall ensure he does not sit above you at supper tonight, Mr Afton. Lord Ravenscar is only a viscount. It was good of you not to make a fuss at luncheon.'

'Mr Ravenscar made enough fuss of his own – I didn't think we needed any more,' said Afton.

'Quite so. But precedence is precedence. I wonder,' Moss sighed, 'why Lord Ravenscar keeps him on. Making trouble below stairs – and I didn't think much of the finish he got on Lord Ravenscar's boots. I don't believe the French really understand good leather. There was a gentleman once, many years ago, who came with a French valet – or was he German? I'll think of his name in a moment—'

'The dressing bell, Mr Moss?' Mrs Webster reminded him kindly.

'Yes, yes, of course.' He went two steps, turned back and said, 'Goossens, that was it. Now is that French or German? Of course, we called him Mr Edgehill down here, but he – yes, yes, I'm on my way.' And he was gone.

Alice was drawing in her room when there was a knock at the door.

'I'm sorry to disturb you, my lady, but Mr Tullamore has called, and her ladyship is out.'

'Oh. Yes, all right, I'll come,' Alice said resignedly. It wasn't that she didn't like Angus, but Rachel was still in Scotland and she was afraid he would ask her awkward questions.

He was in the drawing-room, idly examining the cards on Aunt Caroline's mantelpiece. He came across to shake her hand.

'It's just me, I'm afraid,' she said. 'Aunt Caroline's having a fitting, and everyone else is at the Castle.'

He raised his eyebrows. 'Rachel went straight down to the Castle?'

'No, she's still with Uncle Fergus and Aunt Giulia at Kincraig.'

'I thought she was staying with your other aunt,' he said.

'Aunt Vicky and Uncle Bobo went back to Germany so Uncle Fergus took her over,' Alice said, trying to sound matter-of-fact.

'It must have been a let-down, after hobnobbing with royalties at Glamis,' he said discontentedly.

'I think there's one last big shooting party, and that the King might be going across from Balmoral. He's rather taken a shine to Giulia.'

Angus said nothing, but walked across to the window to stare out at the rainy, blustery day. She went and stood beside him in silent sympathy. The trees in the square had been stripped bare now; people below hurrying along the street were invisible under umbrellas, like travelling mushrooms.

He seemed deep in his thoughts, and she took the opportunity to study him. He had changed since the beginning of the year. When he had arrived at the Castle at Christmas he had seemed like an eager boy, his face like a flame, burning with love and determination. Now he seemed older, his face firm with authority, lines in his forehead and between his sandy brows – definitely a man, not a boy. More serious, too: he did not smile readily any more. The work and responsibility he had taken on for Mr Cowling, she guessed, involved more effort from him than when he was his father's heir and lightly dabbling in his father's business. She liked him better for it, but she had no idea about Rachel's taste in the matter.

'What's going on with her?' he asked at last.

'I don't know,' Alice said. 'Really I don't. She used to tell me things when we were girls in the old schoolroom at the Castle, but all that changed when Mama took her to Germany. I don't know any more what she's thinking.'

Angus stared at her penetratingly, his mouth grim. 'Does she mean to jilt me? Is that what it is?'

She didn't answer. How could she know?

'I gave up everything for her,' he said, in a low, angry voice. 'My brother Fritz turned twenty-one and married Fiona Culross in August and my father's officially made him his heir. I'm cut out of his will, thrown out of the family! I wasn't even invited to the wedding.'

'I'm sorry,' she said.

'I did it for her! I got myself a position. I work hard, I'm giving satisfaction, I'm saving every penny I can, and by next year, when she's twenty-one, I shall be able to afford a decent house, and we can get married. It won't be near what I could have had if I'd bowed down to my father and married Diana Huntley. But what of it? I loved Rachel, and she was all I wanted. And she said she loved me.'

'I'm sure—' Alice began helplessly.

'She's changed, you know,' he said abruptly, interrupting

her. 'She was terrified of being separated from me. She wanted to run away with me. She talked about Gretna Green, but I persuaded her it wouldn't do. I said, "You only have to hold on, that's all, and we'll be together for ever." Now, all she seems to care about is dancing and parties.'

'You mustn't be hard on her,' Alice began, but again he interrupted.

'God knows, I want her to have all that – nice clothes and jewels and a carriage and servants. I'd be a cad if I wanted her to be less comfortable marrying me than she might be otherwise. And I *will* give her those things! I'll work my fingers to the bone for her. She only has to be patient. Is that too much to ask?'

'No,' she said sadly. 'It's not too much to ask, to be with the man you love.'

He stared again, and his nostrils flared. 'You're saying she doesn't love me any more?'

'I'm *not* saying that,' she said quickly. 'I'm sure she does love you. It's just —'

'Just what?'

'It's hard for her. She's always enjoyed dressing up and balls and so on. I never did. When we were girls together, it was what she dreamed of. I just dreamed about horses. And Mama gave her a taste for it when she brought her out and – well, it's hard for her, that's all I'm saying.'

He was silent a moment. 'It seems as though I picked the wrong sister,' he said, with a wry twist of his lips.

'Oh, don't say that!' she begged.

'No, no, of course I don't mean it. I love her, and I always will, even if she loves dancing more than she loves me. I just need to know where I stand. If—' He broke off, and started again with difficulty. 'If she's had second thoughts, if she wants me to release her, I will. I only want her to be happy.'

She doesn't deserve you, Alice thought. She said, 'All I can tell you is that I believe she loves you too.'

'You *believe*?'

'I haven't spoken to her in months,' Alice defended herself. 'I think you have to take your own advice, and just hold on. Be patient. Let her get the dancing out of her system, and she'll settle down. She'll come back to you.'

He looked at her a long moment more, and gave a wry smile. 'You're kind. I shall like having you for a sister.'

'I shall like having you for a brother.'

He sighed and turned away. 'I'll see myself out. If you speak to her, or write to her, tell her . . .'

'I know.'

'I gave up everything for her,' he said again, quietly. And left.

CHAPTER TWENTY-ONE

In the train on the way down to Portsmouth, Mr Cowling broke a long silence to say, 'It's been a good summer. Don't you think so, my dear?'

Nina looked up from the magazine she wasn't really reading, not sure what he was referring to. He was looking at her intently.

'I mean, spending so much more time with you,' he said. 'First the Isle of Wight—'

'I wasn't sure you really enjoyed that,' Nina said. 'Bobby's family can be rather boisterous.'

'Oh, I don't mind a bit of good, honest family fun,' he said. 'I'm not such a dour old fossil, am I?'

'None of those things,' she said, with a gallant smile.

'And then the trip to Paris. We must do it again, and see the sights. Notre Dame and the Louvre and so on. The Eiffel Tower – you'd have liked to go up that, eh?'

'I expect the view from the top is wonderful,' Nina said.

'Tallest structure in the world when it was first built. People said it'd never stand up. And, d'you know, the French nobs and artists and such hated it! Said it was ugly and ridiculous and an insult to French good taste.'

'How do you know that?' she marvelled.

'Oh, I read it somewhere. There was some famous French writer or other who had lunch in the Eiffel Tower restaurant every day, because he said it was the only place in Paris where you couldn't see it.' She laughed. 'There's always people who will stand in the way of progress.'

'I suppose you need a brake on a motor-car. The faster the car, the more it needs the brakes.'

'That's cleverly put,' he said. 'Yes, we must go back to Paris some time. And how would you like a trip to Italy?'

'I would love it. Is there some reason you're mentioning it now?' she asked.

'I've been thinking it was time I rearranged my life a bit. I've got Decius, and Truman, and young Tullamore in London, and good people in all the factories. I ought to spend more time enjoying my money instead of making it.'

'Not *instead of* making, it, surely.'

'Oh, you're too sharp for me! You know what I mean. Next month, for instance, the hunting will start. There'll be lots of dinners and parties to go to, but why shouldn't we give one?'

'No reason that I can think of,' she said.

'And make it a prime 'un, too – one that everyone'll talk about.'

'You should buy a horse, and come out with me,' Nina said generously, on the basis that he would like to be asked but would never do it.

But he said, 'Aye, well, I might, at that. I'm no great horseman, but I dare say I could stick on all right. See what it is all you folk get so excited about.'

'Well, do,' she said, and looked away, out of the window, while she got her expression under control. She'd had an image of Giles on horseback, and for an instant saw herself riding at his side. In that other world, a world where history had happened differently.

'Are you all right, Nina dear?' Mr Cowling asked. 'You're quite well, aren't you?'

'Quite well, thank you,' she said, and turned back to him to smile.

'Only you looked uncomfortable for a moment there.'

He had seen her face reflected in the window. She had to say something. 'I just thought about Trump for an instant.'

He took her hand and pressed it. 'I'm sorry, my love. I should have thought. Dragging you to Portsmouth – it's bound to bring it all back.'

'No, really, I'm quite all right. Don't worry about it, please.' She changed the subject with determination. 'It will be a very grand celebration, I suppose?'

'I should just about think it will! A hundred years since Trafalgar? The navy have Trafalgar dinners in their messes every year, but for the centenary it's got to be a bit special.'

'What goes on at these dinners?'

'Oh, there's a grand spread, of course, and they generally have a band playing while they eat. And there's the parading of the beef.'

'Goodness, what's that?'

'The main dish is always the roast beef of old England, and the chef brings it in on a trolley and parades it round the table for everyone to see before it's carved. All very jolly. At the end of dinner there are speeches and toasts. The chair says, "Mr Vice, the King," and the vice chair stands up and proposes the Loyal Toast. And then the guest of honour proposes a toast to the Immortal Memory.'

'Immortal memory of what?'

'Of Lord Nelson and those who fell with him, of course.'

'Ah! It all sounds very . . .' she wasn't sure how to put it. It sounded like something from a gentlemen's club, or a university dining hall '. . . interesting,' she concluded. 'But there aren't any women in the navy. How can I be invited?'

'This is a special Trafalgar dinner, and it's not being held in a mess. There'll be all sorts of dignitaries and their wives. It was hoped the King might come, but he's got engagements in London. I expect he'll send someone to represent him.'

★ ★ ★

HMS *Victory* had been rotting at her moorings for years, and in 1903 she had been accidentally rammed by HMS *Neptune*, and only by the skin of her teeth had been prevented from sinking. Emergency repairs had been carried out, but she was too frail to accommodate a centenary celebration. The best that could be done was to dress her overall, not just with flags but with electric light globes, which were powered from a submarine moored alongside.

The special dinner was held in Portsmouth's grandest hotel, with the Princess Royal and the Duke of Fife representing the King. There were two long tables, joined at the top by a short one at which the princess and her husband were seated along with the chair and vice chair, the port admiral, the mayor of Portsmouth and various other 'high-ups', as Mr Cowling called them. Nina and Mr Cowling were seated quite far down one of the long tables. The menu was extensive, beginning with oysters, then consommé, fillets of sole Grand Duc, braised sweetbreads Demidoff, and pheasant *à la Reine*. Then came the roast beef of Old England, with the promised parade and, since suitable wines had been served with each course, considerable noise and jollity. After that came the sweet and the savoury – *omelette surprise* and *barquettes de foie gras*, then dessert, speeches and toasts.

Nina, with Mr Cowling opposite her on the other side of the table, had on her left a young captain who was just back from Malta and was happy to tell her everything she wanted to know about the island's history and culture. On her right was a Portsmouth man of the law who had plenty to say about starting a campaign to save HMS *Victory* 'since the Admiralty clearly won't'.

'It would be a scandal if our most famous ship were allowed to perish,' he said.

The captain leaned forward to agree. 'And foolish, too. If the old girl was put into good enough shape to allow visitors, she'd make enough money from entry fees to pay for her keep. Back in the eighteen forties she was attracting over twenty thousand visitors a year.'

'That's an interesting idea,' the lawman said. 'It would be good for the rest of Portsmouth, too, bringing people to the city, to stay at hotels and eat in restaurants, hire cabs and boats and so on.'

Nina looked at her husband and saw that he had overheard the exchange and was bursting to join in with the discussion, had etiquette not forbidden speaking across the table. More people spending money was an ideal close to his heart.

It was a late evening, and with so much food, drink, talk and noise, Nina felt very sleepy when she and Mr Cowling finally left. They stepped out under the hotel's canopy to have a cab summoned to take them back to their own hotel. The streets were shiny and wet. It was not very cold, but a blustery wind was blowing a light rain in from the sea. The air smelt wonderfully fresh after the banqueting room, and slightly salty; the strings of electric lights the hotel had put up for the celebration rocked alarmingly overhead.

'Did you have a nice time?' Mr Cowling asked, when they were seated in the cab.

'Very nice,' she said.

'You had a couple of interesting people to talk to,' he suggested.

'I did. Didn't you?'

He didn't answer that. 'The young fellow on your left,' he said. 'He had a lot to say for himself. Seemed to be very taken with you, too.'

'Taken with me?'

'Hogging your attention. Leaning towards you. I was afraid he was going to end up in your lap if he got any closer.'

He was jealous, she realised with surprise. 'I spoke to the man on my right too,' she said. 'When we turned.'

'Aye, but then blow me if the young whippersnapper didn't

lean right forward and poke himself into *that* conversation as well.'

'It was about saving the *Victory*. I saw you were interested.'

'Interested in why he couldn't leave you alone for long enough to attend to the lady on his other side.'

'Ah, here we are at the hotel,' she said, hoping to break the chain. 'It isn't far, is it? I'm so sleepy, I'm more than ready for bed.'

He said nothing more, but got out to help her down. The hotel porter had emerged to open the cab door and hold an umbrella over Nina, but as she stepped onto the pavement, a strong gust of wind snatched it inside-out, and the rain hit her face as the porter wrestled with it. At the same moment, a small dog scuttled out from the alley at the side of the hotel and ran past her across the road. A dray with a tarpaulin-covered load was passing the stationary cab at a smart pace. Nina, who had closed her eyes momentarily against the fine blowing rain, heard the dog's shrill scream, cut off short, a shout from the dray's driver, and the snorting of the horses.

Her eyes flew open. She was on the move before Mr Cowling could catch her arm to hold her back. 'No, Nina!' he called.

The dog was lying on its side in the road. Other people were hurrying across, but Nina got there first. She heard voices, heard the dray driver's protest, felt the nervous movement of the two big horses, was aware of their steaming bulk and the smell of manure and chaff and the scrape of their iron-clad feet on the road. The dog was panting shallowly, its eyes staring straight ahead. She couldn't see any damage on it, and was bracing herself to touch it when it gave an *oof* of expelled breath, and was still.

Mr Cowling reached her, and pulled her to her feet. 'Your gown! The wet road!' he protested. 'Come away, there's nothing you can do.'

'No,' she said. 'It's gone. Poor thing.' She heard her own

voice, and it sounded quite calm. It seemed to reassure Mr Cowling, who led her back to the hotel.

People were passing them the other way, going to look at the accident. The doorman was one of them: Mr Cowling had to open the door himself. 'Perhaps a brandy-and-soda, for the shock,' he suggested.

'I'm all right,' she said. 'I just want to go to bed.' Still she sounded normal.

She took his arm and they went upstairs in silence. Tina and Moxton were waiting. Moxton took Mr Cowling through into the adjoining room, while the maid undressed Nina. It was only when Tina saw the marks on the coat at knee level and the state of the gown's hem that she broke silence. 'Oh, madam, what happened?'

'I knelt down for a moment. In the road. Can you do anything about it?'

'Don't worry about it, madam. I'll brush it when its dry,' Tina said, her voice puzzled, longing to ask more. But she restrained herself. 'It'll be all right, you'll see. Oh, madam, don't upset yourself,' she concluded, seeing Nina's expression.

Mr Cowling came back in in his dressing-gown, assessed the situation, and took charge. 'You can go,' he told Tina, and she was glad to scurry away. When she was gone, he said, 'My love. What is it?'

She was trembling. 'I'm cold,' she stammered, between clenched teeth. 'I'm so cold.'

He stepped close and put his arms round her. 'Get into bed,' he said, guiding her there. He helped her between the sheets, hesitated, then turned off the lamps, took off his dressing-gown and got in beside her. 'My love,' he said, drawing her against him. 'Let me warm you. My poor darling. I'll stay with you.'

He held her close against him, and for once she was glad of the solid heat of him. There was comfort in his strong arms, his kind words, and she let herself relax against him.

He kissed the crown of her head, and she felt as though her heart would break. 'It's your poor little dog, of course,' he said. 'I should have thought. It's bound to bring it all back to you. There, there. Don't cry, my Nina.'

But she did, even as his warmth crept into her and the shaking stopped. She cried her sadness and guilt and loss, lying in the darkness and staring down the long lonely years ahead, exiled from what she loved. Aunt Schofield had asked her if she had thought enough about it when she had accepted Mr Cowling, and she had said yes, she had. But she had been so young, how could she have? Now she knew. This was what there was for her, for the rest of her life. She was wife to this kind but utterly separate man, whose thoughts she could not read, and who could not read hers.

Eventually the tears stopped. He kissed her hair again, and then her cheek, and she felt the difference in his breathing. He nudged her face round to kiss her lips, and she let him. 'My love,' he whispered. He caressed her neck, and then her breast. She did not pull away. His hand was on her bare skin now, inside her nightgown. How could she help remembering the last time she had been touched so? But this was her husband, and she had a duty to yield to him. She made herself move into his embrace.

And for a wonder, this time, he seemed to have no difficulty. She could not respond to it, but she allowed it: she owed him that. He possessed her, and she held him lightly, her senses silent, her mind blank. He cried out softly at the end, a small sound of helplessness that hurt her heart. And then it was all over and he was holding her tightly, covering her unresisting face with kisses. 'My Nina! My Nina!' he murmured passionately again and again.

For the rest of my life. This, now, for ever.

He did not go back to his own room. With her in his arms he slept, quiet with accomplished joy; woke early, remembered, and lay with her warm softness cradled against him, savouring the memories. There had been no struggle, no difficulty. It had been natural and easy, as he'd always hoped it would be. He felt a page had been turned. What was it that had made the difference? He was not one for self-analysis, but he knew without words that it was because she had needed him. He had been jealous of her pleasure in other men's company at the dinner, and she had been cool towards him, as always. But then there was the accident to the dog, which must have brought memories rushing back to her. And in her distress she had turned to him. She had needed him, and he had been able to comfort her.

The balance of power between them had changed. He had always been the unworthy supplicant, she the proud, inaccessible goddess. Now, he was a man again, with a man's pride in a man's proper role – providing, protecting, nurturing, comforting. Now she was his wife in truth. He looked down the long happy years ahead, in union with what he loved. Her aunt, he knew, had been doubtful about the match, but he had sworn to himself that he would make her happy, and now there was nothing in the way of that intent.

Lord and Lady Leven were immensely rich, and great patrons, especially of fine art. One of the ways in which they supported it was to invite the pupils at the Blackwood School to visit their impressive permanent collection. The young ladies came in groups to study the paintings close up, to copy them, to discuss them with the attending teacher.

Alice and Bron were in a group that went at the end of October.

'I've heard they serve refreshments,' Bron said eagerly, as they walked in crocodile to the Levens' house in Portman Square.

'I've heard that's not true,' Alice countered.

'Oh, well – it will be fun anyway. They have some very important paintings. They say Lord Leven is richer than the

King. When a great Old Master comes on the market, he buys it up to keep it in the country.'

'I want to see the Holbein portrait of Henry the Eighth,' Alice said.

'It's only a copy.'

'Well, of course it is. The original was painted on a wall in Whitehall Palace and it burned down. Miss Deeks told me.'

'I know,' Bron said vaguely. 'Oh, I remember what I was going to say to you. Next term, what would you think about living in lodgings? There's a house in Bloomsbury that lets out rooms to girls from the Blackwood. There's a live-in housekeeper, so it's all very respectable, and I've heard that there's a room for two sharing that's going to be available from January.'

'Bloomsbury? That's further away than I am now,' Alice said.

'But think what fun, to be just all girls together! Oh, do say yes – I'd sooner share a room with you than anyone else.'

'I don't suppose I could get permission,' Alice said.

'But I told you, it's frightfully respectable – it has to be, otherwise *no-one* would get permission. It's owned by the school, you know, so it's official. I bet if you asked they'd say yes – why not?'

'I expect my aunt would like to have her house to herself sometimes,' Alice said doubtfully. Aunt Caroline had never hinted anything of the sort, and seemed not just resigned to, but actually to relish her role as the family's free hotel. 'All I can do is ask.'

'You can do what I do – keep asking until they say yes just to get some peace and quiet,' Bron said, with a grin.

There were, in fact, no refreshments, but Alice was soon too absorbed in the wonderful paintings to mind or even notice. Among them she was intrigued to discover a pair of very brown eighteenth-century romantic oils by Hubert Robert, called *The*

Flight of Galatea and *The Trial of Cicero*, whose provenance noted that they had once been owned by her father. Sold, she supposed, before she was born, to pay off a debt.

Passing into an anteroom, still searching for the Holbein, she saw something that made her call excitedly to Bron. 'Come and look, come and look!'

'Goodness,' Bron breathed into her ear, gazing over her shoulder. 'It's a Wentworth!'

'Ivor Wentworth,' Alice marvelled. 'One of our teachers!'

'Seeing it here makes you realise properly that he is a famous artist. To think that we know him!'

'Well, not "know" really,' Alice said, in fairness. 'But we've seen him in the flesh. Passed him in the corridor. Spoken to him.'

'I count that as "knowing",' Bron said. 'And he praised your drawing at the Hampstead Heath outing. That makes you practically family!'

Alice examined the painting. 'It's not much like his usual work. Not much colour.'

'*Cicero Denouncing Catiline*,' Bron read the title.

'The Levens seem to have a particular interest in Cicero,' Alice said.

It showed two banks of seats facing each other across a marble floor, those on one side populated by men in various poses of listening or whispering to each other, and on the other side only by one man, chin in hand, staring at the floor looking dejected. Standing in the middle was a man with his arms flung out in oratorical mode. All the men were wearing white togas; the only colour came from the faces, the wooden benches and the mild variations in hue of the marble floor and walls. Usually a Wentworth was full of rich blues and crimsons and lashings of gold. 'It's clever, though,' Alice said, as she studied it. 'Every face is different, and there must be fifty of them. And their poses and expressions are very natural-looking – it must have taken a very long time to paint.'

'Are you going to copy it?'

'It would take weeks! Besides, I've got my heart set on Henry.' Alice glanced around, and saw a footman at the far end of the room – there had been several dotted about, perhaps to help the young ladies in their endeavours – or perhaps, less liberally, to stop them touching anything. 'I'll ask that man if he knows where it is.'

But before she could act on the thought, someone came in through the door just beside her, made a sound of surprise, or perhaps annoyance, at the sight of her and Bron. He was immediately withdrawing when, seeing Alice's face as she turned to look, he stopped, smiled, and came forward with his hand out.

'Miss Tallant? Well, goodness! I was told there were some young ladies wandering about, and was warned to avoid them. To think of its being you!'

'Mr Farocean,' Alice said. 'To think of its being you!' Bron gave a very small cough, and she introduced them. 'We are two of the wandering young ladies. Why were you told to avoid us? Are we likely to annoy you, or was it vice versa?'

Bentham Farocean grinned. 'I imagine the idea was that the young ladies are of such unworldly delicacy I might fatally shock them, being myself entirely terrestrial. Of the earth: earthy.'

'We are students of fine art, Mr Farocean. Nudity, lust and murder are all around us, every day.'

'By Jove, yes. Those Old Masters didn't hold back, did they?'

'But you haven't said what you are doing here,' Alice said, enjoying herself. It was nice to talk to a man again, after a diet of girls and female teachers. He reminded her a little of Richard, which was comfortable.

'I've been visiting Oliver – Oliver Leven. Grandson.' He waved a hand to indicate the entirety of the Leven house as a shorthand way of indicating whose grandson Oliver was.

'He's laid up in bed with a busted bone so I was relieving the boredom. We were up at Balliol together.'

'That explains everything perfectly,' Alice said. 'I'm sure if in five years' time Bron was laid up in bed I would feel duty bound to go and visit her.'

Bron laughed and excused herself, walking away briskly to give them privacy.

Bentham didn't seem to notice she had gone. 'So, what are you doing here?' he asked. 'Yes, looking at the paintings, no need to be literal. Any in particular?'

'I'm looking for Henry the Eighth,' Alice said.

'Oh, he's on the stairs. Enormous great thing, no space for it in a room. Shall I show you?'

'Thank you – if you don't mind.'

He ushered her through the anteroom door onto a staircase. 'Not this one – t'other side of the house. I know a short-cut. So, you weren't in Scotland, like your sister?'

'You saw her there, did you? She went with my aunt Vicky, who'd taken her on holiday to the South of France, and then went on to Glamis. I had to be here for the start of term. Were you staying at Glamis?'

'No, but we were invited once or twice. We were staying with the Eassies – do you know them?'

'Yes. They're my uncle's neighbours, and friends of our cousins, the Tullamores.'

'Ah, yes. We saw them, too. Everyone knows everyone else down there: Scotland's a small place. Your sister seemed to be having a tremendous time,' he went on, giving her a curious look.

'She loves dancing and parties,' Alice said.

'You disapprove?' Alice shook her head without answering, not wishing to expose family secrets. 'She's a very beautiful girl, your sister,' he went on thoughtfully. 'My brother certainly thought so, at any rate.'

'Your brother?'

'Jervis. They danced together in several houses – whenever we happened to meet at a ball.'

'She was flirting?'

'Oh, now – well – I wouldn't go so far as to say that. Such a harsh word. It's natural for a beautiful young woman to want to enjoy herself. Quite harmless, really.'

'You know that she's engaged.' It wasn't a question. He bowed slightly in acknowledgement. 'Does your brother know?'

He hesitated. Then he said, 'There is something especially delightful about an engaged woman. Her anxieties are all behind her, she is able to relax in male company and be herself. So much more pleasing than the buttoned-up, fearful, daren't-open-her-lips caution of the unattached female.'

'Pleasing,' Alice said.

'Fun,' he said.

They walked on in silence, and came out onto another, grander staircase where, immediately opposite and in full splendour, was the immense copy of the Holbein *Henry VIII*. '*Voilà, mademoiselle*,' Bentham said, with a flourish. '*Le roi vous attend.*'

Alice looked at it in silence for a moment. 'It's much bigger than I expected.'

'Large as life and twice as ugly. How could a man with a face like that persuade six different women to marry him?'

'He *was* the king,' Alice pointed out.

'Yes, well, as a younger son myself, I don't enjoy the idea that it all hinges on position.'

'And money,' Alice said.

'Indeed.' He flicked a glance at her. 'I hope it was only flirting,' he said quietly, his bantering tone absent. 'I know Jervis, and that's all it was for him. He's not serious.'

'Did you think she was?'

He paused, thinking. 'Sometimes it seemed as though she might be wanting something more from him. I hope I was wrong. My brother has a very clear notion of his own worth.'

Alice was offended. 'My sister is an earl's daughter,' she said.

'And beautiful but – forgive me – rumour says . . . Your father's financial woes are known about. It's said she has no dowry.'

'And that's all that matters,' Alice said flatly, looking at him.

'Not to me,' he said gently. 'Being a younger son has the virtues of its defects. Thrust out into the world like an unwanted pup to fend for myself, I can admire where I will.' She was staring at the Holbein again, but not as if she was seeing it. 'I mentioned it only so that you could put her on her guard, *if* you believe she has any expectations of the situation.' He examined her expression. 'I had no wish to offend you.'

'You haven't offended me,' she said absently. She would have to try to talk to Rachel, but whether she was just enjoying the last burst of pre-marital freedom, or whether she really was hoping to exchange for a better husband, she would not heed anything Alice said.

She sighed and changed the subject firmly. 'It's a pity it's hung over the stairs like that. I won't be able to get up close to study it.'

'I stand rebuked,' he said meekly.

'No, not at all,' she said.

They turned back towards the door.

'Is there any hope that I shall see you again, Miss Tallant?' he said. 'We are in Town for some weeks – a sister of mine being prepared to be brought out, no end of parties. Or you are from Buckinghamshire, I believe? Do you hunt?'

She smiled. 'It's strange you should ask that. My family is giving house parties for the hunting all next month, and I was thinking of going home for them.' Aunt Caroline had urged her to go and have fun – it was only an hour away on the train, after all – and she was longing to go out on her darling Pharaoh.

'Not such a very great coincidence,' he admitted. 'Ashridge Park is near you, I believe.'

'You know Lord Shacklock?'

'I know his son, Brandon. Younger son,' he added, with a grin. 'We're all invited for a hunting weekend on the seventeenth. Apparently there's going to be a splendid ball, most of the county invited. I do hope you'll be there.'

'If the county's invited, I'm sure we will be,' she said.

'And dare I hope that you'll spare a dance for a despicable younger son?'

'If you have any desire to dance with a penniless younger daughter.'

He bowed. 'The pleasure will be entirely mine.'

They chatted inconsequentially until he delivered her in front of Cicero again and, assured she knew her way from there, clattered off down the staircase.

Alice remained staring at the painting for some time, but she was not thinking about brush strokes or colour or Cicero or indeed Ivor Wentworth. She was thinking that if she and Bentham Farocean were at the Shacklock ball, then Rachel and Jervis Farocean would be too. And the face she saw in her mind's eye was Angus's.

'I am not a very confident horsewoman,' Lepida had written, 'but I agree it is the best way to see the countryside. I'll ride, if you promise not to go out of a walk.'

So Nina had borrowed a horse for her from Bobby, and they rode out every morning.

'I don't want to keep you from your hunting,' Lepida said.

'It doesn't matter. I can always hunt – I won't always have you.'

'No, that's true,' Lepida said.

It was a cold, sunny day, and the slanting sunshine threw Lepida's face into planes that made her look thinner than ever. 'I'm so glad you've found time to come and stay,' Nina said.

'I'm having a delightful time,' Lepida said serenely.

Apart from the sedate rides, they had walked about the garden and into the town, and otherwise mostly sat and read or talked together. Bobby was hunting three times a week, so vigorously that on the days in between she was almost prostrate, but she had had them to an informal dinner on a non-hunting day, and they had been once to tea with Lady Clemmie. Nina had invited Clemmie to join their rides, but she had declined charmingly, saying she would be *de trop*. They were on their own for most of the first week, Mr Cowling being away on business: his intention to spend more time at home had not accounted for business activity already planned.

Nina had ridden Lepida's mount, Florence, before, and knew that while gentle and even-paced she did have one fault, which was a liking sometimes to go down and roll when crossing water. Riding side by side, Nina felt she could intervene if that appeared likely, and her groom, Daughters, said stoutly, 'Don't you worry, ma'am – I won't let anything happen to Miss Morris.'

He already adored her, fussed over her and checked Florence's girths a dozen times before each ride. All the servants loved Lepida. She had a natural grandeur about her that commanded respect, allied to a sweetness of manner that made her approachable – a winning combination. Nina's lady's maid Tina, who was dressing Lepida during her stay, was concerned about how thin she was and reported her anxiety to Mrs Deering who, already shocked at how little Miss Morris ate, concocted wonderful delicacies for every meal to tempt her. The housemaid, Polly, who went in to light her fire in the morning, thought her an angel. Lepida did not sleep well and was always awake when Polly arrived, and was very soon possessed of all Polly's secrets. And Deering raided the garden, neighbours' hothouses and even the hedgerows to bring fresh floral offerings for her every day, which he left shyly in the kitchen for Polly to take up to 'the visiting young lady', a title he pronounced with a touch of awe.

They had just come out of a wood when they saw, crossing a hillside two fields distant, the hunt streaming away – the low forms of the hounds, the scarlet splashes of the hunt servants, and the main body of the field, already strung out by the differing abilities of the riders. Bobby would be there among them, Nina thought, trying to work out which of the undistinguishable shapes was her. One of those near the front, for sure.

Lepida mistook her concentration for wistfulness. 'You're wishing you were with them, aren't you?'

Nina turned to smile, and said peacefully, 'Not at all. I am content exactly where I am.'

Lepida examined her face. 'You've changed, you know,' she said. 'I've been noticing it ever since I arrived.'

'Changed how?'

Lepida thought about it, seeking the right words. 'You just said you're content. I think that's it. There was always a restlessness about you, as though you might suddenly burst away, like water from a breached dam.'

'And you don't see that any more?' Nina asked, amused.

'Something has changed you. And I think you know it. What is it?'

Nina did know, but she was impressed that Lepida had noticed it. She wasn't sure how to express it, however. And Lepida, however wise and learned she was, was unmarried.

'I've decided to accept my lot,' she said at last, 'instead of railing against it.'

Since that night in Portsmouth, Mr Cowling's difficulties seemed to have disappeared. He had successfully completed the act many times since then, and the difference in him was noticeable. The tense, faintly anxious look he had always carried had gone. He seemed to have grown and filled out – it was absurd to think that, but it was the only way she could describe it to herself – like trodden grass straightening, or a pinched bud opening in unexpected sunshine.

It had made her feel guilty to realise how much he had been affected by what she had considered unimportant, even faintly ridiculous. And she wondered, guiltily, whether she had added to his difficulties. She had always withheld herself from him – not obviously, but there had been a core of herself that she had kept back for herself, and she wondered now whether in some way he had always known it. She had married him, but she had never been his. He had fulfilled his part of the bargain, but she had kept only the letter of the contract, not the spirit. She had not been fair to him.

Secretly, she had been waiting for her life to change and present her with her hidden desire. But Portsmouth had made her realise that this marriage was not a temporary aberration. It was her life, for the rest of her life.

Lepida was waiting for more explanation, and she said, 'I kept thinking, 'Is this all there is?' I kept thinking that at some point I would be woken from a dream and my real life would begin.'

'You were very young when you married,' Lepida observed.

Nina shrugged. 'Most girls are.'

'The great pity,' Lepida went on, 'is that there is no way to prepare a female for it. They dream of palaces with gilded turrets and knights on white horses. Reality is decisions about mutton or beef, when to get the chimney swept, whether the cook is using too much butter. Reality is a man who's bad-tempered in the morning and complains if his favourite shirt isn't ironed just right.' She smiled at Nina's expression. 'Don't look so surprised! I live with my mother and father. I've observed them for years. There isn't much I don't know about marriage in our wonderful age.'

'Well,' Nina said, with reservation.

'Yes, of course, there is the other side of it that no-one will ever talk about,' Lepida went on. 'But even I know it is not a sigh and a languishing gaze, but flesh and blood and sweat and smells and pain and discomfort.'

Nina didn't want to ask her how she knew that. 'Did you never dream of palaces and sighs?' she asked.

'Never,' said Lepida. 'It's the consequence of reading too much. They are right about that, at any rate – educating females only makes for misery. If we are to endure a woman's lot, better we have nothing between our ears at all.'

'You don't believe that,' Nina exclaimed.

Lepida gave a small quirk of a smile. 'Yes and no. In reality, women have minds and some of them have enquiring minds, and once you start to think you can't go back. So we have to do what we can to make things better. But part of that is understanding the limitations of what's possible. It seems to me that you have reached that understanding by yourself.'

Nina didn't answer. But she thought, *Yes, I'm married to Mr Cowling, and I must make the best of it.*

They rode on. It was a small enough thing, she thought, to make him happy. It took up very little time. She could not be part of it, but she had to receive him, because he was her husband and it was her duty. And, because she understood now, she had let him *think* she was part of it, and that it made her happy too.

The tragedy was that she now knew what the physical act could mean. In that sense, Lepida was right – better not to know. But however difficult it made it to adjust to her life as it was, she would not have missed that. She buried it deep in her mind and tried never to think about it, but it was there, like a distant source of warmth, like the faint luminosity of the sun behind the solid cover of clouds on a winter's day.

CHAPTER TWENTY-TWO

Lepida saw how glad Mr Cowling was to be back, and how tenderly he kissed his wife – he had always been fond, but now there was a confidence in his caresses. She studied him that first night as they waited in the drawing-room for dinner to be announced. She had known him through her father for many years, and he had been just another business acquaintance of her father's age, no-one of particular interest to her until Nina had taken his fancy and accepted his offer of marriage. He was a pink-faced, healthy-looking man with greying hair, not handsome but not repulsive; a man of decided opinions, not highly educated, a great expert in an area that did not interest her very much. She had no need to ask herself why Nina had married him – it happened all the time. Nina could have been a teacher, but had no great liking for the idea. Instead she chose a rich man to give her the freedom of his money and name. And so she had to live with him, and obey him, mould herself to his wishes, sleep in the same bed with him and endure those activities Lepida knew about as a matter of biology.

The human condition, she thought, was very strange.

On the second evening, Decius joined them for dinner, and Nina invited a local couple, Mr and Mrs Girton, to make it more of a party. They were acquaintances of Mr Cowling, and not the most fascinating people, but it was a full-moon night so everyone else was engaged. But Mr Cowling was in great good humour, and Decius was always an asset in company. Nina had cherished an idea that something might develop between him and Lepida, that her dear friend might fall in love and marry him and become part of her home circle. But though there seemed a spark on Decius's side, her recent conversation with Lepida convinced her that she had no interest in marriage. It was a pity.

At dinner, the conversation inevitably touched on the increasing likelihood of a general election. The coalition, which had been in power since 1895, was looking worn out; the Conservatives under Arthur Balfour were increasingly unpopular; the Liberals had split over free trade and tariff reform. There was rising unemployment, and the working classes were worried about the price of bread. Recruitment for the Boer War had exposed the poor general health of the population – 40 per cent of recruits had been found to be unfit for service – and the Rowntree survey of 1902 had shown that a third of the population lived below what the report named 'the poverty line', which had led to increasing calls for social reform. That was expected to favour the Labour Representation Committee, which had won only two seats in the 1900 election.

So it was widely assumed that Balfour must call an election in the next few weeks, and protest meetings, marches and demonstrations were gathering pace all over the country. It was in answer to a question put by Lepida, which Nina didn't catch, that Decius mentioned the protest that had taken place in October in the Free Trade Hall in Manchester.

'Oh, it seems the WSPU felt that the general excitement about an election was pushing the women's issue to the margins, so they had to do something to get themselves into the news.'

'Oh, you're talking about women's suffrage,' said Mrs Girton. 'There was something in the newspaper about a disturbance – didn't you mention it, dear?'

Mr Girton didn't look pleased with the subject. 'Some misguided females made a display of themselves at a public meeting, that's all. Nothing important.'

'But what did they do?' Nina asked.

Decius answered her: 'Interrupted Sir Edward Grey – who was addressing the meeting – to ask him, "Will the Liberal Government give women the vote?"'

'Ask him?' Mr Cowling said. 'They stood on their seats and yelled and shrieked like banshees, so the meeting couldn't go on. The chief constable had to go and quiet 'em down, said they could send up a written question like civilised people.'

'When they did,' Decius said, 'Grey ignored it.'

Mr Cowling eyed him indulgently. 'Aye, I know you're soft on the subject, but they'll not get anywhere behaving badly. No-one likes to see a female show herself up like that.'

'Thirty years of asking nicely has got them nowhere,' Lepida said mildly. 'Perhaps a new strategy is needed.'

Mr Cowling admired Lepida and didn't want to argue with her. So he said in an end-of-conversation tone, 'Well, they got arrested for their trouble, so perhaps they've learned their lesson.'

She didn't take the hint. 'But they wanted to be arrested. Their whole purpose was to be sent to prison.'

'How shocking!' Mrs Girton murmured.

'The magistrate would have let them off with a fine, but they refused to pay and were given seven days in Strangeways.'

'Disgusting!' said Mr Girton.

'Strange ways indeed,' Mr Cowling said. 'I don't like the idea of ladies being put in prison, but it has to be said, they didn't behave like ladies.'

'The plan worked at all events,' Decius said. 'When they came out they were met by an adoring crowd, held a mass rally in Free Trade Hall with a speech by the Labour leader, and the whole thing was reported in *The Times*. So I expect they count it a success.'

'It's a very unpleasant state of mind that considers going to prison a success,' said Mr Girton. 'Revolutionary ideas coarsen the character and destroy civilised manners. I sincerely hope this society of women, whatever it's called, *doesn't* manage to spread its evil influence.'

Lepida seemed about to speak, but Nina saw Decius catch her eye and give a tiny shake of the head and she subsided.

Instead, throwing himself into the breach, Decius said, 'I read a most interesting report in the newspaper the other day. It seems two brothers in America have successfully tested a flying machine. Are you at all interested in aeronautics, sir?'

Mr Girton merely looked blank. Mrs Girton, slightly puzzled, said, 'Do you mean, a balloon? We saw a balloon ascent once, didn't we, dear? The balloonist was a very handsome man. I particularly remember that he had very fine moustaches.'

'Not a balloon,' Decius said, as Nina suppressed a giggle. 'A proper machine, with an engine – like a motor-car, but with wings.'

Mr Cowling said, 'People have been building flying machines for years – I remember when I was a nipper there was an exhibition of 'em at the Crystal Palace, all sorts of wonderful contrivances, but they never managed to get them off the ground. Or if they did, they came straight back down again.'

'Motive force was always the problem,' Decius said. 'Steam engines were too heavy, and pedalling or winding a screw didn't give enough power. But things have changed. A small, light petrol engine is a different matter.'

Mr Cowling looked amused. 'You know all about it, eh?'

'I'm interested in the subject. I read anything that comes my way. These brothers in America actually kept their machine in the air for over half an hour!'

'You must be jesting,' said Mr Cowling.

'And not just flying in a straight line, either, but guiding it and performing figures of eight. *And* landing it safely at the end.'

'If it's true at all,' said Mr Girton, 'it can only be a flash in the pan.'

'Half an hour, sir,' said Decius. 'If it could stay aloft for that length of time, I think we can be sure it wasn't a flash in the pan. I believe it is the start of something tremendous for mankind.'

'Flying motor-cars, stuff and nonsense,' said Mr Girton, discontentedly.

But Mr Cowling looked thoughtful. 'If there's anything in it, it would be something to get in on. Look at railways – they were new once, and some folk said they'd never catch on. Other folk put their money into 'em. If flying machines really work, there'd be fortunes to be made.' He looked indulgently at Decius. 'And I warrant you'll be one of the ones up there driving 'em, am I right?'

Decius smiled. 'I would dearly love to fly. It's been man's desire from time immemorial.'

'I sometimes dream I'm flying,' Mrs Girton said unexpectedly.

'How odd,' said Nina. 'I do, too.'

'I believe it's quite common,' Lepida said.

'I wonder why that is,' Nina said. 'When I dream of flying, it's like a memory, as if it was something I used to be able to do but forgot. When I wake, I feel dreadfully sad, knowing that I can't.'

'You ladies have a great deal of imagination,' Mr Cowling said. 'I never dream at all.'

'I don't either,' said Mr Girton, impatiently. 'And I can't see that flying machines will make a jot of difference to the country, except to litter it with broken engines and broken heads. It's just another way for young men to risk their necks. Sir Bradley Graham's nephew was killed last year while out with the Quorn. His poor sister has never been the same since. Riding recklessly, on an over-corned new horse! I believe Sir Bradley warned him, but of course he didn't listen. Young men are always mad for speed.'

'It's been so remarkably mild this autumn,' Mrs Girton said. 'Do you know, there are actually roses blooming in our garden?'

Nina was bemused. Was she deliberately calming the atmosphere, or was it the random pipings of a vacant brain? Was there more to Mrs Girton than was apparent? 'We have some, too,' she said. 'I'd like to pick them and bring them in, but they're so frail at this time of year, they die very quickly.'

'Put a little aspirin in the water,' Mrs Girton said. 'That keeps them fresh.'

'Aye, flower-arranging – now that's a nice, ladylike occupation.' Mr Cowling said approvingly.

Kitty heard about it in a roundabout way. Uncle Fergus had written to both his sisters, and Aunt Caroline relayed the news in a letter that arrived in the mid-week lull between hunting house-parties. Kitty had enjoyed October and was enjoying November even more, since she didn't care about shooting but loved hunting. And this season she was not pregnant, so could ride to her heart's content. She adored the beautiful horse, Apollo, that Giles had bought her when they were first married, and now there was also her mother-in-law's Queen Bee, left behind on the dowager's marriage. It couldn't be sold as Maud might one day send for it, so meanwhile Kitty had a second horse to hunt.

And with the Castle entertaining again, other houses in the neighbourhood had followed suit, so the season was lively, and Kitty was enjoying the consequence of being at the top of everyone's guest list. For the first time she felt that she really *was* the countess, that she was accepted in the role she had married into, and was a success. Little Kitty Bayfield, too stupidly shy to speak a word to her partners at her come-out, was now the chatelaine of Ashmore Castle, mother of two fine little boys, and issuer of invitations that were prized in the neighbourhood.

Aunt Caroline's letter was full of inconsequential chat – she had grown up in the era when a young lady was taught to make a little matter go a long way – and Kitty read without engaging her full attention, until a new paragraph stopped her dead.

I heard yesterday from my dear brother Fergus, who writes from Venice to say that they will not, after all, be coming to London in December, nor, I am sorry to say, be spending the Christmas Season at Ashmore Castle, as I believe had been discussed, or at least mooted. The cause of what I know will occasion disappointment to all is, yet, a cause for general rejoicing. It is not ill health, far less disinclination, but an advice from a medical consultant that travelling at that time would not be advisable, for the most delicate of reasons. In short, my dear Kitty, I am delighted to tell you that Fergus and Giulia are expecting a child in the spring or early summer. She—

Kitty's first, guilty little thought was relief, as if being with child placed Giulia further out of Giles's reach than simply being married. Absurd! There *had* been talk of their coming to the Castle at Christmas, and a part of Kitty had dreaded it – dreaded having that luminous, clever, striking woman under the same roof, invoking shared memories with Giles, falling into Italian with him, that damnably romantic language, which flowed so fluently from both their tongues and which no-one else could understand . . .

Kitty had believed Giles when he said he did not care romantically for Giulia. But – she raised her head to look at him over the breakfast table, absorbed in the newspaper, pretty much unaware of his wife's existence – there was no saying that his feelings couldn't change. He was not in love with Kitty. And if he was not in love with her, didn't that mean there was a vacancy?

Anecdote said that men of rank and fortune, once they had secured the nursery, more often than not took a mistress. Giles had never shown any interest in other women, but he no longer visited her bedroom, and men had needs, as her stepmother had warned her. At some point, in likelihood, he *would* take a mistress. He would be discreet. But, loving him as she did, she was sure she would know. That would be bad enough – so much worse if it was someone she knew. So she was glad there would be a baby – the first, she hoped, of many – to dim Giulia's radiance.

She went on reading. Maud was recovered from childbirth and the Usingens and Linda were going to the Wachturm, home of Aunt Vicky and Uncle Bobo near Darmstadt, for the Christmas season. Darmstadt was the home of Grand Duke Ernie of Hesse, so there would be glittering parties. Vicky had written, said Aunt Caroline, to say that it was expected to be an especially lively season, being the first since the grand duke had remarried. He had – shockingly – divorced his first wife, Princess Ducky of Edinburgh, Queen Victoria's granddaughter and his first cousin, in December 1901. The only child of the marriage, a daughter, had died of typhoid in November 1903, so to secure the succession Ernie had remarried, in February 1905, to Princess Onor of Solms-Hohensolms-Lich. Princess Ducky, Aunt Caroline went on chattily to note, had also just remarried, to another cousin, the Russian Grand Duke Kirill Vladimirovich. Unfortunately, Ernie's sister, the tsarina, blamed Ducky for the divorce and had persuaded the tsar to strip Kirill of his titles and exile the couple, so they'd had to go and live in Paris. Not that *that* was a terrible disadvantage, things being still very unsettled in Russia, with strikes and violent demonstrations, and a mutiny of the navy in Sebastopol, according to Paul Usingen, who had many Russian relatives . . .

'You're very engrossed in that letter,' Giles's voice interrupted her. 'Interesting news?'

She looked up. 'You can read it later,' she said. 'It's from Aunt Caroline.'

'I might forgo the pleasure,' he said. 'She never uses one word where ten will do.'

Kitty thought that was rather a skill than a fault, when you had pages to cover.

'You can give me a digest,' Giles went on.

So she said, 'Giulia's having a baby.'

He walked up the hill, slashing at dead cow parsley stems with his stick. The dogs dashed about, lost in their own rich world of smells, remembering him now and then, running up to check that he was all right, then away again. It was a mild, damp November day, with an uninteresting sky of unbroken grey, like dish-rags, and the sort of intermittent fine prickle that couldn't decide whether to be rain or not. It gathered on the dogs' thick winter coats in a silver mist. The air smelt of leaf-mould and wet grass.

He was enough of a farmer by now to think absently as he trudged, *That tree looks as though it's been struck by lightning: the split branch ought to be trimmed . . . Damage to the hedge there – probably the hunt. That whole stretch ought to be re-laid . . . The cows should come off that field, it's too wet, they're cutting it up . . . Marbeck's sheep on the turnip field: looking healthy . . .*

At the top he turned along the crest, and stopped to take in the view. Tiger came and leaned against his leg; grey Isaac was snuffling madly in a clump of dried thistle stalks, which might or might not be masking a rabbit-hole. That made him think of the rabbit activity at the motte. He had had the hole boarded over and a barrier of hurdles put round it to stop anyone going too close. There simply had not been time yet to explore it further – and the weather was against him now. He thought of his friends and the light-hearted talk of an excavation. The place had cost poor little Arthur his life. If he'd arranged for the boy to go away to school, it never would have happened. Perhaps it was just as well he'd had no time for excavation: it might have looked heartless. Next year, perhaps, in summer, the tragedy would be far enough in the past . . .

His thoughts reverted to Kitty's letter. Giulia pregnant? Well, of course it was to be expected. She was young, and Uncle was only – what? – forty-two. She was his aunt by marriage; the child would be his cousin.

But it was not because of Giulia that he had escaped on this solitary walk. It was because Kitty had looked at him for a guilty reaction. Nothing inside him cared about Giulia, but the look had reminded him of where his guilt truly lay. He had done wrong by Kitty, though she didn't know it. And it was all the worse because he could not regret it. If he could go back, he knew he would do the same thing again.

Nina! She glowed in his mind like a light in a window on a dark night. In these cases, he supposed, one must always ask *why*. Why this person and not another? Why this one person, and no other? There was no explanation. He loved her, he wanted her, and no-one and nothing else could fill her space. He ached with wanting her, simply her presence. How fortunate were they who could be with the one person, see them, talk to them, touch them? Hold them in their arms through the night, as he did Nina, for that one, irreplaceable, unrepeatable, utterly sustaining night. To be with her was everything he needed, it was the very sustenance of life, it was everything he wanted and could not have.

He lifted his face to the prickling rain and felt his throat stiffen with the howl he could not let out. He wanted to shout with all his strength and have it echo off the sky. But he was not quite so far gone as to do it, not even on his own land. No, he was confined, circumscribed by the rules and laws and customs and manners of the country and the society and the class he was born into. Gentlemen did not shout. They did not make a fuss. They did not abandon their wives and run off with someone else's.

Tiger made a small sound, looking up at him, sensing his tension, and he forced himself to relax. He put down a hand to the dog and felt it licked consolingly. He had so much, he was lucky beyond the lot of most men. He had a loving wife, two little sons he adored, an estate to run, a purpose in life and enough money to pursue it. Lucky, lucky, *lucky* man. He stared around at the horizon, the line of the hills and treetops that blurred into the misty sky like a watercolour. She was somewhere out there, perhaps thinking of him. She lived in the same day, under the same sky, in the same world, and that was all he could have. 'Can we make this one time pay for everything?' she had said. Can it be enough? No. But it was all they would ever have.

The rain had decided to be rain. It was getting heavier, the dogs' coats were darkening, and his hands, clenched over the head of his stick, were wet and cold. Both dogs were looking up at him now, awaiting his will. 'Come on, then,' he said aloud, and his voice sounded strange. As soon as he moved, they leaped into action, glad to be turning for home. Home! But he must be content. They had known it was the only time. He must shut it away, and never look at it, and get comfort only from knowing that it was there.

The dogs were running on ahead, and the rain was really setting in – he could hardly see them. They'd be back before him, more surefooted than him on the slippery path. And he thought of being indoors, lamps lit and a fire blazing. *Never forget*, he thought, *that you're a lucky, lucky man.*

Oh, Nina.

Kitty's letter invited Nina and Mr Cowling to spend Christmas at the Castle. Nina's first instinct was to refuse and not even tell him about it. He would be sure to insist they accepted, believing she would want to go. And, of course, she would love to see Kitty, and her little boys, and Richard, and the girls.

To be with Giles, to see him and talk to him, to lie in bed at night knowing he was under the same roof – that would be a different pleasure, more potent, and edged like a honed knife with the potential for disaster.

If, during their stay, Mr Cowling should come to her bed – how could she refuse him? How could she bear not to? It was all too difficult.

But if she refused the invitation without telling him, sooner or later he would know they had been asked and want to know why she had kept it from him. No, she would have to tell him, and he would want to say yes. So she would have to go, and hope her new-found acceptance and contentment in her lot would stand the test.

She went on reading. Rachel was dividing her time between parties in London and the hunting weekends down at Ashmore. Alice had come down to hunt once or twice. Mother-in-law Maud and Linda were spending Christmas with the Wittenstein-Glücksbergs, thank goodness. Oh, and Uncle Fergus and Giulia would not be coming after all, because Giulia was expecting a child. How pleased Lord Leake would be to have an heir on the way. Maud had hated the thought of the title going to a distant cousin, so she would be pleased too that Giulia was pregnant—

Her thoughts stalled. She put the letter down, staring at nothing. Then she went upstairs to her bedchamber, to a certain drawer, where she kept her diary. Underneath it, and underneath a concealing cloth, for modesty's sake, were the webbing sanitary belt and the napkins. She leafed through the diary, thoughtfully.

At dinner that evening, she said, 'You are going to London tomorrow, aren't you?'

'Yes – but only for the day. I shall be home in time for dinner.' He gave her a fond smile.

'I wonder if I might travel up with you,' she said diffidently.

'Of course. It'd be grand to have your company. What are you going for?'

'Oh, I've one or two errands to do.'

'Secrets, eh? Nothing to do with Christmas coming up, I suppose?'

She smiled, and let him think it was that. She would have to do some shopping. Afterwards.

'I thought I might look in on my aunt.'

'Yes, do,' he said. He approved of Nina's aunt, though he found her intimidating. Perhaps *because* he found her intimidating. 'But you must promise me you won't get too tired. I know what ladies are when they start shopping. They lose all track of time. You must take cabs, and not try to manage the Underground. I'll give you plenty of cash, so there's no excuse.'

'I'll take cabs,' she promised, wondering at his characterisation of her. When had she ever been interested in shopping? Or forgetful? But perhaps that was what he wanted her to be – the helpless, fluffy-minded female of male fantasy.

'I shall wait for you outside the station,' he warned, with a twinkle, 'and if I don't see you arriving in a cab . . .'

Fortunately, he believed in reading on the train, and bought her several ladies' magazines at the station newsagent, so there was no need to talk to him or even look at him during the journey. He saw her into a cab and gave the jarvey her aunt's address, so she had to wait until they'd turned the corner to rap on the hatch and change it. She'd decided to go to Dr Grossman, her aunt's physician, the doctor of her childhood because, being robustly healthy, she had never consulted a doctor in Market Harborough, and knew nothing of them. Somehow she didn't want a stranger at this moment.

Grossman had aged since she last saw him – he looked very grey and lined, and he wore spectacles now, but his large, bushy moustache did not hide his warm smile as he came forward to shake her hand. 'Miss Sanderton, what a delight. It's been – how long? Many years, at any rate, since I last saw you.'

'It's Mrs Cowling now,' she said. 'I gave your nurse my maiden name so that you'd know it was me, but I'm married now and living in Market Harborough.'

'Yes, I believe your aunt did mention that you had married. How is she, by the way? Well, I hope.'

'Very well.'

'Yes, you both always enjoyed good health. If I had depended on you and your aunt for a living, I should have been on poor pastures!' He enjoyed his own joke, and repeated it. 'Very poor pastures! One of the seven lean kine, ha ha!' She laughed too, obligingly. He ushered her to a seat, went behind his desk and sat down, steepled his fingers and said, 'Well, well, what can I help you with? Nothing concerning, I hope. You are looking well – very bonny.'

Nina tried to compose a sentence, but in the end nothing seemed better than just saying it. 'I think I might be pregnant.'

'Ah,' he said. He folded his fingers into a clasp and surveyed her from behind them. 'Well, you are a married woman, and that is only to be expected.' There was the breath of a question there, to which she did not respond. 'And why do you think you might be?'

'My monthly flux has – has not occurred.' It was harder than she had expected to say it aloud to a man, even if he was a doctor.

'When was the last one?'

'At the end of September. I didn't notice that it didn't happen at the end of October, but something has made me think about it, and there was nothing at the end of November either.'

'And the absence is unusual?'

'Yes. It has always been regular.'

'Very well.' He paused, studying her face. 'May I ask why you have come to me, instead of your own physician?'

'You *are* my own physician, Dr Grossman. The only one I've ever consulted.'

His face cleared. 'Ah, indeed. Well, I am honoured by your trust, Mrs – er – Cowling. It sounds as thought you may well be pregnant, but I shall examine you to make sure.' He stood up and went to the door to summon the nurse.

It was unpleasant and embarrassing, and she was glad of a time to herself afterwards, behind the screen, dressing slowly and composing herself. Then, back in their previous positions, he told her.

'When?' she asked.

'From what you have told me, and my own examination, I calculate the baby to be due in July. Now, you may want to consult a physician at various points along the way, to check that everything is going as expected. You are a healthy young woman so there is no reason to suppose there will be any problems, but it is prudent to keep an eye on things. I don't suppose you will want to travel to London every time to see me.' Again, a faint question mark, to which she did not respond. She was deep in her own thoughts. 'But when you get home you should seek out a physician to undertake your care. I expect your husband can advise you on that?'

She registered at last that he had asked her something. She focused on him. 'Hmm?'

He waited, and then said, 'You are understandably distracted by this good news. It will take a little time to adjust to. But please remember that it is an entirely natural process and one that you are designed for by nature. You are young and healthy and should experience no difficulties. Now, is there anything you wish to ask me?'

'Yes,' she said. He waited. 'When— I would like to know when I – I conceived.'

'Some time in the month of October,' he said, as if puzzled by the question.

'But can you . . . Is there any way to tell exactly when it happened?'

Now a faint disapproval clouded his look. 'If there were – multiple possible occasions, then, no.' He examined her face. 'Does it matter? Your husband will be delighted, I am sure. Your first child . . .'

'Yes.' Nina looked at her hands. 'He'll be delighted.'

'I'm sure he will,' said Dr Grossman, and the relief was evident in his voice.

She walked from the doctor's rooms to her aunt's house, and was not entirely sorry to find her out.

'If only she'd known you were coming, Miss Nina,' said Haydock, with a hint of reproach. 'But we're not expecting her back until after teatime, and then it's only to dress and go out again.'

'It doesn't matter,' Nina said. 'I was in Town and called on the spur of the moment.'

'You look tired,' Haydock said, with the privilege of an old servant. 'Why don't you sit down and let me get you a glass of sherry? Mrs Roth can make you a nice bit of luncheon – a drop of soup and a nice omelette. You know you like her omelettes,' he added coaxingly.

The familiar petting made Nina feel tearful, but she tightened her face. 'No, thank you, Haydock. It's kind of you, but I must be off. I have a lot of errands. I shall just write a note to Aunt, if you don't mind.'

She sat at her aunt's desk and drew pen and paper towards her, but couldn't think what to say. It was not news to be conveyed in a hasty note. In the end she just said she had called on a whim and was sorry to have missed her, that she was well and hoped her aunt was too. Then, with a day to fill, she left.

She walked without noticing where she was going, and found herself in Knightsbridge, outside Harrod's store. It was a good place to use up time, and she wandered from department to department, rode up the moving staircase for the novelty of it, and finally thought she had better buy something for Mr Cowling, since he assumed she had gone to shop for Christmas presents. She wandered and examined and probably exasperated several hopeful assistants, and finally purchased a tortoiseshell and silver dressing-table set – clothes brush, two hair brushes, moustache comb and studs cup – and had them wrap it for her, which used up some more time.

Her wanderings took her past Manicure and Chiropody, and the thought of sitting down – her feet were aching by then – led her to go in and have a manicure for the first time in her life. The manicurist did not conceal her disapproval of Nina's hands, which had not been rendered more lily-white and exquisite by handling reins on a daily basis, and it took a usefully long time to get them into a state that did not break the practitioner's heart. On leaving the chair she discovered that she was very hungry, so she went to the restaurant for what was either a very late lunch or an early tea – a pot of Darjeeling and a Welsh rarebit. On her way out of the store, she stopped in Confectionery and bought a box of Carlsbad plums, which Mr Cowling loved, and then it was time to get a cab to the station.

All the time she had shut her mind to the idea of being pregnant. It was too big, she wasn't ready to think about it; she was afraid of being afraid of it. But when the cab drew up outside the station, Mr Cowling was there and came hurrying to open the door for her and hand her out, and she felt her head fill and her throat tighten, and struggled to hold everything back.

'My goodness me!' he exclaimed, taking her packages from her and drawing her hand through his arm. 'Is that all you've bought? Not worth coming all this way for. Or couldn't you find what you wanted? And you look tired! You've worn yourself out for nothing. I'm sure you could have got something in Market Harborough just as well. I'm not a hard man to please. There, there – you're tottering! You must be exhausted, my poor Nina. Here's our compartment. Let me help you in, and then you can put your head back and sleep all the way home if you want.'

He was not usually a chatterer, and she saw that he was covering his anxiousness for her, that he had sensed something was wrong. He loved her too much not to be aware that she had said nothing since she got out of the cab. And suddenly she lost her grip, tears flooded her eyes, and it was there, standing on the station platform by the open carriage door, with his hand under her elbow ready to help her up the steep step, with the engine hissing steam and the evocative smell of sulphur on the air, that she told him. She didn't even phrase it properly, but just blurted out stupidly, 'I'm pregnant.'

He didn't say anything, and she looked up, and saw his face suffused by a joy so intense it was almost holy. To be able to occasion such emotion in another person was beautiful and terrible, more responsibility than she thought she could bear. The tears rolled over, and that was a good thing, because he helped her into the carriage and sat beside her and put his arm round her and didn't expect her to speak.

And all he said was, 'Oh, my Nina. You've made me so happy. So very happy.'

CHAPTER TWENTY-THREE

There was end-of-term excitement at the Blackwood. Not a great deal of work got done. Some of the girls had decorated the common room with paper garlands; others had brought in holly, laurel and ivy and made Christmas wreaths to hang on the doors and in the windows. Yet another had contributed dried flowers, teasels and pine cones from home, and a magnificent decoration had been contrived to be tied to the newel post at the foot of the stairs with gold ribbon. Within the common room there was an exchange of hand-drawn Christmas cards, some of them extremely elaborate, and some gift-exchanging between close friends.

Finally, on the last afternoon, there was the Christmas party. The girls crowded into the Studio, the only space in the house that could hold everyone, where they were regaled by the staff with fruit punch, dainty sandwiches and mincemeat pies. The servants came in and the principal, Mrs Brightwell, gave each of them a small gift 'on behalf of everyone at the school'.

'It's paid for out of our fees,' Bron whispered to Alice. 'Someone said they used to take a collection but by this time of the year a lot of girls had no money left, so they do it this way.'

The high voices of the girls echoed off the glass roof, and the heat and noise grew. Julia Stevens appeared at Alice's elbow and whispered, with much giggling, that one of the senior girls had put something in the punch. 'I think it was brandy,' she imparted breathlessly, 'so now everyone's going to get squiffy! Isn't it fun?'

'I couldn't taste anything,' Bron said. 'Couldn't have been very much. I don't suppose it'll make any difference among so many.'

'But I saw Mr Ffolliot with something that looked like a hunting flask,' Alice said, 'so perhaps he'll pass that round the staff.'

'Shocking!' said Bron with a grin. 'What an example to set to impressionable young women! I say, have you asked yet about living out next term?'

'I did ask my aunt, and she said she didn't mind, but I don't think she was really listening. The main thing is I have to ask my brother, because he's really responsible for me, with my mother away in Germany.'

'Is she really never coming back?'

'Not to live. I suppose she might visit sometimes.'

'Don't you mind?'

'She was never a very motherly sort of mother,' Alice said.

'So why haven't you asked your brother?'

'There wasn't a suitable time,' Alice said. 'I don't suppose he'll mind, really, as long as it's respectable. There's bound to be a time over Christmas when I can ask him.'

'I'm worried we may lose the room if we don't fix it soon. We can't wait until term starts.'

'I *will* ask him,' Alice said. 'I'll send you a telegram as soon as I know.'

'Well, do it as soon as you get there. All these weekends you've been going home—' She broke off, staring over Alice's shoulder. Alice felt the hair on the back of her neck stand up, and turned to see Ivor Wentworth looming over her.

'Some very important confabulation seems to be going on here. Miss Strachan, Miss Tallant – what are you plotting?'

'Nothing, sir,' Bron said quickly.

'I hope it wasn't you who put the brandy in the fruit punch?'

'How do you know about that?'

He laughed. 'Someone does it every year. I'm afraid it was a rather half-hearted effort – not nearly enough to go round.'

Alice tried to think of something intelligent to say. 'I wonder why there isn't any brandy in the punch to begin with,' she said. 'I'm sure every one of us has wine and sherry at home. We aren't children.'

'No, indeed,' he said, with a hint of amusement. 'Not by a long chalk. I fancy the embargo has more to do with economy than morality. May I speak to you for a moment, Miss Tallant – if Miss Strachan will excuse us?'

Bron made a complicated face at Alice as she followed his beautifully suited back. In a quiet corner, he stopped and waited for her. Her heart was beating rather faster than usual, just from being singled out by *the* Ivor Wentworth – and also because he was young and handsome and male and most of the teachers were not. 'What *were* you talking about in a lowered voice?' he asked her. 'It looked like a conspiracy to overthrow the monarchy, at least.'

'Oh, I would never do that,' she said. 'It would upset the Queen, and my grandmother knows her quite well.'

He laughed. 'You are an original! Don't you find yourself rather out of your place here?'

'Why?' she said, a little hurt.

'I didn't mean you are not a promising artist,' he said. 'I've seen some of your work, and heard the other teachers talking about you. I only meant that you always appear to be just a little outside every group, the observer looking on. You have an unnerving way of smiling at the wrong things, Miss Tallant, as if you've come from another place where things are done differently. It's intriguing.'

Alice didn't know how to respond to that. She said, 'Bron

– Miss Strachan – and I were talking about living in lodgings next term, that's all.'

'An excellent idea,' he said.

'Why?'

'Such a blunt question. Because to get away from home influences opens you to other influences, which allow you to grow. And growth is essential for an artist.'

Alice frowned, trying to work out what he meant. He watched her, with that same gleam of amusement, as if he could follow her thoughts and they entertained him.

'A true artist is always an outsider,' he went on. 'The detached observer, looking into the lighted room through a window, himself unobserved, outside in the dark street; separate from but witnessing life in all its glory, tragedy and absurdity. You have that quality, Miss Tallant, in embryo. It should be nurtured, allowed to grow to its full potential.'

His talk fascinated her, and not only because she didn't entirely understand it.

'You think I have potential?' she asked hesitantly. There was something of subtle mockery about him. She didn't want to take him at face value and find she had misunderstood or misjudged. She didn't want to make a fool of herself – especially not with him.

But as if he had understood her doubt, he said more kindly, 'I know that you do. Your work shows great promise.'

She felt her face glow with pleasure, and knew that he had observed her blush. He gave a little nod, as if a question had been answered.

'When school resumes next term I should like to give you some extra tuition. I invite a few special girls to tea at my studio each week, for discussion and instruction. You will come on the first Tuesday, at four o'clock.'

'I have a class every day at four,' she said awkwardly.

'That is not a problem. It is understood by the rest of the staff that my chosen girls will be released for my tea parties.

There will be no difficulty.' He gave her a bend of the head that was almost a bow, and walked briskly away.

Bron was soon by her side and asking what had been said. 'Oh, you lucky thing!' she said, when Alice told her. 'Extra tuition – from Ivor Wentworth! I'd give my hair for that! He must think you're very talented to bother with you. You could be the next Angelica Kauffman or Laura Alma-Tadema!'

Alice laughed. 'I don't think so! He said he takes lots of girls, and they can't all become famous or we'd know.'

'Well, it's an opportunity, anyway. And you might get to see him at work. If you do, be sure to notice *everything* and report back to me. You never know if you might pick up something that helps – some trick or other.'

'Great art isn't a trick,' Alice objected.

'Of course it is. They all have their little secrets – that's why they have us copy the Old Masters. Genius is a knack.'

'I thought it was a gift from God,' Alice said solemnly.

'Oh, goodness! Don't say that to him or he'll think you a simpleton.'

'You are far too world-weary for a young girl,' Alice said.

'Great artists are always world-weary. Hadn't you heard?' said Bron.

Mr Cowling did not understand Nina's wish to keep the news secret. His inclination would have run more to banners across the street and employing the town crier.

'Just for a little while,' she begged. 'Just until after Christmas. I need time to get used to the idea.'

'Get used to it?' he said, but good-humouredly. 'It's the best news anyone could ever have.'

'Yes, but it will change my life in so many ways. I need to think about it.'

'You think too much about everything,' he said, still kindly.

'Please, Joseph.'

The fact that she used his given name, and that the

conversation was taking place in bed, tilted the balance in her favour. 'Very well,' he said. 'You know I can't deny you anything. But I was looking forward to telling everyone at the Castle this Christmas.'

Yes, she had been right that he would want to accept the invitation. In fact, as soon as she relayed it to him, he assumed they would be going.

'But just think,' she beguiled him now. 'We shall be sharing the Christmas after that with a child of our own.'

'A child of our own,' he repeated, his tone rapturous in the darkness. 'Oh, Nina!' And he gathered her in to hold her close. 'You've made me so very happy,' he whispered.

She lay quiet in his embrace and thought, *Yes, the child is yours*. The other, slight possibility she had dismissed from her mind. It had raised itself briefly and painfully, but she would not contemplate it – not now, not ever. She had made her peace. This was her life now, and she would go to the Castle as Mrs Cowling, Kitty's schooldays friend. It would be lovely to see Kitty again.

'Next year they can come to us, here,' he said, almost as if he had kept pace with her thoughts. 'I've got some plans in mind for improving the house, building on a new wing. After Christmas we must get that architect-feller back and see what he thinks. I've made a sketch – not that I'm any artist, but I'll show it to you tomorrow.'

The new footman, Frederick, was tall, with very dark hair and blue eyes, and had the maids in a flutter.

'He's so handsome!' Doris moaned.

'Like a prince in a story,' Daisy agreed. 'I can't believe he's real.'

'He's real enough,' said Mabel. 'I wouldn't mind a kiss and a cuddle with him.'

Rose, passing by, growled, 'You'd do it with a one-eyed dog, so that's not saying much.'

Frederick, so far, had regarded the maids with lofty detachment, like a sultan looking over an unpromising new batch of slave girls. It was a relief to Afton that he did not seem inclined to dive into their giggling, bosomy sea of promise.

'He's very self-contained,' Afton said. 'That's unusual in a servant.'

Mrs Webster had been discomposed by the way he looked directly into her eyes when speaking to her, something hardly anyone ever did. 'He quite put me out of countenance,' she said to Afton.

'But Mr Moss likes him,' Afton noted.

Despite Frederick being the same height, which meant Moss could not loom impressively over him, he had taken to him. Frederick had never worked in a big house before, having been the sole male servant in the household of a rich, single, elderly man, but though he did not always know how things were done, he learned quickly.

'You never have to tell him anything twice,' Moss had said. 'And he's quick and handy, and asks questions when he doesn't know. I like that.'

He liked, too, the brisk way Frederick moved, unlike William, who had never been the same since his brush with the law. To see his languid movements and vapid, drooping carriage annoyed Moss, but telling him off didn't seem to help, only made William more miserable. 'Frederick bestrides the downstairs world like a colobus, as Shakespeare says,' Mr Moss had remarked to Afton. 'Just to see the vigour he puts into every job is a tonic.'

'He doesn't look at all put out when he's corrected,' Mrs Webster went on now. 'And if you praise him he doesn't . . .' She couldn't think of the right words.

'Wag his tail?' Afton smiled. 'No embarrassment, no shame, no anxiety, no desire for approval – is this a human being we're talking about? Can it be a visiting demi-god walking among us?'

'He's no demi-god, the way he packs his food away,' Rose said, passing. 'I've never seen anyone get outside his dinner so quick. Not that he shovels it in, like that Wilfrid. He eats nice. But his hands move so quick it's all done and dusted and a clean plate left. I don't know how he does it.'

'Perhaps he came from a large family,' Afton said, 'where if you don't eat quickly you don't eat.' His childhood in the orphanage had worked in the same way. Make sure of your portion, before someone else snaffled it.

'All the same,' Mrs Webster said thoughtfully, 'there's something strange about him. I can't put my finger on it.'

'I think he'll bear watching. He has an air of having secrets,' Afton said.

'Everyone's got secrets,' Rose said impatiently.

'There I can't agree with you,' Afton said. 'Most people's lives are too small and cramped for secrets. They'd have nowhere to put them. Present company excepted, of course,' he added, with a bow.

'*I* don't have any secrets,' Rose objected.

'I know very well that you do,' Afton said. She glanced at him with quick suspicion, and he went on blandly, 'You are not a small person, Rose.'

'Stuff and nonsense!' she said, with a toss of the head, and left.

Christmas Day was on a Monday, and Kitty had wanted to hold a large party on the Saturday before, but the Shacklocks had got in first with a ball, to which the whole neighbourhood was invited. 'We can't compete with that,' Giles had said, amused at her disappointment.

'I wouldn't dream of trying,' Kitty said. 'It's going to be very grand. And we don't have a proper ballroom, so ours would only have been dancing in the great hall.'

'Shall I buy you a ballroom?' Giles offered.

She hesitated for a telling moment before saying, 'Don't

be absurd. But your title is older than Lord Shacklock's. He ought to have checked that you didn't want the date before inviting everyone.'

'Dear Kitty, just enjoy a large entertainment that you haven't had to do the work for.'

'I like doing the work,' she said briskly. 'It keeps me busy.'

Giles knew the good of being kept busy, and said no more.

Nina and Mr Cowling were invited to arrive on the twenty-third so as to be able to attend the ball. 'It's a full-dress occasion,' Nina warned.

'Don't say that as if it's a drawback,' said Mr Cowling. 'I'm perfectly capable of putting on breeches and stockings, and Moxton knows what's what, all right. But you, my love – is there time to get a new gown made?'

'There's no need. I have my sea-green taffeta,' she said. 'That's never been seen down there.' She could see he was restless to buy her something new, and she added, 'I can wear my emeralds.' Over the years he had given her necklace, earrings, bracelet and hair clips in emeralds and diamonds, so it was an impressive set.

He was about to say something, then obviously changed his mind. 'So you can,' he said peacefully, and went away.

She discovered what he'd been thinking when he presented her, on the eve of travel, with a new pair of green morocco shoes 'for dancing in' – he had lasts of her feet in both his factories, and could have new shoes made for her in very short order.

'You're so thoughtful,' she said. 'Thank you.'

'That reminds me,' he said. 'You're to tell me as soon as your shoes start to feel too tight. Pregnant ladies' feet swell, you know, so I'll have to have larger shoes made for you for the while.'

'How do you know that?' she asked, amazed.

'How wouldn't I know it? I've been making shoes since I was a lad,' he said. 'I know all about it. I remember the first time Mrs Chamberlain came to complain that her shoes pinched, and blamed the workmanship. She was carrying her first, and a very smart, fashionable woman she was.'

'I don't suppose she liked being told she had bigger feet,' Nina said, amused.

'Well, she didn't, but I had her last and could prove it. However, why are we talking about feet, when I've another present for you?'

It was a tiara. Nina was surprised into silence. 'Don't you like it?' he asked anxiously.

'It's beautiful!' she protested. It was – very light and delicate, with diamond flowers set against emerald leaves. 'But it's too much!'

'Everyone will be wearing tiaras, if it's a dress ball,' he said. 'Don't be afraid I can't afford it. I know you were brought up frugal, my Nina, but there's no need to hold back now. All my businesses are doing well, and what do I make it for, except to spend it?'

She smiled at him rather unevenly. 'To have a fortune to hand on to your son?' she suggested.

He stepped close and took her in his arms. When he was able to speak, he said, 'He'll have that all right. I've enough for him and for you, so don't you worry. And the mother of my child is going to have a tiara to wear to a dress ball, and that's that.'

Aunt Caroline was going to stay with friends in the country for Christmas, and Richard went to London to escort Grandmère down to the Castle on the twenty-second, so that she could be settled in and rested before the ball.

'Of course I want to go to it! The Shacklocks do not entertain nearly enough for their position. Do you think I would miss this opportunity of seeing them *en grande tenue*? And I do not know how many more chances I shall have to wear my rubies. They were made by Fabergé, you know – the father, not the son. Nobody understands rubies like the Russians.'

'It's hardly fair on the young females, who will be hoping to shine at the ball, to have you gather every man's attention to yourself,' Richard said.

'Your compliments become more extravagant the less you mean them,' she said severely, but he could see she was pleased.

He lifted her hand to his lips. 'I mean every word. Who could look at some unformed, simpering girl when *la vraie beauté* is before them?'

'You are absurd,' she said. After a moment's silence she added, 'You have not heard anything?'

'Not a word. You?'

Grandmère sighed. 'Nothing.'

'Who would have thought we were so easy to forget?' Richard said lightly. 'You and he had decades of shared memories.'

'When a man of a certain age falls in love with a young girl, he forgets everything else,' she said. 'I hope when he finally takes the fortress, he finds it worth the sacrifice. But you, *mon pauvre* . . .' She eyed him sympathetically. 'Is your poor heart broken?'

He exploded in indignant laughter. 'Granny! I thought you didn't believe in hearts. Except as organs to pump blood. What is it you always say? "Music lasts. Kisses do not."'

'In my arrogance I thought I had both music and kisses. Now I have neither. And what is left of my heart is too tough to break, but it splits. *Ça déchire, enfin.*'

Richard was moved. 'If he ever comes back to England, the devil, I will boot his bottom all the way down Piccadilly, I promise you. On both our behalves.'

She smiled faintly. 'I believe you would. And in the mean time, there is dancing. Though the world ends, we shall dance. Have they invited that girl again, for you, the Miss – what is this her name is?'

'Miss Rawlins?' he said innocently.

'Rowsham,' she corrected him sternly.

'And you pretended you couldn't remember! I don't know if she will be there. And don't care, either.'

'"Don't care was made to care" – did not your nanny tell you? There will be girls at this ball, and if you don't ask them to dance, I shall make you dance with me.'

'Oh, but that would be my pleasure.'

'I'm so glad you will be here for Christmas Eve,' Kitty said to Nina. 'I do think bringing in the tree and dressing it is the best part of Christmas. And the boys are just old enough now to enjoy it.' Louis was two and a half, and Alec sixteen months. 'Come up straight away and see them,' she said, tucking her hand through Nina's arm.

On the way up the stairs, Nina said, 'Have you heard any more from Germany? How does – Giles' she made herself say the name, 'feel about having a new baby brother?'

'I think he got over the shock when she first announced she was pregnant. He has a great capacity for burying himself in his work to the exclusion of everything else.'

Nina thought she heard a hint of wistfulness, but though she loved Kitty, she didn't think she could stand a conversation about her relationship with Giles. Instead, she said, 'Any news of Linda?'

'Nothing directly, but Aunt Caroline said Aunt Vicky wrote that Paul's Cousin Pippi was spending Christmas with them. I don't know whether Aunt Vicky invited him for Linda's sake, or whether he invited himself. We hope the latter, because that would mean he was interested in her.'

'We?'

'Giles would dearly like to have her married and settled. Otherwise there's always the risk that she'll come back and impose herself on him. She *was* difficult,' she confessed. 'But

I feel sorry for poor Arabella. She liked it here. She didn't want to leave.'

'Children have to go where their parents take them,' Nina said. 'I didn't want to leave India.'

They reached the nursery. Kitty paused with her hand on the doorknob and said, 'I'm so lucky to have my boys. I often think of poor little Arthur. And my little brother Peter. Children are so easily lost.'

She opened the door. The two little boys were up at once, Louis running, Alexander tottering with new baby gait just behind. Louis had a very strong look of Giles about him; Alec was more ambiguous, though there was something of Kitty about his eyes. Nina felt a pang deep in her stomach – or was it her womb? Next Christmas she would have a baby in her arms.

Kitty, thoroughly engaged with her children, spared several glances for Nina. She had always known her friend was not beguiled by babies, but had hoped for a change. Now she thought she saw it. 'Oh, Nina, wouldn't it be wonderful if you had one too?' she couldn't help exclaiming. 'Imagine if our children could grow up together, and be friends the way we are friends.'

'Yes, it would be wonderful,' Nina said. There were too many complicated ideas behind that sentence for her to say more.

The ball at Ashridge Park was magnificently staged, with lamps and candles enough to light a village, and pots of shrubs brought in from the famous Ashridge greenhouses, including some of gardenias in flower, which helped to disguise the slightly musty smell inevitable in rooms not often used. In any case, the guests were all too ready to enjoy themselves to notice any deficiencies. Lord and Lady Shacklock, with two sons, Elliot and Brandon, and the two daughters who were out, Cecilia and Agatha, were in the receiving line – Lord Shacklock, tall, dark and saturnine, was scowling, his much younger wife vibrating with excitement. The ball, it might be concluded, was her idea, agreed to reluctantly by him, perhaps in the hope of advancing the marriage prospects of the daughters, who unfortunately favoured their father in looks rather than their mother.

Every important family in the neighbourhood had been invited, along with others from further afield to add elegance to the mix. Lord and Lady Ballantine from Aylesbury were there with a son and daughter and a house guest, who was the son of a marquess. Lord and Lady Ravenscar had come from Wendover, and Miss Rowsham was with them looking hopeful in a new gown. There were even some families down from London: the Lathams with a son and daughter; and, as Alice very quickly noticed, the Faroceans – father, mother, the two sons she had already met, Jervis and Bentham, and a tall young woman she supposed was the sister who was being brought out, Hermione.

That Rachel had spotted them too was evident. She seized Alice's arm in a fierce grip. Alice saw Bentham's roving gaze snag on her. He said something to his brother, who was chatting to Louisa Latham, and a moment later they were coming over.

Bentham bowed deeply to Alice, slightly to Rachel, and said, 'I hoped we were going to meet in London, but you don't seem to go to the same parties as us.'

'I don't go to parties at all, really. Too busy,' Alice said.

'But here you are,' he said, waving a hand around the glittering scene, 'and I'm suspecting now that you only go to the very grandest of affairs, and I was looking too low down.'

'The Shacklocks are neighbours. We have to come.'

'*Noblesse oblige,*' Bentham said, with a theatrical sigh. 'The things one has to do for mere politesse, to oil the wheels of society! You are too good, Lady Alice.'

'But what are you doing here? That is the more interesting question,' she said.

'My father knows Lord Shacklock. And I was up at Oxford with Brandon Shacklock. In fact, I was at school with him, so I've known him for ever.'

'You said you were at Balliol with Oliver Leven,' she reminded him.

'So I was. There were three hundred undergraduates at Balliol when I was there. Did you think it was just me and Oliver?'

She laughed. 'You are absurd! But it's nice to see a friendly face here.'

'Aren't all your neighbours friendly?'

'Oh, it isn't that. It's just that I'm not very good at balls, so I always feel out of my place.'

'Well, ma'am, you look very much the part,' he said, with a bow, 'so if you don't tell anyone, they won't know. May I solicit the honour of a dance? If you have any left.'

'You're the first person who's asked me, so you can have your pick.'

'Then I'll take the first, and keep dancing with you until I'm dragged away,' he said, with a grin.

Rachel had been talking all this time with Jervis, in low, intimate tones. Bentham now glanced at them, and said to Alice quietly, 'I'm afraid my brother is trespassing on someone else's estate again. Is the fiancé not here?'

'He is supposed to be coming, but he was at the office this morning so perhaps he's been delayed.'

'Then I hope for his sake he's hurrying, and gets here soon,' Bentham said.

After her dances with Bentham, Alice was surprised and a little gratified to be asked by several other men, and since she enjoyed the activity of dancing, being an energetic sort of girl, she was pleased to be occupied on the dance-floor. She tried to keep an eye on Rachel, but caught only glimpses of her in the crush. She had a variety of partners, but Alice saw her several times with Jervis Farocean.

A dance had just finished when she saw Angus standing in the doorway, looking about. She thanked her latest partner, excused herself and hurried over to him. 'Angus! I'm so glad you came. You're very late.'

'I had to go up to the Castle first to drop my luggage and change,' he said. 'And there was a lot to do, closing the office for three days, so I was late starting out. Is Rachel here?'

'Of course. She's longing to see you.'

He looked at her oddly. 'Is she? Strange that you spotted me straight away and she didn't.'

'I just happened to be looking this way,' she said. 'Come on, let's go and find her, before another dance starts.'

It was unfortunate that when they came upon Rachel, she was with Jervis, having just finished a dance with him, and they had their heads together, the drooping marabou feathers on her headpiece touching his cheek as they whispered.

She straightened quickly as she saw Angus, and her cheeks reddened, but she smiled and came straight to him, her hand out. 'Oh, Angus, you managed to get here!'

'Yes. Are you disappointed?' he said.

Rachel bit her lip. 'What on earth do you mean? Of course not. I've been hoping and hoping you'd come.'

Angus took the hand she had extended and used it to turn her away from her former partner. 'I have to talk to you privately,' he said, and drew her away.

Jervis watched them go, caught Alice's eye and shrugged. 'So that's the fiancé.'

She gave him a stern look. 'You knew she was engaged.'

'So did she,' he retorted.

'Well, I should keep out of the way if I were you. Angus is very strong.' She eyed Jervis, who was more the willowy sort. A Town beau, where Angus had been brought up to strenuous activities on wild moorlands.

He laughed, showing admirable teeth, and shaking his beautifully cut, glossy locks. 'You don't suppose I'm going to engage in fisticuffs with him? Or pistols at dawn? This is 1905, not 1805!'

'You shouldn't have flirted with her,' Alice said reproachfully.

He shrugged. 'I have a dance free now, Lady Alice. Might I persuade you to take a turn with me? If you're not promised to my clod-hopping brother.'

'I wouldn't dance with you even if I wasn't,' Alice said, and marched away as determinedly as dancing shoes and a gown with a train allowed.

Angus had meant to be angry with Rachel, but when he found a quiet corner and turned to face her, he saw that there were tears in her eyes and his rage slipped away like water. 'What is it, darling? Don't cry. Did that oaf say something to you?'

'No, it's not that,' Rachel said, fumbling out her handkerchief. 'It's just that you looked so angry, I was afraid.'

'Afraid of me?' He was appalled.

'I thought you were going to shout at me.'

'I'm sorry. Forgive me. I'm a brute. But, Rachel, you must admit—'

'Oh, now you're going to lecture me!'

'I've hardly seen you this whole year.'

'Whose fault is that? You're always working!'

'For us! I'm working for us. Then you went to Germany—'

'My mother sent for me. I *had* to go.'

'Did you have to go to the South of France? And then Scotland? And since you got back, you've been spending so much time at Ashmore—'

'Only the weekends. I'm in London all week.'

'When I'm at work. You know I only have Saturday afternoon and Sunday free.'

'But that's when Kitty and Giles have parties.' She looked at him anxiously, and saw not just pain but resignation in his face, and that frightened her more. She didn't want him to give up on her. 'I'm just trying to have a little fun,' she said pathetically. 'That's not wrong, is it?'

'No, it's not wrong,' he said sadly.

'I want to enjoy myself while I can,' she protested. 'Before—' She broke off.

'Before you marry me? You don't think there'll be any more fun after that?'

She wriggled. 'Oh, don't look like that, Angus! Everyone likes parties and dancing and—'

'Flirting?'

'I don't flirt!' she said indignantly. 'I can't help it if men are attracted to me, and pay me silly compliments.'

'Rachel, I don't want to hold you against your wishes. If you've changed your mind about marrying me, I'll release you. But you must be honest with me.' She said nothing, chewing her lip, frowning. He spoke very gently. 'I think you wanted to marry me because you were forbidden to. As soon as your mother withdrew her opposition, you lost interest. Isn't that the case?'

'No!' she cried. 'I didn't know there'd be opposition when I said yes to you.'

'In the heat of the moment, at a ball,' he said. 'It was my fault. I should never have proposed to you in those circumstances. And without finding out how our parents felt about it.'

'Well, if everyone had to ask their parents first, no-one would ever propose to anyone,' Rachel said crossly.

He took her hand. 'Tell me – and I promise I won't be angry whatever you say – do you love me?'

'Yes, of course,' she said.

'Not "of course". You love me?'

'I just said so.'

'And do you want to marry me?'

She hesitated the merest fraction of a second, but it was enough. She saw he had noticed. 'Yes, I do,' she said hastily.

'Of course I do. I mean – I do. But you know I can't marry you until I'm of age. And you can't expect me to sit with my hands in my lap until then. It's another eight months!'

He lifted her hand to his lips, and gave it back to her. 'I understand. I've been a brute.'

'No!' she said, afraid now.

'So here's what we'll do. We'll release each other from our engagement. And next August, when you're of age, I'll come and ask you again. If you haven't accepted someone else by then.'

'Angus, I would never—'

'Oh, I think you might,' he said. 'But we'll see, shall we?'

'You're – *jilting* me?' she said, in horror.

'Not at all. I'm setting you free. When you try to tame a wild animal, there has to come a point when you let it go, and see if it comes back to you of its own accord. Otherwise you'll never know, will you?'

'I'm not a wild animal,' she said indignantly.

But he only smiled and walked away. And his back view was so strong and upright and manly, she felt a sob rising up her throat. He had never looked more attractive to her than at that moment.

CHAPTER TWENTY-FOUR

'And then he just packed his bag again and left,' said Addy, on her knees in front of the morning-room fire. 'Went back to London.'

Mildred was leaning against the mantelpiece, housemaid's box in hand. 'Well, where's he going to spend Christmas, then?'

'Wherever he lives, I suppose,' said Addy. 'It's a shame for him – he won't be getting a feed like he'd have had here. Bread and cheese more likely,' she added, with relish for other people's disasters.

'How's Lady Rachel taking it?'

'Daisy says she's quiet, but not crying. More like mad, I reckon. I would be.'

'But she's lost her love, hasn't she?' Mildred said, with a sniff. 'I'd be bawling my eyes out.'

'Naw, she's mad at him for telling her she can't dance with anyone else, Daisy says. Well, what does he expect? Just because a girl's spoken for, doesn't mean she's got to say no when a chap asks her to dance. Specially when he's not around to give her a good time.'

'I think it's a shame,' Mildred said. 'He's ever such a nice young man, ever so good-looking.'

Eddie, the house boy, arrived with a basket of logs nearly as big as him. 'Not good enough for her,' he joined in. 'She's an earl's daughter and he works in an office.'

Addy went on laying the fire. 'Where d'you get that idea? You never thought of that for yourself.'

'Wilf said. The gardener's boy. When I was getting the logs. He said Mr Allsuch said it. She's a earl's daughter and real beautiful, so she could have anyone.'

'Well, if she could have anyone, how'd she end up with Mr Tullamore?' Addy said triumphantly.

Mrs Webster was suddenly there, retribution on silent feet. 'You've more than enough to do without wasting time gossiping. Mildred, stop leaning and get on with the dusting. And wipe your nose. *Not on your sleeve!* Addy, you've got the drawing-room and hall fires still to do, so stop dawdling. And Eddie, those logs are for the hall fire. You ought to know that by now. Take them away. What are you doing afterwards?'

'Front-door brasses, Mrs Webster,' he said, staring resolutely at the floor.

'Hurry up, then. They're to be done before breakfast.'

She was gone, Mildred was gone, and Eddie shuffled away with his burden. 'How does she do that?' Addy asked the air, as she brushed up the last trace of ash from the hearth and heaved herself to her feet. 'Blummin' mystery she is.'

'I do feel sorry for the poor child,' the blummin' mystery paused to say to Mr Afton, as they passed on Piccadilly. 'How is she supposed to know her own mind when she's told what to do all the time? First she's forbidden to marry the man, then told she can, then as I understand it, hauled about the ballrooms by her aunt to be auctioned off to anyone with a title who might take a fancy to her.'

'That's very harsh,' Afton said mildly. 'Her mother wants the best for her, as any mother would.'

'He was a perfectly respectable match in the first place,' said Mrs Webster grimly, 'with a fortune to inherit. If she'd supported the match he wouldn't have lost it.'

'As I understand it, it was *his* father who opposed the match first,' said Afton.

Mrs Webster shrugged. 'First or last, she forbade it. She'll have that poor girl left on her hands, and it'll be her own fault.'

Afton patted her arm comfortingly as he moved on. 'She'll marry someone, sooner or later. A girl like that won't get left on the shelf.'

She walked on briskly to the kitchen, where the level of activity would have suggested to the untrained eye that a natural disaster, such as a volcanic eruption, was taking place. 'Have the trays gone up?' she asked.

Mrs Terry, the cook, answered, without looking up from the béchamel she was stirring. 'Yes, Mrs Webster. Nursery breakfast just about to go up now.'

'Those boys will have been awake since five o'clock, if I know children. They'll be hungry. What are you giving them?'

'Sausages,' the cook said. 'That'll peg 'em down.'

There were sausages at Wisteria House, too, and buttered eggs, kidneys, which the master was partial to, and fried ham. Crooks stood at the buffet and attended to the coffee pot. He liked things to be done properly: now he was the sole male servant in the household, he regarded himself as keeper of the flame, as well as butler, footman and valet, and did his best to run the small house like a great house. It had been a new lease of life for him. He felt ten years younger.

'You cried out in your sleep again last night,' Sebastian said.

Dory looked up. 'Did I? I don't remember.'

'Were you dreaming?'

'I suppose I must have been. It was something about being chased, trying to find somewhere to hide.'

'The old dream. Was it *him* you were running from?' She hesitated to answer, and without turning, he said, 'Would you bring fresh toast, Crooks? This has got cold.' When he heard the door click quietly he said, 'When will you stop dreaming that he's coming after you? When will you feel safe?'

'I do feel safe,' she said. 'You can't help your dreams.'

'We had such a nice day yesterday,' he said. They had gone for a long walk by the river – the grass had been rimed with frost and crunched under their feet, there were skims of ice on the puddles, their breath had clouded on the winter air, and Dory had put her hand in his pocket to keep warm as they tramped along. He had looked down at her, and seen her cheeks and nose pink with the cold and her eyes sparkling, and thought her beautiful. After luncheon they had gone out to cut greenery and brought it back to decorate the house, and after dinner he played carols on the piano and they sang together.

'It was a nice day,' she said. 'The best day ever.'

'So far. They'll keep getting better, you know.'

'I know. And I am happy – happier than I ever thought I could be. The dreams will stop coming one day.'

'It's done you good with the staff, you know. Mrs May is now your champion, Crooks tells me. Poor sweet creature, she says, and longs for Crooks to tell her what sad thing from your past haunts you. He would never tell, of course, even if he knew. She wants to pet you, and refers to you to Olive as "the mistress". So you are established, my love.'

'I did wonder at the number of times she offers me cups of tea,' Dory laughed.

'And the ginger pudding last night? It was an experiment of mine. I mentioned – oh, so casually – to Crooks the day before that you liked ginger, just to see what happened.'

'I know there's one thing that would establish me for ever,' she said, looking at her plate, 'and I long for it as much as they possibly can.' She looked up. 'I so want to give you a child. I thought it would have happened by now. I'm beginning to wonder . . .'

'My love,' he said, his voice a little shaky, 'I didn't marry you for children. If they come, I will be very, very happy. But if they don't, it won't matter. You are enough for me. You are everything I want.'

'It's early days, still – isn't it?'

'Of course it is.'

She changed the subject. 'So, what happens today? Do you have traditions here?'

'Little ones. After breakfast I give the servants their Christmas presents. Then we walk to church. We have our Christmas dinner at half past one, and then the servants are off for the rest of the day, so we shall have a dear, cosy time alone together. Mrs May will lay a cold supper for us before she goes, and Joe will make sure the coal scuttles and log basket are full. We shall be as snug as puppies in a basket.'

'Where do they go?'

'Mrs May goes home with Olive – her mother makes Christmas dinner for them all. Joe has his own family. I don't know what Crooks will do. At the Castle all the servants got together in the servants' hall for a party – those who didn't go home.'

'I hope he won't be all alone,' Dory said.

It was like her, he thought, to worry. Crooks returned with the hot toast at that moment and, to put her mind at rest, Sebastian asked, 'How will you be spending Christmas afternoon, Crooks?'

He looked faintly surprised to be asked, then pleased, and said, 'Olive's mother, sir, has invited me to join the family party. It was a kind invitation, which I felt I could not refuse without causing offence.'

Which left them to suppose that he would have been happier reading alone in his room. Sebastian chose to believe that was not the case. Dory was sure it wasn't.

★ ★ ★

The estate workers and tenants came up to the Castle in the morning to receive their Christmas boxes and be served with mulled wine and mincemeat pies in the great hall. Rose had gone out of the back yard with some pastry crumbs to throw for the birds, when she saw Michael Woodrow coming by, presumably on his way home from the ceremony, as he had a package under his arm. He stopped when he saw her, and they looked at each other in silence for a moment. He looked tired, Rose thought, or perhaps sad, with lines she didn't remember in his face. She felt . . . She didn't know what, but it was not anger or dislike. It might be something like . . . Pity? Regret?

As the silence extended itself, she began to doubt that he would speak at all. It was a cold day, with a grey, heavy sky and a sharp, gusty breeze – not Christmas weather. There had been no snow yet, and with the wind not even any frost to make things pretty. It was a day to be indoors. He was bundled in a warm coat, but she had only slipped someone's jacket over her grey morning uniform dress. If she didn't want to freeze, she would have to get things started, or abandon them. And she discovered she wanted him to talk.

'What did they give you?' she asked.

'I haven't opened it. But I think it was gloves for the men and handkerchiefs for the women.' He glanced at her hand. 'Feeding the birds? I didn't know you liked birds.'

She shrugged. 'Why shouldn't I?' She had spotted from the corner of her eye the little blur of wings as the robin flew down onto the top of the high wall that enclosed the yard. Now she heard his quiet, hopeful tweedling above and behind her. She yielded. 'There's a robin,' she said. 'He's prac'ly tame.' She turned her back on Woodrow and scattered the crumbs at a little distance, and the robin was down immediately, pecking. 'They're hungry this weather,' she said defiantly, turning back.

He was smiling. 'I think it's lovely. You're so tough and practical, but this proves you have a heart, too.'

'Heart!' she said, with a *pff* of disdain. But he went on smiling. 'How's your sister?' she said roughly. She didn't know how to do soft talk.

'Just the same,' he said, the smile disappearing. 'They don't think she'll ever improve much.' He chewed his lip, and then said, effortfully, 'It was coming a long time. I should have realised.' He shrugged. 'Probably I couldn't have done anything about it. But sometimes I think – p'r'aps I could have.'

She nodded, not knowing what to say, trying to convey sympathy. She didn't blame him any more. People were the way they were. You couldn't change them. It must be lonely for him, living in that house on his own. His sister had been company, even if she was difficult. 'I heard you got someone to come in and clean,' she said.

'Molly Gale,' he said. 'Beattie's sister. Younger sister. She cleans and cooks something for my dinner.' He gave a crooked smile. 'She's not much of a cook. Watery stew mostly. But, then, I'm not much of an eater, these days.'

Rose spoke briskly to cover her feelings. 'No need for a stew to be watery. Easiest thing in the world to make tasty. You could shoot some rabbits or pigeons to go in it. There's still mushrooms about. Herbs – I bet Mrs Gale's got some in her garden. And potatoes'll thicken it, if they're cooked long enough.'

'I bet you'd make a delicious stew,' he said, smiling again.

'Well, I would!' she retorted. The breeze gusted, and she shivered. 'I got to go in.'

He took a step closer. 'Rose,' he said, 'couldn't we start again? I miss you.'

'You just want me to come and cook meals for you,' she said suspiciously.

'No! That's not what I mean. Look, could we go for a walk, like we used to – just that? See how it goes. We used to talk and talk. I miss talking to you.'

She would have held out longer, but she was really cold. The wind was bitter. 'All right,' she said. 'We'll give it a try. No promises, mind.'

Now his smile was wide. 'When's your afternoon off?'

'Thursday.'

'I'll come and call for you.'

'No, I'll come by your house. Three o'clock?'

'Three o'clock. Thank you!'

'Soft!' she snorted, and hurried away. Her face and hand were frozen, but there was a queer warm spot somewhere in her stomach that had nothing to do with the temperature.

At the Castle, Christmas gifts between adults were exchanged after dinner, but Mr Cowling couldn't wait. Before they went down to breakfast, he sent Tina away, took Nina's hands, and smiled at her in such a particular way that she said, 'Please don't ask me to tell everyone our news. I'm not ready.'

'No, no, it's not that. I wanted to tell you about your Christmas present from me. It's something I couldn't wrap up.'

He seemed almost gleeful, so she said, 'Tell me, then. Shall I be excited?'

'I hope so. Our next neighbour in Market Harborough, Utterby, is going through a bad patch, and he's decided to sell some of his land. He's got debts to pay off. So I'm buying the twenty acres adjoining our garden. It used to belong to Wriothesby House once upon a time, as Deering will tell you if you ask. It's enough to make a proper park for the house. What do you think? It's my Christmas present to you – and to celebrate the baby. I want him to grow up a proper gentleman, and to have everything a gentleman should have.'

'You've decided to stay at Wriothesby House, then?'

'You like it, don't you? You want to stay?'

'Yes, I do. But I thought you were still – migratory.'

'It's time I settled down, and there's as good as anywhere.

The railway connections are good, it's a genteel place, and if it's home to you, it's home to me. So,' he looked at her face, hungry for affirmation, 'what d'you think about that?'

'It's the biggest Christmas present I've ever had,' she said, smiling. 'Better than diamonds. It's wonderful. To plan a park – who ever gets an opportunity like that?'

'Aye, we'll get one of those landscaping fellers in to do the job, but it'll be how we want it – how *you* want it.' His smile grew shy. 'You've given me the best Christmas present a man could have – telling me there's a baby on the way. This is small beans beside that.'

She saw then that the land was not just meant to please her – it was to tie her down. Not that he had any doubts about her fidelity – just that he couldn't quite believe his luck. Giving her land to make her house into an estate made it harder for her to wander away.

She felt a tremor of unease. His love was a great responsibility; and it was a great deal to be riding on one small baby, barely established yet in her womb. If anything should happen to it . . . She remembered Kitty telling her that after Louis was born she'd known fear for the first time: babies were so fragile, and the things that could go wrong so multitudinous, she never stopped worrying after that.

A bell sounded below. *Send not to know for whom the bell tolls*, she thought. But she was glad of the interruption. 'That's the breakfast bell,' she said. 'We'd better go down.'

'This is so lovely,' Nina said.

The children had their presents after breakfast. She was sitting with Kitty and watching the little ones' happiness and excitement. The tree filled the hall with its wild scent; the fire burned with a smell of good woodland smoke. The dogs followed the children around protectively, swinging their tails, poking their noses into everything and making them giggle.

Kitty said, 'I look at my boys and I feel so lucky. I wish

you could have the same, darling Nina. But it will happen, I know it will. Sometimes it takes time, that's all.'

'Oh, I'm sure it will,' Nina said peacefully.

Kitty glanced at her doubtfully, a question forming in her mind. Nina *looked* different. But surely if there was something to tell, she would have told it. There would be no reason to keep it a secret.

'Look at Alice,' Nina said, 'sketching us all. What a picture that would make – in oils, over the fireplace. All the colour and sparkle, and all the people.'

Giles was now sitting on the floor by the tree with the boys, inspecting their treasures with them, the dogs leaning against him from either side as if the slightest encouragement would have them climbing on his lap. She thought for a moment of poor Trump. Perhaps she was ready for another dog. Giles seemed to feel her stare, and looked up. Their eyes met, and there was a moment of intense connection. She remembered, like something revealed in a lightning flash, that night together, the intensity of it, the joy. She pushed the memory away. She must not think of it now. And she knew she could not be near him when he found out that she was with child. She had been right to keep the secret. It must be by letter, when she was far away. She owed that to Mr Cowling, and to Kitty. For all their sakes.

Rachel, Richard and Grandmère were sitting together, being part of Alice's tableau.

'It's strange without Mama here,' Rachel said. 'And Linda.'

'And Uncle Sebastian and his wife,' Richard added.

'I don't see why they couldn't have come,' Rachel said. 'His marriage wasn't so very disgraceful, was it? I mean, it's not as if he's anyone important – not an earl or anything.'

'I do not believe he stayed away from shame,' Grandmère said. 'He followed his heart and married exactly who he wanted to. Where is the shame?'

'There you go, talking about hearts again,' Richard teased her. 'I'm wondering if we ought to be calling Dr Arbogast to you. You're not yourself.'

She didn't smile. 'I am *not* myself. Myself was bound up with certain other – *vérités*. The world has changed. I must change with it.'

'Please don't change too much,' Richard said. 'You are one of *my* verities.'

'I am too old to be that for you. You must make your own way,' Grandmère said crossly.

'Now I know you need to see the doctor. You *never* admit to being old.'

Grandmère tutted at him, and turned to Rachel, who was not following their practised conversation. 'And you, Miss, you need to decide what you want, and do it quickly. Life will not wait for you. *C'est un fleuve large et puissant qui roule rapidement et cruellement.*'

Rachel stared in perplexity, not having caught her grandmother's rapid French.

'It will wash you away,' Grandmère translated for her. 'What is your intention around this young man?'

'Which young man?' Rachel said.

'Do not pout! You know very well. Your fiancé, who came so far to spend Christmas with you and went away unpleased and unfed. Is it at an end with you?'

Rachel flushed, unhappy and uncomfortable. 'I don't know.'

'*You don't know?*'

'He said – he said he would ask me again when I am of age.' Her eyes filled with tears. 'He's completely unreasonable! A girl is allowed to dance at a ball, for Heaven's sake! I think he wants me to be locked up all day and see nobody.'

'If that is so,' Grandmère said, in measured tone, 'you must think: do you want to marry him?'

The tears began to brim over. 'He was so unkind. After I risked everything for him. Defied Mama and endured months of her scolding, and – and *oppressing* me. And then he talks to me as if . . . He called me a wild animal!' Richard began to laugh softly, which did not help her mood. 'He's not the only man in the world, and he'd better learn that. I shall have many other offers to choose from.'

'Any creature less oppressed than you would be hard to find,' Richard said. 'My silly little sister! A wild animal, eh? You must have depths kept hidden from me all these years.'

The tears went back to their source. 'You're not to make fun of me,' she said crossly.

'*Tiens*, you must not,' said Grandmère. 'It is not gentlemanly to tease.' But she was laughing too.

The carriages were got out to take everyone to church, but Alice said she would walk. 'I've been sitting too long, I need to stretch my legs.'

'I'll come with you,' Giles said. 'We'll work up an appetite for the turkey.'

'Can we take the dogs?' Alice asked. 'They do so love to go out. We can tie them up in the porch.'

Warm coats, mufflers, gloves and hats were the order of the day. Giles had a deerstalker, and turned the flaps down to keep his ears warm. Alice unearthed a knitted hat from her childhood in preference to something more grown-up and fashionable, and they set off under the dreary grey sky with the brisk, cold breeze pushing them from behind and the dogs racing about, puffing out their breath in small clouds. Everything was very still, no birds anywhere, only the moving bare branches of the trees breaking the monotony.

'The sky is so low. Do you think it will snow?' Alice asked.

Giles looked about and sniffed the air. 'I don't think so. Not the right sort of cloud. I hope not, anyway.'

'I hope so a bit, but not entirely. What age do you have to be before you stop looking forward to snow?'

'You must know that better than me. You're closer to it.

All I think of is the nuisance, all the animals to cart feed to, and the flood when the snow finally melts.'

'That's a very dull way of thinking,' Alice said. 'I suppose you're very grown-up now.'

'You're pretty grown-up yourself,' he laughed, 'if you can talk to your elders and betters so boldly. I remember when I came home after Father died, there were two very shy, mouselike girls in the old schoolroom who wouldn't say boo to a goose.'

'Why would anyone say boo to a goose? Such an odd expression! The snow is lovely for painting, though, you must admit that.'

'There was a picture of a snowy landscape in the nursery when I was a child,' he remembered. 'I never liked it. Too chilly!'

'Without snow there'd be no Christmas cards,' she said solemnly. 'No lamplit inn with a stage-coach pulled up outside it, the wheel-tracks in the snow, the ladies in crinolines with big muffs . . . I must say, a muff would be a good idea on a day like this. Gloves don't really seem to help much.'

He pulled her against him. 'Put your hand in my pocket and tuck the other under your arm. There, is that better?'

'Much. Thanks.' A pause. 'I'm glad to have the chance to talk to you,' she began.

'Oh dear. I sense a request coming,' he said.

'I didn't mean that. I meant *really* talk to you. We don't often have the opportunity.'

'We don't, little sister, especially now you're in London so much. How's art school?'

'Wonderful.'

'Still keen, then?'

'More than ever. I think . . .' She hesitated. 'I believe I could make my living at it one day.'

'What will your husband think about that?'

'Oh, you know I'm never going to get married. I'm not the sort.'

'You only think that because you haven't met the right man. When you do, you'll be the sort all right.'

'We'll see. But, actually, there is something I wanted to ask you.'

'I knew it! Ask away, then, while I'm in a good mood.'

She told him about the lodgings, and he asked a lot of probing questions. They had reached the bridge before he had finished. 'What does your aunt say? Have you asked her?'

Alice stopped on the bridge and looked down into the black water. There were patches of ice at the sides of the river where the vegetation halted the flow. 'She doesn't mind,' she said. 'I think she'd be glad to have one less person to bother about – assuming Rachel is going to be there after Christmas.'

Giles frowned. 'I thought we'd got Rachel all squared away. Thank goodness Aunt Caroline is willing to chaperone her, if she's going to be back on the market.'

'On the market?' Alice said, wrinkling her nose. 'What a horrid expression.'

'Well, you know what I mean. All right, this lodging thing, if it really is respectable, I suppose you can do it. You're a sensible girl – not like your sister.' A splash distracted his attention. 'Oh, my God, has that stupid dog really jumped into the water? It must be freezing! Hi, Tiger! Here! Heel! Get out of that, you old fool!'

The dog was already scrambling up onto the bank and shaking himself vigorously. 'He's found out how cold it is,' Alice said. 'He's coming.'

'Yes, and he'll be ready for his second shake just as he reaches us,' Giles grumbled.

The service was everything a Christmas service should be. All Alice's favourite carols were sung, the rector's sermon was cheerful and not too long, the church was full of greenery, with splashes of red from the holly berries. There was the smell of pine and candle-wax, the smell of incense, and the choir singing the descants and bass lines to leaven the hearty bellowing of the congregation.

Afterwards there was a blockage at the church door, of everyone who wanted to talk to everyone else, or exchange a word with the rector without going out into the cold. Kitty and Grandmère and Rachel were absorbed into a group of ladies in smart hats, Richard was buttonholed by Mort Gregory from Shelloes Farm to talk about skimmed milk for pigs, and Giles was kidnapped by the Bexleys from the Grange who wanted to talk about the Shacklock ball and their own intended lawn meet on Boxing Day. Alice might have enjoyed talking about the latter, but she was conscious of the dogs being tied up in the porch, mouthed to Giles that she was going home, and slipped out.

Tiger and Isaac were enraptured to see her, and Tiger didn't seem to be suffering from his icy dip – he'd got out so quickly the water probably hadn't penetrated his thick coat. She untied them and walked out into the graveyard and, taking the path to the side gate, came upon the choir streaming out on their way home.

And suddenly Axe was there. She stopped dead, he saw her and stepped out of the flow, then came the few steps towards her, almost reluctantly, as though pulled by a rope. The dogs jumped and tugged at their leashes, wanting to get to him. Every living thing wanted to be near Axe Brandom. He was like a big fire in the dark of night – instinctively you edged closer.

And then they were only a foot apart, staring at each other. She thought he looked tired, and rather pale around the edges. A skinned sort of look. 'You've had a haircut,' she said, idiotically.

'No, not recently,' he said.

She had forgotten his voice, the richness of it. It made the hairs stand up on the back of her neck.

'How are you, Lady Alice?'

'Well,' she said. 'Are you well?'

He didn't answer that. 'You've been in London all this time?'

She was about to answer, and then saw that he knew she hadn't. She'd been back many times. She'd hunted. But she'd never gone to see him. She had decided that it was best for both of them if she cut him from her life. And mostly it had been easy. He suspected that, and was sad.

'How's Dolly?' she asked, to avoid anything harder. 'And Della?'

'All right,' he said. 'They miss you.' *I miss you.*

'Have you got any animals at the moment?' He usually had some creature he'd rescued – young and abandoned, or hurt – that he healed, raised, fed and set free.

'Two baby owls. Nearly ready to be let go.'

'I suppose you trap mice to feed them,' she said.

'Everyone's got to eat,' he said. And then, 'I kill 'em quick. I don't give 'em alive now.'

'Thank you,' she said. She had objected to the practice. It warmed her perilously that he'd cared enough to stop it. She understood that, telling her, he was making her a gift. 'I – I haven't been to see you,' she began with difficulty.

'I know,' he said.

He seemed to have edged a little nearer. She was looking up into his face now; she could feel the heat of his big body, the draw of his presence. She looked at the curve of his lips, the soft curtain of his eyelashes, and knew that the whole year away had been wasted, had done nothing to lessen her desire to put herself in his arms and press herself against him, and be held and consumed.

'It wasn't because—'

'I know,' he said again. He made a little movement of his hand, as though he would have touched her, and stopped himself. 'You thought it was for the best.'

'Was it?' she asked helplessly.

He was a long time answering. 'I expect so,' he said at last. His hand moved again. This time, very delicately, he picked a loose strand of hair that was sticking to her cheek and pushed it back into the mass over her ear. She felt herself trembling. Or was that him? 'I miss our talks,' he said. 'Dolly's company, but she's got no conversation.'

She drew a breath of pain. 'I—' she began.

But he said, 'No. 'Tis all right. There's a whole world out there. You've got to explore it. You're – you're too big for this little space.' He meant, *too big for my little place in it*. 'You're like one of those explorers in Jules Verne, off to see the world. It's right. It's right.' She could feel tears starting in her eyes. 'No, no, don't you fret. We're all right. All will be well.' He stepped back a pace, and smiled, and the smile was healing, and at the same time made her feel desperately hungry for him – for more.

'I'll give Dolly your love,' he said in valediction. 'Merry Christmas, Lady Alice.'

She felt her lips say merry Christmas, but no sound came out. He turned and walked away, carrying the warmth of the sun with him, and she stood stupidly in the greyness that was left and watched him go. Because there was nothing else to do. Nothing to say. Nothing it was possible to say.

The dogs stood up, watched him go, then looked up at her.

'Yes, all right,' she said. 'Let's go home.'